A messenger approached the Captain's Table and handed a telegram to Captain Barthou, who noted it was marked "For the Captain Only," in the handwriting of the *Normandie*'s chief wireless operator. This cannot be good news, Barthou thought to himself. He finished his champagne and opened the envelope. As he read the message, his blood ran cold.

Private to Barthou:
Urgent warning! French government says its analysis of German radio signals indicates the *Normandie* is being tracked across the Atlantic by German ships. Purpose of tracking unclear. Government has issued you the following orders:

1. Immediately break off visual contact with any German vessels.
2. Radio news of such contacts to Paris.
3. Establish all-quarters, round-the-clock U-boat watch.

Good luck. Signed Henri Cangardel.

Barthou folded the telegram neatly and replaced it in the envelope. He signaled the wine steward to refill his glass. Then he looked around the table at Mrs. William Randolph Hearst, the violinist Jascha Heifetz, Ambassador Joseph P. Kennedy, and his other important guests, watching them conduct their business — and their pleasure — with great verve and impressive skill.

How would they be acting, Barthou thought, if they knew German U-boats were following the ship?

BLOCKBUSTER FICTION FROM PINNACLE BOOKS!

THE FINAL VOYAGE OF THE S.S.N. SKATE   (17-157, $3.95)
by Stephen Cassell
The "leper" of the U.S. Pacific Fleet, SSN 578 nuclear attack sub
SKATE, has one final mission to perform—an impossible act of
piracy that will pit the underwater deathtrap and its inexperienced
crew against the combined might of the Soviet Navy's finest!

QUEENS GATE RECKONING   (17-164, $3.95)
by Lewis Purdue
Only a wounded CIA operative and a defecting Soviet ballerina
stand in the way of a vast consortium of treason that speeds toward the hour of mankind's ultimate reckoning! From the best-
selling author of THE LINZ TESTAMENT.

FAREWELL TO RUSSIA   (17-165, $4.50)
by Richard Hugo
A KGB agent must race against time to infiltrate the confines of
U.S. nuclear technology after a terrifying accident threatens to
unleash unmitigated devastation!

THE NICODEMUS CODE   (17-133, $3.95)
by Graham N. Smith and Donna Smith
A two-thousand-year-old parchment has been unearthed, un-
leashing a terrifying conspiracy unlike any the world has previously known, one that threatens the life of the Pope himself, and
the ultimate destruction of Christianity!

*Available wherever paperbacks are sold, or order direct from the
Publisher. Send cover price plus 50¢ per copy for mailing and
handling to Pinnacle Books, Dept.17-362, 475 Park Avenue
South, New York, N.Y. 10016. Residents of New York, New Jer-
sey and Pennsylvania must include sales tax. DO NOT SEND
CASH.*

THE FINAL CROSSING

HARVEY ARDMAN

PINNACLE BOOKS
WINDSOR PUBLISHING CORP.

PINNACLE BOOKS

are published by

Windsor Publishing Corp.
475 Park Avenue South
New York, NY 10016

First printing: June, 1990

Printed in the United States of America

This book is dedicated to

Catherine and Nicholas

Special Thanks to My Fellow Writer, Barbara Bauer

Prologue

He'd thought it was going to be easy.

Just a few quick snips and he'd be rid of the most visible symbol of his beliefs, the forelocks he had cultivated since childhood. He'd be free of the reddish brown strands that dangled from his temples to his jaw, which in obedience to the word of God, he and others of his faith had pledged to leave eternally untrimmed.

Then he would shed the costume he had always worn: the *shtreimel* — the black fur hat — the black overcoat, and the black shoes of the Orthodox Jew. And he would don the brown felt hat and the brown herringbone-tweed overcoat that had lain unclaimed in his uncle's tailor shop for nearly two years.

In these few brief moments, he would transform himself from Reb Pinchas Nachman, son of the chief Rabbi of Prague, into a middle-class *goy*, a shopkeeper, perhaps, or even a landowner.

He'd thought it was going to be easy. And it would have been easy if it were easy to abandon his heritage and convictions.

As it was, he recoiled from the scissors. It was the Sabbath, after all. He shuddered at the thought of changing his

7

identity, even temporarily, even for the most desperate reason.

He heard his mother's voice through the bathroom door. "Pinchas? It's time."

"Yes, Mother, I know. I'll be ready soon."

Reb Pinchas Nachman examined himself in the tiny bathroom mirror one last time, then seized the scissors and severed his forelocks with two swift cuts. He watched the strands fall into the white porcelain sink. Then he continued cropping his hair to fit his image of the name on his forged identity card: Casimir Sulkowski.

He did not shave off his curly red beard, however, though he did trim it back to what he hoped were appropriate proportions. He could not part with his beard. Without it, he himself would not know who he was.

"Are you ready, Pinchas?"

"Yes, Mother."

Reb Nachman opened the bathroom door. His mother stood before him, eyes averted, the brown overcoat hanging from her outstretched arm. As he slipped on the coat, it crackled with the sound of the banknotes sewn into it, the savings of the entire community.

They embraced with the heartfelt tenderness of a mother and son who knew they were about to be separated forever. Then the young man broke away, grabbed the brown fedora, and left the shabby two-story gray stone building that had always been his home.

He walked quickly through Jewish Town, along Rote Gasse, a narrow cobblestone street that twisted its way between a large cemetery filled with tombstones tightly jammed up against each other and a row of dingy stone buildings with worn clay tile roofs. The windows were shuttered and the streets deserted. Many Jews had fled since the Nazis had occupied Prague in March.

Ahead of Reb Nachman now was the Altneushul synagogue, with its one-story gray stone base and rows of small barred windows, its odd crenellated brick gable, and its sharply pitched faded red tile roof. As a child, he'd thought it was a huge, imposing structure. Now he knew how small it really was, its size an illusion created by the fact that it sat in an open square across from the Town Hall and its tall baroque clock tower.

Reb Nachman entered the ancient synagogue through the rear door and walked downstairs to the main floor. Here, as in many European synagogues, the floor was well below street level — an architect's trick to evade the government-imposed height restrictions intended to diminish Jewish houses of worship in comparison to churches.

Before him lay the main hall — two naves of three bays each, divided by rectangular piers that rose to support the rib-vaulted ceiling. A wooden *bema* — a raised platform with a reader's desk from which the Torah scroll was recited to the congregation — filled the central space between the two main piers. The sight still filled him with awe.

On any other Saturday, Reb Nachman's father, Rabbi Herschel Nachman, would be standing at the reader's desk. He would be leading the congregation in prayer, chanting in his strong, clear voice, a tiny black *yarmulke* perched precariously atop his unkempt white hair.

On this Sabbath day, however, Rabbi Nachman and nine other old men, prayer shawls draped over their fragile shoulders, were huddled against the eastern wall, near the high-backed chair built for the sixteenth-century rabbi, Judah Loew ben Bazalel.

Rabbi Loew. That name had a special hold on Pinchas Nachman's imagination. Legend had it that Rabbi Loew, resorting to alchemy, had created the *Golem*, a monster, an artificial being, to shield the Jewish community against attack.

The *Golem* legend, as Reb Nachman's father had told it, sprang from the hopes and fears of East European Jewry, after so many of them had perished during the Chmielnicki massacres of 1648–49. From that time on, it was said, a wise and righteous rabbi could call forth the *Golem* to defend any Jews who were threatened.

Rabbi Hershel Nachman was certainly a wise and righteous man. Of this his son had no doubt. And the Nazis were certainly the most fearsome threat the Jews of Eastern Europe had ever faced. But Rabbi Nachman had not summoned the *Golem*. Instead, he had called upon his own twenty-four-year-old son.

Reb Pinchas Nachman knew himself for what he was — not a supernatural being with terrifying powers, but a quiet and peaceful fellow devoted to the study of the *Talmud*. He was tall and strong, yes, but he was otherwise ill equipped to be the savior of his people. Of course, he wasn't being asked to save his people. Not exactly.

"Ah, Pinchas," his father called to him. "We are ready for you."

"We have been waiting for you," Josef Frankel added pointedly. Reb Frankel was a temple rarity — a *fat* old man. He was the richest Jew in Prague, the founder and owner of Frankel's Department Store.

Reb Nachman crossed the stone floor to the ten old men. A *minyan*, he thought, always a *minyan*. These were the graybeards, the soul of the congregation. They spent their days here, wrapped in their *tallithim, davening* — mumbling in constant prayer, swaying back and forth in their devotion.

At their feet was a rough pine box about the size of a valise. Its handles were made of rope. There were words stenciled on the two longest sides, in English: *Salesmen's Samples*. Reb Nachman knew the box would be waiting for him, but he was shocked to see it nonetheless.

The hush that had filled the nave now intensified into total silence. Reb Frankel abruptly stooped and opened the box. Pinchas couldn't stop himself from glancing inside. The interior was sumptuously lined and cushioned in blue velvet interwoven with gold threads.

Two other old men now stepped forward, Reb Karel Freuler and Reb Joseph Delmedigo. They were the oldest male members of the congregation and they had been entrusted with its greatest treasure. They carried it now, jointly, cradling it in their arms.

It was a piece of stiff yellowed parchment 137.3 meters long, carefully rolled up on two walnut scroll pins, which were bound together with silk ribbons embroidered with prayers. This was the original handwritten manuscript of the *Mishna Torah*, the code of Jewish law devised in 1165 by the legendary medieval Jewish philosopher, Moses Ben Maimon — Maimonides. It was the Altneushul's greatest treasure and the single most valued possession of the Jews of Czechoslovakia, a relic of historic and holy significance.

While everyone else watched, Reb Freuler and Reb Delmedigo bent slowly toward the box. They delicately lowered the scroll into its blue velvet cushioning. It fit perfectly. An instant later Reb Frankel closed the box and sealed it with a small steel padlock. He handed the key to Reb Pinchas Nachman, who accepted it uneasily.

The others now stepped back from the box. Rabbi Nachman knelt before it, placing his hands near the rope handles. *"Sh'ma Yisroayl Adonoy elohaynu, Adonoy ehod,"* he chanted, the others murmuring along with him.

Then the rabbi stood and took his son's hands in his own. He looked searchingly into the young man's eyes.

"You are ready for your trip, Pinchas, in your heart and in your soul?"

"Yes, Father."

"You have the map . . . and the train timetables?"

"In my pocket, Father."

"The names of the *landsmen* who will meet you at each stage of your journey?"

"Also in my pocket, written in Hebrew."

"You know you must arrive in Le Havre no later than Wednesday morning, August 23. The *Normandie* will sail at

11

about one o'clock."

Pinchas nodded. He had heard these instructions at least six times.

"Are you listening to me? Do you have the twenty-five dollars for the boat?"

"It is in my coat, Father, in the lining."

Rabbi Nachman glanced at the other old men. Reb Frankel stepped forward and took Pinchas's hand.

"We have given you the grave responsibility of safely conveying our treasure to Rabbi Herzberg in Brooklyn, USA," he said solemnly.

"Yes, sir," Reb Nachman replied. He became aware that he was having trouble breathing.

"I know you will succeed, Reb Nachman." The fat old man was trying to be encouraging.

"I would give my life to accomplish my mission," Pinchas said, his voice louder than he had intended.

Reb Frankel paused briefly, then responded. "We all hope that will not be necessary."

Everyone had been trying to delay the moment of departure, but now there was simply nothing more to say. Rabbi Nachman clasped his son's hands once more. "Go with God, my son," he said softly.

Pinchas didn't have enough air in his lungs to reply.

He forced down a deep breath, picked up the box by its rope handles, and started up the stairs, aware that every one of the old men was watching him. He did not look back.

Day One

Monday, August 21, 1939

The young girl in the gingham jumper slowly and sadly walked down the desolate country lane, a suitcase in one hand and basket in the other. A small dog trotted happily beside her, unaware of her problems.

Soon the girl came to a little wooden bridge. On the other side, just off the road, a broken-down circus wagon sat among the weeds. Faded letters on the side announced that it belonged to "Professor Marvel, acclaimed by the crowned heads of Europe. Let him read your past, present, future in his crystal." As the girl approached the wagon, she heard cheerful humming coming from within.

Soon a man in a frock coat and a felt hat emerged from the wagon and spotted the girl and the dog. He greeted them in a friendly manner, calling them house guests and asking who they might be. Then he decided to figure it out for himself.

He sat down on a small upturned barrel near a little cook fire. Tapping his forehead thoughtfully, he asked the girl not to tell him who she was. Then he speculated that she was traveling in disguise. But he immediately dismissed that thought. Another idea occurred to him — that she was going on a visit. Somehow, though, he knew that was wrong, too.

13

Finally, as if he'd known it all along, he ventured one last thought — that she was running away.

The girl smiled for the first time, enchanted by the man. She was amazed at the accuracy of his guess, but the professor denied that it was a guess. He knew such things, he said. Then he began to speculate about why she might be running away — that she was misunderstood at home, that she wasn't appreciated, that she wanted to see other lands, big cities, big mountains, big oceans.

Once more the girl was amazed and delighted. She told the professor that it was as though he could see what was inside of her.

During their conversation, the man had been absent-mindedly holding a stick on which he'd been cooking a frankfurter. Suddenly, the girl's dog snatched the frankfurter and began wolfing it down.

"Toto!" the girl cried out, mortified. She told the dog his nibbling wasn't polite, since they hadn't yet been asked.

David Nathan looked away from the movie screen toward the auditorium entrance. His eye had been caught by two people coming down the aisle, a man and a woman. Briefly, in the theater's darkness, he'd thought it was them. But no, it was just a couple of tourists.

Tourists. Nathan couldn't imagine what still drew them to Berlin. He wouldn't have been here himself if Roosevelt hadn't asked him to come. He hated this place. It had been bad enough three years ago, when FDR had sent him here to handle the Jesse Owens matter. Now it was worse — more organized, more somber, more brutal.

The entire city, it seemed, was covered with propaganda posters. One showed a mother nursing a child, "in the service of the state," it said. Another poster, "Blood and Soil," featured a giant eagle standing on a giant Nazi swastika. A third, a poster that advertised a documentary film entitled

"The Eternal Jew," was dominated by ominous, long-nosed greenish faces superimposed over a red star of David.

In the mid-1920's, when David Nathan was at Columbia, his father had taken him to Berlin, as part of a father-son tour of Europe. It had been a very different city back then. As Nathan remembered it, it was a feverish, turbulent, and recklessly hedonistic place. It was the cosmopolitan crossroad of Europe, the natural sanctuary for thousands of Russian refugees from the Bolsheviks and a second home to scores of writers and artists from England and the United States.

The Berlin of the mid-twenties had been troubled and crazy, with inflation running wild and with no effective government. But it had Bertolt Brecht, Walter Gropius, and Vladimir Horowitz. It had Paul Klee, George Grosz, and Albert Einstein. It had a mind, a heart, and a soul. And except for the streets and the buildings and the parks, it was nothing at all like this place.

Nathan held his watch up to the little light on the side of his seat. They should be here in another ten minutes. Then the fun would begin. He looked around the theater. As he had anticipated, there were about a hundred people in the auditorium, some tourists, some tired shoppers, a few secretaries playing hooky, some children, a couple of assistant envoys from the nearby diplomatic missions, resting after a demanding lunch. Just about the right number for his purpose.

He looked back at the screen. To his surprise, the muted black-and-white image he'd been watching had been replaced by almost garish Technicolor. He saw a fairy-tale village surrounded by a fairy-tale brook, unnaturally large fairy-tale flowers and fairy-tale mountains in the distance. A curling yellow cobblestone road led directly into the heart of the village.

The girl in the gingham jumper—it turned out to be blue—was plainly as astonished at the sight as Nathan was.

15

While birds twittered sweetly and choral music swelled, she walked slowly toward the village, carrying her little black dog in her arms. "Toto," she said, gazing at the place wide-eyed, "I have a feeling we're not in Kansas anymore."

Nathan glanced at his watch again. The minute hand had hardly moved at all. It was always like that when the action was about to begin—even trivial action, like this playlet he'd worked out with his charges.

His charges. The words had a slightly rancid taste. Since he'd gotten involved in that near catastrophe in Miami in 1932, he'd undertaken a dozen difficult and dangerous missions for the President of the United States, against gangsters, spies, assassins, corrupt politicians, and dictators. But this was the first time FDR had ever asked him to babysit.

No, that was unfair. FDR had never yet given him a trivial assignment. No doubt this one was also crucial. But the President hadn't seen fit to tell him exactly why it was so important to get this man out of Berlin and bring him back to America.

Nathan had not found it easy to travel abroad, to leave his mother and brother so soon after his father's funeral. But it was something to do, something that could keep his mind occupied. And maybe that's what FDR had in mind.

So last Friday night he had dropped everything, hopped on Pan Am's Yankee Clipper—a majestic seventy-five-passenger Boeing 314 flying boat—and spent twenty-nine long hours flying to Marseilles. In the process, he had missed out on the opportunity to take some girl named Margo ("such a beauty," his aunt had told him) to see Tallulah Bankhead and Florence Williams in "The Little Foxes" at the National Theater.

Then, on Sunday, while the Yankees had played a twin bill with the Athletics, his season box seat behind first base conspicuously empty, he took a Deutsche Lufthansa Junkers Ju 52/3m to Templehof Airport, just outside of Berlin. It wasn't until this morning, when he had picked up a copy of the *International Herald Tribune* at the Adlon newsstand, that he'd learned the Yankees had split the doubleheader and that DiMaggio, whose career he was following avidly, had gone two-for-nine for the day.

That wasn't all he'd learned, of course. The *Trib* had been full of dire news about the European situation. Hitler had ordered one hundred thousand German and Slovak troops to Czechoslovakia's Polish border. Pope Pius had made one of his frequent fervent pleas for peace. And Switzerland had decided to strengthen the garrisons on her German and Italian borders.

The news from home had been somewhat more pleasant. Robert Moses was offering two new plans to remodel Coney Island. Unlike his 1937 proposal, they preserved the amusement park and hot dog stands. In another article, he read that attendance at the World's Fair in Flushing Meadow had been pretty good last weekend. And one of the Fair's best attractions, Billy Rose's Aquacade, which starred Johnny Weissmuller, Eleanor Holm, Morton Downey, Gertrude Ederle, and "a cast of 500 girls," tallied 2,705,054 visitors.

Up on the movie screen, a troupe of midgets clad in brightly colored fairy-tale costumes were prancing through their gingerbread village, singing, in their cute, chirpy little voices: "Ding dong, the witch is dead. Which old witch? The wicked witch. Ding dong, the wicked witch is dead . . ."

Once more, David Nathan held his watch up to the light. They'd be here in five minutes, assuming they were on time. No, he was being petty. Victor Meisner—*Doctor* Victor Meisner, that is, the boy wonder scientist—might be an obnoxious and egotistical young man, but there was no evidence that he wasn't punctual.

There was evidence, however, that he was an infuriating person. Plenty of evidence. For instance, there was the matter of the plainclothes Gestapo agent who followed Victor wherever he went. Nathan had spotted the agent—a tough, square-shouldered woman in a gray raincoat—soon after he'd first met Victor at the prearranged table at Cafe Josty on Potsdamer Platz.

Identifying her hadn't exactly been a shining example of detective work. She'd come in on Victor's heels, followed him to the restroom and back, and stolidly stared at him while he and Nathan talked. She had all the subtlety of an anvil.

"Ever seen that woman before?" Nathan had asked the thin, scholarly-looking young man.

"Oh, her. Yes. She's always around somewhere."

"I think she's following you."

"Well, I suppose she is."

Nathan was taken aback. "You knew you were being followed?"

"I suppose I did. They follow all the Institute people they don't fully trust. The Jewish ones especially."

Infuriating.

"Why didn't you tell me earlier?" Nathan asked, not bothering to hide his annoyance.

"Well, I'm the scientist and you're the secret agent. I didn't want to—how do you say it?—poach on your territory."

"When both of our lives are at stake, I expect you to tell me everything that could possibly matter. Got that?"

"Whatever you say, Mr. Nathan." There was just the faintest hint of contempt in his voice, the tone twenty-five-year-old men like Victor used to convey their low opinion of an elder. Infuriating.

And then there was the business of Victor's sister. "You know, of course, that my younger sister lives with me in Berlin and that I won't leave the country without her."

Nathan hadn't known. No one had bothered to tell him. "Your little sister?" he asked, groaning inwardly, imagining a frightened little girl who could endanger them all. "There are other ways to smuggle a child out of the country. . . ."

18

"She's going with us or I'm not going. That's final."

It was infuriating.

"My orders," Nathan said evenly, "are to get you safely to the United States. I don't know exactly why that's so important, but those were my orders. No one said anything about a sister."

"Well, then," Victor said with that slight smile of his, "why don't you tell her yourself that you intend to abandon her, a Jewish girl, in Nazi Germany. That's her, coming in the door now."

Nathan swiveled around to see a startlingly attractive young woman striding toward them, grinning broadly, waving to a friend on the other side of the crowded cafe, stopping briefly at a table to say hello. Everyone was looking at her.

She was in her early twenties, slender but well-proportioned, slightly taller than average. Her shoulder-length honey-blond hair swung freely as she looked around the room for friends and acquaintances. She had the face of an angel, a mischievous angel, a face dominated by large and expressive emerald-green eyes. A bit of stage makeup was still visible on her cheeks. She was *not* a little girl.

"Hullo, Victor," she said, hardly acknowledging her brother. "Sorry it took me so long. The rehearsal ran late. And you, you must be Mr. . . . ah . . . Cameron. That's what we're supposed to call you, I understand. You're much younger and better looking than I imagined. I thought you'd have scars and a beard." Smiling gaily, she extended her hand. Nathan shook it awkwardly.

"This is my sister Tina, Mr. Nathan," Victor announced coolly. "Was there something you wanted to say to her?"

Up on the movie screen, there was a sudden clap of thunder, a burst of portentous music, and an explosion of red smoke on the village square. A black-hatted, green-skinned witch emerged from the smoke, waving a broomstick. The midgets scattered, screaming in terror.

19

"I thought you said she was dead," said the little girl to the lovely gowned woman standing next to her.

"That was her sister, the wicked witch of the East," the woman cooed. "This is the wicked witch of the West. She's worse than the other one."

Nathan checked his watch again. They should be walking into the theater anytime now. And if everything worked out as planned, they'd be out of Germany in a few hours. Then, home.

It had gone very smoothly this morning. Nathan's contact at the American Embassy had delivered false passports for Victor and Valentina Meisner on schedule, as promised. Then Nathan had quickly found and purchased exactly the sort of automobile they needed — a '37 Citroen 11 CV. "The gangster's favorite," the used car dealer had told him.

And then, at the Meisners' apartment, he had found Victor's and Tina's trunks packed and ready, as agreed. The luggage office at his hotel — the Adlon — had accepted them without hesitation and guaranteed their delivery to Le Havre by the next day. Nathan had even called to double-check the arrangements at the German/Netherlands border crossing. Everything was ready for their arrival.

Then, after a pleasant, uneventful lunch of Wiener schnitzel and Botzow beer at the Ashingers Bierquellen on Friedrich Strasse, he'd driven to Hermann-Goering Strasse, parked the car, and walked the two blocks to the Ufa Kammerlichtspiele, the cinema on Potsdamer Platz.

Unfortunately, Nathan had arrived at the theater before the box office girl was ready to sell tickets. He'd had to wait several minutes for her to break his twenty-reichsmark note and, even then, had been forced to accept so many coins that his pockets sagged with them. Still, he was the first person to enter the movie house, so he was able to choose exactly the seat he wanted. Everything was going just as he had planned.

Nathan looked toward the auditorium entrance again.

Just then, young Dr. Victor Meisner walked into the theater, thin, gawky, and unkempt as usual. If central casting had been searching for someone to play Einstein's smartest student or one of Germany's top scientists—both of which he actually was—they would have been delighted with Victor Meisner.

Victor walked down the aisle without even glancing at Nathan. He took a seat at the far side of the auditorium, as planned, and focused his attention on the screen. An instant later, the female Gestapo agent entered, her raincoat buttoned up to her neck. She was a stocky, grim short-haired lady with a face like a baked potato. She sat down three rows behind Victor, where she could easily keep an eye on him. There was an empty seat on either side of her.

On the screen, the pretty lady in the white gown pointed her star-tipped wand at the girl's feet. The girl looked down and was amazed to find that she was wearing glittering ruby-covered shoes.

The witch demanded her slippers back, insisting that only she knew how to use them, that they would be useless to the girl. She commanded the girl to return them.

But the pretty woman advised the girl to keep her feet inside the slippers, saying that their magic must be very powerful or the witch wouldn't want them so badly.

The pretty woman's advice angered the witch, who told her to stay out of the argument or she'd fix her as well.

The lady dismissed the witch's threat with a laugh, calling it rubbish. She told the witch that she had no power there and to be gone before somebody dropped a house on her, too.

Nathan looked toward the theater entrance just in time to see Tina stroll in. She was wearing an adorable little blue sailor suit and her hair was pulled back in pigtails. All in all, she looked about thirteen.

Pausing at the head of the aisle, Tina spotted David Nathan and winked broadly. He frowned and gestured toward the front of the auditorium. Tina shrugged and walked on, sliding into the row in which the Gestapo agent was sitting. She sat down directly beside the woman.

Nathan looked toward the movie screen. The little girl was now in the country, at the fork of the yellow cobblestone road. She appeared to be having a conversation with a scarecrow.

At that instant, a young girl's voice rang out in fear—not from the screen, but from the auditorium. "Stop that! Don't touch me there!" It was Tina, doing a very credible imitation of an adolescent.

The chunky Gestapo woman stared at Tina in shock and disbelief, and the other patrons turned to see what was going on.

"It was you!" Tina cried out, pointing at the Gestapo woman. "You put your hands between my legs and you—"

"Young woman, you are mistaken, I assure you. . . ."

"Liar! Filthy liar! Stop touching me, you queer!"

"Leave that girl alone!" Nathan shouted angrily.

"But I—"

"Mother said only my husband could touch me there!" Tina screamed at the top of her voice. "What have you done to me? What have you done?" She began sobbing loudly.

By now, everyone in the theater had turned to see what the commotion was about. Several men had left their seats and were hurrying toward Tina and the Gestapo woman.

"Young lady, I assure you—"

"You dirty Jew!" Tina screamed.

"Grab her!" yelled one of the theater patrons.

"Get the manager! Call the police!" another screamed out, running toward Tina and her alleged molester.

Three men reached the Gestapo woman almost simultaneously and began grappling with her. With an angry roar, she pushed them off. Then two other men joined the fray and an elderly woman began pummeling the Gestapo agent with her purse.

Up on the screen, ignored by everyone now except for few children in the very front row of the theater, a man in a tin suit was singing and dancing, insisting that he could be kind of human, if he only had a heart.

In the bright August sun outside of the theater, a small troop of *Deutsche Jungvolk*—a bunch of eleven-year-old boys in brown shirts, black ties, and short black pants—picked its way through the automobiles and trolleys that clogged Potsdamer Platz, marching past the giant department stores and the clock tower in the middle of the square.

They were members of the junior division of the Hitler Youth, fresh from a rally at the Lustgarten. And their leader, a sickly-looking man in his forties with hairless legs and knobby knees, was taking them to see a movie.

The troop of *Deutsche Jungvolk* pulled up to the Ufa Kammerlichtspiele, in front of a poster of a little girl wiping the eyes of a tearful man in a lion costume. The troop leader approached the box office window, his boys crowding into the lobby beside him. "Fifteen children, please," he told the woman, shoving bills under the window.

"Yes, sir. You do know that the movie started about a half hour ago, don't you?"

"The *Deutsche Zeitung* said two o'clock."

"No, sir, one o'clock."

The troop leader angrily pointed at his newspaper. "It's right here," he said. "*The Eternal Jew,* at two o'clock, four o'clock, six o'clock, eight o'clock, and ten."

"No, no," the box office woman protested. "We're playing *The Wizard of Oz,* at one, three, five, seven, and nine. It's a Premiere Showing."

"Impossible!" screamed the leader of the *Deutsche Jungvolk* troop. He was getting overwrought.

Inside, while the Gestapo woman was scuffling with the angry moviegoers, Tina slipped away and hurried toward the back of the theater. Victor was only a few steps behind her. They joined Nathan and headed for daylight, only to run into the *Deutsche Jungvolk* kids clogging the lobby.

They'd almost pushed through the crowd of little boys and out onto the street when the Gestapo woman emerged from the auditorium, disheveled and bleeding from the nose. "Get them," she screamed, pointing at Nathan and the Meisners. "Stop them! They're enemies of the Fatherland!"

Nathan broke into a run, pocket change clinking loudly with every step, Victor and Tina on his heels. They were heading toward a canary-yellow trolley about to depart from its stop in front of the stately Palast Hotel. And they were being chased by a gaggle of midget Nazis in short black pants.

Nathan dipped deep into his pocket. If they're anything at all like American kids, he told himself, this ought to slow them down. He flung a huge handful of change into the air. It came down like a shower of little bells, clinking and pinging off the cobblestones and bouncing in dozens of different directions.

The front-runners among the brave little lads tried desperately to scoop up the change on the fly, but that proved impossible. As they bent down to retrieve it, the boys coming up from behind crashed into the front-runners, sending everyone sprawling. In a few seconds, the troop of *Deutsche Jungvolk* had turned into a reasonable facsimile of two football teams trying to recover a goal-line fumble.

Nathan, Victor, and Tina hopped on the trolley at the last possible second, and it pulled away from the unruly mound of little boys and out of reach. The other trolley passengers, mostly staff members from nearby embassies and rich matrons loaded with packages from nearby stores, casually looked out the windows in other directions or buried their faces in their newspapers.

The trolley turned sharply north and rumbled up Hermann-Goering Strasse, through a block of fashionable shops and on past the edge of the Tiergarten and its inviting greenery and winding paths. Nathan stood at the back window, watching the sprawling boys trying to untangle themselves and resume the chase. They had almost managed it when one of the little Nazis spotted another cache of coins and initiated a second round of diving and stumbling.

At that instant, Nathan felt a tap on his shoulder. It was the conductor, a small red-cheeked old man with a huge walrus mustache. He held out the fare box and Nathan dumped in another handful of coins. "Ah, boys," said the conductor pleasantly, "they can be so troublesome sometimes."

"Yes indeed," Nathan agreed.

The conductor briefly touched a finger to the brim of his cap, in a wry salute, and went on his way.

Victor and Tina, both a little wide-eyed and winded, had found themselves seats near the door. "A little closer than I would have liked," Nathan remarked.

"It certainly was," Victor said coldly.

Nathan handed the false passports to his charges, shielding the exchange with his body. Then he looked back in the direction they'd come from. No little Nazis were in pursuit. Everything seemed quite normal.

Ahead of the trolley now, to the right, loomed the massive eighty-five-foot-tall sandstone monument known as Brandenburger Tor, its twelve gigantic Doric columns supporting a mighty sandstone Attica, itself crowned by a copper sculpture of four horses drawing the chariot of the Goddess of Victory.

The trolley squealed to a stop at a red light, to allow auto traffic to pour between Brandenburger Tor's Doric columns and into Pariser Platz, at the head of Unter den Linden.

"Here," Nathan commanded, abruptly realizing that the light would be green in a moment, since Berlin traffic signals operated on a hysterically accelerated thirty-second cycle.

The three of them stepped off the trolley and walked briskly through Brandenburger Tor, into Pariser Platz, a

huge paved square filled with pedestrians, bicyclists, automobiles, and trolleys. The imposing Academy of Art, a fine
example of neoclassic architecture, occupied the south side
of the square, beyond a little rectangle of closely cropped
grass, reflecting pools, flowers, and sculpted shrubs. On the
north side, beyond a second, identical little park, lay the
French Embassy.

"Where are we going?" Victor asked, ready to criticize.

"We're circling back to our automobile," Nathan replied
brusquely. He was not fond of explaining himself.

"What kind of car did you buy us?" Tina asked. "I hope
you got us a Bugatti. Or maybe a BMW Cabriolet. That's
my favorite."

"A Citroen 11 CV."

"Oh, ugh!"

Nathan turned toward Tina, ready to reprimand her. But
her appearance startled him. She'd shed her sailor suit
jacket, revealing the simple, well-filled white blouse beneath. She'd also undone her pigtails and somehow — evidently on the trolley — had managed to put on lipstick. The
thirteen-year-old girl had vanished. In her place was this
lovely young woman, glowing with life.

Tina smiled disarmingly. "Tell me, Mr. Cameron, was I
all right in the movie theater?"

Nathan's annoyance evaporated. "Just fine," he admitted.

"She always fishes for compliments," Victor told Nathan
maliciously.

"I'll stop fishing on the day I get one from you," Tina
parried.

Victor groaned.

By now, they'd reached the beginning of Unter den Linden — The Linden, most people called it. It was surely the
most famous and probably the most beautiful boulevard in
Berlin, a kind of German Champs-Elysées. The Linden was
really three thoroughfares: a pedestrian promenade in the
middle and a broad street on either side, lined with first-

26

class hotels, exquisite shops, handsome palaces, university buildings, art galleries, and sidewalk cafes.

The street had been named for the two rows of linden trees that ran down the center of the boulevard. When Nathan had come here to deal with the Jesse Owens matter, he recalled, the trees had been healthy and full. But the beautiful old lindens had been ripped out during the construction of a subway, and their replacements were still small and scrawny.

Nathan also noted other changes. The three rows of electric arc lights that lit up the Linden at night were now permanently capped by Nazi eagles. And Nazi flags—black swastikas in a circle of white, on a field of red—hung from every third building.

There was nothing surprising about this, nothing particularly ominous. It was just that the Nazis considered the Linden an ideal parade route. On every likely occasion, they marched battalions of goose-stepping Storm Troopers from Brandenburger Tor at one end of the street to the Lustgarten at the other end. There, in the enormous open plaza between the Altes Museum and the domed Royal Palace, Hitler enjoyed fulminating in front of the multitudes.

Blending in with the shoppers and tourists, Nathan and his charges strolled down the central promenade, past the square, bulky Adlon Hotel, the Berlin equivalent of New York's Waldorf-Astoria, past the reading room of the Berliner Lokal-Anzieger, past stationers, trunk makers, furriers, and jewelry shops. No one paid the slightest attention to them—or at least not to the men. Everyone noticed Tina, but that was to be expected.

Then, behind them, Nathan heard the irritating singsong cawing characteristic of European sirens. It was distant at first, then closer. "This way," Nathan quietly told Victor and Tina. "Briskly, but not in a panic. Laugh and smile if you can."

27

As the siren grew louder, Nathan led the Meisners across the promenade, to the south side of the street. They entered Conrad Felsing's clock and watch shop.

A fat, balding man in his mid-fifties approached at high speed. He was impeccably dressed in a white summer suit made of raw silk. There were watches on both of his wrists and his vest was festooned with several gold chains, each no doubt leading to still another watch. His entire shop was ticking.

"Can I assist you?" he asked in a lilting, high-pitched voice.

"Well, yes you can," Nathan replied, affecting a slight Texas twang. "This is my niece, Lilly, and her fiancé, Jack. They're getting married next month and I want them each to have a fine timepiece as a present from me. Do you think you can handle that?"

"Oh yes, sir," the fat man said, scarcely able to conceal his glee.

"Good. Now, why don't you young people just look at the man's wares and pick out something expensive. I'll go down the street, get myself a cigar, and be back in a minute. That okay with you, kids?"

"Just fine, Uncle Frank," Tina cooed. "And thank you so much. You're just the nicest man."

Victor just grunted.

Nathan sauntered back down the Linden, toward Brandenburger Tor. The sirens were louder and closer now, and he was starting to get worried. Had that Gestapo Brunhilde sounded a city-wide alarm? Would there be hundreds of Gestapo agents—or even worse, SS officers—crisscrossing Berlin, searching for them, complicating all his plans?

Two motorcycles with sidecars came roaring through Brandenburger Tor, the traffic scurrying to make way for them. They slowed down and split up as they hit the Linden, one taking the north avenue, the other the south. The men in the sidecars, who were wearing the fearsome black

28

uniforms of Himmler's Allgemeine SS, carefully scanned the sidewalks and the promenade.

As the motorcycles approached, Nathan scampered across the street, forcing one of the motorcycles to swerve. The driver shook a fist at him but did not slow down. Well, Nathan decided, if they're looking for me, they don't have much of a description.

Back at the clock shop, Tina and Victor examined a tray of Swiss watches. "How many jewels do these have?" Tina asked.

"These have seventeen," Herr Felsing told her, indicating a group on the left side of the tray. "Those have twenty-four." He pointed to the group on the right.

"Don't you have any with more diamonds?" Tina asked innocently.

Victor shot her a dirty look.

"In the safe in the back room, yes," said Herr Felsing.

"Could you get them for me, please?"

Felsing hastened away, thinking about Patek Philippes, Vacheron-Constantines, and high profits.

"We shouldn't wait here very long," Victor told his sister.

"What do you mean? He said he'd be back for us in a few minutes."

"If the Gestapo doesn't have him already."

"Oh, I'm sure they don't," Tina said. "He's much too clever for them. Look how he got us away from the *Deutsche Jungvolk*."

"You think that was clever? I think it was lucky."

"Oh, Victor, you think everyone is stupid except you."

"I think *you're* stupid if you trust that man."

"He's risking his life to get us out of Germany. Isn't that worth something?"

"It is his job, you know."

"He's a very unusual man, Victor. Don't you sense it?"

"You mean because he's Roosevelt's private agent?"

"No."

"Every man you meet is special, Tina," Victor said.

"I think there's something very sad about him," Tina went on, ignoring Victor's sarcasm.

"Sad? Oh, God, here we go again."

Herr Felsing appeared at the door to the back room, balancing half a dozen trays of watches against his stomach. "I think I've found just what you want," he said, beaming.

Sitting on a bench on the promenade, Nathan watched the motorcycles move slowly toward the Royal Palace at the far end of the Linden, scanning the pedestrians. Then he saw two large black vans pull to a stop two blocks ahead of the motorcycles. Each disgorged about a dozen black-uniformed SS men, who immediately fanned out among the pedestrians and began demanding identity papers. Nathan glanced back toward Brandenburger Tor, instinctively seeking an escape route. Two more trucks. Two dozen more SS men. But no little Nazis in short pants, thank God.

Nathan sighed deeply. He should have known this wouldn't be easy. What was it his father liked to say? "Every downhill has its uphill." How true, how true. He stood, stretched casually, and strolled back to Felsing's clock shop and walked in.

"I hate to interrupt you kids," Nathan said, "but I guess we all forgot that Lilly has an appointment in a few minutes to get her wedding dress fitted. Your mother must already be there, young lady."

"Oh dear," said Herr Felsing.

"We'll be back later," Tina reassured him.

"But we have to hurry now," Nathan said. "Jack, you shouldn't be in on this. Bad luck, you know. Why don't we meet you somewhere afterward?"

"Wait a minute, I—"

"I'm afraid we don't have time to take a vote on this, Jack," Nathan said pleasantly. His eyes said shut up and do what you're told.

"But—"

"We could pick you up at the tower," Tina suggested.

"The tower?"

"Do you know how to get there?" Nathan asked.

"Of course, but—"

"How long will it take?"

"About a half hour, I think, but—"

"We should be there shortly afterward," Nathan said. "And if we're not there in an hour, leave without us. We'll catch up."

"I'd rather wait for you there," Victor insisted. He was barely managing to contain his anger.

Nathan gave in. "Whatever you say, Jack, but we gotta run now."

He hustled Tina through the door. "See you later, darling," she said to her brother, cheerily.

"Of course."

Their eyes met. A profoundly tender expression flickered across Victor's face, then faded away. "Promise me," his father had said just before they took him away, "promise me you will take care of her no matter what." And Victor had promised. It was the deepest commitment he had ever made. And now he'd turned her over to this American, to this man he barely knew. Had he done the right thing? He simply did not know.

Herr Felsing was looking at him strangely. "She has a very poor memory," Victor said.

Felsing smiled and shrugged. "Not a fatal flaw." He began to gather up the watch trays.

"No, not a fatal flaw," Victor agreed.

"In fact, rather charming."

"Yes."

Victor walked out of the shop and headed for the new S-Bahn subway kiosk half a block away, resisting the powerful impulse to look for Tina and David Nathan. There were SS men everywhere, checking identity papers at random. One was standing at the subway entrance. Victor examined the false passport Nathan had given him. It bore his picture and the name Jack Cameron. It looked authentic enough, but the SS man would be the final judge of that.

When his turn came, Victor presented his passport to the young SS officer at the S-Bahn entrance. He had no choice. He watched, heart pounding, as the pimply fellow looked first at the picture, then up at him, then handed the passport back and reached for the next one. A little weak-kneed, Victor headed down the subway steps, relieved and rather impressed by Nathan's ability to come up with convincing forged documents.

David Nathan and Tina Meisner walked down the Linden arm in arm, talking animatedly, frequently laughing. They passed the Linden Cabaret, Van Santen's gift shop, the Invalidendank box office in front of the Metropolitan Theater, and the fussy little Kaiser-Galerie shopping arcade. They didn't run into any SS officers.

"Where is this tower?" Nathan asked.

"In Potsdam. About a twenty-minute drive. What was the idea of sending Victor off on his own?"

"Is the autobahn out of Berlin near Potsdam?"

"Not far. I'm worried about Victor."

"He should be fine." Nathan said. "His new passport will get him past anyone who doesn't know him personally."

"How can you be so sure?"

"The passport is genuine German government issue — except for the name and the picture."

"I see. But I still don't know why we had to split up."

Nathan realized that the only way to shut her up was to explain. "Well, they were looking for two men and a little girl," he said, hoping that would do it.

"Yes?"

32

"Well, if I knew Berlin well enough, I would have sent us all off in separate directions. But I had to stick with one of you. If I'd stayed with Victor, that would have been two men together—a suspicious combination. We could have dumped the little girl somewhere. But one man, that's okay. So is a man and a woman. Understand?"

"I suppose so."

They stopped for a red light at the corner of Unter den Linden and Friedrich Strasse, the busiest intersection in Berlin. A stream of automobiles, trolleys, double-decker buses, and bicyclists flowed past them for thirty seconds, then, after a flash of yellow, the light turned green again and traffic moved down the Linden for thirty seconds. Across the street and about a block ahead, a line of SS men was methodically making its way down the street.

"What now?" Tina asked.

Nathan pointed to the Cafe Unter den Linden across the street, on the corner. "We go in there," he said. "We sit at separate tables. Order coffee and biscuits. Don't talk to anybody. And act old."

"I'll be positively ancient."

"And if the SS comes in and asks for your passport, show it to them and pretend to be bored."

"Yes, master."

"When the SS sweep has passed," Nathan continued, "we'll retrieve the automobile and pick up Victor."

Inside the cafe, they both found tables beside the huge picture windows, which provided a fine view of the Linden. Nathan ordered a cup of coffee and had the waitress bring him a copy of the *Voelkischer Beobachter*. If the SS decided to question him, it would do no harm to be reading a Nazi newspaper.

Tina sat two tables away, facing Nathan, occasionally catching his eye and winking. When the waitress arrived, she ordered—loudly enough for him to hear—a plate of pastries, some ice cream, a glass of chocolate milk, and a

33

straw. When the waitress started to walk away, though, Tina called her back and changed her order to a cup of black coffee and a hard roll. Nathan wanted to spank her until she cried.

He sighed and unfolded his newspaper. "POLAND REJECTS GERMAN PEACE OFFER" read the banner headline. Among the other headlines: "GERMAN PASSENGER PLANES SHOT AT BY POLES" and "SLOVAKS MOBILIZE ARMY, DEMAND POLAND RETURN STOLEN LANDS."

Nathan knew what this must portend: a German invasion of Poland—within weeks, maybe days. And that, no doubt, meant war between Germany, France, and England. Well, it had been coming. The signs had been there for at least two years. He'd seen a particularly ominous sign himself last night, an air raid dress rehearsal in the heart of Berlin: anti-aircraft guns blazing away with blanks at imaginary bombers, firemen dousing make-believe fires, first-aid crews bandaging the sound arms and legs of placarded "wounded," red flares, black flags, and roped-off streets indicating places that had been "hit."

According to the papers, exercises of this sort were going on throughout Europe. In the last few months, England, France, Poland, and Italy had all mobilized their reserves for various periods. And there'd been practice blackouts in Paris and practice evacuations of children from London. How long before pretense turned into reality?

Nathan opened the paper to the second page. Now, here was a very strange item: Germany and the Soviet Union had signed a trade pact. They'd agreed to buy each other's goods and Germany had agreed to lend Russia the necessary funds at five percent per year. Now, this was highly unlikely, Nathan thought. Germany and Russia were blood enemies. But if it were really true, if Russia and Germany actually did intend to make some kind of deal, that was an ominous sign—even if it was just a commercial treaty. He just hoped nothing would prevent the three of them from getting out of Germany today.

Nathan looked up to see two SS men entering the cafe, a lieutenant and a corporal. They immediately began examining papers. The cafe patrons, evidently accustomed to such inquisitions, offered no protest.

The lower-ranking SS man, a tall, manly-looking fellow with blond hair and pale blue eyes, started down the row of tables by the window. He skipped an old lady, two priests, and a Japanese businessman. When he got to Nathan, he extended a hand and the American surrendered his passport. At that moment, however, the SS man spotted Tina. His eyes narrowed. He returned Nathan's passport without opening it and made his way to her table. Nathan casually crossed his legs and rested his hand on an ankle, just below the Smith & Wesson .38 Special revolver he had tucked in his sock.

"Papers, please," the SS corporal said to Tina. He took the liberty of standing very close to her.

Without a glance at him, Tina fished the new passport out of her purse and handed it over. She continued drinking her coffee while the SS corporal examined the document.

Nathan watched—and listened to—the conversation, glad, at least, that it was within earshot. Just what could he do to save them if things turned bad, if Tina couldn't handle the questioning? And he had no idea if she could. This wasn't playacting in the protective darkness of a movie theater or on the stage of some little playhouse, after all. This was the real thing.

"Is this *your* passport, Fräulein?" the SS corporal asked. His expression was hard and cold.

"Of course it is," she replied. She spoke as if addressing a moron.

Nathan considered the situation. He had a gun, but so what? What could he do with it? He certainly couldn't shoot *both* SS men. He might take a hostage, perhaps Tina. But how could they get away, with the streets full of SS patrols?

"You are Lilly Cameron?" the SS corporal asked Tina, reading the passport.

"Yes."

"Born where?"

"Berlin."

"I don't think Cameron is a German name."

Tina looked at him directly for the first time and fired off a smile, full force. "My father was a Swedish diplomat."

"Ah. And you were born . . . when?"

"In 1916. I am twenty-three years old."

The SS corporal leaned over and studied Tina's face carefully. "You look like you could be younger," he said.

"Thank you."

"Please stand."

Tina rose. In her simple white blouse and navy-blue skirt, she was lovely, elegant, and without question, womanly.

Nathan decided what he must do, if it came to that. He would shoot out the cafe's picture windows. In the noise and confusion, the SS men would almost certainly think someone on the street was shooting at them. While they were reacting to the threat, he and Tina would have a pretty good chance of slipping away. Nathan reached under his pant leg and slipped the Smith & Wesson from his sock. He was breathing heavily now.

The SS corporal examined Tina as she stood, taking special note of the white stripe on her navy blue skirt. "Without all that makeup," he said at last, "you might look like a teenager."

"Yes," Tina said demurely. "And without balls, the king would be queen."

The SS corporal jerked backward, his face flushing with embarrassment.

"Corporal Brunner," called the SS lieutenant. "We are looking for two men and a twelve-year-old girl. No grown women, however attractive. Are you finished over there? We have much territory to cover."

"I . . . yes." He handed back Tina's passport. "My compliments, Fraülein Cameron."

Tina bestowed another smile on him, a going-away present.

Nathan shook his head in wonderment. He simply had no idea what to make of this girl. Everything she did surprised him. He slipped the gun back into his sock and took a long sip of coffee.

When the two SS men left, David collected Tina and paid the checks. "You handled him quite well." He was uncomfortable dispensing compliments, but this one was deserved.

Tina dismissed it with a tiny shrug of her shoulders. "I've had a lot of practice with men asking me questions."

"So it appears."

"Where to now?" Tina inquired brightly.

Nathan once again felt the urge to spank her. "To the automobile," he said gruffly.

Outside, Nathan hailed a taxi. He held the door for Tina and climbed in after her. "Wertheim's, please," he told the driver.

Tina looked at Nathan in surprise. "We're going to a department store?"

"Briefly," Nathan said. He withheld an explanation, hoping that if he kept her in the dark, she'd behave. But he knew he really had no idea how to control her, how to get her to take their situation seriously. What a puzzling creature she was.

Tina boldly inspected the man sitting beside her in the back seat of the taxi, this American, this special agent. He was not especially impressive, as men go. He was thirty, possibly thirty-two, she guessed. He was broad-shouldered, but not particularly tall. His features were regular enough, although they were too stern to be called handsome. His hair, carefully parted on one side, was dark brown, almost black. He had an olive complexion. His eyes were gray-green and *much* too serious. His nose was slightly too big for the rest of his face, but it did soften him a bit. There was a slight blue tinge to his jaw, the product of a heavy beard.

He was wearing a light gray business suit—expensive, probably British, and almost identical to the brown one he'd had on yesterday. In fact, that's what bothered her most, even more than his obvious disapproval of her: He was *all* business. He wasn't even willing to banter with her, much less flirt. He had a sense of humor—she'd seen it in his eyes—but it was very well concealed.

Still, he had a certain quality about him, a certain energy and strength. What was the word Mr. Neustadt had used in acting school? A rare attribute he said he saw in every really talented actor or actress? Oh yes, *presence*. That was the word. That's what David Nathan had: presence. Tina was pleased with herself for remembering the word. Somehow, it made her feel a little less baffled by the man.

The taxi drove south for a couple of blocks on Friedrich Strasse, a busy commercial street lined with banks, haber-dashers, businessmen's hotels, and liquor stores and confec-tioners. There were no SS men in view.

At Leipziger Strasse, Berlin's central shopping street, they turned west and drove along a block of discount stores and unpretentious restaurants, then past the gigantic Reichspost Ministry and the even larger Luftwaffe head-quarters.

The taxi pulled up in front of Wertheim's department store, an eight-story granite palace with domed towers and gabled windows that occupied a full city block. Tina and David hopped out and joined a crowd of shoppers entering the store. It was an extraordinarily opulent place, in the current style of Berlin shopping emporia, with marble-lined walls, crystal chandeliers, and fountains made with tiles from the Kaiser's own ceramic works.

Nathan steered Tina onto an escalator, a recent and novel addition to the store. They glided up to the second floor, where they were met with a large sign that said "Women's Wear."

"As long as we're going shopping," Tina said with a naughty grin, "there are a few things I need. . . ."

Nathan interrupted curtly, "We're not going shopping."

"Well, then, what?"

"We're taking a shortcut. And we're making sure we haven't been followed."

"I see. No time, then, even to buy a nightgown?"

Nathan finally lost his temper. "Tina, I'm sick of all this joking around. Don't you realize the situation we're in?"

Tina studied Nathan, her stunning green eyes cold and dangerous. "I think I do realize that, Mr. Cameron. Remember, I've seen the Nazis take away every member of my family except my brother. So I think maybe I realize it even better than you do."

Once again, Nathan was taken aback by the girl. "Good," he said at last. "Good."

Nathan and Tina took a circuitous route to the down escalator, not saying a word to each other. They exited via a back door, on Vos Strasse, a narrow street that led directly to the more fashionable Hermann-Goering Strasse. Very shortly, they arrived at the Citroen 11 CV Nathan had purchased that morning.

"Oh yes," Tina said, breaking the chilly silence. "A Citroen. I'd forgotten."

"You don't like it?" Nathan asked. He was glad she was speaking again. "Why?"

"It's so ugly I'd be embarrassed to be seen in it."

Nathan forced a little chuckle. "Well, let's hope you're not."

They drove back up Hermann-Goering Strasse, toward Brandenburger Tor. Just before they turned west, into the Tiergarten, they stopped at a traffic light. To Nathan's dismay, a troop of *Deutsche Jungvolk*—the troop of *Deutsche Jungvolk*—was crossing the street in front of them.

"Quick, down!" he told Tina.

She ducked, but not before one of the little Nazis had looked their way, blankly at first, then with recognition.

"Look! The enemies!" the towheaded youngster sang out in a bell-like soprano. He waved an arm at them. One or two of his friends turned to see what he was pointing at.

Just then, the light changed. Nathan swung the Citroen onto Charlottenburger Chaussee, cutting right through the center of the Tiergarten, leaving the little boys in the distance.

"Did they see us?" Tina asked.

" 'Fraid so."

"Is that a problem? I mean, we left them behind okay."

"It's a problem if they give the SS a description of our car. They could be looking for us at the border or even before."

Tina was quiet.

"No matter," Nathan said, not wanting her discouraged. "We'll get Victor and get out of Berlin."

They drove through the wealthy neighborhoods in the western part of town, then caught the Automobile Strasse, the handsome new highway that ran through Grunwald Forest.

"Tell me about this tower we're going to," Nathan said, trying to restart the conversation and ease the tension.

"It's a very silly building," Tina said. "Einstein lived there. It was designed for him, I think."

"Why silly?"

"It looks like a big boot made out of concrete. There are windows leading up the boot, where the lace holes would be. And on the top, there's an observatory. Einstein hated the place. He thought it was the ugliest building he'd ever seen."

"You also know Einstein?"

"Of course. I haven't seen him since he went to America.

But we were great friends. I used to play in the tower while he and Victor and the other students worked in the observatory."

"What's he like?"

Tina giggled. It sounded like the tinkling of a wind chime. "He's a tickler."

"A tickler?"

"We used to get into tickling battles. You see, we're both terribly ticklish. We'd try to tickle each other into . . . 'crying Uncle,' I think you say."

"Who won?"

"Me—usually. I'd pull off his shoes and socks and start tickling his feet. He couldn't stand it. He'd end up gasping with laughter."

Nathan glanced over at Tina. Her eyes were sparkling again.

Over the clatter of the Citroen's engine, they heard a familiar and frightening sound coming from somewhere up ahead of them—the singsong siren of a police or emergency vehicle. It was faint at first, but it grew steadily louder. Soon they could see it approaching—a police car coming at them at high speed.

"There's only one," Nathan said. "We should be able to handle it." He reached down and took his Smith & Wesson revolver out of his sock.

Tina was amazed. "You've had that all the time?"

"Just a tool of the trade."

The police car sped toward them, then shot by without slowing, bent on some other urgent errand.

Nathan restored the gun to its hiding place.

"I didn't like that much," Tina said.

"The gun?"

"The police car. I could learn to like the gun."

They exited the Automobile Strasse about ten minutes later and drove on, into the pleasant, sleepy suburb of Potsdam, Tina providing directions. Before long, they came to

41

Einstein's concrete house, a distinct oddity in a neighborhood of gracious turn-of-the-century mansions.

Victor was sitting on the grass, his back propped up against the concrete structure. He was reading a book. He was so engrossed in it, in fact, that he hadn't noticed their approach. Nathan honked.

"You took your time getting here," Victor said, sliding into the back seat. "Was there any trouble?"

"They may have a description of our car," Nathan told him.

"Now, that's wonderful news," Victor said.

"Do try not to be so snotty, Victor," Tina told her brother with a mocking, saccharine smile.

In half an hour, they were on the autobahn, Hitler's four-lane homage to the motorcar. Nathan chose this route over the back roads because he thought it might be possible to outrun their pursuers, if any.

"If we're lucky enough to average fifty miles an hour," Nathan told Victor and Tina, "we should reach Gronau, on the Netherlands/German border, in about five hours, just after dusk."

"If we are not intercepted," Victor said.

"Yes, if we are not intercepted."

Tina dug through her purse and came up with a tube of lipstick. She began applying it.

Victor's eyes narrowed. "Why are you doing that, Tina?"

"Well, if we're intercepted, I want to be ready."

It had not been a good day for Lt. Kurt Jaekel. For the last ten hours, he'd been waiting to be admitted into the august presence of Grand Admiral Erich Raeder, Commander in Chief of the German Navy. All this time, he'd been sitting on a hard wooden bench in Raeder's outer office, trying to guess what the admiral wanted.

In the late morning, the admiral's pretty blond secretary

had taken pity on him and told him that Raeder had been summoned to an urgent meeting with Hitler. But he was "eager" to see Jaekel and would return "any time now." Jaekel had no choice but to stay.

During his wait, Jaekel drank seven cups of coffee, read and reread the only printed matter in the office — a set of ancient leather-bound Navy manuals — and awkwardly tried to flirt with the secretary, without any real success. He had not dared to leave the outer office, except for a single hurried trip to the men's room. Hunger was ever-present now.

The young officer had been thrilled when he'd gotten Raeder's summons at the officer's quarters last night. Finally, he hoped, he would have the opportunity to be of service to the man who had done so much for him, who'd told Jaekel about his father's heroic deeds in the World War, who had testified on his behalf at the trial, who'd gotten him into the Naval Academy and then Commando School, who'd sent gifts every Christmas and who'd always brushed aside Jaekel's halting thank-yous. "Just keeping a promise to an old friend," he would say.

"Care for a piece of pastry?"

Jaekel was startled out of his reverie. Raeder's little blond secretary was standing in front of him, holding a plate.

"I was getting ready to go home," she said, "and I found this in my desk. It isn't very fresh, but I know you haven't had anything to eat today, so —"

Jaekel immediately started gobbling down the pastry. "Thank you, I —"

"Also, I just received a call from the *Führer's* office. The meeting has finally adjourned. Admiral Raeder should be here soon. Sorry you've had to wait so long."

Though his mouth was full of pastry, Jaekel tried to smile at the girl. She looked at him with motherly concern, as if making sure he finished the pastry. He wondered, as he often did, how he could be so self-confident, so commanding with men and so inept with women? Why was it that the

43

more he was attracted to a woman, the more helpless he felt?

"Good-bye now," she said as the last of the pastry disappeared from the plate.

Jaekel sat down again on the bench, picked up a manual on artillery trajectories, and began leafing through it. The pages were neatly filled with endless columns of numbers.

Suddenly, the office door burst open and a tall, expansively smiling Grand Admiral Erich Raeder strode in, resplendent in his perfectly tailored, perfectly pressed navy-blue uniform, with its rows of medals and gold braid. His pudgy face glowed with manly vitality and purpose.

Trailing on Raeder's heels were his aides, a perfectly matched pair of hulking blond gods, each worthy of Phidias. Everyone called them Hansel and Gretel, although not to their faces. They differed only in height, Hansel being about six feet four, Gretel a mere six feet one.

Jaekel leaped to attention and Raeder's eyes clouded momentarily. Then he remembered. "Ah, Kurt. I am delighted that you're here."

The admiral dismissed Hansel and Gretel with a dramatic wave and marched briskly into his office, beckoning Jaekel to follow. Raeder's office was a cavernous chamber lined in black walnut and carpeted with a thick Oriental rug. A huge mahogany desk dominated the room. The admiral settled into the swivel chair behind it and motioned broadly to Jaekel to sit down in one of the red leather chairs facing the desk.

"It has been an incredible day, Kurt," Raeder said a little manically, his blue eyes blazing. "I have just come from the *Führer's* office. Great events are about to occur, events that will shake the world. I have much to do to get ready for them."

"The war will begin soon?"

Raeder was surprised by the innocence of Jaekel's question. Despite the spit and polish and the erect bearing, the young Navy officer was still a country boy.

"Yes, my young friend, there will be war very soon. More importantly, there will be victory, a glorious victory over all of our enemies and all of the rabble of the earth."

"Is that why you've summoned me? Is there a role for me to play?"

Raeder smiled. How good-looking Kurt Jaekel was, how naively willing. How much he resembled his father, Horst. And there it was again, the memory he always associated with this young man, the vivid recollections of the French destroyer, the depth charges, and the terrible fire that had swept the tiny submarine on which he and Jaekel's father had served.

Must it always be this way? Must those thoughts always intrude whenever he saw young Jaekel? Must he forever remember, in excruciatingly vivid detail, how the boy's father had rescued him from the fire, then died?

"Admiral?"

Raeder snapped back. "Yes, I may have a role for you to play, Kurt—a vital role. Are you prepared for duty? Are you in sound physical condition?"

"Yes, sir!"

Raeder had reviewed Jaekel's file a dozen times. He had studied the files of seven other commandos as well. None was the equal of this young man, but he still wanted to reassure himself. Raeder lifted a monocle to his left eye, opened Jaekel's file, and started to read through it again.

"Have you been swimming much lately?" he asked casually.

"Fifty laps a day, sir. My usual."

Raeder looked up at the young man on the other side of the desk. Except for his gleaming black hair, Jaekel was the model German man: tall, handsome, strong in mind and body, capable, eminently likable; a truly glorious specimen, and so very different from the fellow Raeder had met eight years ago.

The admiral recalled the Jaekel he had seen then: a devastated and defeated youth, an accused murderer who had snapped the neck of his opponent in the final round of the 1930 All-European Greco-Roman Wrestling Tournament. What would have become of the boy if he had not intervened?

"Tell me honestly, Kurt, could you still swim the channel?"

Jaekel laughed modestly. "Oh yes, sir, I am quite sure I could do it. But perhaps not as fast as in 1934."

"Of course. But as I recall, you used animal grease to keep yourself warm then. The rubber suits we have today are more efficient, are they not?"

"Yes they are." Jaekel said. "They retain body heat better than grease, which means swimmers have more energy for swimming."

Raeder nodded. He looked down at Jaekel's file. "I see you have excellent scores in unarmed combat."

"Yes, sir." Why all these questions?

"And you are a qualified marksman?"

"That is correct. Handguns and rifles."

"Tell me about your experience with explosives, please."

"Yes, sir. I have taken the basic and advanced explosives courses given in commando school, including placement, damage maximization, fusing, timer operation, concealment, booby-trapping." What was Raeder planning for him, some kind of sabotage mission?

Raeder smiled. He *liked* this young man. He liked what Jaekel had become and he gave himself some of the credit. He turned another page. The boy had excellent grades at the Academy, especially in math and navigation. His behavior record was spotless, except for that time when he'd seriously injured a classmate during an unarmed combat exercise—an accident, it was decided. Of course, Raeder knew better. He knew about Jaekel's temper.

"Your mother. She's still living on the farm?"

46

"Yes, sir. I saw her about a month ago. She tends the chickens and the pigs." He was perplexed by all these questions. Was Raeder ever going to get to the point? And what was the point, anyhow?

"As I remember," the admiral continued, "your farm's egg production was really quite exceptional." He was enjoying the young man's growing impatience.

"Yes, sir. It still is."

"That's nice," Raeder said. The only quality the boy was missing was worldliness. But in its own way, that was useful.

"Any girlfriends?"

Jaekel shrugged uncomfortably. "Not really."

"A robust, handsome fellow like you?"

"I never seem to meet any attractive women."

Just as well, the admiral thought. "I understand," he said. "Not many girls in commando school, eh? Tell you what, when you come back, I'll introduce you to my secretary. You'll like her."

"When I come back?"

"Yes, when you come back. And that brings me to the reason I asked you here."

Jaekel practically snapped to attention in his chair.

"When you leave me, I want you to proceed directly to Le Havre, France. I have put an automobile at your disposal for this purpose, a very special automobile."

"I'm to go to France?" Jaekel had hardly expected a pleasure drive.

"That is correct. When you arrive, you will find waiting for you a first-class ticket for the next voyage of the ocean liner *Normandie*. Of course, you know of her."

"Yes, sir. She steams from Le Havre to New York, does she not?"

"She does indeed. But the next time she departs from Le Havre, she will not arrive in New York."

The light dawned in Jaekel's eyes. "That is my mission?"

"Yes. You will take a bomb aboard the *Normandie* and

47

detonate it at a specific, predetermined point during the voyage."

"I will sink the ship?"

"The *French* ship, Kurt, remember that. The *French* ship. You will avenge your father at last." Raeder saw the wave of emotion pass over Jaekel's face, then the tears forming in his eyes, as he knew they would. He was, he reminded himself, an extremely good motivator of men.

"Just before the detonation," Raeder went on, "you will don a rubber suit and jump out of a porthole. A U-boat will be standing by to pick you up. Are you with me?"

"Yes, Admiral."

"Good. You will find the rubber suit in your luggage, which is already packed in the auto, along with everything else you will need, all the proper attire, including a tuxedo."

Jaekel was awed by the suddenness and enormity of all this, by the compliment and the responsibility. But he had questions.

"May I ask, sir, the underlying purpose of my mission?"

Raeder was pleased that the young man had recovered from his initial surprise and was beginning to think. "There are several purposes," the admiral replied. "First of all, the loss of the *Normandie* will be devastating to French morale. They call it their 'floating colony,' you know. They have invested their heart and soul in the ship."

Jaekel framed his next question carefully. "There will be hundreds of people on the *Normandie*, people of many nations," he said, "men, women, and children. What will become of them?"

"They must die." Raeder said bluntly. "There can be no survivors to tell the world what has happened. We must be free of any taint of suspicion. Remember, we are still at peace with France."

Jaekel was satisfied with this answer, but he had other questions. "You said the bomb had to be detonated at a predetermined point. Why?"

Raeder took a cigar out of the humidor on his desk, clipped off the end, and began to smoke. The boy might be a country bumpkin, but he was nobody's fool. He must be told.

"There is something else you should know, Kurt. We have learned that the French are sending the bulk of their gold reserves to America—three hundred billion deutsch marks' worth. They want to prevent our armed forces from capturing it, in the event of war. They are sending it abroad on the *Normandie*."

In his mind's eye, Jaekel saw bars of gold piled high in the ship's hold. "What a devastating loss to France."

"Exactly."

"But why not order a submarine to sink the ship?"

"We considered that, of course. But I decided against it. Why don't you tell me why?" Raeder wanted the young man to reason it out for himself.

Jaekel contemplated the question. He enjoyed being tested, perhaps because he almost always knew the answers. "The biggest problem would be the *Normandie*'s speed, I suppose. She cruises at about twenty-eight knots. A U-boat's best speed is about eighteen knots."

"And so—?"

"And so a U-boat would have to lie in wait for the passenger ship—and it would get only one shot at her. If the torpedo missed, or if it didn't sink the ship, *Normandie* would report the attempt and Germany would be vilified in the Western press."

The admiral was very pleased with his student. Every moment he spent with Jaekel increased his confidence. He took another long puff on his cigar.

"But there is another way, though," Jaekel said excitedly. "Both of our battle cruisers—the *Gneisenau* and the *Scharnhorst*—are just as fast as the *Normandie*. You could order one of them to intercept the French ship and *capture* the gold, instead of sending it to the bottom."

The admiral leaned all the way back in his chair, enjoying Jaekel's performance. "That is true," he said, "but there are problems with that idea, too."

Jaekel quickly saw the reason. "Control of the seas, you mean."

"Just so. The *Normandie* would certainly radio for help as soon as our warships appeared. British and US ships and planes would rush to her rescue before we were able to transfer the gold."

"The whole thing would stir up public opinion, too—especially in America," Jaekel added.

"It would be worse than the *Lusitania,*" Admiral Raeder agreed.

"What about hijacking the ship? A small force of commandos could seize the vessel and sail it back to Germany or to a friendly South American port."

"Yes," Raeder said. "We also considered that. But there are several flaws in the idea."

"Public opinion, you mean."

Raeder took a puff on his cigar. "Well, there's that, of course. But the French are bound to have troops aboard, guarding the gold and positioned to forestall any attempt to interfere with the ship's operation. It would be a very bloody battle and the ship would no doubt have time to radio for help. We couldn't be sure of success. No, the bomb is the only way."

"But all that gold," Jaekel went on. "What a shame to send it to the bottom of the ocean. What a loss. Wouldn't it be better to seize it and add it to our own gold reserves?"

"It certainly would." The admiral smiled, his face a mixture of amusement and cunning.

There was a knock on the door. "Enter," Raeder called, frowning.

Hansel entered the room timidly. "Admiral, you have a visitor in the outer office. . . ."

Raeder was thoroughly annoyed. "Tell whoever it is that I

cannot be interrupted now. He'll have to make an appointment like everyone else."

The aide waited respectfully until Raeder's little tantrum had subsided. "Sir, your visitor is Reichsmarshall Goering."

Raeder eyes opened wide, then he sprang to his feet. "Have him come in."

But Goering had already sauntered into the room. A huge man in a lovely dove-gray uniform, he was an even more imposing presence than the admiral. But he was also more odd; his eyes were too bright and his cheeks were unnaturally red. And he emitted a sweet, perfumy smell. He walked right up to Raeder's desk and leaned his stomach against it. The desk, massive as it was, slid back slightly across the Oriental rug toward the admiral.

Raeder quickly put his cigar in an ashtray. "An honor to have you visit, Reichsmarshall, a real honor."

"Yes, yes, yes. I know. I just dropped by to tell you that the *Führer* and I continued to discuss your *Normandie* project after you left."

"I see."

"I tried to talk him out of it. It is a stupid venture, after all, almost certain to fail." Goering went on without pause. "But he is mesmerized by the gold. So you still have your approval."

"Well, I—"

"I am warning you, Raeder, you are conducting this operation at the riskiest juncture in the history of the Reich. If anyone gets the slightest whiff that our nation is involved in the disappearance of the *Normandie,* we could lose everything. Everything! Do you hear me?"

"Yes, I—"

"Excellent. Now, can you guess what will happen to you if your operation misfires?"

Raeder finally found his spine. "I will be fighting for my job, I suppose."

"You will be fighting for your life, Admiral. Your life."

Jaekel had been sitting unnoticed in the red leather visitor's chair, watching without a word. But this was too much for him. This perfumed fat man was actually threatening the admiral's life! He stood suddenly, eyes blazing. Goering, sensing the movement, whirled toward Jaekel with surprising grace.

Admiral Raeder saw it all coming. "Reichsmarshall Goering!" he called out loudly. "I wish to present Lt. Kurt Jaekel. He is the young man I mentioned at the meeting."

Jaekel paused, startled by Raeder's voice. But Goering had already realized that the young man had intended to attack him. The Reichsmarshall grinned slyly at Raeder. Then he extended a smooth, fleshy hand toward the young naval officer. Jaekel hesitated, then shook it.

"Well, well, well, what have we here?" Goering asked. He circled Jaekel, openly appraising him. "A fine young sailor boy, with a fine young temper."

"Lt. Kurt Jaekel, sir!" Jaekel said.

"Yes, I know. The swimmer. And, as I recall, the wrestler."

Jaekel felt the color rush to his cheeks.

"And you're going to sink the *Normandie,* I suppose."

"I will do whatever Admiral Raeder orders me to do."

"Yes. Or at least you will try. Well, see to it that you succeed. For your sake and his. *Heil* Hitler!"

Goering strutted out of the room without another word, leaving Jaekel and Raeder staring at each other in wonder. Jaekel was the first to break the silence.

"I will succeed, Admiral Raeder," the young man said softly. "I promise you that."

"And I believe you, my young friend," Raeder responded, more calmly than Jaekel had anticipated. "But don't you worry about Reichsmarshall Goering. I can handle him. I handled him in the meeting with the *Führer* today, and I'll handle him after you've completed your mission."

"Yes, sir," Jaekel said, catching his breath.

"Now, let us get back to our business. We were talking about the gold, I believe. There is still much to tell you."

Jaekel's head was still swimming, but he managed to get back on track anyhow. "Yes, the gold. Can it be saved? It *must* be saved."

"You tell me, Lieutenant Jaekel. How would you sink the ship in the middle of the Atlantic Ocean but save the gold nevertheless?"

Jaekel had encountered such problems frequently enough at the Naval Academy. "The Atlantic Ocean is over five thousand meters deep," he said to himself. "At that depth, there is no salvage ship. . . ."

"At that depth?"

Jaekel stopped in mid sentence. "Wait a minute. The Continental Shelf. Parts of the Continental Shelf are less than one hundred meters deep."

"Go on." Raeder was pleased. Jaekel was catching on faster than most of the General Staff had that morning at the *Führer's* headquarters.

"You told me that you wanted me to detonate the bomb at a predetermined point. May I assume that you have chosen a spot on the Continental Shelf?"

"Yes," the admiral said. "Thirty-five kilometers east of Sable Island, off the coast of Newfoundland." He waited for Jaekel to ask another question.

"You will send a submarine to pick me up—and a salvage ship to retrieve the gold."

Raeder clapped his hands together. "Excellent! That is my plan exactly."

"And the salvage ship will raise the gold before anyone realizes the *Normandie* is missing. And eliminate any passengers or crew members who may have survived the explosion."

"That is precisely correct." Raeder was filled with pride.

"But I have one question, sir," Jaekel continued. "How can we be sure the *Normandie* will be where she's supposed to be, at the right time?"

"That is a good question, my young friend. First, as you know, passenger ships travel fixed tracks, at more or less fixed speeds—the most economical rate of travel. . . ."

Jaekel interrupted for the first time. He was gaining confidence. "What about weather or other emergencies? . . ."

"In addition," Raeder went on, "I have arranged for a string of merchant ships to track the *Normandie* most of the way across the Atlantic. And you will also be able to keep us informed, by sending coded messages through the ship's radio-telephone system—until you destroy it, of course."

"Destroy the radio-telephone system? How?"

Admiral Raeder gave Jaekel a knowing look. Then he rose from his seat. "I will provide you with the means. Please wait here."

Jaekel watched Raeder leave the room and close the door behind him. The young man marveled at what he had seen and learned in the last fifteen minutes. He was amazed at his good fortune. He had been given a remarkable mission, a chance to avenge his father's death, to repay his patron and to perform a great service for the Reich.

Hansel and Gretel were waiting in the outer office for Raeder's next command. When the admiral emerged, they both leaped to attention. "I need to see your pistols," he told them. They each unholstered their weapons and presented them without surprise or comment.

Raeder examined the pistols carefully. Both were standard issue DMW P.08 Lugers, but Gretel's was practically new, while Hansel's was well-worn. He returned Gretel's weapon and kept Hansel's. Then he asked to see the holsters. He chose Gretel's black leather model over Hansel's brown leather holster. Then he inserted Hansel's gun into the holster. He examined the combination and found it quite satisfactory.

"I have a need for this weapon and holster," he told his aides. "Why don't you put in for new ones tomorrow."

"Yes, Admiral," Hansel said. Gretel saluted briskly.

The admiral nodded at them absently and walked back into his office, hiding the holstered pistol behind his back.

Jaekel rose automatically. "Sit, sit, my boy." Raeder said. "I've brought you something . . . something I treasure."

Jaekel looked at him inquisitively.

Raeder held out the pistol to Jaekel. "I have been keeping this for you for years," he went on quietly. "It was your father's. Just before he died, he asked me to give it to you when the time was right. I think that time is now."

Jaekel took the weapon as though it were a fragment of the True Cross. His eyes misted over, to Raeder's immense satisfaction.

"Put it on, my boy, put it on."

Jaekel buckled the weapon around his waist. Raeder helped him adjust it, then stepped back a few paces.

"You are the spitting image of your father," Raeder said, truly struck by the resemblance.

Without warning, Jaekel buried his head in his hands and started sobbing. Raeder watched briefly, then decided to put an end to it. "Lieutenant Jaekel!"

There was a momentary pause, then Jaekel regained control. "Yes, sir!"

"Lieutenant, I am briefing you on a mission of the utmost importance. Are you ready to continue?"

"Yes, sir."

"Before you trigger the bomb, you are to shoot out the *Normandie*'s radio aerial grid. That is why I have given you your father's pistol. Do you understand me?"

Jaekel's eyes met Raeder's. "I do, sir."

"Good."

"What about the pistol shots?"

"There is a silencer in your luggage."

"I see," Jaekel said. "Now what about my opponents?"

"I think I can say with great confidence that no one aboard the ship will have the slightest idea of what you plan

55

to do. Therefore, you will have no opponents," the admiral told him. "Still, there's no need to take chances. So we have prepared a fictitious identity for you—and a curiously delightful one at that."

"I must warn you, sir, I'm not much of an actor."

"You won't have to act. You'll hardly have to speak. All you'll need to do is mumble a little."

"Mumble?"

"Yes, in the ship's synagogue. Otherwise, you will play the role of a recluse."

"Synagogue? What do you mean?"

Admiral Raeder couldn't help chortling a little. "Well, now, we have arranged for you to pose as Simon Rothmann, the only son of a wealthy Jewish businessman from Vienna."

"You want me to pretend to be a *Jew?*"

"Think about it, Jaekel. What could be more innocent? On Friday night, you go to the synagogue with the other Jews and mumble a little when they all pray. The rest of the time, you'll keep to yourself. I've had the chief purser notified about the tragedy you're trying to deal with, so you won't be bothered."

"Which tragedy is that?" Jaekel was confused and doubtful.

"The one that happened to your family. They were killed by the Nazis, every last one of them. Isn't it a pity?"

"But I don't know anything about Jews," Jaekel protested. "I'm not a Berliner. I grew up in the country. The only Jew I ever met was an old junkman."

The admiral shrugged. "No matter. You won't really have to act the part. The fictitious identity is just a way of diverting suspicion. Besides, it's all set up already." Jaekel's bucolic background was another reason Raeder had chosen him. He had never come into contact with the sort of people he'd meet on board the *Normandie*. The chances of his real identity being discovered were quite remote.

Jaekel bowed to the inevitable. "Rothmann, you said,

Simon Rothmann?"

"That's right. Think about it. You're going to be a very remarkable Jew, Herr Rothmann. You're going to control more gold than all the Jews in history combined. Wonderfully ironic, isn't it?"

"Yes," Jaekel said, squirming. "I suppose it is."

Admiral Raeder took a folder from his desk. "This contains all the details of your Rothmann background and some other information you'll need, such as communication codes, how to operate the bomb, exactly where to place it, and precisely when and where it should be detonated. Please read it now."

Jaekel took the folder and began to study it. Admiral Raeder watched him carefully. Once more, he found himself approving of what he saw: fierce and unwavering concentration, a burning determination to master what he was looking at. After about ten minutes, Jaekel closed the folder and looked at Raeder expectantly.

"Any questions?"

"Yes, sir. What type of explosive will I be using? How will I carry it on board the ship?"

"The explosive we have chosen for this mission is cyclotol. You are familiar with it?"

Jaekel was back on solid ground again. "Yes, sir. Cyclotol has the highest known shattering power of any explosive substance—four million pounds per square inch."

"That is correct, Lieutenant. And we have calculated that a detonation of three hundred fifty pounds of it, properly placed, will blow out thirty-seven percent of the ship's bottom in an instant. The ship will sink within five minutes, long before any lifeboats can be lowered."

Jaekel was flabbergasted. "Three hundred and fifty pounds of cyclotol? How in the world will I get it onto the ship?"

"That's very simple, my friend," said the admiral. "Remember that automobile I mentioned? Well, it is a

Mercedes-Benz typ 770 limousine. It is stuffed with approximately four hundred twenty-seven pounds of cyclotol — in the trunk, in the door panels, under the seats, even under the hood. The vehicle was prepared for the Chancellor of Austria, but it proved unnecessary."

"So I will *drive* the explosives aboard." Jaekel was impressed.

"Just so. And you will see to it that the vehicle is parked in a particular spot in the forward hold."

"What should I do if another automobile is in that spot?"

"Whatever you need to do," Admiral Raeder said.

"Yes, sir. I understand."

"One last thing, Jaekel. You will leave immediately. I'm afraid you have a lot of driving ahead of you."

"I will leave immediately?"

"That's right, my friend. The *Normandie* — and the gold — sets sail from Le Havre at one P.M. Wednesday afternoon, the day after tomorrow."

Jaekel rose from his chair. "I understand my job, Admiral Raeder. And I will not fail you." He glanced down at the Luger strapped to his waist. "Or my father."

"Good luck, Kurt." He leaned across the desk and shook hands with the young man. ⸺⸺

Jaekel then stepped back three paces. *"Heil* Hitler!"

The Citroen 11 CV turned off the autobahn and onto a narrow, winding country road at Osnabruck, about fifty miles from the border. It was seven P.M. They'd been driving for four hours without incident. There'd been a mixture of civilian and military traffic, but no sign whatever of the SS.

"By my calculations," Victor said, "we'll be at the border in about an hour."

"Right. But it will be about two hours before we can cross," Nathan told him. "We have to wait until the nine

P.M. guard shift comes on duty. They're the ones we've made arrangements with."

It was just past eight-thirty when the Citroen came to the border crossing sign: "Attention! Customs check four thousand meters ahead! Prepare to stop!" The customs house was not yet in view.

Nathan slowed the car to a creep, looking for a place to hide until the shift change. He soon found a narrow dirt path leading into the woods. He backed down the path and shut off the engine. From the main road now, the Citroen was invisible amidst the trees and the gathering darkness.

Tina started to ask a question, but Nathan held a hand up for silence. They rolled down their windows and listened. They could hear voices up ahead, although they could not pick out the words.

"The border guards," Nathan whispered. He checked his watch. "The shift change should take place in about twenty minutes."

"And then Tina and I will leave this Godforsaken land forever," Victor said with unexpected intensity.

Nathan looked at him wryly. "I'll be leaving, too," he said.

After a few minutes, they heard a car approaching from the same direction they'd come. Shortly afterward, an automobile sped by, leaving a shower of laughter and beer bottles in its wake. Then, up ahead, there was the sharp squeal of brakes, followed by angry commands to get out of the car.

"That doesn't sound like a customs check," Nathan said.

He got out of the automobile, closing the door soundlessly, and crept toward the customs house, picking his way through the trees near the side of the road. Tina and Victor followed close behind. What they saw came as a very unpleasant surprise.

A Citroen very much like Nathan's was stopped at the striped wooden barrier at the German border, only this one was packed with young boys and girls. Two black-uniformed

SS men were training their semi-automatic Mauser rifles on the vehicle.

The SS man nearest the driver, a husky sergeant with hair so blond it was almost white, banged his weapon against the door. "I said, get out of the car, *Jews*. Now!"

The driver, a gawky-looking redhead eighteen or nineteen years old, had rolled down his window. "But we're not Jewish."

"He's telling the truth," said a pretty blond girl in the back seat.

"Tell him we have nothing to declare," another female voice suggested.

Tina came up next to Nathan. "How did the SS get there? They didn't pass us."

"Local garrison," Nathan said, speaking very softly. "Probably been here for hours. No doubt, SS units are waiting for us at every western border crossing."

"And how do you plan to get us by them?" Victor asked.

"I guess I'll have to think up a way, won't I?"

The white-haired SS sergeant pulled open the driver's side door. "Out, I said!"

The passengers — a pair of young men in their late teens and two much younger girls — exited the automobile now as if it were about to explode.

"Stand over here near the lights, *Jews*," the other SS man ordered, waving his machine gun at them. He was a tall, hawk-faced man with a first lieutenant's insignia on his lapels.

The young people did as they were told. The boy who'd been sitting in the back seat, a chubby, goofy-looking kid, round-faced and dark-haired, attempted a bit of levity. "No Jews here, General. They're all at temple," he said.

The SS lieutenant slowly raised his rifle until it was pointing directly at the goofy kid's chest. "Prove it," he said with a chilling smile.

"Prove it? Well, listen, I'm Dutch. We don't mark our

passports with our religions. I mean, my name is Broederwart. Does that sound Jewish?"

"We're looking for two Jew men and a little girl Jewess," the SS sergeant said. "You two could be the Jew men. You could have gotten rid of the little girl. Killed her, maybe."

"Killed her?" the gawky red-haired boy said, horrified. "Not us. We're just tourists."

"That's right," said his companion, a slender, pretty, pale-skinned fifteen-year-old blonde. "We spent the day in Bremen. My cousin lives there."

"I said," the hawk-faced SS lieutenant repeated, "you'll have to *prove* you're not Jewish. If you do, we'll let you pass." He and his colleague smiled snidely at each other.

The other girl — Broederwart's companion — finally spoke up. She was a short, mousy kid with a surprisingly deep voice. "And just how can we prove that?" It was a challenge, not a question.

"*You* can't," the lieutenant said. "But *they* can." He pointed to the boys.

"Drop your pants," the white-haired SS sergeant commanded.

Tina looked at Nathan, confused. "What's going on here?"

"I'm afraid I know, but there's nothing to be done about it."

"Drop my pants? Why?" the Broederwart boy asked.

"Because I say so," said the lieutenant, brandishing his Mauser rifle.

The two boys, both terrified now, unbuckled their trousers and let them fall to their ankles, revealing two pairs of stringy thighs, knobby knees, and grimy boxer shorts.

"Now the shorts," said the SS sergeant.

Broederwart opened his mouth to protest.

"Now!"

Terrified and humiliated, both boys gingerly slipped down their shorts. The SS sergeant shined his flashlight on their crotches, spotlighting their pubic hair, their testicles, and their completely unremarkable penises. Broederwart's was about the size of a breakfast sausage.

The girls averted their eyes.

From their hiding place in the woods, Nathan, Victor, and Tina watched, Nathan hoping for a clue to their own escape, Victor outraged . . . and Tina absolutely spellbound.

There was something strange about the way these young fellows were built, Tina thought, something odd about their organs. She'd seen her father and Victor, and their organs were definitely different from these. This was bizarre and puzzling.

The lieutenant lowered his rifle to the groin of the first boy, the red-haired driver. He probed the boy's penis with the rifle barrel. "Well, well, well," he said pleasantly. "A good uncircumcised Christian boy."

He moved on to Broederwart, the goofy-looking kid. "And what do we have here? Isn't that interesting? Another nice little uncircumcised Wiener schnitzel. In fact, very little. You should let it out more often. Exercise it. Put it to good use."

The sergeant chuckled rudely. "Let someone else play with it for a change." He winked broadly at the pretty blond girl, who instantly turned bright red.

"So that's what an uncircumcised penis looks like," Tina murmured in wonder, half to herself. "I've never seen one before."

"And I if I have anything to say about it, you will never see one again," Victor whispered, disgusted. "Come on, let's go back to the car. We're in danger here."

At the customs house, the boys were hurriedly pulling up their pants.

"Can we go now?" the girl with the foghorn voice asked, her voice vibrating with anger.

The lieutenant smiled. "Yes, of course."

"Try to keep your pants buttoned from now on," the SS sergeant told the boys. "Unless your girlfriends have other ideas, of course."

The mousy girl glared at the noncom, then hopped back into the car. Her friends piled in after her. They drove off as quickly as they could.

Nathan led his charges back through the trees to the Citroen, Victor mumbling all the way. "So we're stuck, right? The arrangement with the border guards has fallen through, isn't that so? And now you're going to ask us to find our way through the forest, I suppose."

Nathan decided not to respond. What good would it do?

"I have an idea," Tina said brightly.

"I'm sure you do," Victor shot back, "and I'll bet I know where you got it."

Nathan was getting tired of all this. "Would you two please stop bickering?"

Victor lapsed into sullen silence. And Tina, confident now that her brother would let her talk, told them about her idea. "It occurred to me when I heard them say they were looking for a little girl . . . still!" she said. Then, giggling, she described her plan. Nathan, dubious at first, finally agreed to it.

A few minutes later, Tina came loping out of the woods right beside the customs house, caught in its lights like a frightened deer. She was screaming in terror. Her blouse was unbuttoned, her skirt was missing, and her slip was ripped open, exposing quite a bit of firm, tawny thigh. Twigs and leaves clung to her lovely long hair. She was the picture of innocence defiled.

"They attacked me!" she cried out, "They tried to rape me!"

Both of the SS men, startled, whirled toward Tina, instinctively raising their rifles, only to lower them sheepishly when they realized they were aiming at a damsel in distress.

"Calm yourself, Fräulein," the hawk-faced lieutenant said

sternly, taking Tina by the arm.

She pulled loose. "They're coming after me," Tina screamed. "They're going to kill me!" She broke into heart-rending sobs.

The SS lieutenant softened. "Who molested you, Fräulein? Where is he?"

"In the woods," Tina managed to say.

The lieutenant waved the white-haired noncom into the woods to investigate. He switched on his flashlight and hung it on his belt. Then, rifle at the ready, he lurched through the trees, crunching twigs with every step, the light bobbing in front of him.

"There were two of them," Tina said, still crying.

"Two? Two men?" The lieutenant was becoming extremely interested.

"Yes. They had a gun and they tried to force me—"

"A gun! Whitey, wait for me!" the lieutenant called. "I think we've found the Jews."

He crashed into the woods.

Half a minute later, the Citroen rolled up to the customs house, engine off, lights off, Victor at the wheel, Nathan pushing. Tina silently opened the front door on the passenger side and slipped inside. Nathan took over the driver's seat and Victor got in back.

There was a shout from the woods. "How far in, Fräulein?"

Tina looked at Nathan, a flicker of real fear in her eyes. He held a finger to his lips and hit the ignition. The car coughed and died.

"Fräulein!" The shout was closer, and it was quickly followed by the sound of footsteps running toward them, crashing through the woods.

Nathan pushed the ignition button again. Two coughs this time, then nothing.

The bobbing glow of the German's flashlight was visible now through the trees.

The Citroen coughed again and the engine finally sputtered to life. Just then, the SS lieutenant emerged from the woods. "Halt!" he shouted.

A little old man in a comic-opera uniform came hobbling out of the customs house, waving his arms theatrically.

"I suppose that's our friend," Victor said.

"No doubt," Nathan allowed. He put the car in gear, then tramped down on the accelerator. The Citroen moved lazily toward the striped wooden barrier at the border crossing.

"I said *halt!*" yelled the SS man. He fired at them three times. The Citroen's left taillight exploded. Tina screamed, this time for real.

The Citroen smashed through the wooden barrier, losing a headlight in the process. Behind them, the SS lieutenant fired several more shots in their direction. One shattered the rear window, harmlessly sprinkling Victor with broken glass and frightening another scream out of Tina.

Then they rounded a corner and the shooting stopped. Up ahead was another customs house and another striped wooden barrier.

"That's it?" Tina asked, her voice small and hopeful, "That's the Netherlands?"

There was a note in her voice Nathan had not heard before, a certain vulnerability, as though—for just an instant—she *was* that little girl the SS was looking for.

"Yes it is," Nathan told her gently.

"It's funny," Tina said, as though she'd given the matter quite a bit of thought. "I've always wanted to see the Netherlands."

There was a derisive hoot from the back seat.

As they approached the customs house, a young boy ran out of the building and lifted the barrier. A man in his late twenties, evidently the boy's father, appeared at the customs house door. He waved them on with a big smile. "Welcome," he called. "Welcome."

At *Kriegsmarine* headquarters in Berlin, Grand Admiral Erich Raeder paid a visit to the central code room, where dozens of junior officers sat at odd typewriterlike machines, each of them clattering away.

The admiral walked into the glass-walled booth in the middle of the room from which Col. Heinz Reitfeld, a stooped, professorial type, supervised code operations.

"What have we heard from the U-42 and Kommandant Zentner?" Admiral Raeder asked.

Reitfeld shuffled through a stack of manila folders, removing one and reading the contents. "Last report at 1200 hours today," he said. "The U-42 and the salvage ship *Otto Wunsche* are on course, on schedule, proceeding without incident."

"That's good, Reitfeld, very good. Let me know as soon as Zentner reports again."

On time and on schedule. That's what he had come to expect from Zentner. No U-boat kommandant was more reliable and few were more skilled. If any man could do this job, it was Zentner.

Day Two

Tuesday, August 22, 1939

Nathan, Tina, and Victor spent the night at a half-timbered commercial boarding house in Enschede. The next day they were up just after sunrise. It was a perfect, cloudless late August morning, already showing signs of turning hot and humid.

After a breakfast of potatoes and meat pie at a downtown restaurant frequented mainly by shopkeepers and tradesmen, Nathan gassed up the Citroen and they headed west, over the lowlands of North Brabant, on a country road dotted with sixteenth-century windmills.

By late morning they'd reached the edge of Flanders, on whose rolling green fields, a little more than twenty years earlier, hundreds of thousands of young men from Germany, France, and England had fought and died in the terrible artillery and machine gun battles of the Great War.

By now, the heat waves were shimmering up from the grassy fields, and Nathan and his charges were baking inside the Citroen, even with all four windows down. Tina dozed in the back seat, while Victor navigated and Nathan drove.

There was really nothing to worry about, Nathan told himself. The Germans certainly weren't on their track now.

They were as safe as a Kansas farm family on a Sunday drive. Yet he was worried. Which was a good thing, since in this business, there was a direct connection between worrying and surviving.

They passed into France at Wattrelos, then turned southwest toward Dieppe, toward the ocean, hoping it might be a bit cooler. By early afternoon they'd entered the Caux region of upper Normandy, where the road curled out across the chalk cliffs of the Alabaster Coast, with vast farms on the inland side, protected by hedges and curtains of beeches, elms, and poplars.

In the back seat, Tina stirred and stretched, catlike. "What's that smell?"

"Salt air," her brother told her. "We're driving along the Channel now."

She stuck her head up, looked out, then closed her eyes again.

They drove through the fashionable seaside resort of Dieppe, past its gaily striped beach tents, its beach casino, and its lovely, fragile thirteenth-century castle. Then, more farms. Then through the fishing town of Fecamp, and past more medieval castles and cathedrals.

They arrived at the great seaport of Le Havre just before dinner, coming in on the heights, with the red roofs of the city spread out below them, along with the whole of the mouth of the Seine. Looking across it, they could see Honfleur and Trouville and a pair of lighthouses.

Half a mile below them, towering over the cluster of red roofs, dominating even the ancient cathedral, was the Gare Maritime, a thousand-foot-long concrete railroad station shaped like a quonset hut, surmounted by a two-hundred-sixty-two-foot tower that displayed tidal readings in numbers ten feet tall. Le Havre's boat dock—a concrete platform almost half a mile long—was right on the ocean, immediately adjacent to the Gare Maritime.

And tied up to the boat dock was the *Normandie*, the

largest ship in the world, an immense black iron structure ten stories high and seven blocks long, topped off by three red funnels, each the size of a small house. An army of longshoremen was carting steamer trunks up the gangways, like worker bees servicing a queen.

Tina was sitting up now and looking at the scene in awe. "So that's the *Normandie,*" she marveled.

"That's it," Nathan replied.

"What woke you up?" Victor asked.

"I had no idea how big she was — or how lovely," Tina said.

"We'll board tomorrow morning," Nathan said. "We have first-class tickets waiting for us under the name of Cameron."

"When does she cast off?" Victor asked.

"One o'clock tomorrow," Nathan replied. "Our trunks should already be aboard."

"Did they also have to outwit the SS?" Tina asked.

Nathan grinned. He steered the Citroen down the cobblestone road toward the docks, then coasted past the ramshackle buildings at the waterfront. He parked in front of a seaman's boarding house next to a dilapidated warehouse.

"All right, you two, out of the car," Nathan said.

Victor was puzzled. "Out of the car? Why?"

"Because we're staying here tonight."

"Here?" Tina exclaimed with horror and astonishment. "With the rats and the cockroaches? When there are nice hotels downtown?"

"I agree with my sister," Victor said. "I don't see why we shouldn't be comfortable."

"Has it occurred to either of you that the Gestapo almost certainly has informers at the major hotels?"

Tina sighed. "Well, I hope they have soap in the bathrooms."

"I want you two to go in first. Take a room together. Pretend you're lovers. I'll get rid of the car, then come back and get a room for myself."

Victor was aghast. "Pretend we're *what?*"

Tina laughed. "Don't be so stiff, Victor. He's got a good idea."

"But—"

Tina messed up her hair, then kissed her brother full on the lips, leaving his eyes bulging with shock and his face smeared with lipstick. Then she got out of the Citroen. "Come on, Victor. Curtain going up."

Victor climbed out of the car, dazed but obedient. Tina put her head on his shoulder, her arm around his waist, and walked him into the boarding house. She winked at Nathan just before the door closed.

Day Three

EARLY MORNING

First there was just a vague sense of vibration. Then it intensified, into a definite rumble.

David Nathan lay on the lumpy cotton mattress, listening, trying to make sense of the sound. It was, he decided, the low growl of truck engines, dozens of them. And they were getting closer.

He sat up, pushed the rough curtain aside, and peered out of the window, through ancient panes of glass dotted with bubbles and blurred with distortion. It was a night without moonlight, and the street lamps were so dim they were just about invisible. He could see practically nothing.

The engine sounds were getting very loud now. Whatever was out there was coming right past the boarding house. He could now distinguish an additional sound: the clanking of *tank* treads. By this time, he thought, he should be seeing headlights, but the street remained dark.

Then he spotted a faint yellow glow bobbing in the distance — more like flashlight beams than headlights. He realized then that they were headlights — *shrouded* headlights. Even though the night was hot and sticky, he felt

71

a chill sweep over him.

Nathan was considering waking the kids when he saw the first vehicle rumble by, a dark, shapeless mass. It was followed by another and another and another. He counted four tanks, fifteen large trucks, and at least three smaller vehicles, staff cars maybe. What was this? Some kind of secret military convoy?

Perhaps war was even closer than he thought. Perhaps this convoy was being sent to reinforce the coastal defenses at Le Havre. Perhaps the French had more steel in their backbones than he'd suspected.

Nathan pulled the curtain back across the window and let himself sink back into the misshapen mattress. The convoy had reassured him. He felt as though something had arrived to protect them.

Capt. Pierre Barthou didn't like it one bit. And he hadn't kept his feelings a secret. He'd complained bitterly to the managing director of *Compagnie Generale Transatlantique,* who had hired him twenty-four years ago. He'd protested to the assistant Minister of the Merchant Marine, who'd been his roommate at the Academy. He'd even made his objections known to his son-in-law, a promising assistant to the deputy Foreign Minister.

He'd told them all the same thing: He would not compromise the safety of his passengers, not for any reason, not even if he was commanded to do so by the President of France. But everyone had responded in more or less the same words: You have no choice. You must do your duty to France. And how could he argue with that?

Now, in the middle of the night, it was happening. More than a dozen huge military trucks had trundled onto the concrete boat dock. Four menacing tanks stood guard over them, their gun turrets pointed outward, toward each main point on the compass.

The contents of the trucks were being carefully transferred to the *Normandie*'s forward hold—not by the cursing, ill-tempered longshoremen Barthou had come to love, but by uniformed soldiers. Each carried a single small and obviously heavy wooden crate.

"They are very efficient, no?" observed Henri Freppel, the ship's chief purser, one of Barthou's shipmates from the *Paris*.

Barthou couldn't take his eyes off the troops. "I've never cared much for soldiers," he said. "And I don't like having a detachment of them on board, stationed in my wheelhouse, my engine room, and my cargo hold—all to 'thwart any attempt to hijack the ship.' It just makes me nervous."

"Well, I don't share your prejudice," said the dapper little purser, his neatly waxed mustache bobbing as he spoke. "Who knows, if we'd had soldiers guarding the *Paris* . . ." He shrugged expressively. It was a charming gesture. In fact, if you were one of the tens of thousands of passengers who had crossed the Atlantic on one of the ships in his care, it was a famous gesture.

Barthou's ruddy face turned a shade redder. He didn't like to be reminded of the *Paris*, even though he still thought about her obsessively. In the last few days, she'd been on his mind constantly. He'd seen her in the harbor when he brought the *Normandie* in. He'd seen her each day the *Normandie* was in port. He would see her again this morning, at first light.

The *Paris* was lying helplessly on her starboard side about three hundred meters away from the dock, half submerged, looking more like a dead whale than a gay and glamorous ocean liner. Brackish waters licked at her funnels and filled her rotting staterooms.

The day the *Paris* had sunk, just five months ago, had been the bitterest day in Pierre Barthou's life, the first and only time he had ever lost a ship in his command. Again and again, he had told himself he was not to blame.

But who was? The local firemen who had pumped too much water into her? The ship's patrol that had failed to spot the fire before it spread, that had not noticed the jammed locks on the storerooms? The criminal, the unknown saboteur, who had committed the monstrous deed?

Barthou finally tore his thoughts away from the *Paris* and looked down again at the pier. He and Freppel were standing on the *Normandie*'s port bridge wing, one of two small, graceful open-air platforms that extended out from the wheelhouse. From this high perch, the soldiers unloading the trucks looked like midgets.

"Of course," Freppel went on, unaware of Barthou's train of thought, "I'm no happier about our cargo than you are. It is just one more example of French stupidity and weakness. It shows how much we have been weakened by the Jews and the Communists."

The husky silver-haired captain sighed tolerantly. Freppel was about to launch yet another political lecture. How was it that such a charming, witty, and efficient man, such a diplomat, such an essentially decent human being, could spout such crack-brained, right-wing rhetoric?

"Please refrain from sharing your political opinions with our passengers, Henri." It was a gentle request, not a command.

"Our passengers!" Freppel exclaimed with contempt. "If you mean the Jewish stockbrokers, the degenerate movie stars, and the drunken artists and writers, never fear. They will learn the truth in time, but not from me."

Barthou knew it would be better not to respond.

MID-MORNING

Embarkation time at Le Havre usually combined elements of a Royal Wedding, a national political convention, the beginning of Napoleon's march into Russia, and the sailing of the Spanish Armada.

It was raucous and gay, it was crowded and confused.

It was the moment when you forgot everything familiar and

began a wonderful adventure. It was the first leg of a bitter-sweet return to familiar surroundings.

It was confetti, champagne, and giant baskets of fruit.

It was farewell hugs and let the hunt begin.

It was the end of care, it was the beginning of peril.

It was "Where's the porter?" and "Is that Greta Garbo?" and "Are the seas rough?" and "You did get us a better cabin than last time, didn't you?" and "Who's that woman with Neil Gilchrist?"

It was five thousand people — travelers and well-wishers and crewmen.

It was fifteen thousand pieces of luggage, waiting to be carted into the hold and stuffed away by platoons of redcaps. It was a couple of dozen dogs and cats and the occasional snake or monkey. It was fifty luxurious automobiles and a few limousines, going abroad or coming home with their owners.

It was a phalanx of arrogant celebrities, anticipating slights and already furious. It was little knots of schoolteachers and clerks and shop owners and their wives in a semipermanent state of awe. It was commercial travelers on R & R, before the battle or afterward. It was the rich and the mighty, showing off the spoils.

That's what embarkation usually was. But on this twenty-third day of August, 1939, on the *Normandie*'s one hundred thirty-ninth transatlantic crossing, there was a new and un-welcome note, a note of panic. Many of the thousands who had assembled here to board this magnificent machine and sail away to America thought this was their very last chance to hightail it out of Europe, to slip away from the coming confla-gration and escape with their lives.

Captain Barthou and Chief Purser Freppel stood on the bridge, taking care of last-minute details, watching people board and studying the passenger list to prepare themselves for the pleasures and problems it promised.

"That lady looks faintly familiar," Barthou said, pointing to a woman on the dock who was wearing a fox fur coat and carrying a white poodle in each arm.

"Ethel Merman," Freppel said. "The Broadway star."

"And that one?" Barthou indicated a dowager under full sail, approaching the first-class gangway at the head of a retinue of luggage-toting servants.

"The leader of that particular safari is Mrs. William Randolph Hearst," Freppel replied. "I believe she's occupying the Fecamp Suite."

Now a convoy of Paris taxis drove onto the dock and pulled up at the first-class gangway. "Dietrich," Barthou said. "On time for a change, thank God."

All in all, it was not a particularly illustrious passenger list—just the usual sprinkling of celebrities among the multitudes: Walt Disney, Carl Loeb (the investment banker), Jascha Heifetz, Walter P. Chrysler, Cole Porter, Arthur Murray, Olivia de Havilland, Thomas Watson (president of International Business Machines), James Stewart, Sonja Henie, Edward G. Robinson, Ramon Novarro, Erich von Stroheim, and George Raft, plus a number of lesser lights.

"Shall we go down and do our duty?" Chief Purser Freppel asked his captain.

Barthou sighed. "If we must." On this trip, his social duties seemed especially frivolous.

David Nathan stood on the balcony of stateroom number 67, watching the boarding passengers through a small pair of field glasses.

"What are you looking for?" Victor asked.

"Friendly faces," Nathan said. Actually, he was looking for *unfriendly* faces, but he saw no reason to tell that to Victor.

"Think you'll find someone you know?" Tina inquired brightly.

"Lot of Americans travel on this ship," Nathan said. He didn't give a damn about the Americans. He was looking for Germans. If, somehow, they'd been followed, Nathan wanted to know it. That's why he'd made sure they were among the first to board and why he'd immediately taken up residence on the balcony. Better the hunter than the prey.

Ordinarily, perhaps, he might not have been so vigilant. But he'd managed to get a look at this morning's *International Herald Tribune*, and the news was so ominous that he felt he couldn't let down his guard for a moment. According to the newspaper, Hitler and Stalin were about to follow their commercial treaty with a nonaggression pact, of all things. If the *Trib* was right, these sworn enemies were about to make friends, no doubt with terrible consequences for the rest of the world. Of course, the idea was preposterous, but the paper said Ribbentrop was already on his way to Moscow. Fantastic and frightening, if true.

The rest of the front page had been filled with news of blackouts and troop movements and planned evacuations. Practically the only item to cheer him up was on the sports page: The Yankees had won a night game at Comisky Park, 14–5, with five home runs, including a round-tripper by Joe DiMaggio, who'd gone three-for-six. Maybe he'd make .400 yet. And it was beginning to look as though the Yankees had the pennant locked up, even without Lou Gehrig.

Tina walked out on the balcony to join him. She'd changed into a deep blue silk dress that made her eyes look even greener than usual.

"Why don't you stay in the cabin," Nathan said. "At least until we're under way."

Tina shook her head sadly. "I feel badly for you, Mr. Cameron. No one ever taught you how to relax."

"Listen, my job is to get you to New York."

"And you always do your job," Victor sang out. He was sitting in an art deco armchair, studying a brochure on the *Normandie*'s propulsion system he'd gotten from a steward.

Nathan found himself starting to seethe. "That's right," he said casually.

She teased him. "I know what it is. You're just petrified that

77

someone is out there, waiting to take a potshot at me."

Nathan thought about it. They were six decks above the gangway entrances, perhaps eighty feet up. There were a dozen stateroom balconies on this side of the ship alone, with people on every one of them. Perhaps he was being too cautious. "All right," he relented. "You can stay out here. But don't draw attention to yourself, okay?"

"You know I'd never do anything like that," she said blithely, leaning over the rail, the silk dress clinging to her like ballet tights.

Kurt Jaekel eased the huge black Mercedes-Benz typ 770 through Le Havre's cobblestone streets, top down, wind in his hair, wearing the expensive Navy blazer and gabardine trousers Raeder had provided, looking more like a matinee idol now than a Navy officer.

It had been an all-night trip, but he was exhilarated from the journey. Despite the extra weight the automobile was carrying, it had been a pleasure to drive. He'd been able to keep up a steady 115 km/h — a little more than 70 mph — thanks to the Mercedes's supercharged engine, which put out 200 horsepower.

The typ 770 was a refined version of the famous Grosser Mercedes, the statesmen's Mercedes. It was a truly monumental machine, seventeen feet long, weighing about three-and-a-half tons and powered by a huge old-style straight-eight. They were not for sale to ordinary people, only to heads of state and celebrities of whom Daimler-Benz approved.

During the trip, Jaekel had run into only two problems.

The first was petrol stations. He'd had a hard time finding enough of them. At 70 mph, the vehicle got only six miles to the gallon.

The second was all that cyclotol under the hood and in the trunk. The thought of the explosives made him wary on rough roads, even though he knew it would take an exceptionally strong jolt to set them off.

Just after eleven A.M., Jaekel steered the Mercedes into the line of cars waiting to be admitted to the boat dock. When his turn came, he showed his ticket to the guard, who waved him onto the quay.

It was a sight Jaekel had not been prepared for: the thousands of people, the taxis, the steamer trunks, the army of porters and redcaps, the massive bulk of the *Normandie* tied up to the pier.

Aware that the pretense was about to begin, he had a sudden attack of nerves. He would not be boarding this vessel as himself, as Kurt Jaekel, sailor, athlete, commando, country boy. He would be boarding as Simon Rothmann, Viennese Jew, a merchant's son, a grieving husband and father.

With an effort of will, Jaekel reminded himself of his mission. He recalled the words of Admiral Raeder. He remembered his father. He thought about the Luger in his luggage.

Up ahead, a junior officer waved him into a line of motor cars waiting at a loading platform. Chains at each corner of the platform connected it to a gigantic electric crane on the dock.

Jaekel was confused. He'd thought he'd be able to drive the automobile right into the ship, through a dockside cargo port. Then he could have parked the vehicle in the designated place in the ship's hold. But this was different. Now the motor car would be lowered into the hold and parked, no doubt, by a deck hand. He could do nothing about it. Not yet.

He sat in his motor car and watched as a number of automobiles were loaded aboard the ship. The procedure was simple enough. The automobile's owner—or chauffeur—drove it onto the loading platform, guided by a junior officer. The driver then got out, while a deck hand shoved chocks under the wheels and porters removed the luggage, if any.

Meanwhile, the junior officer on the dock consulted a list on his clipboard and, using a telephone that put him in touch with the crane, told the crane operator what the vehicle weighed.

The crane operator made some kind of adjustment and slipped the machinery into gear. Then slowly, with a growling whir, the boom began to rise. The chains grew taut, then began clanking as they rolled around the take-up drum. The platform lifted off the dock, car and all. It slowly rose to deck level, the boom ascending above it.

Once the platform had cleared the ship's rail, the crane gradually swung the platform inboard, until it was directly in line with the open hatch above #1 hold. At that point, the boom dipped down, the chains played out, and the platform and its cargo disappeared beneath the deck. A few minutes later, the platform reappeared, empty.

Jaekel watched from his motor car as an Austro-Daimler ADR 6 saloon, a Dusenberg SJ Rolston convertible sedan, and one of those oddly streamlined Panhard Dynamics were lifted into the hold.

For the *Normandie*'s crew members, loading automobiles was entirely routine, almost boring. But not for the passengers and the well-wishers who had come to see them off. Small boys, especially, watched in fascination, apparently amazed that the crane's boom, with its lacy girders and its almost delicate network of chains, could raise such heavy loads.

Eventually, Jaekel's turn came. He drove the Mercedes onto the platform, set the brake, and hopped out. A porter removed the three brown leather suitcases Jaekel had stashed in the back seat. While the deck hand pushed the chocks into place, the officer consulted his list. "It's a heavy one, Jacques ninety-five hundred kilos," he said into the telephone.

Jaekel shot the man a startled glance, then looked away. The cyclotol, he knew, added nearly a thousand kilos to the vehicle's normal weight. But, of course, that was something he couldn't tell the deck officer.

He studied the crane, trying to estimate its capacity. Surely it had lifted heavier cargo than this into the *Normandie*'s hold. Surely a ten percent weight difference wouldn't matter.

The deck officer gave a wave to the crane operator, who put the machinery into gear. The engine growled, the boom rose, the chains tightened. The platform didn't budge.

"What's going on up there?" the deck officer said into the telephone.

"I'll try it again."

The crane operator shifted into another gear. The engine noise rose to a higher pitch. The platform trembled, then at last began to creep skyward, millimeter by millimeter.

The deck officer was not satisfied with this progress. "What the hell is wrong up there, Jacques?"

"Power fluctuation, I think," the answer came back. "Nothing to worry about."

The platform came to a dead stop ten feet above the concrete Boat Deck. Once again, the crane shifted gears, the engine taking on a new note of urgency. The platform reluctantly resumed its rise, swaying slightly.

Jaekel watched, eyes cold. Had he overestimated the crane's capacity? What would he do if he could not get the automobile aboard the ship? My God, what if it fell?

By now, the little dockside drama was beginning to attract attention. The little boys who'd been peering through the portholes or watching from the Sun Deck's open expanses had been joined by their fathers. Even Tina Meisner was watching from her balcony, thoroughly fascinated.

"Are you going full out, Jacques?" the deck officer asked.

"Damn right, I am," the answer came back over the phone. "You want me to burn out the engine?"

"Yes, if you have to . . . yes! Just don't drop that motor car!"

The cargo platform crept upward incrementally, bearing Jaekel's Mercedes-Benz typ 770, with its huge bug-eyed headlamps, its gleaming black paint, and its chromium-trimmed running boards. The chains were quivering with the load, the crane engines crying out in protest.

"What in God's name is wrong, Jacques?" the deck officer

asked, concern in his voice.

The answer came back through the phone, weak and distant. "I'm giving it everything I have, sir. That thing must be a lot heavier than ninety-five hundred kilos."

"So reset the crane," the deck officer replied angrily. "Do I have to tell you everything?"

The platform ground to a stop three feet from the top. The crane operator tried three times to raise it further. He failed.

The deck officer was furious. "You've sure got us into a fine mess, Jacques. How do you intend to get us out of it?"

"I'm going to swing it over the hatch," the answer came back. "I think it will clear. I hope it will clear."

"It had goddamn better clear," said the deck officer.

High above the pavement, the crane's boom slowly swiveled inward, toward the rail at the edge of the main deck, tugging the loading platform along with it.

For a moment, it looked as though the platform would clear the rail — though only by inches. Then it hit, with a sickening screech, metal against metal, the bottom of the platform scraping against the top of the rail. One of the four supporting chains snapped, the freed chain curling around the crane boom faster than the eye could follow.

The platform, which until now had been perfectly level, abruptly sagged downward at one edge, threatening to dump the huge automobile over the side of the ship and onto the dock. At the same time, the huge Mercedes jerked forward, toward the sagging edge of the platform, the motor car's progress barely checked by the chocks at her front tires. And there it stopped, quivering dangerously.

"Mon Dieu," the deck officer said under his breath. His words were drowned out by the gasps of the onlookers. A woman on the Sun Deck screamed and fainted, Children watching from the portholes began shrieking in fear and shock. Hundreds of bystanders and passengers on the dock scattered and ran, terrified that the wildly teetering platform would fall on them.

Moments before, the dockside scene had been dominated by a mood of eager expectation. Husky porters had been efficiently trundling steamer trunks toward the holds, friendly, smartly attired stewards had been directing passengers to the proper gangways, and well-wishers had been bestowing good-bye hugs and kisses. Now, suddenly, everything was chaos and panic, with crew and passengers alike fleeing the motor car's potential impact point, dropping luggage as they ran, dragging their screaming children with them.

One figure hardly reacted at all — the tall, handsome, and beautifully dressed owner of the automobile, Kurt Jaekel. He stood where he was, gazing up at the dangerously wobbling platform high above him. He was thinking. He was calmly, fatalistically calculating the radius and force of the explosion that would occur when the automobile smashed against the concrete pier.

Jaekel figured the blast would annihilate about a third of the dock and at least as much of the *Normandie*'s port side. Hundreds of men, women, and children would die terrible deaths, not all of them instantaneous. He, himself, would be instantly crushed or blasted into oblivion. His mission would be a catastrophic failure, and he would bring shame on himself and his family. A literally golden opportunity for Germany would be lost forever, and his hero, Admiral Raeder, would fall from power.

Jaekel could do absolutely nothing to prevent this appalling calamity but stand his ground, knowing that at least he would not have to live through the consequences of what he was certain was about to occur.

But Jaekel had not figured on the bravery and efficiency of the *Normandie* crew. Even as his mind filled with images of the explosion, the screaming, the pain and mutilation, the confusion and the death that would accompany the blast, a dozen deck hands were running across the forepeak to prevent the impending accident.

"Pierre! Jean! Albert! Maurice!" the senior man shouted.

"You and Marcel . . . help me lift! The rest of you, up on top, quick! Quick! Quick!"

Half-a-dozen pairs of strong hands grabbed the loading platform. Half-a-dozen powerful men threw their weight onto the high edge. A regiment of stevedores and cargo handlers raced from their stations to help. With agonizing slowness, they managed first to stabilize the platform, then to level it off. But no one knew how long they'd be able to hold it.

"Get that automobile off the rail!" the deck officer shouted into the telephone. "Get it off! Lift it! Raise it! NOW!"

"I'm trying, goddammit! I'm doing everything I can!"

The crane operator slipped his machine back into gear and attempted once more to raise the boom, the engines shrieking with the strain. The platform quivered, then rose — half an inch, an inch, two inches. The sweating deck hands, half of them sitting on the platform to level it off, half of them crouched underneath it, lifting with their shoulders, somehow manhandled it off the rail until it hung free, over the deck.

The men guided the platform toward the hatch. When it was perfectly aligned with the cargo hatch, the crane began to lower the platform into the hold. In a few minutes, it was gone. Then, in a surprisingly short time, the platform reappeared, empty. Scattered applause came from those who had been watching, those who had envisioned catastrophe.

Jaekel took a deep breath. After a moment, he realized he'd better say something to the deck officer. "That fool of a crane operator almost destroyed my automobile," he said angrily.

"I'm sorry, sir. I don't know what happened," the deck officer apologized.

"He also endangered my life, not to mention the lives of many other innocent people," Jaekel went on, warming to his task.

"With all due respect, I think you may have overestimated the danger," the deck officer said carefully.

"Overestimated?" Jaekel was icy. What would this petty creature have said if he knew how great the danger really had been?

"Well, as you can see, nothing actually happened," the deck officer said, trying to pacify this obviously important passenger, who, he realized, had a good reason to be upset. "Nothing at all."

Jaekel was unappeased. "I intend to report this incident to the captain."

The deck officer knew an angry Captain Barthou would be demanding explanations — whether or not this particular passenger made his displeasure known. "Of course, sir. As you wish."

Jaekel spun away sharply from the deck officer and stalked off toward the gangway, motioning the porter to follow him with his luggage.

With that, normal embarkation activities resumed. In a few minutes, it was as though nothing had happened.

"Did you see that?" Tina asked.

"What?" David Nathan didn't take the field glasses away from his eyes.

"He never moved. He just stood there, looking sad."

"Who?"

"The very handsome man with the very expensive automobile."

"What automobile?"

"Are those binoculars painted over or something? Didn't you see what just happened?"

"What was that?"

"The crane almost dropped a car. A big black Mercedes. You really didn't see it?" She was incredulous.

"Too busy looking for friends."

Tina examined the roughly handsome, stern-faced man standing beside her on the balcony. He was so intent on whatever he was looking at through his field glasses that he didn't seem to realize she was looking at him. He hardly seemed to

85

realize she was there.

"Are you aware that you haven't said more than a dozen words to me since we've been out here?"

"Not my job," David Nathan said. "My job is—"

"I know, 'to get us to New York safely.'"

"That's right."

Well, she thought, enough of this. She flounced back into the stateroom, leaving Nathan to his bird watching, which suited him just fine. She'd been disturbing his concentration.

Nathan was systematically searching the docks for the German agent he feared might be tracking them. Obviously, Dr. Victor Meisner was a big fish—God knows why—and the Nazis were determined not to let him slip through their fingers, as they'd proved both in Berlin and at the border crossing.

That's why he'd taken every possible precaution when they'd reached the *Normandie* that morning. He'd sent Tina off to help an old woman board the ship, to pretend to be her traveling companion, and he'd found crutches for Victor, which he made him use while boarding the ship—over the young man's strenuous protests. But there'd been no trouble at the pier.

But they weren't home free yet. The Nazis might be just determined enough and clever enough to get an agent—or even a team of agents—on board the ship. They'd probably keep Victor under surveillance throughout the voyage, then grab him at the last minute, very likely just as the ship was docking, so they could make a clean getaway. At least that's what I'd do if I were in their position, Nathan thought.

And so he scrutinized the face of each boarding passenger through his field glasses, searching for someone wearing a disguise, or someone who was obviously out of place, or someone carrying a weapon. He was looking for a ringer.

Actually, the car incident had been quite helpful. Several passengers had come to his notice because they hadn't reacted normally—that is, first with fascination, then with fear. These might be people with other agendas, perhaps threatening ones.

Three individuals, in particular, had caught Nathan's eye. The first was an overdressed aristocratic type, a tall, thin white-haired man with a white goatee and a gold cigarette holder. He was accompanied by a startlingly voluptuous blonde teenager swathed in jewelry and furs, a spoiled brat who kept demanding that their three servants immediately bring all of her luggage to their room — all twenty-three pieces of it.

Nathan briefly thought they might be father and daughter, then he saw them exchange smiles of mutual adoration. Each expression, he thought, exactly depicted one of the seven deadly sins — avarice for the girl, lust for the man. They seemed made for each other, but as far as he was concerned, they were a bit too obvious. It was as though they were play-acting. Who, exactly, were they trying to fool, and why?

Next to catch Nathan's eye was a slightly stout fellow in a rumpled summer-weight business suit, a dowdy, unimaginative sort who looked like an insurance agent or an electric motor salesman. But this man had something furtive about him. He was as alert as an Indian scout in Sioux territory. Either he was trying to spot someone without being noticed, or he was worried about being spotted himself. At any rate, he was not who he appeared to be.

Then there was the gangster. He'd seen enough of them in his time to know. This one was tastefully dressed — no pointy shoes, no shiny silk suit, no star sapphire pinky ring. But he was a gangster nonetheless, and an important one at that. The two bodyguards at his elbow made that clear. Or were they a team? Italians, sent by Mussolini at Germany's request?

Nathan put the field glasses down for a moment. He was starting to feel suspicious of everyone. The word reminded him of one of his father's epigrams: "In ordinary life, you are either suspicious or you are normal. In this business, you are either suspicious or you are dead." He picked up the glasses again.

Then . . . what was this? Nathan's gaze was arrested by a tall, bearded young man wearing a brown herringbone tweed overcoat — odd attire for the middle of August. He was awkwardly carrying a strange wooden box. Unlike the aristocrat, the businessman, and the gangster, who were all traveling first class, this one was headed for the crewmen's gangway, at the stern, just above the waterline.

Nathan focused his field glasses on the fellow. The man's stride was purposeful, even athletic. The coat was too small for him and the shoes weren't right, either. He might simply have been a Jewish refugee, a victim of the Nazi takeover of Czechoslovakia or Austria, but most of those refugees had an unmistakable frightened look in their eyes. They seemed lost, confused, beaten. This man was carrying himself with pride and determination. He was on a mission.

He was not an ordinary refugee, he was simply disguised as one. So what was he? And what was in that box of his? No one would carry a toilet kit and change of clothing in such an awkward and heavy container. It more likely concealed something else — maybe a disassembled submachine gun or a semi-automatic rifle or even a satchel charge.

Nathan followed the man until he disappeared into the ship, trying to imprint the face in his memory. He could do nothing more for now. And, of course, the man might be exactly who he seemed to be.

He resumed his study of the boarding passengers, methodically scanning their faces with his field glasses, sweeping from left to right, then right to left, probing farther into the crowd and farther from the ship.

Then his mouth went dry. Two more bearded men, dressed almost exactly like the first, were standing near the train station, half concealed behind some benches. These also looked exactly like refugees, like Orthodox Jews trying to conceal their identities. He would have assumed they were, except for their behavior. They were scanning the pier as methodically as he was. He was sure they were part of an operation of some kind.

Were these the members of a Nazi team sent to track down and capture Victor? They looked like Jewish refugees, not SS men, but that would be a perfect disguise for Nazi agents.

Nathan considered his options. There were two.

He and the Meisners could jump ship just before the gangways were taken up, evade the men on the dock somehow, and find another way back to America. They could head for Marseilles or Lisbon, and catch a Pan Am Clipper to America or a freighter to South America.

On the other hand, they could stay on the *Normandie* and take their chances with the one member of the Nazi unit who had boarded — assuming, of course, that he actually was an SS man and that his mission involved Victor.

If he chose the first option, Nathan realized, they'd be right back in the soup, facing all kinds of unknown risks and dangers. If they stayed put, at least the threat was limited.

The ship's powerful whistle gave two short toots and one long, ear-piercing blast. On board, visitors said their last good-byes in a final flurry of kisses, hugs, and tears, then hurried toward the gangways. On the dock, a few stragglers rushed toward the ship, while the throng of well-wishers waved to those on board and shouted their farewells. The two bearded men near the train station made no move at all.

This was the moment for him to depart and take the Meisners with him. There would be no other.

Nathan decided to take his chances with the single SS agent on board — if that's what the man turned out to be. Once they were under way, the SS man would be on his own, while Nathan could get help from ship's security.

The *Normandie*'s whistle emitted one more long, deepthroated blast. On the dock, deck hands ran up the gangways and stevedores began casting away the mooring lines that held the ship against the pier. The floor beneath Nathan's feet began throbbing. Soon the enormous vessel would begin to move, as though part of the land itself were breaking off and floating away.

Nathan walked back into the stateroom, shutting the balcony door behind him. Victor was studying the engine brochure. Tina was sitting at a mirrored vanity table, fussing with her hair.

"Listen, Mr. Nathan—ah, Cameron—would you mind if I got an officer to take me down to the engine room?" Victor asked. "This is the only major passenger ship in the world with turboelectric engines, and I'd like to see them."

"I'm afraid we have more important matters to talk about," Nathan said.

Tina looked up from the mirror.

"I think we may have some unwelcome company aboard."

"You mean the crutches didn't do the job?" Victor said acidly.

Nathan ignored him. "I can't be sure, of course, but I think I saw a possible SS agent boarding the ship."

"What makes you think so?" Victor asked.

"He didn't fit any of the usual categories. Something about him just didn't ring true."

"I suppose this means we're confined to quarters," Tina said petulantly.

"No," Nathan replied. "I don't think that's necessary. If I'm right about this guy, he won't act until just before we arrive in New York, when he has a reasonable chance of escaping."

"So we can forget about him until then?" Victor asked skeptically.

"*You* can forget about him until then. With any luck, I'll take care of him before he becomes a problem. Meanwhile, you stay near me when possible and keep to crowds at other times. Agreed?"

Victor thought about it a moment. "Agreed," he said.

They looked at Tina. "Well, of course agreed," she said with a toss of her head. "Anyhow, I *like* crowds."

AFTERNOON

It was just after the stroke of noon that Captain Barthou gave the "cast off!" order. The smoke from *Normandie*'s stacks turned black. Three strong little tugs, the *Titan*, the *Ursus*, and the *Minotaure*, began the extraordinary effort necessary to separate the gigantic mass of the liner from the pier.

The ship's public address system squawked, then a recording began to play, a brass band giving a raucous rendition of "Sailing, Sailing, Over the Bounding Main."

Stewards bearing hundreds of cornets of confetti and rolls of streamers passed among the passengers, who were lined up three and four deep along the railings. Unrolled by a toss toward the dock, these brightly colored streamers provided one final, fragile link between those on board and those ashore, held on each end until they were snapped by the growing distance between pier and ship.

Usually, it was a moment marked by wisecracks and shouted good-byes. Today, there were poignant little waves and somber farewells.

Barthou turned to Chief Purser Freppel. "And so we begin . . . what number voyage is this, Henri?"

"It's the one hundred thirty-ninth crossing," Freppel said.

"Not so gay as some of the others," the silver-haired captain observed.

"I'd say there's a great air of expectation."

"What I sense is fear, Henri—fear and uncertainty about the future."

Freppel shrugged his charming shrug.

"What's the passenger count?"

"We have a good load, Captain. We're carrying three hundred thirty in third, six hundred nineteen in tourist, and seven hundred thirty-four in first class—sixteen hundred eighty-three, all told."

"A high total for August."

"Just a lot of Americans headed home from their European tours," Freppel said.

"Heading home a little early, I'd say." Barthou turned to the harbor pilot. "Okay, Maurice, get us out of here."

The pilot snapped off a salute and went about his business: guiding the thousand-foot vessel through the jetties and breakwaters of Le Havre harbor into the open seas of the English Channel.

In addition to her sixteen hundred eighty-three paying passengers, *Normandie* carried nearly thirteen hundred crewmen, divided into three entirely separate armies: one to run the ship, a second to care for the passengers, and a third to prepare the tens of thousands of meals the ship served on each voyage.

To feed this human cargo of nearly three thousand people, *Normandie* routinely carried seventy thousand eggs, seven thousand chickens, and mountains of potatoes, meat and fish, plus two hundred thousand pounds of ice cream, twenty-four thousand liters of table wine, and seven thousand bottles of vintage wine and champagne.

She was also equipped with tens of thousands of glasses, plates, cups and saucers, knives, forks, and spoons, and enough bed and table linen to supply all the hospitals and restaurants in Paris.

It was a cliché to call her a floating city. Anyhow, she was more than that. She was a *moving* city. Her turboelectric engines developed one hundred sixty thousand horsepower — enough to propel her across the Atlantic at twenty-eight knots, or a little more than thirty-two mph. When driven hard, she could hit thirty-two knots, or thirty-seven mph. She was a floating Chrysler Building, able to steam across the Atlantic at the speed of a New York taxi.

The *Normandie* had begun life in 1935 as the largest, fastest, and most beautiful liner in the world. Since then, the *Queen Mary* had taken the speed title from her, by the barest fraction of a knot, but in terms of size and glamour, she was still unrivaled.

When the *Normandie* passed the last jetty in the harbor, the pilot hopped aboard a small launch, which sped back toward Le Havre, and the tugs dropped away. "Full speed ahead," the ruddy-faced captain said into the speaking tube.

At the ship's stern, *Normandie*'s four huge bronze propellers began revolving faster and faster. The shores of France grew faint in the afternoon fog.

There was a knock on the door.

"Who is it?" Nathan asked suspiciously.

"Your steward, sir," came the reply. The words had a pleasant French accent.

Nathan motioned Victor into the bathroom and directed Tina to the balcony. He took a seat in the cabin's Art Deco armchair, his hand on the pistol in his sock. "Come in."

A boyish-looking steward entered the room. He was outfitted in a white jacket and black trousers creased to a knife edge. "I'm your steward, Maurice Cosset," he said, friendly as a cocker spaniel.

He bowed and handed Nathan some ship brochures. "For your reading pleasure, sir."

"Thank you." Nathan quickly leafed through the brochures. One booklet caught his interest. "What's this? A passenger list?"

"Yes, sir. Hot from the printer."

"Good." Nathan sat down on a bed and began studying the booklet, pen in hand, circling some names, putting question marks after others.

Tina walked in from the balcony, unsummoned.

"I've come to help you unpack," the steward told her.

"Help me unpack? How wonderful!" She rummaged through her purse, found the key to her steamer trunk, and handed it to him.

The cheerful young man opened the trunk, which had been

93

placed near the cabin door, and began to neatly and efficiently transfer its contents to the drawers of a handsome mahogany chest. Tina directed him and assisted.

Victor came out of the bathroom, surveyed the scene with obvious disinterest, and returned to his engine brochures.

"Do you always unpack for the passengers, Maurice?" Tina asked the steward, smiling.

"Oh yes, mademoiselle. When they are willing to have me do so." Maurice opened a trunk compartment filled with lingerie, and he blushed.

Tina laughed. "Go ahead. It's okay."

The steward daintily removed a pile of lacy silk slips from the trunk and deposited them into a drawer.

"Doesn't everyone appreciate your help, Maurice?"

"Most people, yes. Not everyone."

"But who would refuse?"

The steward finished with Tina's trunk and closed it. He turned to Victor. "Your key, monsieur?" Victor reached into a pocket and tossed the steward a key, hardly looking up from his reading. Maurice opened the trunk and continued his work.

"As a matter of fact, a man refused me not fifteen minutes ago. The young Viennese gentleman, the one whose motor car . . ."

"He wouldn't allow you to open his trunk?" Tina said, interested.

"He said he preferred to be alone. But, of course, I understood."

"What is his name?" Nathan asked, looking up from the passenger list.

"Simon Rothmann," the young steward replied.

"What did you mean, you understood?" Tina asked.

"Well, because of what the purser told me about him."

Tina was fascinated. "What was that?"

"It was told to me in confidence."

Tina flashed a smile at the young man, which could have

94

melted granite. "I swear I won't breathe a word of it to anyone," she said conspiratorially.

The steward basked in her glow. "It's a very sad story. He's very rich and wealthy, heir to the Rothmann Department store fortune and all. But his wealth has done him no good."

Now Victor's curiosity was aroused. "What do you mean?"

"His wife and young daughter were killed. His parents, too."

"Car accident?" Nathan asked.

"Nazis. They seized his family right after *Kristallnacht*. Missed him because he was on a buying trip. The bodies were waiting on his doorstep when he returned."

Tina was aghast. "How horrible."

"Yes," the steward agreed. "But now he is sailing to America to forget. And we have been asked to assist him in any way we can."

Cosset finished emptying Victor's trunk and looked at Nathan. "And you, monsieur, can I unpack your luggage for you?"

"Yes, thank you." Nathan got up and stuffed the passenger list into his inner jacket pocket. "Why don't you two wait here for a while. I have some errands to do."

"You're actually going to leave us alone and unprotected?" Tina asked innocently.

Nathan didn't like being teased. "I'll be back in fifteen or twenty minutes."

"Thank heaven."

After Nathan left, Tina turned toward her brother. "That was a very sad story, Victor, about the man from Vienna."

"Yes, but how many times have we heard it before?"

"Still, you could see that he was troubled, just by looking at his face."

"When did you see his face?"

"He was on the dock, with his motor car."

"You know, you have amazing eyesight — at least when it comes to men."

95

"Don't be mean, Victor. He's a lost soul. You could see it in his eyes."

Victor was fed up with his sister's charitable impulses, especially toward men. "Why is it that you are so attracted to lost souls, Tina? What is it, your maternal instinct?"

Tina glared at him. "Sometimes I think you don't have a shred of human kindness in you, Victor."

Her brother just laughed.

In the corridor, David Nathan consulted a diagram of the ship, which he'd found among the brochures the steward had given him. He spotted the radio-telephone room on the upper deck, forward, one level down from his stateroom.

Instead of going there directly, he chose a route that would take him through some of the *Normandie*'s most important public rooms. It was time to take a closer look at this ship, about which he had heard so much. It was time to begin getting his bearings. He might need them.

At the end of the corridor, Nathan took a small stairway up a level, to the Boat Deck. Turning the corner, he stopped in his tracks and stared in wonder. He found himself standing at the top of a flight of steps that seemed almost as broad and imposing as those at the average county courthouse. A larger-than-life bronze statue stood next to him. And this, he reminded himself, was *inside* a ship!

Nathan descended the heavily carpeted stairway, feeling downright regal. Ahead of him was a chamber the ship's plan had called "the Smoking Room." A few waiters were laying out trays of canapés and filling some punch bowls, but the room was almost devoid of passengers. Everyone must be unpacking, he thought. *I'm* unpacking, even though I'm not there.

He walked across the luxuriously thick carpeting to the middle of the room, then stopped once more to survey his surroundings. The room was longer, wider, higher, and certainly more opulent than most churches or theaters.

Nathan glanced toward the walls, which were decorated with scenes of sports events, hunting and fishing, harvesting and other pastimes, carved into . . . what . . . wood? No, the walls had a distinctly non-wooden glow to them.

He threaded his way through arrangements of brown Morocco leather club chairs and lacquered card tables, walking over to the nearest wall. What is that glow? Studying the wall's surface, he saw what it was. It was gilt. The damn walls were made out of gold.

Nathan found a coin in his jacket pocket and tapped it against the wall. It made a thunk rather than a ping. No, he corrected himself, the walls were wood. They were merely *covered* with gold.

He dropped the coin back into his pocket, where it clinked against a number of others. Curious, he pulled out a handful. They were a mixture of ten-, twenty-five-, and fifty-pfennig pieces. He recalled how they had gotten into his pocket and smiled at the memory.

Looking at the loose change in his hand, Nathan felt the tug of another memory. It was the hand itself—the wide thumb, the blunt-tipped fingers, the wrinkled palm. It was exactly like his father's hand, the hand he remembered holding so often, so many years ago, with his own pudgy little paw.

That had been an important part of his childhood, holding onto that big, strong hand for dear life, going off with his father on some wonderful adventure or another—to the aquarium, the museum, or the ball game.

Of all the afternoons they'd spent together in his childhood, one was exceptionally vivid in his memory, that first Saturday afternoon father-and-son excursion into Manhattan, when he was seven or eight at most. They'd boarded the dark, mysterious, and terrifyingly loud IND subway a few blocks from their house, at the Fordham Road exit, and taken it all the way down to Broadway.

There, after lunching at a hot dog stand—he was thrilled, but his mother would have been appalled—they'd spent the day at a place even gaudier and more magnificent than this one, the largest movie house in America at the time, the Strand Theater. His father, who had always believed in going first class, had gotten them two seats, front row center.

At one o'clock, the curtain had gone up, revealing a full-sized orchestra on the stage, surrounded by plants and fountains. His mouth had dropped open in awe and it remained open until the curtain fell again. It was in this state of wonder that he'd seen the first full-length film comedy, *Tillie's Punctured Romance*, with Charlie Chaplin and the Keystone Kops. He remembered it still. And he recalled his Dad delling him that it was nice to see his "over-serious" little son laughing with such abandon.

But it was what had happened afterwards that made that afternoon such an indelible experience. They'd eaten at a Broadway delicatessen, then spent a few minutes in an entertainment arcade, where his father had bought him a huge bag of marbles. Then, finally, they'd hopped back on the subway for the ride home.

The Concourse train, mainly empty on the weekends at this time of day, had gone just three or four stops before a commotion had broken out in the next car — thumping, banging, and shouts of "stop thief!" Then the door between the cars had crashed open and a big, evil-looking fellow had come barreling down the aisle, a woman's alligator purse in one hairy fist.

Nathan's dad had gone after him immediately, but before he could chase down the thief, the train had screeched to a stop and the doors had slid open at the Columbus Circle station. The thief had bolted out of the train, followed moments later by the Nathans, father and son, hand in hand.

Unfortunately, Nathan senior hadn't stood much of a chance of catching the thief, not with a little boy in tow. As all of them ran down the concrete subway platform, the thief had steadily pulled away from him. Then the elder Nathan had gotten an idea. "The marbles, Davy, give me the marbles."

Nathan had responded as requested, and his father had flung them all — shooters, flints, cloudies, cat's eyes, aggies — down the subway platform, clinking, pinging, and bouncing toward the fleeing crook. Unable to avoid stumbling on them, the thief had come crashing down hard.

Nathan's dad had been on him in a second, getting him in a hammer lock, then lifting him roughly to his feet. He'd tossed the purse to his son. "Well, Davy boy," he'd said — and Nathan could hear the words even now — "it looks like we've made our first joint arrest."

The first, but not the last.

Nathan looked around the room, the memory fading now. It was hard to believe the old man was gone. He sighed, got up from the leather chair, and walked on.

On the way to the next room, he passed through a sliding wooden partition big enough to accommodate two locomotives side by side. The Smoking Room side of the partition was carved with hunters and animals in jungle scenes and lacquered in brilliant colors. The other side was covered in stucco with images of angels and clouds. What kind of a mind conceived this place? he wondered. And what kind of people was he trying to please?

Nathan now found himself in a room even larger than the one he had just left. He consulted his map. This must be the Grand Lounge. And it wasn't just grand, it was awesome. It was a Madison Square Garden of a room, twice the size of the smoking room and at least twice as extravagant.

Nathan stood, flat-footed, at the room's entrance, trying to absorb the scene — the vaulted two-story ceiling, the gargantuan carpet with its intricate red and orange flower-basket pattern, the four ruffled glass lighting towers that dominated each corner of the room, the floor-to-ceiling glass panels that depicted mythical sea scenes in shades of gold, silver, and bronze.

In one corner, three elderly women, incongruously dressed in glamorous gowns designed for females perhaps a third their

99

age, were sipping drinks, nibbling appetizers, and quietly chatting. They were sitting on chairs covered in red, orange, and gray flower-patterned tapestry. More than a hundred similar chairs and couches filled the room, arranged in perfectly tasteful little groupings.

It was spectacular, it was breathtaking, and it was just a bit much. It looked like a scene from a fairy tale — in fact, it reminded Nathan of the movie he'd seen in Berlin. The colors were too bright, the decorations too lavish, the room just too darn big. It felt like a stage set.

Maybe he'd like the place better when it was filled with festivities — jabbering passengers in evening clothes, a dance band, waiters carrying drinks and canapés. As it was, it was so quiet and empty that he felt conspicuous. He walked purposefully toward the forward end of the room, feeling like a single pigeon crossing the Piazza San Marco in Venice.

Picking up speed, Nathan passed through another enormous set of doors, into a slightly more modest concoction, a softly lit area called the Gallery Lounge. Its walls were covered with paintings and carved stone panels. What was so familiar about this place? Ah, he had it. It reminded him of the decorative arts exhibit he'd seen last year at the Museum of Modern Art.

Continuing forward, Nathan entered yet another lavish hallway, this one with a domed ceiling, from the middle of which hung a modernistic light fixture. Four peculiar gilded wrought-iron cages stood at each corner, with graceful stairways between them. No, not cages . . . elevators!

He was still slightly amazed by his discovery, when one of the elevator doors opened. Nathan hopped in and consulted his map again. "Main Deck, please," he told the red-jacketed, red-capped operator. A few moments later, he exited at the lower hall, where he was confronted by marble walls, inlaid marble floors, and more carved stone bas-reliefs — Viking warriors at work and play, no less. Was he actually on a ship or was this some remote section of the Louvre?

100

Just aft of the elevators, he spotted the information kiosk. Just behind that, according to his map, would be the radio-telephone booths. He headed down a corridor, and sure enough, there they were. Six or seven people were standing nearby, waiting their turns.

To Nathan's genuine surprise, the group contained no less than two of his "suspects"—the old aristocrat and the nervous businessman. This was quite an interesting development. Who could they be contacting? What urgent messages could they be sending? Unfortunately, there was no way to eavesdrop.

Soon it was his turn. He entered the booth and picked up the phone. "Please connect me with the White House, in Washington, DC," he said.

Kurt Jaekel got off the elevator at the lowest level it served—E deck. Here, according to the diagram his servile little steward had given him, was the gymnasium and the swimming pool. Here also was an entrance to the freight elevator that served cargo hold #1, where his Mercedes-Benz had been taken.

He opened a door marked "utility passageway" and found himself in a simple corridor, with gray-painted riveted metal walls and floors. It was illuminated by a string of unshielded bulbs. It was a great relief from the oppressive and ridiculous luxury of the upper decks. At last he felt himself in familiar surroundings, in what finally looked like and felt like a ship.

He turned a corner and ran headlong into a man in oil-stained coveralls. "Monsieur! I beg your pardon, but this is no place for passengers."

"It's all right, my friend. I need something out of my automobile. The freight elevator is up ahead, am I right?"

"Yes, monsieur, but passengers are not allowed—"

Jaekel reached into a pocket and came up with a ten-franc note. He pushed it into the crewman's hand. "My wife left her nerve pills in the glove compartment. She'll drive me crazy if I don't get them for her. You understand, don't you?"

The crewman glanced at the ten-franc note and laughed sympathetically. "Can I help you find your motor car?"

"Not necessary, but thanks," Jaekel said, returning his smile. He continued down the corridor, wondering if he would have trouble finding the vehicle.

He took the freight elevator down two decks, exiting in the midst of a dark, grimy, and cavernous cargo hold filled with crates and boxes of all kinds. Up ahead, through a sliding steel door, he could see parked automobiles.

Jaekel made his way toward the automobiles, avoiding the main aisles. When he reached the next chamber forward, he saw about fifty motor cars neatly parked among the stanchions and girders.

It took Jaekel several minutes to spot the Mercedes. It was tucked between a blue Citroen roadster and a silver-colored Alfa-Romeo Berlinetta. It was three rows away from the inboard aft corner of the hold where he'd been told to park it — the weak point. And it was on the other side of the room.

Jaekel considered the problem. A sleek red-and-white Delahaye Cabriolet was parked in the corner where the Mercedes had to go. Fortunately, there were several empty places. All he had to do was park the Delahaye in one of these and move the Mercedes into the Delahaye's former spot.

He was making sure the Delahaye's keys were in the ignition, when he heard the footsteps. He turned to find a husky cargo supervisor staring at him malevolently. The man was carrying an oversized pipe wrench.

"No passengers are allowed on this deck," the cargo supervisor said truculently. "You must return to the public areas immediately. I will escort you."

Jaekel smiled engagingly. "Of course. Just let me move my automobile first."

"Why?"

"Well, it's parked between two motor cars. I prefer it to be in

102

a corner. Safer that way."

"It's safe where it is."

"I'm sure it is," Jaekel said, a little annoyed with the man, "but there could be a storm and it could be damaged. . . ."

"We have never damaged an automobile," the cargo supervisor said haughtily.

"I don't doubt you take the greatest care possible, but at sea, there are acts of God. . . ."

"Which automobile is yours?" It was more an accusation than a question.

"The Mercedes-Benz over there." Jaekel was beginning to get angry.

"Then why are you tampering with this car?"

"I wasn't tampering," Jaekel said, struggling to control his temper. "I was looking for the keys, so I could move it."

"Why did you want to move it?"

Jaekel could feel the rage taking over and he could do absolutely nothing about it. "I wanted to put my automobile in this spot," he said evenly.

The cargo supervisor considered Jaekel's response, absently smacking the pipe wrench against the palm of his hand. "Because you think it will be safer here."

"Yes, that's right."

"Can you prove you own the Mercedes?"

"Prove it?" Jaekel said, his voice trembling despite his best efforts to control it. "It's registered in my name. I'm a passenger on the ship. A first-class passenger. Isn't that enough?"

Jaekel didn't like the way the conversation was going. He couldn't seem to convince the man of his good intentions. He was beginning to feel boxed in.

"What is your name, sir?"

"Rothmann, Simon Rothmann."

"We've had thieves among the passengers before, Monsieur Rothmann," the cargo supervisor said, eyes narrowing. "And I do not have a good feeling about you."

Jaekel swallowed his growing fury. "Tell you what. Why

don't *you* move the car for me." He produced a roll of francs.

The cargo supervisor acted as though he'd been slapped. "You Jews are all the same," he snarled, "but you can't bribe a Frenchman, no matter how much money you have."

"I'm not a . . . it's not a bribe," Jaekel protested. "I'm just trying to pay you to do a job." He was breathing hard now. He knew his face must be flushed. Nothing he said was working. He was getting himself into another no-choice situation.

"There's something rotten about this job of yours," the cargo supervisor said. "I'm calling the Captain of the Watch."

Jaekel was dumbfounded by what was happening. All he had to do was move the automobile. A child could have accomplished it. Instead, he had managed to draw attention both to himself and to the automobile. In a few moments, he would be confronting more hostile questions. He had lost control of the situation.

The cargo supervisor grabbed the German by the arm and pulled him toward a wall-mounted intercom phone nearby. Jaekel felt a gigantic wave of rage washing over him, submerging him completely. He let the undertow sweep him away.

Jaekel was in combat now. He could feel his opponent's skin pressed against his own, hot and hairy. The crowd was cheering, the referee circling, ready to score the point.

The cargo supervisor reached for the phone, but Jaekel jerked his hand away from it. Startled, then angered, the cargo supervisor swung the pipe wrench at Jaekel's head. Jaekel plucked the wrench out of the man's hand and sent it crashing to the floor.

The crowd roared its approval. The referee, crouching, slammed his hand down on the canvas. "One!" he shouted.

The brawny cargo supervisor whirled to challenge Jaekel face-to-face. He was grinning broadly, as if he'd wanted a physical confrontation all along. Jaekel grappled with the man, one arm behind his head, the other at his shoulder. The crowd began to shout.

Jaekel flung the man to the floor and held down both of his

shoulders. Once more, the referee slapped the mat with his hand. "Two!" he shouted. Then he blew his whistle. Jaekel released his hold.

The cargo supervisor staggered to his feet. He was a wounded bull, bewildered but still ferocious, determined now to kill, not just to hurt.

Once more they grappled, the crowd screaming for blood. Jaekel stepped backward, pulling the cargo supervisor toward him. Then, with breathtaking speed, he whirled back, behind the man, wrapping his arm around the supervisor's neck.

"Help! Help me!" the cargo supervisor cried out, his voice ringing with terror.

"Break!" the referee yelled. "Break!"

Seeing nothing but red now, Jaekel jerked his forearm backward with all of his considerable power. There was a sharp crack. The cargo supervisor's head fell limp.

"Break!" the referee yelled again, even more urgently.

Jaekel released his grip. The cargo supervisor's body fell to the floor heavily and lay still. He stared at it, the tide of anger and exhilaration slowly receding.

My God! Jaekel said to himself. My God, my God, my God! It has happened again! Panic now replaced the anger — panic at the enormity of what he had done, panic at the return of the nightmare, panic at the consequences of the deed.

He ran a few steps, then stopped. He returned to the body and checked it again. He looked at the red and white Delahaye. He simply stood there, not knowing what to do.

Jaekel tried to think. The man had cried out for help. Had someone heard him? Would he be found with the body? How could he explain what had happened? The man had attacked him. No, the man had tried to rob him. No, he had discovered the body and heard the man's assailant running away. No, he'd heard a commotion and had been hurrying to help. No. Nothing sounded convincing. He simply didn't belong here.

He listened. No sounds, no voices, no one coming. Maybe he had time to hide the body. Certainly, it would be discovered sooner or later, but no one could connect him with the death. Wait, there was the crewman in the coveralls who'd confronted him in the corridor. But even he wouldn't know when the cargo supervisor was killed, or why.

That was really the heart of the matter: *why*. Would anybody know, could anybody guess the killer's motive? Not likely. In fact, the captain would probably blame the death on a crewmen's quarrel. After all, the cargo supervisor had been a belligerent sort, no doubt involved in plenty of brawls.

Of course, he admitted to himself, the captain could conclude that the death was connected with some misguided attempt to steal the French gold. But that wouldn't matter. It would be speculation, no more, unsupported by facts of any kind.

Jaekel began to breathe again. If he hadn't killed the man, he'd be trying to explain himself right now to the Captain at Arms and his mission would truly be in danger. So maybe what happened wasn't as bad as it looked. Maybe it wasn't bad at all.

After putting the body between two automobiles, Jaekel went to look for a more permanent hiding place. He would have preferred dumping the body out of a porthole, but he couldn't risk carrying it around one more minute than he had to. On the other side of the auto storage area, he found a small storeroom filled with wooden wheel chocks. A rusty old padlock hung from the hasp, wide open. It looked like the perfect spot.

Gracefully tossing the cargo supervisor's body over his shoulder, Jaekel carried him to the storeroom, dumped him inside, and padlocked the door. The man will be missed, he realized. But the body might go undiscovered for days, and in just four days, it would all be over.

Jaekel returned to the Delahaye. Sure enough, the keys were hanging from the ignition. All he had to do was move the Delahaye to a vacant spot, then re-park the Mercedes. But just as he was opening the Delahaye's door, he heard voices approaching. He quickly crouched beside the motor car.

"As long as we have two people on shift at all times, that's enough for me," one of the voices said.

"To protect something that valuable?" the other voice asked.

"There's really nothing to worry about," the first voice replied. "It's safer here than it was in the Bank of France."

"I suppose so," the second voice said glumly.

There was the sound of a match being struck, then a few moments of silence.

"I can tell you this," the second voice went on. "I wouldn't want the responsibility for all of that gold."

The first man sighed. "All part of the job."

Still crouching, Jaekel moved toward the cargo hold door, away from the voices.

"Where's Pierre?" the second voice asked. "Isn't this where he was supposed to meet us?"

"Let's give him another ten minutes," said the first voice.

"I hope he's not off drinking again."

Jaekel slipped out of the automobile storage area and made his way toward the freight elevator. When he was younger, he thought, he would not have hesitated to dispose of these two as well as the other. But that truly would have endangered his mission. And his mission was more important than anything else, even life itself.

After the *Normandie* cleared the French coast, Captain Barthou retired to his quarters, which were just behind the bridge, on the Sun Deck.

Because his duties often required him to entertain lavishly and because, according to convention, Captain Barthou was every bit the social equal of his most prestigious passenger, his three-room suite was every bit the equal of the high-priced mini-mansions that overlooked the tourist-class promenade and outdoor swimming pool.

Now, however, the suite was merely a welcome refuge from

complaining passengers, curious little boys, and junior officers as eager to please as puppy dogs.

Barthou was playing Chopin's "Étude in F Major" on the piano that one of his predecessors had installed in the stateroom, when there was a knock on the door. He reluctantly lifted his fingers from the keyboard.

"Enter."

It was Rene Champeaux, the radio officer, horse-faced and beetle-browed, but immensely likable. "A cable for you from *Compagnie Generale Transatlantique.*"

"You could have taken it to Deputy Captain Martel, Rene."

"Sorry, sir. It was addressed to your personal attention."

Barthou nodded. What was it the home office wanted from him now? Why couldn't it have contacted him while they were still in port? "Thank you, Rene. That will be all."

He put the telegram on the piano lid and resumed the étude. When he finished — and only then — he opened the envelope.

"Private to Barthou: Foreign Office sources have informed us that the European political situation is becoming increasingly unsettled. France has ordered a partial mobilization. Your orders are to tighten internal security and report all sightings of German shipping. Signed Cangardel."

Barthou studied the telegram for almost a minute. Then he sighed and picked up his telephone. "Please have Deputy Captain Martel report to the captain's quarters."

Martel, a well-built man in his mid-thirties, with a face like the Arrow shirt man, arrived less than a minute later. Without a word, Barthou handed him the telegram. Martel read it and handed it back, his brow furrowed.

"Marius, I want you to set up a meeting here for four-thirty," Barthou told him. "Please invite the chief purser, the security officer, the chief engineer . . . and, oh yes, that government intelligence agent, the one from the SDECE, Jean-Louis what's-his-name."

"The man who's guarding the . . . ah . . . special cargo? Lieutenant Segonzak?"

"Segonzak. Yes. I suppose we have to have him here, too."

"I agree. I'll take care of it, sir." Martel saluted and left the room.

And Barthou knew the matter would be taken care of—no fuss, no problems, no silly questions. It was such a pleasure making a request of Marius Martel, he thought. But, of course, that had not always been so.

Five years ago, he had accepted Martel aboard his ship only at the persistent entreaty of the company director, a friend of his family. The young man hadn't seemed a good prospect. He'd been cashiered from the Navy, even though he'd graduated first in his class at the Academy.

Making discreet inquiries among his Navy friends, Barthou found out that Martel had run into trouble on a submarine training exercise in which he'd been given the command. He'd been unwilling or perhaps unable to fire the torpedoes. Because of his outstanding academic record, he'd been given a second chance, but he had failed that one, too.

As a result, the young man had been dismissed from the Navy as "not suited to combat." Bitterly disappointed, Martel had decided to give up the sea altogether. He'd tried government, then business, failing at both. It was at that point that his father appealed to his old friend, the director of the French Line.

Barthou had accepted the handsome young man on the condition that he start at the bottom, as the junior deck officer in a staff of thirty. On their very first voyage together, Martel's alertness had saved them from a devastating collision with a fully loaded oil tanker.

From that moment on, Martel had gained stature with each trip. He personally rescued a drunken sailor who'd fallen overboard. He figured out a way to reduce fuel consumption by better than three percent. He dived overboard and managed to free a stuck rudder. He became the man his colleagues turned to when they came up against problems they could not solve.

During the last five years, Barthou reflected, he and Marius had spent countless hours together on the bridge, talking, arguing, and laughing together. It had been his chance to gradually impart everything he had learned about the sea over the decades — not just the tangible lessons, but the intangible ones as well.

Over time, they had grown to trust each other and care for each other. In a way, they had become father and son, Martel replacing the boy Barthou had lost during the Great War. Now, Martel was second in command of the *Normandie*, not only Barthou's chief assistant, but also his closest colleague.

After Martel left his stateroom, Barthou folded the telegram neatly and put it into his inside jacket pocket. He then resumed his seat at the piano. He began playing Chopin's "Ballade in G Minor."

"Would you zip me, please?" Tina asked, presenting her back to David Nathan. He complied without comment.

Victor was surprised. "Changing your clothes again, Tina?"

"You have to change outfits at least three times a day on an ocean liner, Victor. Don't you know anything?"

"Nope," Victor admitted sarcastically. "Not a thing."

"You two ready?" Nathan asked. "Or would you like a few more minutes bickering time?"

"All ready and waiting for you," Tina shot back. She wasn't about to give him an excuse to change his mind about letting them take a look about the ship. "We have a lot to do, you know."

Nathan was taken aback. "Like what?"

"Well, for example, we have to see the chief dining room

steward and get a table reservation, and we have to go to the Promenade Deck and reserve our deck chairs."

Nathan didn't like it. His trip to Europe aboard the Yankee Clipper had been nowhere near this opulent or complicated. "How do you know about all of this?"

"You'd be surprised at what I know," Tina said mischievously. "But that was in the booklet Maurice gave us."

Nathan led them through the same route he had taken earlier, watching their reactions with interest. While Victor did his best to act blasé, Tina was openly entranced by everything and everyone she saw. And the few passengers they encountered were equally entranced with her.

This time, they took the elevator down two decks, to the marble-walled, marble-floored upper hall. At the aft end of the cavernous chamber were two bronze doors, each almost two stories high, each decorated with five enormous bronze medallions depicting Norman scenes—the church at Saint-Lô, Rouen's famous clock tower, the fortress at Dieppe.

The chief dining room steward, a thin-lipped, school-masterish sort of man, was sitting at a table just inside the doors, a huge seating chart spread out before him. An elaborate screen blocked the view to the dining room.

They approached him. "Names please?" He asked without looking up.

"Cameron," David Nathan said. "I'm David, she's Lilly, and he's Jack."

Now the steward raised his eyes in an appraising gaze. He lingered a moment on Tina. "Married or single?"

"Well, I don't know about them, but I'm single," Tina replied slyly.

"A brother, a sister, and an uncle," David explained.

"Ah," said the steward, perusing his chart. "German?"

Nathan smiled. "No, American. The kids have lived in Germany a long time. But they're coming home now for good."

"Mm hmm." The steward studied his chart. "Any friends on

the ship?"

"Don't think so," Nathan responded.

"Special dietary needs?"

Nathan's eyes narrowed. After a moment's thought, he decided that the steward was merely seeking information so he could serve them better. "None."

The steward hesitated between two spots on the chart. He looked up at Tina again, as though he were measuring her. Then he made his decision and began writing in their names. "I think I have the perfect table for you," he said. "For all three of you, that is. Number 34. It's quite close to the Captain's Table. I think you'll like your table companions."

"Excellent," Victor said. "And who will they be?"

"Other people very much like yourselves." The steward had heard the question a thousand times before, and he had a practiced answer. "You'll all introduce yourselves to each other at dinner tonight."

"Thank you," Nathan said. Who could there be on this ship, he wondered, who was "very much" like us?

They took an elevator back up to the Grand Lounge. There, Tina led them through some tall glass doors out onto the enclosed promenade, a wide roofed-over hallway with huge windows that overlooked the ocean.

Lined up on the red and black checkered rubber tile was an almost endless row of steamer chairs, three deep. A few of them were occupied by passengers who were reading, talking, or simply basking in the sunlight flooding through the picture windows.

Tina spoke briefly with a deck officer, who gave them steamer chair assignments and led them toward their seats, amidships.

"You know," Tina said after he'd departed, "this is really lovely. Let's sit for a while."

Nathan wasn't certain. "I don't know if we should hang out here."

Tina studied the tough-guy face like a doctor. "This problem you have with relaxing . . . is it congenital?"

Nathan's eyes met hers. "All right, we'll sit for a while." They settled into their steamer chairs and began watching the passengers strolling by.

After a few minutes, a man dropped into the chair beside Victor. It was none other than the nervous businessman Nathan had noticed boarding the ship, the dowdy, unremarkable fellow he'd seen again at the radio-telephone booth.

The businessman put his feet up and opened a book—a copy of H.G. Wells's *The Shape of Things to Come*. He read intently, chuckling, shaking his head, turning pages quickly and eagerly. He must have been aware that he was making a bit of a spectacle of himself.

"Amazing," the man said under his breath. "Hard to believe." He looked over at Victor and smiled. Victor nodded almost imperceptibly, doing his best not to encourage the man. The tactic didn't work.

The man read a little more, then spoke again. "Now I say, this is really remarkable."

Tina couldn't contain her curiosity. "What's that?"

"The future—or at least what Mr. Herbert George Wells thinks the future will be. He says there's going to be a dictatorship."

"Oh yes?" said Victor skeptically, drawn into the conversation in spite of himself. "Is that what he thinks?"

"The Air Dictatorship, he calls it. He says it will run the world."

"You mean like the Nazis?" Tina asked.

"Not really. He says they're a passing phase. The Air Dictators will run a world of plenty, a world where people live longer and have better lives."

"Sounds like a pipe dream to me," Nathan put in.

"I know," the businessman admitted. "But there's a terrible new World War first, with all sorts of terrible new weapons, like atomic energy bombs. Frankly, I think he might be right. I think that very well could happen."

Victor gave the man a long, interested look. "In our lifetime? I doubt it." But, he wondered, had the man somehow heard of the work of Werner Heisenberg, Ernst Strassman, and Otto Hahn? Did he know whom he was talking to? No, there could be no way.

"Well, I certainly hope you're right," said the businessman. "I'm Hans Hatzfeld, of Bern, Switzerland. And you?"

Nathan was curious about the man's apparent interest in Victor. What was going on here? Who was this person and what was he up to? He listened carefully, casually looking out to sea, hoping Victor could handle this.

Victor shook Hatzfeld's hand. "I'm Jack Cameron." He cocked his head toward Tina and David Nathan. "My sister Lilly and uncle David."

"Well, hello, hello," Hatzfeld said cheerfully. "It is a beautiful day and a beautiful ship, no?"

"It certainly is." Tina smiled pleasantly.

Nathan acknowledged the man with a simple nod, and for a moment, their eyes met. Was this just a friendly shipboard interchange, or was he being challenged somehow? He didn't know and he didn't like it.

To Nathan's relief, Hatzfeld returned to his book. And after a while, he got up, excused himself, and went below.

"Maybe we'd better go back to our cabin," Nathan suggested.

Tina put a hand to his forehead, concerned. "Maybe you're right. I think you're getting a little too relaxed."

"Okay," Nathan said sourly. "We'll stay out a little while longer. You don't mind if I walk around a little, do you?"

"As long as you don't get lost," Tina said like a concerned mother talking to her little boy.

Nathan got up and strolled over to the window, peering forward. To his surprise, the *Normandie* was approaching the English coast. He could see the docks of Southampton in the distance. It had been a very quick trip across the channel.

Before long, the *Normandie*'s engine note changed, growing

114

lower and less frenzied. The distinct vibration that Nathan had felt underfoot from the moment the ship had left Le Havre faded away, almost to nothing. After a while, the vessel came to a dead stop and the bow anchor was rung out.

They were in Southampton's outer harbor now. Like many other large ships, the *Normandie* drew too much water to tie up at the Southampton docks. So she steamed to within about a half mile of the port city — close enough for cutters to bring out mail, passengers, and a harbor pilot to take her back out through the crowded shipping lanes and into the open seas.

No sooner had the *Normandie* dropped anchor than Nathan spotted three little steamboats approaching the liner from Southampton. The first to arrive immediately began off-loading mail bags through an open port in the ship's starboard side. Just as it departed, the second boat arrived. It dropped off a single person, a weathered-looking man in a blue uniform, evidently the harbor pilot.

While Nathan watched from the enclosed Promenade Deck, the third vessel pulled up to the giant liner. It was the *Lorna Doone*, a little cracker box of a boat, with one big black funnel amidships and enclosed paddle wheels on either side.

This was the tender that brought passengers from Britain out to the *Normandie*. Some seventy or eighty of them were milling around on the *Lorna Doone*'s tiny deck, impatiently waiting to board the liner.

One of the passengers, a bantam rooster of a man in a gray fedora, was quite unable to contain his impatience. He was chewing out the deck officer in charge of the off-loading operation, pointing to himself and gesticulating angrily at his luggage.

From his position high above the *Lorna Doone*, Nathan couldn't hear what the furious little man was saying, but he could guess. He was demanding to be taken aboard the *Normandie* immediately, before anyone else. He was demanding that his luggage be sent to his room this very minute. He was demanding special treatment and special attention. No doubt, he was demanding that the captain come down there himself and carry his bags.

Nathan could imagine what the little man was saying because he knew him. Not personally, of course, but as well as every other American knew this famous and offensive character from his nightly radio shows and weekly newspaper column. He was none other than the gravel-voiced Wallace Westbrook, Jr., America's best-known scandalmonger and news commentator, the loudest and most obnoxious right-wing public figure in the land.

If Westbrook had been an ordinary passenger, Nathan was sure, all of his protests and posturing would have been politely ignored. As it was, the ship's officer kowtowed to him, as though he were a major French Line stockholder, escorting him to the front of the line. As soon as the gangplank was secure, Westbrook strutted across it. Three porters followed him, struggling with his bags.

Nathan glanced at his watch, then turned toward Tina and Victor, both of whom were contentedly sitting in their deck chairs. "Time to go back to the cabin," he said.

"Did anyone ever tell you you're a spoilsport?" Tina asked.

Nathan was ready for her this time. "I assume you want to dress for dinner . . . or do you want to show up in those clothes?"

Instead of answering him, the girl jabbed her brother in the ribs. "Race you back to the room," she challenged.

Before Nathan could speak, brother and sister were up and running. He trotted along behind them, confounded.

EARLY EVENING

Captain Barthou surveyed the group. "We are agreed, then? Even if the bombs are falling in Europe and the armies are marching, we should take no action, except to report any German ships we may encounter and avoid prolonged contact."

He looked one by one at the men around the table in his private dining room, waiting to see if anyone had any contrary ideas or other suggestions. So far, every one of them had reacted just as he had expected.

Chief Purser Freppel, a French poodle of a man, had been annoyed by the telegram and hadn't bothered to hide it. He'd called it *alarmist,* a word he used when he was too chicken to say *cowardly.* The way he saw it, the war scare was silly and it upset the passengers.

Deputy Captain Marius Martel, a dead ringer for Tyrone Power according to many passengers — especially the older women — had been ready and willing to do whatever the captain wanted. His comments had been sensible and perceptive.

Chief Security Officer Bernard Nadeau, tall, gaunt, and humorless, had found the wire personally insulting, because it implied the ship's security could be tighter. As far as he was concerned, he didn't need any help or instructions. He knew everything there was to know about the ship's security. He was going to be a problem.

Chief Engineer Gaston LeBrun, a lilliputian man with a W.C. Fields nose, was a genius in the engine room but painfully out of his element on the upper decks. He hadn't been able to understand why he'd been summoned to this meeting and was eager to get back to his engines. But Barthou had invited him because he wanted to keep him abreast of everything that was happening.

Lt. Jean-Louis Segonzak, a lithe, likable, foxlike fellow, had listened to the conversation intently, as if weighing not only the telegram, but also the men discussing it. He hadn't done much talking himself, but everything he'd said had been intelligent and interesting.

"No objections? Good," the husky silver-haired captain said. "Then I declare the meeting adjourned."

The men rose and began to leave.

"Oh, Henri," Barthou said to the purser, "could you please stay? We have a Captain's Dinner to plan, you know."

117

The ceremonial Captain's Dinner normally took place on the first full day at sea. But after the *Paris* had burned, *Compagnie Generale Translatlantique,* the French Line, had moved the dinner to departure day, to reduce the captain's social obligations and give him more time to oversee security matters. Barthou, to no avail, had argued that it had the opposite effect.

On this special evening, about half the seats at the Captain's Table were usually reserved for the "obligatories," the important or influential people who needed special coddling or attention. Barthou and Freppel were allowed to choose the rest according to their personal preferences.

"How many obligatories?" Barthou asked his chief purser.

Freppel produced his annotated copy of the passenger list, plus the "hot sheet" CGT's Paris office had sent to the ship, and made a quick count. "Twelve," he said.

"Which leaves us with eight."

"Correct. Do you wish to invite anyone in particular, Captain?" Freppel asked.

Barthou thought about the unusually subdued atmosphere at departure. "Is there anyone aboard," he asked, "who might be able to lighten the mood a little? Someone who could provide a little fun — for all of us?"

Freppel grinned slyly. "I think I know just the right people," he said. He pointed to two names on the passenger list.

"Perfect," Barthou said happily. "Invite them both."

A few minutes before, at six P.M. on August 23, 1939, the *Lorna Doone* had finished off-loading the luggage of the seventy-three Southampton passengers who had boarded the *Normandie*. Shortly afterward, the *Normandie* gave three rumbling blasts on her whistle and weighed anchor. Guided gingerly through the crowded Southampton shipping channel by the English pilot, she steamed across a sea as calm as glass, toward the rocky formation outside of the harbor known as The Needles.

Near The Needles, a small boat picked up the pilot. And then, with another clamorous blast on her whistle, the huge French express liner raised steam and headed for the open ocean, slowly accelerating. In a hundred hours or so, God willing, she would arrive at the outer limits of New York harbor.

Nathan and his charges arrived at the dining room reception area at about seven-thirty, only to find themselves in a longish line of passengers waiting to be seated. And as they waited, they looked past the *grande descente* that led down into the first-class dining room and tried their best to absorb the fantastic sight before them.

It was really nothing more than a restaurant, Nathan thought, trying to suppress his feeling of awe — a mammoth, spectacular, and immensely active restaurant. But what a pitiful word that was to describe this palatial setting and its scintillating collection of People of Consequence.

The room was a glittering grotto of pink and gold and red and blue, an Ali Baba cave as high as the nave of St. Patrick's and as wide and long as the football field on which Nathan had played at Columbia University. It was an Art Deco version of the Hall of Mirrors at Versailles, a human rendition of the main chamber of the Carlsbad Caverns.

And like the Carlsbad Caverns, the *Normandie*'s dining room had no windows. Instead, its walls were covered with shimmering glass tiles. It was illuminated by monumental wall sconces and by a dozen elaborate glass lighting towers that stood among the tables like sentries. High above them, the coffered ceiling glowed with gilt. And at their feet, the floor gleamed with polished tiles of India rubber.

Spread out in this vast space were at least one hundred fifty dining tables, each graced by custom-designed Christofle silverware, Daum crystal, and Haviland china — a table service that would not have embarrassed Louis XIV.

At the moment, Nathan noted, the dining room was about half occupied by first-class passengers, the men in the monochrome of formal wear, the women in peacock-colored evening gowns, sparkling with diamonds and emeralds.

An army of waiters, wine stewards, and busboys gracefully insinuated themselves through the tables, performing their appointed tasks with efficiency and assurance.

The scene reminded him of a ballet, complete with spectacular — if somewhat overblown — stage sets and a full-scale symphony orchestra.

At the top of the grand staircase stood the Arturo Toscanini of the place, a rotund man in full-dress uniform, the *Normandie*'s famous maitre d', the redoubtable Oliver Nafferchoux. It was he who appeared to be conducting the activity below.

With a wave of his hand, it seemed, silverware tinkled. A nod of his head brought the percussive pop of a champagne cork. An arm gesture appeared to inspire an outburst of laughter at a distant table. A quick glance produced twitterings of delighted recognition between two Society Ladies at the foot of the staircase.

And at his imperceptible signal, a chorus line of waiters pranced through the room, carrying roasts in silver-domed platters. At the same time, a treble clef of busboys busied themselves cleaning tables and refilling empty water goblets. The piece climaxed with a cymbal crash of falling dishes.

All this, Nathan reflected, in what — if it had truly been a concert hall — would have been the most extraordinary concert hall in the world. All this somewhere on the Atlantic Ocean, on board a ship. All this in a world with painfully fresh memories of the Depression. All this in a world hurtling toward war.

"Mr. Cameron?"

The waiter's voice startled him. "Oh. Yes?"

"May I escort you and your party to your table?"

"Certainly."

The waiter led them through the maze of tables, toward the

120

center of the room. As Tina glided by, a murmur of approval rose up from the elderly men in their dinner jackets, as if Nafferchoux had pointed his baton in their direction. Except for the faintest little smile, she seemed completely oblivious to their admiration.

Tina's sleek black satin gown exposed her slender neck and golden shoulders and, at the floor, revealed ten inches of fault-less calf and ankle. Little jeweled barrettes held her shoulder-length honey-blond hair back behind her ears. Her green eyes were filled, as usual, with mischief and promise.

She was breathtaking, there was no denying it, easily the equal of the better-known beauties aboard the *Normandie* on this voyage, women such as Olivia de Havilland, Constance Bennett, and Sonja Henie. And beside her, Victor and David Nathan, in their simple rented tuxes, were totally invisible.

The waiter seated them at table 34, according to the plac-ard, a table for ten, almost within earshot of the Captain's Table, not far from the giant bronze statue of a toga-clad woman which dominated the room. They were the first to arrive at their table. The waiter distributed menus, then went off to escort other passengers to their tables.

Nathan's gaze darted around the room, stopping first at the Captain's Table, where an odd collection of movie stars, fin-anciers, business tycoons, and diplomats were showing off for each other in every way possible. Even at a distance, the scent of power, money, and sex was almost overpowering.

He reluctantly discontinued his sightseeing and started do-ing his job, which was looking around the room for the people who'd attracted his attention at boarding time. He found the first one three tables away, near the wall. It was the gangster with his two bodyguards.

The man seemed even more familiar than before. Nathan had seen his picture in a newspaper or perhaps a magazine — more likely, on a wanted poster. He had a good memory for names and faces, but the identity of this one eluded him.

As he watched, the three men ate their appetizers, not

looking at each other, not exchanging a word. In fact, their faces were totally expressionless. It was odd, even menacing.

The waiter brought their dinners to the table, serving the gangster first. He began eating immediately. The others were so unimportant, evidently, that he felt no need to wait for them.

Then Nathan noticed a man approaching the gangster's table. The bodyguards stiffened instantly and reached into their jackets. For a moment, Nathan thought gunfire would break out, then he remembered that this was the *Normandie,* not some Brooklyn street corner.

Then the gangster, grinning broadly, stood and stuck out his hand. The visitor shook it. Nathan could see his face now and he knew it immediately. It was a face tens of millions of Americans could have identified without a second thought. It was George Raft, the movie actor.

After some casual chitchat, the gangster evidently asked Raft for some kind of favor. Raft, a little embarrassed, demurred. The gangster repeated his request. Raft shook him off again, but the gangster insisted.

Resigned, Raft reached into his jacket pocket and became an actor. His expression ominous and threatening now, he pulled out a silver dollar, flipped it high into the air with a thumbnail, and caught it with sinister grace. Nathan had seen him repeat the gesture in a number of movies.

The gangster clapped his hands together in childish glee — and apparently asked Raft for the coin. Then he clumsily tried the same trick, missing completely. The silver dollar bounded down the tile floor of the dining room, both bodyguards scrambling after it on their hands and knees.

When the coin was finally retrieved, the gangster, still smiling, handed it back to Raft. Relieved, Raft slipped it back into his pocket, said his good-byes, and walked on. The atmosphere of conviviality that had momentarily prevailed at the gangster's table vanished without a trace.

Nathan had no doubt that he was watching the antics of a

very dangerous man. But could he be a threat to Victor? Nathan had no specific reason to suppose so, but no reason to forget about him, either.

Nathan was trying once more to put a name to the gangster's face when the waiter reappeared, two women in tow. They introduced themselves as Claire and Daphne Stickney "of the Philadelphia Stickneys." They were identical twins — tall, flat-chested, horsey-looking unmarried women of indeterminate age, dressed in similar flowered gowns, one predominately green, the other mainly blue. It soon became apparent that they were given to inappropriate outbursts of merriment.

"We've been seasick," Claire said, giggling.

"That's right," Daphne said with a cackle of her own. "At the rail all afternoon. But we decided to come down to dinner anyway."

"Wouldn't want to miss the first night," Claire added, trying to muffle a snicker.

"Well, we're very pleased to meet you," Tina told them. She chuckled sympathetically and all three women burst into outright laughter. Victor rolled his eyes at Nathan, who shrugged helplessly.

While Tina and the Stickney twins entertained each other, Nathan continued to scan the dining room for suspects. After a few moments, he noticed a waiter leading the aristocratic gentleman and his *coquette* to a table for two. The girl was wearing a red silk gown, which was wrapped around her voluptuous figure so tightly that a doctor could have examined her as she was.

She was pouting . . . no, wheedling. She wanted something from the old man but he held back, preferring to tease her. But whatever it was she wanted, it was important to her, important enough to let her lower lip droop and tremble.

Eventually, the aristocratic gentleman relented. He reached into his pocket and handed her a small rectangular packet, which she unwrapped eagerly. She popped the contents into her mouth. It took Nathan a moment to divine the exact nature of this treat, and he was disgusted when he did. The man obviously had her addicted to drugs.

The waiter now reappeared with yet another tablemate for the "Camerons." He was Arthur Shepard, an apple-cheeked college junior from Northwestern University. Instead of sitting next to one of the Stickney sisters, in the seat the waiter pulled out, Shepard plopped down beside Tina.

"Well, hello," he said with an ingratiating grin, his eyes never leaving her face. "I'm Arthur Shepard. And you?"

"Lilly Cameron." She returned the smile reflexively.

"You're traveling by yourself, Lilly?" he suggested, full of hope.

"No, with my brother and my u.. le." She indicated Victor and David Nathan.

"No boyfriends, though?"

"You mean *men*friends?" She responded pointedly. "Well, not on the ship. My fiancé lives in New York. I'm going to meet him."

The college boy was crestfallen. "I see. Well, maybe we could have a dance after dinner anyway."

Tina became his big sister. "I'd like that, Arthur," she assured him. Then she opened her menu, a gesture that everyone else at the table took as permission to do the same.

Nathan studied the giant cardboard folder, trying to find his way through almost endless lists of *poissons, legumes, pommes de terre, pâtés, rôtis, buffet froid, salades,* and on and on and on. Fortunately, given his weak French, the right-hand side of the menu was in English.

"Shall I order for the three of us?" Tina asked, apparently quite at home both with the language and with this mind-boggling compendium of alternatives.

Nathan was relieved. "Fine by me."

Victor simply shrugged.

The waiter now appeared once more, bringing with him a tall, attractive brunette in a striking strapless red gown that was perfectly suited to her slender, high-breasted figure.

Evidently, someone had once told her that she looked like Myrna Loy. As a result, she had done everything possible to heighten the resemblance, parting her hair in the middle, using her lipstick to give herself bow-shaped lips, and plucking her eyebrows into oblivion.

"Karla Kirkland," she said, smiling coyly, gracefully extending a smooth, tanned hand in Nathan's direction. "I'm a commercial traveler for Tussy Cosmetics."

"David Cameron," Nathan said. "How's business?"

"Not so hot, Mr. Cameron," the lady replied. "Hitler detests cosmetics. But then, this is my first trip abroad. Maybe it's always this bad."

There was a small commotion at the entrance to the dining room, evidently a passenger protesting his table assignment. Nathan could see Nafferchoux smothering the man with compliments, apologies, and promises. Then, the maitre d' himself led the man down into the dining room. To Nathan's surprise, the protester was none other than Wallace Westbrook, Jr., the obnoxious passenger from the *Lorna Doone*. And he was being brought to their table.

"Well, hello Mr. and Mrs. United States and all the boats in the ocean," Westbrook proclaimed in his radio announcer's voice. He went on in normal tones. "I was supposed to be seated at the Captain's Table, but I guess you're going to be my tablemates tonight." He sat down between Nathan and Karla Kirkland, to the lady's undisguised annoyance.

The waiter began taking orders now — duckling *à l'orange*, fillets of turbot *paiva*, and a two-pound Maine lobster for Victor, Tina, and Nathan; pike in butter for Karla Kirkland and Arthur Shepard; roast beef "and it better be medium rare and I don't mean rare and I don't mean medium" for Wallace Westbrook, Jr.; and a cold buffet for the Stickney sisters.

The table had one empty seat left, but it did not remain so for long. A tall, square-jawed, dark-haired athletic-looking young man walked up, checked the table number placard, then sat down and opened a menu. He was apparently unaware of the interest — and, in Tina's case, the soft-hearted sympathy — that he aroused.

Noticing the silence at last, he looked around the table shyly, almost diffidently. "Oh, hello," he said, reserved and polite. "My name is Simon Rothmann."

"Tell me, Mr. Allen," Captain Barthou said, egging the man on. "Is Jack Benny really as cheap as they say?"

The doleful-looking man rolled his eyes. "Cheap? Jack's so cheap that when he went to the race track and lost, he got mad at the horse."

The captain laughed, then he looked around the table. Jules Bache was smiling broadly, a good sign in these troubled times. Marlene Dietrich was snickering in delight. Even the courtly business executive Thomas Watson, who only moments ago had told the table that he considered most humor coarse and vulgar, could not restrain a grin.

"I was not mad at the horse," a slightly balding man across the table said in wounded protest.

"Then why did you shove your hand down his throat?" Allen asked slyly.

At the other end of the table, the boyishly good-looking Jimmy Stewart slapped his knee and roared. Sitting next to him, Mrs. William Randolph Hearst, matronly now but once a gorgeous showgirl, chortled without restraint.

Benny did one of his patented double takes. "I did it to get my lump of sugar back, if you must know."

To Barthou's gratification, the entire Captain's Table exploded in laughter.

"You know," put in Benny's wife, Mary Livingston, "that stingy stuff is just a running joke for the radio show. Jack's really quite generous. You should have seen his reaction when the cancer fund asked him for a contribution."

Fred Allen produced an engagingly droll expression. "I'll

bet little chunks of stone rolled down his cheeks."

That remark even tickled the two waiters who were beginning to distribute food and drink around the huge table.

Erich von Stroheim squinted through his monocle at Jack Benny. "From what I understand, Mr. Benny," he said with cunning malevolence, "you and Mr. Allen detest each other. Yet here you are aboard the *Normandie*, with your wives, traveling together. Could you explain that?"

"Well—1—1—, I . . ." Benny began.

"He got a package deal on the tickets," Allen interrupted.

Once again, everyone broke out into laughter.

Captain Barthou had taken only one bite from his pike when he felt a tap on his shoulder. It was the gaunt figure of his officious security chief, Bernard Nadeau, a man who had once actually arrested two tourist-class passengers for sneaking into first.

"Trouble?" Barthou asked quietly.

"Perhaps. Clouzot, the cargo supervisor, has been missing for better than three hours."

"Missing? Again? Has anybody looked for him?"

"Of course we have," Nadeau said, stiffening. "I've had a team of men looking for him. It has not yet succeeded."

Barthou sighed. "He's probably holed up somewhere, drinking again or sleeping it off."

"Very possible, sir. But I wanted you to know that he cannot be accounted for. This could become a serious security matter."

A missing crewman a serious security matter? That was a bit much. "Thank you, Bernard," Barthou said. "Let me know when he turns up. Perhaps I should have a talk with him this time."

"I'll discipline him for you, if you like."

"We'll see."

Barthou turned back toward his guests. Marlene Dietrich was speaking in her husky, insinuating, charmingly accented English. She was a frequent transatlantic passenger, and

Barthou had always enjoyed listening to her and looking at her. Tonight, her blond hair was soft, feminine and, as usual, perfectly coiffed. Her gauzy green two-piece suit — with trousers, no less — looked more like pajamas than an evening gown and set her apart from every other woman in the room.

"Tell me, Mr. Benny," Dietrich was saying, "is it true that you are only thirty-nine years old?"

Benny laughed modestly. "Well," he said, rolling his eyes, "I'm not as young as I used to be."

"You're not as young as *anybody* used to be," Allen put in.

"Now cut that out!" Benny objected.

Once more, the table dissolved in laughter. There was chuckling at some of the nearby tables, too. The entire room seemed to brighten perceptibly.

"And what do you do in Philadelphia, Cameron?" Westbrook asked. The man's private voice was the same as his public one, a harsh, barking staccato.

"I own a couple of apartment buildings."

"Whereabouts? I know Philly pretty well."

He certainly was a persistent questioner, Nathan thought. "Actually, they're in Upper Darby. My father built them just before the crash."

"What were your niece and nephew doing in Germany?"

"Germany?"

"The accent, Cameron. I've got a good ear for accents. Hope you don't mind these questions. Don't mean anything by it, you know. It's my business."

"I know. I've heard your show."

"Yeah, I'm sure you have. Anyhow, I'm interested in what's going on in Germany. What did your nephew do over there, anyhow?"

"He was a student. Art history." Why was this man interested in Victor? Victor hadn't done anything to attract the attention of a man like Westbrook. "You gathering material for your next broadcast or your next column?"

Westbrook shrugged. "I'm always gathering material, Cameron. But not from you. I'm keeping an eye on those two over there." He pointed to the Captain's Table.

"Jack Benny and Fred Allen?"

"Nope. Dietrich and von Stroheim. I'm tracking down some mighty interesting stories about both of them. And I think I have something on George Raft, too."

"Is that so?"

The busboy cleared away the empty dinner plates and refilled their wine glasses with the last of the *Bordeaux Blanc Superieur*. Almost simultaneously, the waiter arrived with a silver coffee pot and a platter full of *crème brûlée, bavaroises chocolat,* and *pudding martiniquais*. He began pouring coffee and serving dessert.

"You're from Vienna, Herr Rothmann?" Tina asked.

"Please, *Mr.* Rothmann. I do not wish to be called Herr anything anymore."

Tina reacted very compassionately. "Of course, I understand. What are you planning to do in America, Mr. Rothmann?"

Jaekel was firm but polite. "I'd rather not talk about it." He'd been told to remain as inconspicuous as possible, which meant no idle chitchat with anyone, even this lovely girl. This policy was now yielding a useful side benefit: He was not compelled to experience the awkward embarrassment that normally accompanied his every attempt to make conversation with a desirable woman.

"I saw them loading your motor car this morning, Mr. Rothmann," Tina said, trying again. "It gave us quite a scare."

Jaekel allowed himself the smallest possible shrug but said nothing, closing off any possible conversational opening.

Tina tried again anyhow, unaccustomed to having difficulty getting a man to talk to her. "Have you been enjoying the voyage?" she asked a little lamely.

"It's okay."

The remark did not invite a reply.

Tina was puzzled. Usually, she was the one who did the fending off. The problem had always been how to do it without hurting their feelings. But this man was different. He was keeping *her* at arm's length. That had happened only twice before, with fellows who were not interested in women. Rothmann certainly wasn't one of those. He'd been married, he'd had children. What was the problem, then? It troubled her. She found it challenging.

When Nathan finally managed to disengage himself from Westbrook, he was astonished to find Victor's seat empty. He looked around the room wildly, finally spotting the young man at the Captain's Table, speaking to Barthou himself. What was this? He went over to find out.

". . . always been fascinated with energy and propulsive devices," Victor was saying.

"I see," Captain Barthou said. He was a captive audience.

Victor hardly missed a beat. "So I'm hoping someone could show me the *Normandie*'s electric power plant."

This was a request the captain could deal with. "Well, of course," he said. "Apply to the chief purser and he'll arrange a tour."

"Sorry for the interruption," Nathan said, tugging at Victor's arm. "My nephew is very interested in technical matters."

"Perfectly all right, Mr. —"

"Cameron. David Cameron."

After dinner, Tina persuaded Nathan to take her and Victor up to the Boat Deck, aft, to the Cafe Grill, the *Normandie*'s after-hours restaurant, bar, and dance hall.

"Everyone goes there after dinner," she'd told the broad-shouldered, dark-haired American.

"What for?" Victor asked. "Certainly not to eat, not again."

"They go to drink. And to dance."

"Is that what you have in mind, Tina?" Nathan asked,

130

wariness in his gray-green eyes.

Tina flashed Nathan an angelic smile, a smile with just the faintest trace of suggestion and innuendo. It made him very uncomfortable. "Well, of course," she told him. "Did you expect anything else?"

"I just want you to—"

"You want me to be careful," Tina offered helpfully.

"And don't do anything I wouldn't do," Victor added.

"No," Nathan said. "Well, yes, of course, all of that. But I also expect neither of you to leave the room without telling me and both of you to accompany me back to our stateroom when I say it's time. Agreed?"

"As far as I'm concerned, I could go back right now," Victor said. He glanced at his sister, but she showed no signs of rising to the bait.

She chose instead to tease their escort. "I didn't know you were afraid to go back to the cabin alone, Mr. Cameron. Of course, I'll keep you company. I'll even hold your hand if you like."

What a maddening girl, Nathan thought. "That's fine," he sulked, "just fine."

By the time they got to the Cafe Grill, it was hopping with activity. Many of the passengers, especially the younger ones, had come there directly from the first-class dining room, seeking good company, or romance, or nothing more than an opportunity to dance or drink themselves into the void.

The room had none of the gaudy opulence of the ship's other public areas. It was low-ceilinged, indirectly lit, cozy as opposed to commodious, Bauhaus functionalist rather than Art Deco, filled not with tapestry-covered chairs but with assemblies of leather cushions in stainless steel frames, grouped around tables with stainless steel pedestals.

Against one wall was a streamlined black bar, with black bar stools and a glass bar top, set off against a cast metal bas-relief of game animals. It was crammed with drinkers of both genders. Against another wall was a busy dance band, complete with piano and crooner, positioned between two huge picture windows overlooking the trailing sea.

And in the midst of the room was a polished parquet dance floor, almost every inch of it taken up by couples energetically dancing to the strains of "Frenesi."

"Would you mind getting me a martini?" Tina asked Nathan, batting her eyelashes in his direction.

Nathan frowned, then went to do his duty. Tina and Victor threaded their way through the crowd toward one of the few empty tables.

Victor pointed to one of the dancers. "I recognize that man."

"A movie actor," Tina told him. "Edward G. Robinson. 'Little Caesar.' "

"Oh, yes. What about that woman over there. She also looks familiar."

"That's Sonja Henie."

"Henie?"

"The ice-skating champion, Victor. Do you live inside a box?"

"Frankly, Tina, I'm amazed that you know all these people."

"I'm just as amazed that you don't. The magazines and newspapers are always writing about them."

"While you've been reading the decadent press, I've been studying physics," Victor said.

"You're studying your profession, Victor, and I'm studying mine."

"You mean acting."

"Yes, I mean acting. And I'd appreciate it if you would take me seriously, Victor."

"I do. Believe me, I do."

Arthur Shepard, the college boy, appeared at their table. "I was hoping to find you here," he told Tina. "I've come to claim my dance."

Since there was no avoiding it, she decided to be gracious. She rose and joined him, as the band launched into a rendition of "Body and Soul."

Shepard put an arm around Tina's waist and clasped her hand in his a bit awkwardly. "You never did tell me when you're getting married," he said, still trying.

"Oh, Arthur." Tina dismissed the question with a soft little laugh. "Let's not talk about me. Let's talk about you. Tell me about your girlfriend. I'm sure you have one, a nice-looking boy like you."

"Well, there is this girl at the University of Michigan. . . ."

Suddenly, a figure appeared at Arthur's shoulder, a small, barrel-chested man with distinctly forbidding features: a shaven skull, piercing blue eyes, thin, cruel lips. Tina recognized him instantly. He was Erich von Stroheim, the German actor and director who had played so many hateful film roles.

"I will finish this dance with the lady, young man," he told Arthur Shepard sternly. Shepard, cowed, yielded his prize without protest. And von Stroheim whirled Tina away, into a world of his own creation.

"I am von Stroheim," he said, clasping her to him tightly, masterfully. "And you?"

"I am—" For an instant, she forgot her made-up identity. "I am Lilly Cameron," she said, struggling just to breathe.

"Lilly Cameron is the most beautiful woman on the ship," he told her. "And I know beauty."

"Thank you," Tina said. She was completely disconcerted.

"Have you ever considered acting?" von Stroheim continued.

"But I am—I *am* an actress." She was intensely aware of his body against her, pressed so tightly that she could feel its every outline.

"Of course, I must have sensed that. You are German?"

Tina smelled alcohol on his breath. But Arthur Shepard's breath had reeked of alcohol, and the same could have been said of almost everyone else in the room as well. "I am American," she said, delivering her lines as well as she could. "My father was in the foreign service, and we lived in Germany for a long time."

The music came to an end, but von Stroheim did not release her. Soon, the band resumed. "I didn't know what time it was," the crooner sang, "till I met you . . ."

"I am about to begin a new film," von Stroheim confided. "It will be one of the most remarkable motion pictures ever created, greater even than *Queen Kelly.* And there may be a part in it for you."

Tina was fighting to regain her equilibrium. Here she was, a young, inexperienced, and very much undiscovered actress, in the arms of a great actor and director who thought she might be right for his new movie. It was a heady moment indeed. "What is the part?" she managed somehow.

"Ah, the part." Von Stroheim was speaking into her ear and the fumes were a little intense. "It is a marvelous part. A part for a young Carole Lombard. A part in my film of de Sade's novel, *The Adventures of Adversity.*"

"De Sade?"

"Yes, the Marquis. You must have heard about him — a brilliant man, with astonishing psychological insights. He wrote the book in 1787, but it is as true to life now as it was then." Von Stroheim swept her toward the floor, crushing her breasts against his chest, then swung her back up again to her feet.

"Can you tell me about the part?" The question took every bit of breath she had.

"Ah, yes, the part, Miss Cameron, the part." Von Stroheim's eyes were glittering. "You see, I am looking for a beautiful unknown, a creature exactly like yourself. I want her to play the horsewoman who evolves from a state of total innocence into a state of all-encompassing sexual perversion."

"Sexual what?" Tina asked, not sure she'd heard him correctly.

"Perversion, pretty lady, perversion. So you can see why it is essential that the actress be both surpassingly alluring, yet surpassingly innocent. The transformation must be profoundly shocking to the audience. Of course, that means it must be a transformation in real life as well as on film."

Tina frowned. "What do you mean, in real life?"

"I mean the life the actress is living off the screen. I will direct that life also. It will be an extraordinary experience, I assure you, Miss Cameron, absolutely extraordinary." He was whispering now, his soft voice hypnotically intense.

"I don't know." Tina tried to open some space between them, but she could not loosen his grip on her body.

"Of course, you may not be right for the part," von Stroheim continued. "It all depends on how you look in jodhpurs."

"Jodhpurs?"

"Riding breeches. I have several pairs in my stateroom. We can go back right now and you can try them on. They must be tight at the buttocks and at the calves — *very* tight."

Tina gathered her strength and pushed at the man. He lost his balance but kept his grip. She felt herself falling, falling.

Then strong arms swept her up and away. "You tripped on something," David Nathan was saying.

The air began to clear.

Von Stroheim, sprawled on the floor, was struggling to rise. He was furious, as only someone who has had too much to drink can be furious.

"You all right?" Nathan asked him, extending a hand.

"I will not require your assistance," von Stroheim said, his voice frigid, his eyes fixing Nathan with a malignant glare. They left him up on one knee. Couples danced around him as though avoiding a piece of furniture.

"I think it's time to go back to the cabin, don't you?" Nathan said, his hand gently gripping Tina's arm. He led her away from the dance floor.

"He was offering me a part," Tina began, striving for composure.

"No details, please."

"But you don't understand. . . ."

"What's there to understand? It seems pretty obvious to

135

me."

Tina glared at him, then pulled her arm free. She made her way toward the table where Victor was sitting. "Daddy wants us to go back to the stateroom," she snapped. "He thinks it's time to change our diapers."

"Well, whatever Daddy wants," Victor responded agreeably.

They threaded their way through the crowded room, past flirting couples who'd just met, past playboys on their sixth Rob Roy and going down for the count, past walking jewelry and fur displays, and near the door, past a group of gamblers debating what speed the *Normandie* was making and exactly when she would arrive in New York. It was in this last group that Tina noticed Simon Rothmann, carefully weighing the opposing arguments. For a moment, their eyes met. She smiled. He looked away.

Night fell on the Atlantic. On board the *Normandie*, it was celebrated in various ways. The very young and the very old and a few of those in between simply went to bed. The rest sought amusement, sometimes desperately. Many failed, but many succeeded beyond their fondest dreams.

In third class, the rowing team from Yale University, on the way home from a match against Oxford, stumbled across a troupe of Folies-Bergère dancers headed for a tour of the eastern seaboard. *L'amour, toujour l'amour.*

In tourist class, five middle-aged spinster schoolteachers from Elyria, Ohio, returning from a glorious tour of the Gothic cathedrals of France, found themselves dining with a like number of furniture salesman who'd won trips to Paris by selling more Beautyrest mattresses than anyone else in the United States. They spent the night thrusting and parrying.

In first class, festivities in the Cafe Grill concluded just after three A.M. Three merrymakers had to be carried to their rooms — about the usual number. Before the Cafe Grill closed—and afterward as well—there was drinking, carousing, and assorted hanky-panky in many first-class suites. Some of it was relatively innocent, some of it downright depraved.

The most uninhibited *soiree,* as expected, took place in the Trouville suite, one of the *Normandie*'s four *grand luxe* apartments, this one located on starboard side of the Sun Deck, aft.

Like its companions, the Trouville contained four bedrooms, two full baths, two lavatories, a dining room, a lounge, and a pantry. A large private terrace overlooked the ocean and the ship's wake.

Designed by the renowned artist Jean Leleu, the suite was a study in ovals—an oval dining room lined with ivory Morocco leather, with a polished mahogany oval dining table and green chairs, all set on a white oval rug with a geometric pattern; an oval lounge hung with Aubusson tapestries, with yet another oval rug and another, smaller oval table; even an oval master bedroom, with an oval bathroom close at hand.

These were the quarters Marlene Dietrich customarily occupied when she traveled on the *Normandie.* And these were the quarters where she was now entertaining at least thirty others of mixed ages, genders, occupations, and reputations. They overflowed the dining room and lounge into all of the bedrooms, the bathrooms, the pantry—even the terrace, despite the Atlantic's chill.

In the lounge, two famous investment bankers argued about whether or not the Maginot Line could stop Hitler's legions. In the dining room, a number of minor movie stars discussed the choice of Vivien Leigh to play Scarlett O'Hara in *Gone With the Wind,* set for December release. The consensus was that she'd been miscast.

The rest of Dietrich's guests were mainly congregated in the bedrooms, in pairs, trios, and various other combinations. None were with their spouses, and few were engaged in activities they would have been willing to describe to their mothers or even to their psychiatrists.

Long before Dietrich's party had gotten into high gear, David Nathan had his charges safely tucked into bed, lights out, door locked. Then he changed from his tuxedo into casual clothing and shaved for the second time that day—the only way he could make headway against his stubborn beard. While the Meisners slept, he planned to continue exploring the ship. Despite the map, he'd found her eleven decks and miles of corridors endlessly confusing. Somehow, he had to turn the place into familiar territory. If they ran into trouble, that might be his only advantage.

He entered the first-class elevator near the Smoking Room doors and asked the page to take him "all the way up." The top was as good a place to start as any.

Moments later, he exited on the upper Sun Deck, near the aft funnel. The moon's bright crescent and a hundred million stars eerily illuminated the funnels, with their great bulk, the shimmering radio antenna grid, the shadowy ventilators. Except for a steward walking a dog, he was totally alone. For the first time since he had come aboard the ship, he truly felt he was at sea, truly exposed to the elements, truly experiencing the motion of this great ship as it hurtled toward America.

Nathan walked forward over the wooden deck, along the rail, past one house-sized funnel, continually fighting the wind. On either side of the deck the name *NORMANDIE* rose up in enormous floodlit letters. Below him, one level down, were rows of neat canvas-covered lifeboats hanging from pairs of giant automatic davits, devices designed to lower boats to the ocean's surface at the slightest sign of trouble.

Between the *NORMANDIE* signs, he found a full-size tennis court, surrounded by a wire fence to keep aces and volleys from flying off into the Atlantic. Now this place, Nathan told himself, must be more decorative than recreational. After all, how could anyone play tennis in this cold wind?

Nathan continued forward, stopping once to look into the

windows of a little room at the base of the first funnel. Inside were hobby horses and a Punch-and-Judy stage, but no children at play, not at this hour.

Just ahead was another stairway. He descended, at last escaping from the wind, exiting at the forward end of the enclosed promenade, half a ship's length away from their deck chairs and just behind the *Normandie*'s famous Winter Garden, a kind of observation lounge at the extreme forward end of the superstructure.

Nathan decided to take a look. Entering through the starboard door, he maneuvered his way through groupings of wicker chairs and tables, walking under swirling loop-the-loop trellises that overflowed with rare and magnificent tropical flowers and plants.

It all reminded him of the Botanical Garden in Bronx Park, on Bedford Park Boulevard. He'd protested whenever his father had taken him there—"Come on, Dad, not the plants again"—and he wasn't all that thrilled now.

Then he found something that was completely incongruous but quite delightful, something that belonged not on a ship but in the Bronx Zoo (which, unlike the Botanical Garden, he'd loved visiting with his dad). It was a three-tired crystal and bronze bird cage the size of a subway kiosk, set in a softly burbling fountain.

Two such concoctions graced the room, one on this side, one on the port side. Inside the cages, brilliantly colored tropical birds sang twittering love songs to each other without a care in the world. He envied them.

Nathan spent a few minutes enjoying the birds, then circled through the room, past a pair of elderly gentlemen absorbed in a game of cribbage, past the gracefully curving windows on the forward wall that overlooked the *Normandie*'s handsome prow and the moonlit ocean, exiting through the port side doors onto the glassed-in promenade on the other side of the ship.

A sudden, sharp metallic twang erupted at a bulkhead a few

feet away from him, then there was another, this one a foot or two above his head. Jesus Christ, he said to himself, dropping to the deck instinctively. Someone is shooting at me!

Another ping hit far to his left, then something thudded into the rubber tile to his right, then a shot shattered a large window several yards away. Nathan pulled his Smith & Wesson revolver out of his sock and peered down the dimly lit promenade, searching for a target. Who is shooting at me? Why? Are Victor and Tina safe?

He heard the sound of running footsteps. The deck lights suddenly came on, full force. Uniformed security patrolmen were approaching from both directions, toward a man crouched between a pair of deck chairs fifty yards away with a rifle in his hand. A rifle! What was this? A sniper?

Nathan trained his gun on the man, ready to fire if he took aim again. But the man did not raise his rifle. In fact, he threw it onto the deck and collapsed. It was about this time that the security officers reached the sniper.

"I got him, Étiènne," the senior patrolman told his colleague. "You get the rifle."

Then they saw Nathan.

"It's all right, sir," the other security man called to Nathan, grabbing the weapon. "We have the rifle. The danger is over now."

They hauled the sniper to his feet.

Nathan shoved the revolver back into his sock and approached the man. Then he stopped dead in his tracks, flabbergasted. He could see his assailant now. It was the movie actor who'd been dancing with Tina—Erich von Stroheim. Had he lost his mind?

"Please accebt my humblest apologies," von Stroheim said as Nathan approached. "I vas not sheeting atchu, sur, belief me." The words were civilized, even gracious, but they were slurred almost to the point of unintelligibility. Van Stroheim was drunk as a skunk.

"Nevertheless, you almost hit me," Nathan told him.

"I thank the good Lord thachu vere not injured," von Stroheim told him, besotted and groveling. "I vould never haf forgotten myself."

"I probably wouldn't have forgotten you, either," Nathan allowed. "Where did this man get a rifle?" asked the security officer.

"It's a pellet gun," the officer said, examining the weapon. "Must have come from the shooting gallery. He evidently broke the lock."

"What *were* you shooting at?" Nathan asked van Stroheim.

"Shooding at? Shooding at?" van Stroheim repeated, wild-eyed. "The moon. I was shooding at the moon, whish has robbed me so many times before and whish stole from me again tonight." He slipped out of the security man's grasp and crashed to the deck.

"What is he talking about? Is he insane?" one of the security men asked the other as they lifted him to his feet once more.

"He is obsessed," Nathan said. And I think I know the object of his obsession, he told himself.

The senior security officer turned his attention toward Nathan, realizing that his main task now was placating this justifiably upset passenger. "The captain will hear of this, sir. And he will take the appropriate action. Meanwhile, we will take him back to his room and lock him in for the night."

"And you will fix the lock on the shooting gallery?" Nathan promoted.

"You can be sure of it, monsieur."

"Thank you."

"I hope you have a very pleasant voyage, sir," said the second security man, trying to patch things up.

"I'm sure."

Nathan watched the security men take the actor away, half dragging him. He was very glad that they had come when they did—not because of the danger, but because in another moment be might have been forced to shoot. That would have prompted some very awkward questions. Fortunately, no one else had witnessed this event. No one had seen his gun, and no one would think he was anything other than an unfortunate bystander.

Nathan took a few deep breaths, then walked on. He had a lot more to see. It was time to get an idea of how the other classes were laid out. On the Main Deck, he jimmied a gate intended to keep the lower orders isolated from the high and mighty and entered tourist class.

During the next hour and a half, Nathan reconnoitered the public areas of tourist class, mainly on A, B, and C Decks, peering into the lower-class smoking rooms, dining rooms, and lounges, most of them nearly as luxurious as their sister quarters upstairs.

He wandered down endless corridors, past the endless cabin doors of tourist and third — the cheap seats, the bleachers. All was quiet. How many of the people in these rooms, he wondered, were sleeping peacefully for the first time in months, even years?

All the rooms and corridors reminded him of some big New York hotel — the Biltmore, specifically, that big, undistinguished block of rooms next to Grand Central Station. Nathan had spent a lot of time in the Biltmore, more than he'd ever wanted to.

It had been back in '31 or so, when King Prajadhipok, the absolute monarch of Siam, had seen fit to visit New York City, bringing with him a retinue of eighty-two, a disproportionate number of them young, female, and quite lovely, and over a thousand pieces of luggage. For some reason, Jimmy Walker had decided to put him up in the Biltmore. It wasn't the most glamorous possible choice, but it was fairly cheap, which in Depression times was an important consideration.

In one of his first important police assignments, Nathan had been put in charge of providing security for the young monarch and his flocks of pretty, slender companions. He'd insisted, from the start, that the Biltmore empty out an entire floor for the Royal party. There'd been some sniffing about that, since it would leave some rooms unoccupied, but Nathan had prevailed in the end.

It had been a rollicking week at the Biltmore. The king couldn't have cared less about security arrangements. He hadn't been much interested in fancy dressing, either. He'd wandered up and down the halls at all hours of the day and night, wearing nothing more than a red silk robe, which, Nathan had assumed, he could jettison in a matter of seconds when necessary, which was frequently.

Meanwhile, Nathan and his team — two detectives and six beat cops — had patrolled the corridors, keeping out the common drunks, the hotel thieves, and the misguided multitudes who were entranced by royalty. Someone had been concerned that a group of Siamese insurgents, the Mung people, might make an attempt on the young king's life, but fortunately that had never materialized.

Only one thing had saved Nathan from being smothered in boredom: His Highness's unexpected propensity for conversation. Postprandial frolics made him especially talkative — about the charms of one of his young ladies or another, or several at the same time. He'd also been liberal with his romantic advice. Nathan remembered one line in particular.

"In Siam, we have a proverb," the king had told him. "A woman is a flower, who must give her nectar to but a single man. But a man is like a bumblebee, who must flit from flower to flower and spread all the pollen he can."

Nathan had thought that was good advice, but then, he had been barely twenty-two years old at the time.

A year after his New York visit, Nathan recalled, the young king had been relieved of his state powers but allowed to live pretty much as he always had. He wondered if Prajadhipok still had his red silk robe.

On D Deck, Nathan was stopped by locked doors marked "No passengers beyond this point." He selected one that was particularly inconspicuous, picked the lock in about fifteen seconds, and walked into . . . the biggest kitchen he had ever seen.

Rows of ovens and grills the length of auto assembly lines, together with walls of refrigerators and freezers, filled the room. And no one was in sight, except for two janitors with mops, neither of whom showed the slightest interest in him. Exploring the place, he found whole rooms filled with fruit, or glassware, or baked goods, or coffee brewing equipment.

According to his map, a gymnasium and swimming pool lay ahead, and past them were crew quarters. Instead, he went down to E Deck, where he found the largest wine cellar he had ever seen—thousands of bottles of everything from common table wine to the rarest Bordeaux and Burgundies of St. Emilion.

Nathan descended again, to F Deck, to engine room territory, where no unescorted passengers were permitted. He had to move very carefully now. If he were caught here, he'd have some difficult explaining to do.

He passed through a small watertight door and found himself standing on a cat walk overlooking a cavernous steel-walled, steel-floored space that dwarfed even the huge public rooms high above. Below him, monstrous electric alternators hummed and crackled, and Gargantuan water boilers gurgled and steamed.

Suddenly, Nathan slipped. He lost his balance and banged a shoulder against the cat walk railing, very nearly slipping through. He quickly pulled himself to his feet. Had anyone heard the noise? Had he been spotted? He looked down at the men in front of the control panel. Evidently, his footsteps had been drowned out by the throbbing of the machinery.

The cat walk continued, weaving its way through a jungle of ventilation tubes, steam pipes, and smokestack ducts, some the diameter of the Holland Tunnel. Ahead now was another watertight steel door. Nathan turned the wheel, jerked the door open, and squeezed through.

Spread out before him were interminable stacks of steamer trunks, cartons, and wooden crates and, beyond them, rows

144

of parked motor cars. Nathan walked forward cautiously. Here was another place where wandering passengers would be viewed with suspicion, perhaps even accused of trespassing with intent to steal.

Nathan was looking for a stairway or an elevator now. It was time to go back to the stateroom and get some sleep. Tomorrow, he would concentrate on his suspects. He would find out who they were and whether or not they really posed a threat.

His shoulder brushed against a cardboard box, which crashed to the floor.

"Clouzot?"

Damn.

"Is that you, Clouzot?"

Nathan backed down a corridor of small wooden boxes, away from the voice. He heard a chair scrape against the steel floor. They were coming to investigate the noise.

He turned a corner and collided with someone, head-on.

"Sorry," Nathan said politely, turning away. A burly uniformed soldier was blocking his path, a sergeant. Three other soldiers, all privates, were standing behind him. Nathan turned back, toward the man he'd bumped into.

"Are you lost?" the man asked, smiling slightly. He was a slender, pleasant-looking fellow in a light blue jacket and tan pants. He was about thirty years old, with sandy hair, a pointed nose, and light blue eyes that radiated intelligence.

Ever since he'd knocked down the box, Nathan had been weighing his alternatives. He'd considered telling them he was looking for a piece of luggage, but they'd soon discover there was no luggage here in his name. He'd thought about saying he was simply exploring—but at this hour? In the cargo hold?

"I musta gotten off at the wrong elevator," he said, slurring his words. "Shoudda gone up 'nsteada down."

The sandy-haired young man brought his face very close to Nathan's and sniffed. "Lost, perhaps. But not drunk. In fact, I think you may be one of the very few passengers whose breath does not reek of alcohol tonight."

"What are you really doing on this deck, monsieur?" the sergeant asked. A gun holster was strapped to his waist and his hand was resting suggestively on the pistol handle.

"Looking around," Nathan admitted. "I've never been aboard a ship of this size before."

"There *is* no other ship of this size, monsieur," the sergeant said quietly.

"You are a passenger, sir?" the civilian asked politely.

"Yes, first class. My name is Frank Peters."

"Frank Peters," the civilian security man said. "I wonder if that is true. After all, everything else you have told me is a lie."

Something very curious is going on here, Nathan thought. This man is anything but a normal member of the *Normandie*'s security patrol. He is a professional of some sort—but *what* sort? What is he doing here? Why the soldiers? And how in the world am I going to get myself out of this situation?

"You have me all wrong, I assure you," Nathan said. "I am nothing more than an inquisitive passenger."

"Well, we will see, won't we?" The civilian nodded to the sergeant, who began frisking Nathan, starting at the shoulders.

Nathan stood stock-still, hoping that the sergeant wouldn't find the gun he had in his sock. There was at least half a chance he'd miss it. It had been one of his father's favorite tricks.

"Nothing here," the sergeant said, finishing his job.

The civilian raised an eyebrow. "This is the technique you've been trained to use?"

"Yes, sir. Standard military police technique."

"I see," said the civilian. He suddenly bent down and grabbed both of Nathan's ankles. When he straightened up, Nathan's gun was in his hand. "Very interesting. Tell me, Mr. Peters, what would a first-class passenger aboard the *Normandie* need with a Smith & Wesson .38 Special?"

"Protection against burglars?" Nathan was trying for humor, but he couldn't interest his captors, which had suddenly

146

become the correct word to describe the sergeant and the civilian security man.

"Sergeant," the civilian said, "you remain here at the command post. I'm taking Mr. Peters to see the captain. Anyhow, your relief should be here very soon."

What *was* going on here, Nathan asked himself. Why were there soldiers in the cargo hold? Why was a very professional, very skilled civilian security man aboard the ship? This was big . . . bigger than the business with Victor. Or perhaps it was connected somehow.

The civilian security man led Nathan out of the cargo hold, down a narrow corridor, toward a service elevator. He pressed the call button, then turned to say something to his captive.

At that moment, Nathan suddenly grabbed the man by the upper part of his right arm and the muscles just below his neck, to the left, and jerked up and out, perfectly executing the *major outer reaping* judo throw.

Nothing happened.

Well, not nothing. Instead of feeling his opponent's body go sailing over his broad shoulders, instead of hearing the man crash against the floor, instead of successfully escaping back into the ship's passenger quarters, Nathan shuddered under the simultaneous impact of three powerful blows—to his chest, to his chin, to his solar plexus. He hit the corridor bulkhead full force and crumpled. Somehow, with an almost superhuman effort, he managed to bounce back to his feet, but by then the civilian security man was pointing his own gun at him.

"Do you wish to go another round, Mr. Peters?"

"I guess not," Nathan conceded ruefully.

"That was a good judo move, though," the security man said. "Where did you learn it?"

"I spent a summer in the Philippines during my college days," Nathan told him. "But my move obviously wasn't good enough—or I didn't do it properly."

"Oh, you did it just fine. It's just that judo is no match for *tae*

147

kwon do."

"Which you learned—"

"—when I served in Indochina," the security man said, completing Nathan's sentence.

"What were you doing in Indochina?"

"Ah, Mr. Peters, it is we who must ask the questions of you, not the reverse."

They sat in the captain's suite, waiting. Then, finally, there was a knock on the door. "Enter," the captain said.

It was the *Normandie*'s morose and officious Chief Security Officer Bernard Nadeau. Nadeau had been a cop for most of his adult life and had spent most of his time in the gutter, dealing with the pimps, bums, small-time hoodlums, and other riffraff of the Cherbourg docks. He'd been hired a year ago by a former *Normandie* captain for no apparent reason— he certainly didn't have much experience with the sort of people who traveled aboard the *Normandie*— and now Barthou was saddled with him.

"I was finally able to get through to the White House," Nadeau said, as though it were a considerable triumph and he should be given great credit for it.

"Yes?" Captain Barthou prompted. He was sitting on his piano bench, dressed in an exquisitely tailored pair of gray silk pajamas with red piping.

"The connection was remarkably clear," the security chief said. In addition to his other flaws, he was the sort of man who guarded information the way a child guarded his toys, sharing it only when commanded to do so.

"Go on, go on," Chief Purser Freppel urged impatiently. "Did you get through to anyone important?"

"Of course I did," Nadeau said, distinctly offended. "I had a very nice conversation with Stephen Early, the President's Press Secretary. He was extremely friendly to me."

"Just what was it he told you about Mr. Nathan?" This time,

Deputy Captain Marius Martel provided the nudge.

"I'm coming to that, Deputy Captain. Don't rush me."

Captain Barthou was trying to be calm and patient. "What did Mr. Early say?"

"Mr. Early told me that David Nathan has the full confidence of the President," Nadeau concluded.

Freppel was startled. "The full confidence?"

Nadeau didn't take well to being challenged. "Those were his exact words, Purser."

"Well, *vive la Presidente*," Nathan said with a grin.

Captain Barthou rose from his piano bench, went over to Nathan, who was sitting with the others at the dining table, and shook his hand solemnly. "Please accept my apologies, Monsieur Nathan."

"Of course, none of this would have been necessary if you had identified yourself earlier," the chief purser observed sourly.

"I was hoping I would not have to," Nathan told him.

The captain was gracious. "It seems that we are at your service, Monsieur Nathan. Is there anything we can do for you?"

Nathan thought for a moment. "Well, I wouldn't mind having my revolver back."

Now Nadeau objected sharply. "I'm sorry. All weapons must be locked up in the guard room. That's the policy aboard this vessel, and I enforce it to the letter."

Barthou shook his head. "I don't think the rule applies in this case." The captain gestured to Segonzak, leaving Nadeau grumbling under his breath.

Segonzak returned Nathan's Smith & Wesson. "Cute trick, the gun in the sock."

"Something my father taught me," Nathan said. "Cute trick finding it."

Segonzak smiled. "Something *my* father taught *me*."

"Of course, I expect you to refrain from using your weapon aboard my ship, Monsieur Nathan," the captain said.

"I sincerely hope I will not have to."

"Can we do anything to assure that?"

"Perhaps you could help me identify my suspects."

"Captain, I wish to register an objection." The security chief, Nadeau, was as pompous as a Supreme Court Justice. "Security on the *Normandie* is *my* responsibility. If there is a threat to someone aboard this ship, it is *my* job to deal with it. There is no room here for an independent police authority, especially from a foreign country."

It was Deputy Captain Martel who answered the security chief. "Of course you are absolutely correct, Bernard — at least technically. But in the interests of Franco-American friendship, I don't think it would hurt to give Mr. Nathan a little information."

"I agree with Marius," Barthou said. "But let's say this: If it turns out that there's a real problem, Mr. Nathan will immediately put the matter in your hands. Won't you, Mr. Nathan?"

"I'll contact the security chief at the very first sign of trouble," Nathan promised easily.

The security chief was somewhat appeased by this, but he still felt it necessary to fix Nathan with a "you'd-better-behave-yourself" look.

At that moment, there was a sudden, insistent banging on the captain's door. Barthou glanced at Freppel, who opened the door. Before he could ask the visitor's business, Wallace Westbrook, Jr. had pushed his way into the captain's quarters.

"Which one of you guys is in charge here?" asked the pit bull of New York journalism.

Barthou smiled wearily. "I think you may be seeking me, sir."

"If you're the captain of this tub, you're damn right I'm seeking you."

"How can I be of service?"

"You can give me the room I requested."

"And what room was that, Mr. —"

"Westbrook, Wallace Westbrook, Jr., the radio commentator and newspaper columnist. Surely you've heard of me."

"Certainly," Barthou lied. "I just didn't recall your face."

"Well, I reserved the Fecamp suite and I got Jumieges."

"I see," the captain said evenly. "But they are exactly the same, except for furnishings and decor."

"That's the problem. Jumieges is stuffed with all this fussy French Provincial. I hate it. Makes me feel like I'm sleeping with Marie Antoinette."

"That would be annoying, wouldn't it?" Barthou said with paternal patience. "Can you tell me anything about this, Purser?"

"Yes, Captain, Mr. Westbrook has already discussed this situation with me. Unfortunately, we have no record of his reservation and Fecamp is already taken."

"By whom?"

"A distinguished older lady, Captain, the Countess de Chambord. She is unwilling to change rooms."

Westbrook exploded again. "She had damn well better switch. If I don't get the room I reserved, there's going to be real trouble."

"When did you make your reservation, Monsieur Westbrook?"

"I don't know . . . a week ago. What difference does it make? Your incompetent people evidently didn't take the trouble to make a record of it."

"Very careless of them," Barthou said, ladling out the oil. "I will speak with my reservations people, and I will have a talk with the countess. I can't promise anything, but I will try."

Westbrook was slightly mollified. "That's a little more like it." Growing calmer, the fiery little man finally took a look around the room. He was interested in what he found. "What's this all about, anyway . . . this meeting?"

"It's not exactly a meeting," the captain told him. "Just some friends getting together in the evening for drinks and conversation."

Then Westbrook spotted Nathan. "Wait a minute. What are *you* doing here, Cameron? You couldn't know any of these people. What's going on?"

Segonzak spoke up. "*Au contraire,* Monsieur Westbrook. Mr. . . . ah . . . Cameron and I are old friends. I invited him."

"Who are you?" Westbrook demanded. "You're not a ship's officer. What the hell is going on here? I warn you, if you don't tell me, I'll find out anyhow."

Out of Westbrook's line of vision, Barthou and Martel exchanged murderous glances. "It's just as the captain said," Martel insisted politely. "Old friends getting together."

Westbrook looked them over suspiciously. "I don't believe a word of it," he announced. "An urgent meeting, this late at night, attended by the ship's top officers. Something is going on here, and I'm going to find out what."

Barthou was totally unflappable. "I'm sorry you feel that way, Monsieur Westbrook. But be assured that you have nothing whatever to worry about. And I promise you I shall do my best to get you the Fecamp."

Westbrook's eyes narrowed. "You can't fool me."

Barthou simply smiled. "Of course not. It would never occur to me to try."

The journalist shot him a sour glance, turned on his heel, and slammed the door behind him.

"Very entertaining," Nathan said after Westbrook's footsteps could no longer be heard.

"Perhaps," the captain granted, "if you're merely a spectator."

Freppel was quite apologetic. "Sorry for the interruption, Captain."

"Never mind, Henri. I'll take care of it. Now, what about Mr. Nathan's suspects. Any ideas about their identity?"

Freppel shrugged his famous little shrug. "Yes. I know the names of the people you have described."

"Please tell us," the captain said, sensing Freppel's reluctance.

"Certainly, Captain. The gangster . . . his name is Barzinni. I am certain he is dangerous only to his own kind, if he is really a gangster, which I have no way of knowing. The diplomat is Count Cherbatoff, a White Russian. I am sure that he and his lady friend are exactly what they appear to be — a wealthy man approaching his twilight years, receiving comfort from an appreciative young woman."

"How about Hatzfeld?" Nathan asked.

"Ah, yes, Hatzfeld. The face is familiar," Freppel said, lost in thought. "It will come to me."

"And von Stroheim?"

"I can tell you about Herr von Stroheim," Captain Barthou said. "I visited him in his room after the little incident on the Promenade Deck. He seems obsessed with some pretty girl he met."

"I'm afraid he's referring to the sister of the man I am escorting," Nathan said.

"Ah."

"She's hard to resist," Nathan continued.

Deputy Captain Martel laughed. "Unfortunately, von Stroheim succumbs rather easily to temptation. In fact, we usually have to rein him in, sometimes pretty hard."

"That so?" Nathan was a little surprised.

"I wouldn't worry about him," the captain said. "He'll be sullen but subdued for the rest of the voyage. We've seen it all before."

"Okay. But what about the bearded man? He's the one who worries me the most."

Captain Barthou sighed. "Monsieur Nathan, I know you're concerned. Perhaps you have good reason. But in recent years, we've been transporting all kinds of bearded people to America."

"Some of them are your coreligionists, I believe," Freppel added with a sly smile.

Barthou cut him off. "Do you have any evidence that this particular bearded man means you harm?"

Nathan shook his head. "Nope. None. Just instinct." He turned toward Segonzak, the sandy-haired civilian security man. "The same instinct, by the way, that tells me you are no ordinary ship's security man and that tells me this crossing of the *Normandie* is unusual in some important way."

Security Chief Nadeau rose haughtily to his full height. "With all due respect, Mr. Nathan, this is just a waste of time. There is no assassin on board this ship, Nazi or otherwise. Even if your young scientist is in danger, which I seriously doubt, no one would be foolish enough to attempt to kill him here, where capture is practically certain. Why is he so important to your country, anyway?"

"I'm sorry, that's something I can't tell you," Nathan said. He wished he knew.

"You can't — or you won't? Which is it?"

Segonzak spoke up before Nathan could answer. "My guess is that the young man possesses some kind of valuable knowledge," he said. "But, of course, that's beside the point."

"Absolutely right, Lieutenant Segonzak," Nathan said. "That *is* beside the point. The only important question is, is he safe aboard this ship?"

Nadeau's face darkened. "Of course he is, Monsieur. Everyone on board this ship is safe. Even you."

The chief purser agreed. "Personally, I think all of your suspicions are a little silly."

"How about you, Lieutenant Segonzak?" Nathan asked. "Do you concur?"

"It's Jean-Louis," Segonzak said. "And, yes, I think your young man probably is quite safe on board the *Normandie*. I only know of one murder that's ever been committed aboard an ocean liner and that was a crime of passion. Except for the usual minor thefts, ships at sea are essentially crime-free. That's why we . . . I mean . . ."

"That's why you what?" Nathan interrupted. "Would someone please tell me what the hell is going on aboard this ship?"

Segonzak and the ship's officers exchanged "should-we-tell-him-now?" looks.

Nathan glanced from face to face. He was casting them, as though he were a movie director. It was an old habit, but sometimes it yielded useful insights. Segonzak, with that fox-like French face of his and easy smile, was the hero's best friend. Barthou was the wise grandfather. Freppel was the spendthrift brother, charming but weak, with an uncontrollable penchant for insult. Martel was brave, handsome, and strong—the epitome of the intrepid soldier. Nadeau, tall, homely, and dour, was the perpetually offended spinster aunt.

Segonzak was about to speak when there was a knock at the door.

"At last," said Deputy Captain Martel. "It certainly took him long enough."

Captain Barthou laughed. "You are a man with an endless appetite, Marius. How do you stay so trim?"

"My boss keeps me on the run," Martel said with a grin.

The knock came again, louder.

"You may enter, steward," Captain Barthou called.

A steward brought in a silver platter loaded mainly with desserts and coffee. He handed a *crème caramel* to the captain and served pieces of pastry to Freppel, Nadeau, Segonzak, and Martel.

"And here's your corned beef sandwich, sir," he said, putting a platter in front of Nathan.

"Looks wonderful," Nathan said in admiration. "You even remembered the rye bread."

"The rye bread comes from Lindy's," Freppel said. "So does the corned beef."

Nathan took a bite. "Delicious."

"Unfortunately, sir," said the steward, "we are out of cream soda. I substituted root beer."

"That's fine."

Segonzak shook his head in disbelief. "American tastes never cease to amaze me," he said.

The steward poured coffee for the others then, finally, he

left.

"Listen," Nathan said, returning to the subject at hand, "if you people don't think I'm trustworthy . . ."

"Relax, David," Segonzak said. "No one is questioning your credentials, at least not anymore. But you have no idea how important a secret this is."

"Well, let's see if I can figure it out," Nathan said, taking on the challenge. "Fact one: There's a company of French soldiers in the hold, which means something very important or very valuable is aboard. Fact two: You're carrying a highly skilled agent, no doubt a government man." He cocked a head at Segonzak and took another bite of his sandwich.

"Yes, yes, that's all obvious," Freppel said. "But the explanation is perfectly simple: We've had urgent orders to tighten ship's security."

"I didn't ask for the soldiers," Nadeau said bitterly. "I don't need them. My men and I can take care of everything."

For once, Nathan found himself agreeing with the security chief. "Well, there you are. If it were just a matter of tightening ship security, why would you need troops? No, something else is going on here. And I think it's connected to the political situation in Europe."

"Is that what you think?" Segonzak was obviously enjoying the discussion.

"The way I see it, France must be sending something very important to America, something it wants to protect from the Nazis at all costs—the *Mona Lisa,* maybe, or the statue of Winged Victory, or some other treasure. Do you want me to go on?"

"You know, he could be helpful," Segonzak told Captain Barthou. "Besides, the Americans already know. It wouldn't really hurt to tell this one, too. After all, he is in the President's employ."

Captain Barthou looked at Chief Purser Freppel, who shrugged, and at Security Chief Nadeau. "It doesn't make any difference to me anymore," Nadeau said. Let them tell him anything they want. He no longer cared.

"All right," the captain decided. He got up from the bench and began pacing around the private dining room. "Yes, Mr. Nathan. You are right. We are carrying something of value, something of extraordinary value. It is nothing less than the wealth of France . . . most of the bullion she possesses."

"You mean gold?"

"He means gold," Segonzak said. "Fourteen metric tons of it."

Nathan was speechless.

"Told you it was big stuff," Segonzak said. He liked the surprised expression on Nathan's face.

"But the gold is perfectly safe," Freppel told him. "No one can remove it from the cargo hold."

"If anyone tries," Nadeau put in, "he will have to deal with me."

Barthou agreed. "The gold is safe on the ship. But I am not so sure the ship is safe. Here . . . you might as well know about this, too."

He handed Nathan the telegram from *Compagnie Generale Transatlantique*.

Nathan read it quickly. "Do you fear some kind of attack, maybe a submarine attack?"

The captain shrugged. "I don't know. It depends on what's happening back home. Of course, the *Normandie* can outrun any submarine ever built. Isn't that true, Marius? You know about such things."

The deputy captain sighed. He didn't like contradicting his captain, especially not in front of others. "Technically, yes. No submarine could catch us. Of course, if one were waiting for us . . ."

"There will be no attack," Freppel insisted. "Who would attack us and why? We are a civilian passenger ship, from a country that is at peace with the world."

"According to our most recent radio communication with Europe," Segonzak added. Freppel glared at him.

Nathan had another suggestion. "Maybe this bearded man is part of a joint effort — against the man I'm escorting to America *and* against the gold."

Nadeau shot Nathan a skeptical look.

"I am more worried about what's happening in Europe." Captain Barthou was unwilling to entertain Nathan's suggestion. "Will there be a France left for the *Normandie* to return to?"

"You are all alarmists," Freppel blurted out. "You've been paying too much attention to fools like Churchill and de Gaulle."

"Henri," Captain Barthou said. It was a subtle warning.

The chief purser swallowed hard and collected himself. "I'm sorry," he said. "I really don't know any more about the international situation than anyone else, and my opinions are of no special merit. But I would like to point out that the *Normandie* has a large and well-trained security force, recently augmented by Lieutenant Segonzak, and that it was good enough to catch a professional and like yourself, Mr. Nathan."

"True enough," Nathan admitted.

"So why don't you relax and enjoy the rest of the voyage?" Captain Barthou nodded his assent. "That sounds like a good idea to me, Monsieur Nathan. But if you run into any problems, please don't hesitate to contact the security chief. And I assure you, we will do likewise."

"In other words, don't call us, we'll call you."

"What's that?" Freppel asked.

"An American saying. Forget it."

Freppel smiled. "Of course."

"Listen, Jean-Louis," Nathan said, "why don't you drop by our room sometime soon. I'd like to hear more about Indochina."

"I'd enjoy that — if you'll tell me about the Philippines."

"It's a deal."

Nathan bade them all good night and left the room. He headed back toward the cabin, thinking. Just what the hell have I gotten Victor and Tina into?

Four hundred miles off the coast of Newfoundland, the small but powerful salvage vessel *Otto Wunsche* fought her way through heavy seas, making about seven knots. She was flying the Paraguayan flag.

A few meters beneath the ocean's surface, in much quieter waters, a German *unterseeboote* cruised on a parallel course. She was the U-42, a type IXA submarine, displacing about eleven hundred tons. She was capable of just over eighteen knots on the surface and nearly eight knots submerged. Her armament included three antiaircraft guns of different calibers and six torpedo tubes, four forward and two aft. Normally, she carried twenty-two torpedoes and had a crew complement of forty-eight.

Although the U-42 had been launched just over five months ago from the A.G. Weser shipyard in Bremen, she was not the latest design. She was a direct ancestor of the U-81 of Great War vintage. Nevertheless, but she was reliable and capable.

The submarine's commander was Kommandant Wolfgang Zentner, a slender, hawk-faced veteran of submarine operations and one of Admiral Raeder's favorites.

Zentner was puzzled. Worse, he was worried. The orders he'd been given were both strange and vague. He was to escort the *Otto Wunsche* to a rendezvous point, both vessels arriving within an hour of a designated time, no more, no less.

Then Zentner was to wait for an explosion. Following the explosion, he was to pick up a swimmer. At that time, the *Otto Wunsche* would begin salvage operations at the explosion site.

If, at the appointed time, there was no explosion at the rendezvous, he was to open his sealed orders and follow them precisely.

Why was Raeder so coy about this explosion? Clearly, some kind of ship was going to be blown up. Equally clearly, it was carrying something of great value, something worth salvaging. And this swimmer . . . he was no doubt the saboteur. Didn't Raeder give him credit for being able to put two and two together?

What kind of role was his vessel supposed to play in this operation? Escort service for a salvage ship? That was no mission for the second most efficient submarine in the fleet according to the most recent ranking, no matter how important the cargo the salvage ship was retrieving.

And why had Raeder ordered him to keep secret the details of his orders, not only from his own crew, but also from his immediate *Kriegsmarine* superiors? What the hell was so mysterious about this operation?

Zentner checked with his signals officer, Lieutenant Gerlach. "The salvage ship is still on course?" he asked.

"Yes, sir," the answer came back almost immediately.

He sighed and tried to suppress his worries. He'd often been told he worried too much, and maybe that was true. After all, this really wasn't a dangerous mission, so far as he could see. The world was still at peace, and there were no enemy vessels to contend with.

Besides, this was a special task for Admiral Raeder, a man who had befriended him and done a great deal to advance his career. Zentner was indebted to this man. He owed him his loyalty.

Ah, loyalty. There was a magic word. What would the Navy be without loyalty? What would Germany be without loyalty?

Day Four

It was dawn on the Atlantic, the beginning of a magnificent late summer day. There was hardly a ripple in the surface of the second largest ocean on planet earth. The *Normandie* was plowing through the seas at a steady twenty-eight knots, pitching only slightly and rolling not at all.

Capt. Pierre Barthou stood alone on the great vessel's starboard bridge wing, wind in his face, his eye on the gentle swells. It was his favorite place on the ship, his favorite time of the day.

Here, he felt as though he were really at sea, a sensation all too rare in the liner's great public rooms or luxurious suites. Here, free of the crush of adoring or complaining passengers, he felt truly in command.

Barthou put his back to the wind now and looked eastward, into the sun, back toward Europe — hundreds of miles behind him now. Mathilde would already be up, he knew. The eggs would be gathered, the cows milked. All of France would be stirring. And all of Germany.

He no longer thought of Claude very often. All that had happened more than twenty years ago, after all. But on this particular morning, the image of his son came back to him vividly. In his mind's eye, for some reason, he saw him riding a bicycle, riding a bicycle off to war. His mother had loved him so much, too much.

"Captain?"

161

Barthou turned, startled out of his reverie. "Ah, Martel. Good morning."

"Captain, the lookout has spotted a ship off the port stern."

"A ship?"

"A liner, sir. You can see her from the other bridge wing."

This was decidedly odd, Barthou thought. When they'd passed Bishop's Rock, at Britain's westernmost point, there hadn't been a ship in sight. Now, one had appeared out of nowhere . . . but which one? It couldn't be the *Queen Mary.* Right now, she'd be bound for England, traveling toward them. But what ship had managed to catch up with the *Normandie?* A thought occurred to him, a very unpleasant thought.

"You lead the way, Marius."

They crossed through the wheelhouse and came out the other side, to the port bridge wing. There she was, glinting in the sun perhaps two miles astern, a large, brawny vessel with two squat funnels and a low superstructure. It was the ship Barthou hoped it would not be.

"It is the *Bremen,* isn't it?" Martel asked.

"Yes, it is." This was a ship to be reckoned with. She was huge, less than a hundred feet shorter than the *Normandie.* She was fast, a former Blue Ribbon holder, having crossed the Atlantic on one occasion at better than twenty-eight and a half knots, although she normally cruised at twenty-six. Except for the *Normandie* and the *Queen Mary,* the *Bremen* and her sister ship, the *Europa,* were the most formidable liners in the world. They were Germany's pride and joy.

"She came up on us around five A.M."

"Came up on us?" That was unusual. The *Normandie* had never been overtaken by the *Bremen* before, although the opposite had occurred on many occasions. "We were at normal cruising speed?"

"Yes, Captain, twenty-eight knots. And we're holding that speed now."

"What about the *Bremen?*"

"Also twenty-eight knots — and, to catch up with us, she must have hit even higher speeds."

Barthou frowned. "All right, Marius. We seem to have a problem. What would you do if you were in my place?"

Martel was starting to get used to this. Whenever there was a difficult decision to make, the captain asked for his suggestions. Despite their long association and their deep friendship, despite his proven ability, Barthou was testing him for some reason. Well, there was nothing to do about it except to provide the answer his friend expected. "I'd increase our speed to 30 knots and hold it until the *Bremen* is well out of sight."

"Excellent," Barthou said. As usual, the young man's decision had been swift and sound. "Why don't you go ahead and do it?"

"Yes, sir," the deputy captain said with pleasure. "Immediately." He hurried off to give the order, leaving Barthou alone once more.

Barthou gazed at the *Bremen*. There was simply no innocent explanation for her behavior. She'd been sent to track the *Normandie*. But for what purpose? To radio the *Normandie*'s position to a submarine? Or merely to intimidate?

He didn't like it. But many things had happened on this voyage that he did not like. The gold. The American agent. The disappearance of Clouzot, the cargo supervisor. Damn, he'd forgotten to tell the American agent about Clouzot. Certainly, the man would show up soon. But what if he didn't? What could that mean?

Chief Engineer Gaston LeBrun stood at the main engine room control panel, his tiny body dwarfed by the huge machinery around him. He had the intercom phone at one ear and a finger in the other, blocking out the engine noises. "Yes, sir," he said, nodding as though the man on the phone were right there in the room. "At once."

LeBrun's first assistant, a chinless, jug-eared young man

163

named Jean Gaspard, approached him as soon as he'd hung up the phone. "Is there a problem?"

"Not really. The captain wants us to increase speed two knots. Tell the men to fire up four of the back boilers and get them on line as soon as possible."

"Yes, sir," Gaspard said. Then he chuckled to himself.

"What's so funny, Gaspard?"

"I was just thinking about the ship's pool, sir. I hear there's a lot of money in it."

"I assume you have placed no bet of your own."

"Of course not," Gaspard said, protesting his innocence.

"Well, then, don't worry about the passengers, Gaspard. Someone else will win and someone else will lose. It doesn't concern us."

"As you wish, chief engineer."

"Do you think that's really an appropriate breakfast outfit?" Nathan asked, frowning.

Tina was wearing a backless red sundress that exposed a pair of small, perfectly symmetrical shoulder blades and a sweep of curving, velvety butterscotch-colored skin.

"Well," she reflected, "I could wear these if you liked." She held up a halter top and a pair of shorts that, together, had consumed less than a boll and a half of cotton.

"That's all you have in all of those suitcases?"

"That's all I'm interested in wearing this morning."

"It's useless to argue with her," Victor observed.

"I know," Nathan said, accepting his defeat. "So you're ready to go?"

"Of course." She gave her golden hair one last, unnecessary brush stroke and presented herself at the cabin door with all the alacrity of a ten-year-old heading for a birthday party.

Ten minutes later, they were back in the *Normandie*'s main dining room. Less than a quarter of last night's diners had made their breakfast appearance, but it was only ten-thirty

164

A.M., practically dawn for first-class passengers on a major ship.

They weaved their way through the tables to number 34, where a single diner, Kurt Jaekel, nattily dressed in a white sweater, blue trousers, and tennis shoes, was just finishing a plate of deep-fried French toast and link sausages.

"Good morning, Mr. Rothmann," Tina said pleasantly. "Looks like it's going to be a perfect day."

Jaekel nodded politely, scarcely looking up. Then he touched the linen napkin to the corner of his mouth, excused himself, and left.

"Maybe you should have worn the shorts," Victor told his little sister. She slapped at him with her napkin.

"Now, now, children," Nathan mocked.

A few minutes later, they were joined by a less welcome table mate, Wallace Westbrook, Jr. He was not in a very good humor.

"Good morning," Tina said, looking for at least one positive reaction.

"Yeah."

Nathan couldn't resist needling the man. "What's the matter, Westbrook, still stuck in the wrong room?"

"As a matter of fact, I've got my room. What's bothering me, Cameron, is *you*."

"Me?"

"Yes, you," Westbrook replied flatly. "You're lying about who you are."

Nathan didn't like that at all. "What's that? Lying?"

"I don't know exactly who you are — yet. But I know you're not just an apartment house owner."

Nathan laughed. "I'd show you the deeds, but I left them in my other pants pocket."

Westbrook was not amused. "What was going on in the captain's quarters last night?"

"Nothing special. Just a few friends getting together."

"Yeah, sure. And we're having breakfast on the *Hindenburg*,

"If you say so. You're always very well-informed."

"That's right," Westbrook snapped. "And I'm going to get myself a little better informed—about you. I'm going to do some checking up on you. Then we'll see."

"I suppose we will."

"Where is that damned waiter?" Westbrook grumbled.

"Right here, sir," the waiter said. He'd been standing directly behind Westbrook, waiting for the man to stop fulminating. "What can I get you?"

After breakfast, Nathan led Tina and Victor out of the dining room, away from that nosy pest Westbrook, and back onto the enclosed Promenade Deck. He thought they'd be pleased with the opportunity to see or be seen by their fellow passengers. But he had his own reason for coming here. He had business to conduct, and this was an excellent place to start.

Quite a few passengers had already settled into deck chairs on the Promenade Deck and were enjoying the pleasures of the sunshine without the inconveniences of the wind.

Three chairs down from the deck chairs they had reserved sat a gentleman in summer tweeds, observing the passengers and taking notes in a small green leather notebook. Nathan recognized him as a one-time guest lecturer at Columbia, the American author Ludwig Bemelmans.

Directly beside their chairs sat a dark fortress of a woman, wrapped in sables despite the balmy weather, with a face made of Roquefort cheese and eyes like marbles. On her lap, covered by a small hound's-tooth blanket, asthmatic and dribbly, sat a Pekinese with thyroid trouble; his eyes were completely outside his head.

Tina was genuinely taken with the little beast. "Oh, what a precious little thing. What is his name?"

The woman stirred and looked up at Tina. She smiled fearsomely. "His name is Pichou," she rasped, "and I am the Countess de Chambord. What is your name, child?"

"I am Lilly Cameron." Tina executed a perfect little curtsy.

The old lady extended a hand that looked like a road map. Tina took it gracefully and held it for a moment.

"Pichou, regardez donc la petite fille qu'elle est mignonne," the countess instructed her Pekinese.

The dog licked Tina's hand. "How old is Pichou?" she asked the countess.

"Pichou has been my closest companion for fourteen years," she replied, stroking him affectionately. "He knows me better than anyone else on earth."

"He is very sweet."

"Thank you, my dear."

The dog licked Tina's hand again, then curled up and closed his eyes. In a moment, he was snoring loudly.

"Have you been having a nice voyage, Countess?"

"It has not been one of our better crossings, child. The captain requested us to change rooms. Something about a reservation mix-up."

"You don't like your new room?"

"It is French Provincial," the old lady said in utter contempt. "I took it only as a favor to the captain."

While Tina talked to the countess, Victor stood at the rail, watching the sea, and Nathan took the third of their reserved deck chairs. Next to Nathan, exactly as he had hoped, Hans Hatzfeld was relaxing with his book.

"Good morning Mr. . . . ah . . ."

"Hatzfeld," the businessman said. "And you're Mr. Cameron, I believe?"

"Yes. Lovely day, isn't it?"

"Very. There's nothing like the Atlantic Ocean at the end of the summer," Hatzfeld said.

"You've made the trip before?"

"Oh, yes, many times. On many ships."

"Do you like the *Normandie?*" Nathan was trying to draw him out.

"I believe it is the finest liner afloat," Hatzfeld said, as

167

endorsement mattered.

"...re you traveling to America on business or pleasure?"

"Both." Hatzfeld smiled, apparently enjoying the interrogation.

"And what *is* your business, Mr. Hatzfeld?"

"Oh, I sell things, Mr. Cameron."

"Things?"

"Whatever people need. Would you happen to know anyone who could use a ton of beryllium?"

"I don't know what beryllium is," Nathan said.

"It is a metallic element. A very rare and expensive metallic element."

"Wish I could help you." Nathan had been telling Hatzfeld the truth. He'd never heard of the substance. But maybe Victor had. Maybe there was a connection of some kind.

Hatzfeld smiled ruefully. "That's the trouble with selling. It's a poor occupation, unless you can find a buyer who—"

He paused in mid-sentence. Something had caught his eye. Nathan turned to see what he was staring at. It was a tall, imposing woman in her late thirties or early forties who was slowly walking in their general direction. She was wearing so much gold jewelry she clanked with every step.

"Excuse me," Hatzfeld said as she approached. "Someone from my past I would rather not encounter at this time." He got up quickly and disappeared in a cloud of unanswered questions, through the doors leading into the Grand Lounge.

The Packard Twin-Six had no wheel chocks. For that matter, neither did the Minerva. The crewman checked the Cord, then the Hispano-Suiza limousine, then the Peugeot 402. Not a chock in the bunch.

That lazy, good-for-nothing Clouzot had gone off without doing his job. Well, it was a job someone had to do—or the fury of the baggage chief would come down on all of them. Cursing, he unlocked the chock closet and opened the door.

"Well, now that you've found him, have him report to me immediately," Barthou said, thoroughly annoyed.

"I'm afraid he can't, sir," Security Chief Bernard Nadeau told him glumly.

"Then you bring him to me."

"I don't think that will be possible."

"What are you talking about, Bernard? Would you please get to the point!"

"He's beginning to smell. . . ."

"Smell!?"

"We found him in the chock closet. He's dead."

"Dead?" This was terrible. "What happened to him?"

"The doctor hasn't looked at him yet."

Barthou was getting very impatient. "Was there a wound, a blow to the head? Could it have been an accident?"

"As near as I can tell, his neck was broken. And it couldn't have been an accident. The closet in which he was found was padlocked."

The steward had delivered the message just after Hatzfeld left. At first, Nathan thought of parking his charges in the stateroom. Tina had insisted on going to the beauty shop, however, and Victor had wanted to investigate the library. He'd let them go, with some misgivings, and had followed the steward to the captain's quarters, where he took a seat at the dining room table with the others.

Nathan didn't know it, but there'd been an argument over inviting him. It had been Segonzak's idea. (*He's a professional. We could use his help.*) Martel had agreed, but Nadeau had objected strenuously. (*I'm in charge of security and I don't need any advice from some foreign policeman.*) And Freppel had backed up Nadeau. (*This is an internal matter, a ship problem. We don't need any outsiders, certainly not any glorified babysitters.*) But, in the end,

Barthou had sided with Segonzak.

"All right, gentlemen," Barthou said, calling the meeting to order. "Here are the facts as we know them: Clouzot was murdered sometime yesterday afternoon, probably during the channel crossing. His neck was cleanly broken and his body was stuffed into the chock closet. There were no signs of a struggle, and so far as we can tell, nothing in the cargo holds was disturbed."

"Is the chock closet normally kept locked?" Nathan asked.

The security chief spoke up, his voice as gloomy as his visage. "We keep a padlock on the hasp, but some of the men are careless about using it. I've warned them that—"

Segonzak interrupted quickly. "Was the closet locked this morning?"

"Yes, sir." The security chief was uncharacteristically direct. "The cargo handler found the body when he unlocked the door." He reached into a pocket, pulled out a rusty old padlock, and put it on the table.

"Well," Nathan said, "so much for fingerprints. Were there any bruises on the body?"

"None."

"Did anyone see anything unusual?" Segonzak asked.

"We have questioned the entire cargo crew. No one heard or saw a thing." It was clear that the security chief resented the interrogation.

Nathan had an idea. "What about the man at the guard point in the other room? Someone should ask him."

"I already did," Segonzak said. "Nothing."

Barthou put his hand up to stop the conversation. "My question is this: Who killed Clouzot and why? The answer could be crucial to all of us."

Suddenly, they heard a disturbance in the hallway. It sounded like someone screeching. Barthou raised an eyebrow in Freppel's direction. The chief purser went to see what the commotion was all about. When he opened the door, a woman burst into the room, shrieking. It was the Countess de

Chambord, sables and all. She was screaming hoarsely.

"What's wrong, Countess?" Barthou asked, greatly concerned.

"Pichou has fallen overboard! Stop the ship! Sound the siren! Man the lifeboats!"

Deputy Captain Martel leaped to his feet. "I will put a rescue operation into effect immediately," he announced.

Barthou restrained him. "Just a minute."

"Who is Patou?" Freppel asked. "Your husband? Your son?"

"Pichou. My dearest friend. And he is drowning! Can't you do something?" She was crying now and her makeup was running. It was a terrible sight.

"You saw him fall overboard, Countess?" Barthou asked.

"No, not exactly," the old lady admitted tearfully. "He was on my lap when I dozed off. When I woke up, just a few minutes later, the ship was beginning to roll and he was gone. Save him, Captain. I implore you! I beg you!"

"He was on your *lap?*" Barthou asked.

"You're wasting valuable time, Captain," she said between sobs. "He may be drowning."

"The man on your lap?" Barthou was confused. "What makes you think he jumped overboard?"

"Pichou is not a man, he is a Pekinese."

Captain Barthou was silent for a moment. When he spoke, his voice was very soft. "Countess, I cannot stop the ship to rescue a dog."

"Pichou is worth ten passengers. He is the most loyal, loving creature . . ."

"I am sure he is a wonderful dog, madam," the captain said in his most dignified manner. "But the company has given me explicit orders to proceed to America without delay. These are dangerous times, you know."

"You don't care if Pichou dies?"

Freppel took the countess's hand in his own. "He has not fallen overboard, madam, I am sure of that."

"How can — " she took a great gulp of air, "how can you be so sure?"

"Dogs often wander off on the ship, madam," Freppel said, reassuring her. "We always find them."

"I picture him slipping under the rail somewhere, falling into the ocean, paddling frantically with his little arms and whimpering for my help, then drowning. I cannot bear to think about it."

"Henri, would you personally organize the search?"

"Of course, Captain." Freppel took the countess's arm. Come with me, madam. We will find your Patou."

"Pichou."

The chief purser escorted the countess from the captain's chambers.

"Does that happen often?" Nathan asked Barthou sympathetically.

The captain was rubbing the bridge of his nose, his eyes closed. "Usually just in rough weather," he said.

"I know exactly why Clouzot was killed," the security chief suddenly announced.

Everyone else in the room turned toward him in great surprise.

"Why don't you let us all in on the secret," Barthou suggested.

"It's really quite obvious," Nadeau said with just a trace of contempt in his voice. "If you know Clouzot's reputation."

"Just what sort of reputation did he have?" Nathan asked.

"He was one of the worst troublemakers on the ship — and he had a terrible temper."

"I suppose that's interesting," Barthou said, "but I don't see how it explains his murder."

"It's just a matter of sound police thinking." Nadeau was reluctant to deliver the punch line. Then Segonzak caught his eye, and he went on. "He almost certainly got into a fight with another crew member and got himself killed."

Barthou nodded, unimpressed. "Well, that is the very best

possible interpretation of the evidence."

Nadeau recoiled, as if he'd been slapped.

"Care to hear the worst?" Nathan asked.

"Go ahead."

"He was killed by a Nazi agent."

"What?" Nadeau said. "That's totally ridiculous."

The captain was also skeptical. "I don't think we have any evidence for that," he said.

"Well, I think we can be reasonably sure he was not killed by a crew member," Nathan said.

Nadeau was immediately defensive. "What makes you say that?"

"Because of the *way* he was killed—a broken neck and no bruises. That's not what happens in a fight. That is the work of a trained professional."

"I have to agree," Segonzak assented.

Deputy Captain Martel had been silent for some time. Now he spoke up. "Maybe you're right, Mr. Nathan," he said. "And there is something else that's been bothering me."

"What's that?" Segonzak asked.

"Why did the murderer choose to hide the body in the chock closet, where it was bound to be discovered very quickly?"

Nathan was surprised. "Are there better hiding places?"

"There certainly are," Martel told him. "The *Normandie* has hundreds of nooks and crannies where a body could be concealed, places no one checks for weeks at a time. But the chock closet is emptied out—and filled again—on every voyage. Any crewman would have known that."

"Well, a murderer couldn't very well tote a body around the ship," Segonzak observed. "Are any of these nooks and crannies in the cargo area?"

"I can think of several," said Martel. "In fact, there's a plumbing storage room right next to the chock closet. I doubt anyone's been in it since the ship was launched."

"Is it unlocked?" Barthou asked sharply.

"Yes, sir," Nadeau said. "I checked it myself this morning."

Segonzak drew the obvious conclusion. "That means the murderer could have dumped the body in there, where it was unlikely to be found, then locked the door with the same padlock he used on the chock closet."

"I suppose you're right," Nadeau admitted with the greatest reluctance.

Barthou and his deputy captain looked at each other grimly. Then the silver-haired captain turned to Nathan. "One more thing. You said 'Nazi agent'. Why Nazi?"

"Because it's the only conclusion you can draw from the facts," Nathan said. "We know that the murderer is not a crew member. We also know he's not a common criminal. He's a professional. Now, what would attract a professional agent to this ship?"

It was Martel who supplied the obvious answer. "The gold."

"Exactly. And who would have the motive, the will, and the resources to attempt to steal it?"

This time, Segonzak drew the conclusion. "I'd say the Nazis are the only reasonable candidate."

"That's my opinion, too," Nathan said.

"But it is absolutely impossible to steal the gold," Security Chief Nadeau said, protesting. "It's completely safe as long as it's aboard the ship. For God's sake, we have *troops* guarding it."

Segonzak was confused again. "He has a point, David. The killer may be a Nazi agent, but how could he hope to steal such a quantity of gold when troops are guarding it?"

"I don't know," Nathan admitted. "I haven't figured that out yet."

Martel summed up their progress, which wasn't very impressive. "Then we can't be sure who killed Clouzot — or why. All we can say for sure is that it's a professional."

At that moment, Freppel returned, to everyone's surprise.

"You've found the dog already?" Barthou asked.

Freppel smiled. "It was no great feat of detection," he said modestly. "He was sniffing around the meat locker. A lot of lost dogs end up there."

They all laughed, including Freppel.

"What did the countess say?" Nadeau asked.

"Believe it or not, she thought I jumped into the ocean to rescue her little animal. I denied it, of course, but she didn't believe me."

"Amazing." The captain was tickled.

"Then she tried to give me a hundred-franc note."

"Which you refused," Barthou promoted.

"Naturellement."

"I assume you then had the creature taken to the kennel," the captain said.

Freppel sighed. "I couldn't do that, Captain. The countess convinced me she would not be able to survive the voyage without her pet. So I allowed her to keep him, and she promised not to remove his leash again."

"I understand. Thank you, Henri. Well done."

Freppel, glowing, reclaimed his spot at the table. For a few moments, no one said anything.

Then Nathan spoke up. "It looks like there's only one way we're going to find out why Clouzot was killed."

Every face turned toward him expectantly.

"We'll have to *catch* the killer," he said.

"And how do you propose we do that, Mr. American Government Agent?" the security chief asked.

"It won't be easy," Nathan admitted. "It'll take some long, laborious police work."

Nadeau was instantly ready to argue. "You're suggesting we contact the New York police when we dock?"

"No. Well, only if we have to. I have something else in mind. Perhaps Jean-Louis knows where I'm going."

The fox-faced French agent nodded agreement. "It's standard procedure in cases like this. You start by developing a list of suspects."

"I hope you don't mean Barzinni, Cherbatoff, and the others Monsieur Nathan thinks are suspicious," Freppel said.

"No," Segonzak answered. "He's thinking of something more formal. We start with the passenger list—and a list of crew members. We eliminate everyone we're sure is innocent, then start questioning the rest."

Barthou raised an eyebrow. "We are carrying sixteen hundred and eight-three passengers, Monsieur Nathan."

"Plus twelve hundred fifty-two crewmen," the security chief added truculently.

"Which makes almost three thousand people," Freppel concluded. "How are you going to find a murderer—who has apparently left no clues—in a group that size?"

"New York City has more than six *million* people, gentlemen," Nathan said. "Nevertheless, murderers are routinely identified and arrested."

Freppel was skeptical. "In four days?"

"Sometimes overnight."

Barthou sighed. "I understand what you are proposing, Monsieur Nathan. It is a laborious process, with no guarantee of success. And it is certain to upset some passengers and crew members."

"All true," Nathan agreed. "Nevertheless . . ."

The captain went on as though Nathan had not spoken. "It is my decision not to employ such an extreme measure, at least not yet, at least not unless something else occurs. But I will direct the security chief and the chief purser to make discreet inquiries."

Despite this note of finality, Segonzak had one last suggestion. "Let us at least not alert the killer that we are looking for him. Let us keep the murder quiet and relock the storeroom, in case he checks it."

"That is a reasonable request, Lieutenant Segonzak," the captain said. "Would you take care of it, Bernard?"

"Certainly, Captain." Nadeau pocketed the lock.

Deputy Captain Martel spoke up "It's almost time for lunch, Captain."

"So it is. Meeting adjourned."

The security chief walked back to his office angry and disgruntled. He was certain Clouzot had been killed by a fellow crew member. He was also fairly certain that the man deserved his fate. He was one of the worst malcontents on the ship, no doubt an ex-convict. And he probably would have convinced the captain of this truth if it hadn't been for that interfering American and the simpering little French agent who was accompanying the gold. Why didn't they just leave him alone so he could do his job?

Nadeau summoned the Captain of the Watch, an eager young man named Georges Tardieu. "See to it that the chock closet is relocked," he said, tossing him the padlock.

Tardieu saluted and left. On the way to the cargo hold, he stopped off at the Security Messroom for a cup of coffee.

"What did Aunt Bernard want?" his buddy Philip asked.

"I have to relock the chock closet." Tardieu put the rusty padlock on the table.

"Whew."

"I know."

"You going to use that?"

"Why not?"

"Well, *everybody* has a key to that one. Anybody could open it."

"Hmmm. I'll bet Aunt Bernard didn't think of that."

"What does Aunt Bernard ever think of?"

Philip reached into his pocket and pulled out a brand new padlock. "The keys are in the lock drawer."

"Thanks."

"Now, tell me how you made out with Marie last night."

AFTERNOON

"What have you done to yourself?"

"Done? I've had my hair cut. You don't like it?" She cocked

177

her head toward Nathan, mischief in her surprisingly green eyes.

He looked at Tina critically. The shoulder-length tresses were gone, replaced by a neat golden pageboy that set off her face like a picture frame. Do I like it? he asked himself. Of course like it. It's gorgeous. But I'll be damned if I'm going to tell her that.

"It's fine," he said.

"Fine? What kind of a word is that to describe a hairdo?"

"What word would you prefer?"

"Well, a gentleman might say *pretty* or *attractive* — if he liked it."

"What would a gentleman say if he weren't sure?"

Tina's expression turned playful. "Well, if he were really a gentleman, I suppose he'd say *stylish* or maybe even *interesting*, but I don't really know. No one has ever used those words with me."

She smiled slyly and waited for him to make a fool of himself.

"Ah, you're already here," Victor said, taking a seat. "Nice haircut, sis."

"Yes, very nice," Nathan said, relieved.

They lunched on fillet of sole almondine and veal piccata and chicken pot pie. It was Nathan who had the chicken. Wallace Westbrook failed to make an appearance, which was just as well. But just as they were finishing dessert — *bombe imperiale* all around — Karla Kirkland, the attractive cosmetics saleswoman, took her seat at the table.

"Good morning, everyone," she said brightly.

"Morning?" Tina asked.

"I didn't make it down for breakfast," the tall brunette explained. "It was a late night." She winked at Nathan, who recoiled slightly.

"We went back to the cabin early," Tina explained.

"Yes," Karla said. She put a hand on Nathan's arm. "I saw you in the Cafe Grill last night, but you left before I could make my way over to you. You're very elusive, you know."

"I never was much for night life, Miss Kirkland," Nathan told her.

"Please, make it Karla."

Nathan nodded nervously and took a sip of coffee. "Well," he said, "we have to get going."

"Oh, too bad." The woman was genuinely disappointed. "What's so important?"

Victor came to Nathan's aid. "We're going to the horse race on the esplanade."

"Horse race?" That didn't make any sense.

"That's right," Victor explained. "With model horses, of course. Many liners have them. People bet on them."

"I see. I hadn't come across that yet. It sounds like fun."

"It is, but we're going to be late for the first race if we don't leave now," Nathan told her.

"Well, have a good time," Karla Kirkland said warmly. "Maybe I'll see you up there later."

They left the dining room.

"I think she finds you attractive, although I have no idea why," Tina told Nathan. She parodied the woman's wink.

Nathan winced.

"She's quite pretty," Victor pointed out.

"I'd appreciate it if you laid off the matchmaking," Nathan said, putting an end to this line of conversation.

They walked toward the elevator in silence. "Are we really going to the horse races?" Tina finally asked.

"I suppose we are," Nathan said.

The elevator took them to the Promenade Deck, which was strangely deserted. They walked toward the aft esplanade, the site of the deck games.

At about mid-deck, they passed a small group of people buzzing apprehensively. A little farther down the deck, another knot of passengers was acting pretty much like the first.

At the esplanade, the horses were all set up — lifelike metal models about the size of Chihuahuas, complete with pigeon-

179

sized model jockeys in racing silks. Each horse and jockey was mounted atop a movable pedestal.

The passengers, however, were not quietly assembled at the circular track painted on the deck, awaiting a race. Instead, they were crowded around a deck steward, pushing and shoving and shouting for attention. The deck steward was passing out copies of some kind of printed announcement. Time and again, one passenger or another would get hold of one, read it quickly, cry out in surprise and anguish, and go running off.

It was several minutes before Nathan could get close enough to obtain a copy for himself. It was a news bulletin, mimeographed on the letterhead of the ship's newspaper.

"War?" Victor asked, holding his breath.

"Just about," Nathan replied, thinking that the other shoe had finally dropped. He showed the bulletin to Victor and his sister.

HITLER AND STALIN SIGN FRIENDSHIP PACT ENGLAND ALERTS NAVY, FRANCE MOBILIZES ARMY

MOSCOW, Thursday, Aug. 24 — Germany and Soviet Russia early today signed a non-aggression pact binding each of them for ten years not to "associate itself with any other grouping of powers which directly or indirectly is aimed at the other party."

According to some European political observers, the agreement is not so much a declaration of friendship between the two nations — who have so often proclaimed their undying hatred for each other — but, referring to the Great War and previous conflicts, "the fourth and final partition of Poland."

The French government, convinced that an invasion of Poland is imminent and that widespread war may follow, has called up additional reserve forces to augment those summoned earlier in August.

The British government massed warships in the Skagerrak, called an emergency session of Parliament, ordered a blackout in London, and gave every indication she was ready to go to war with Germany whenever a call for help from Poland should come.

Among the major European capitals, only Rome has displayed no outward signs of war preparation, although the Italian press continued to attack Poland's treatment of its German minorities.

In the United States, President Roosevelt interrupted a vacation cruise to return to Washington to receive a report on American munitions productions.

"Doesn't look good," Victor said.

"No."

"I'm glad we've left Europe behind us," Tina said.

"I'll be happier when we've tied up at the pier in New York," Nathan grumbled. He read the announcement again. This was no commercial treaty between former enemies, he thought. It was a goddamn alliance.

While they were calmly discussing the bulletin, a man ran down the deck, screaming for his wife. That set off first an agitated murmur among those who had gathered on the esplanade, then a rising hysteria — panicky exclamations of woe, nasty arguments over what the bulletin really meant, a fusillade of questions ruthlessly hurled at a passing ship's officer: "What's being done to prevent submarine attack?" "Will the ship be returning to Europe on schedule?" "How soon can we get to New York?"

In a matter of moments, the shipboard atmosphere had changed completely, from one of indolence and indulgence to one of dismay and dread. Of course, every passenger who had boarded this great vessel at Le Havre had known that trouble was coming. Many had taken the voyage for the precise purpose of escaping it. But the reality — which had reached them, unexpectedly, all the way out here in the middle of the Atlan-

181

tic — had still come as a terrible shock.

"I think we should head back to the stateroom," Nathan told his charges.

"What for?" Victor asked. "There's no danger here."

"Yes there is," Nathan said. "There's the danger of hysteria. There's the danger of chaos. If someone wants to do us harm, I can think of no better moment."

Tina was exasperated with him. "Why is it that you always think the bogeyman is just around the corner?"

Nathan took her by one arm and Victor by another. "Come on. We'll talk about it later," he said, leading them off the Promenade Deck and into the Grand Lounge.

Fifteen or twenty men were gathered in one corner of the lounge, engaged in serious discussion. Among them was Arthur Shepard, Tina's hopeful college boy swain. He spotted them and waved.

"Mr. Cameron . . . over here. We could use your help."

Nathan hesitated. Now what?

Another man called him. "We'd like you to join us, sir, if you're willing."

Nathan approached the group, keeping Tina and Victor close at hand.

"You see," Shepard began, "a group of us are going to the captain . . ."

He was interrupted by a well-dressed gentlemen in his mid-sixties, a man of obvious presence and stature. "Mr. Cameron, I'm Milton Motherwell. Continental Oil. We're putting together a delegation to see the captain."

"What about?"

"We're going to demand that he radio for an escort of American warships."

"Or British," one of the other men put in.

"Or airplanes," added another.

"That's right," Motherwell said. "We have no wish to become another *Lusitania*."

"You think the ship is in danger?"

"I do, sir," Motherwell said. "The war in Europe will begin before the day is out—if it has not started already. The U-boats are no doubt already in place, ready to torpedo anything they see."

"You are aware," Victor said, "that the *Normandie* is faster than any submarine ever built?"

Motherwell barely let him finish his sentence. "We know that, young man, but what if a submarine is already laying for us?"

"Or maybe a fleet of them," Shepard added.

"If they are," Victor said, "how could warships or airplanes protect us?"

"I agree. We're one big target right now," Motherwell said. "But what German submarine would be willing to tangle with an American battleship?"

Victor opened his mouth to reply, but Nathan spoke first. "Gentlemen, I understand your concern, but don't you think the captain is already taking every possible precaution?"

"I know the French. Worked with them for years. Sold to 'em and bought from 'em," Motherwell said. "And I just don't think much of 'em."

Nathan nodded. "Well, I just don't share your feelings, Mr. Motherwell. But I am sure the captain will give you a hearing. Good luck to you."

"And good luck to you, sir," Motherwell said without conviction.

Nathan guided Tina and Victor back to their stateroom and parked them. He had intended to tell them about the murdered cargo supervisor. He wanted them to know the dangers they might be facing. But so far he had been unable to find the right moment—and this certainly wasn't the time. Besides, he had something else to do. It was time to make contact again with Washington. "You two stay here for a while," Nathan said. "I have an errand to do. Don't let anybody in."

"Not even Maurice Cosset?" Tina inquired.

"Cosset?"

"Our steward."

"All right, Cosset . . . but no one else."

"When will you be back?" Victor asked.

"Fifteen minutes. A half hour at most."

"We'll miss you desperately," Tina told him.

Nathan locked them in and made his way toward the radio telephone booths. He heard the commotion long before he arrived — angry shouting, men yelling at each other, all the ingredients for a fist fight or even a small riot.

At the radio-telephone booths, a full-scale pushing match was in progress — eighty or ninety full-grown and well-dressed men and a score of women, all adults, some offering good money for a better spot in line, others ready for hand-to-hand combat at the first sign that someone was encroaching on their spot, each desperate to tell someone in New York or London or Paris, to sell, sell, sell, or buy, buy, buy, or vote yes or vote no, or convert the factory immediately, or underbid the son of a bitch if you have to, or drop the suit, or if anything happens look in the green shoebox in the back of the closet, or I hope you'll forgive me, I didn't mean to hurt you, or I miss you and be sure to tell the kids I'm thinking about them. . . .

There was panic in the air.

And there was the handsome deputy captain, Marius Martel, on the scene with half a dozen young deck officers at his side.

"Ladies and gentlemen," he announced loudly, "the captain has asked me to clear the area immediately in the interest of passenger safety."

No one moved.

"Furthermore, the captain has asked me to invite you all to the Cafe Grill, where the bar will be open for the rest of the afternoon."

About a third of the crowd — those at the end of the line — reluctantly began to disperse, heading aft toward the free drinks.

"And now, my assistants" — he gestured to the deck officers — "will take your names. You will be called, in the exact order you are now standing, when your turn to use the radio-telephones has come."

Most of the rest of the crowd now began to surrender to the inevitable, not without grumbling. But a few diehards confronted the deputy captain, begging or bullying.

"It is imperative that I . . . hundreds of thousands of dollars depend . . . my wife is deathly ill . . . do you know who you're talking to . . . a matter of national security . . . friend of the purser, friend of the captain, friend of Mayor LaGuardia, friend of the Governor, friend of Mrs. Roosevelt, friend of the President . . . there's a thousand dollars in it for you . . . crucial to the war effort . . . going to cost you your job . . . secret information about Hitler . . ."

Martel shrugged them all off with a smile that was polite but implacable. In about fifteen minutes, the hallway was back to normal. Nathan was surprised and impressed.

"The passengers are pretty excited," he observed.

"Yes. And it's like this all over the ship. But we're getting it under control."

"You're doing a good job of it."

"Well, practice makes perfect."

"Practice?"

"It's happened before, Monsieur Nathan. A year ago last spring, during the Anschluss, then again last fall, just before Munich."

"I see."

"Now it's all part of the job."

"How's the captain doing, Martel?"

The deputy captain pursed his lips and considered the question. "Captain Barthou is doing very well — except for the lunatics, of course."

"The lunatics?"

"Yes. There was one fellow — a Pole, I believe — who offered the captain fifty thousand dollars if he'd turn the ship around

185

and pick up his relatives. And there was a Jewish girl in third class who tried to kill herself, unsuccessfully thank heaven. Then some men wanted us to call in the British Navy."

"I met that bunch."

"The captain took care of them."

"I'll bet."

"But afterward, he called us together and told us to get everyone quieted down. He wants to run a lifeboat drill."

Nathan was surprised. "He does? When?"

Deputy Captain Martel checked his watch. "In about a half hour," he said, "which means I have to go. I'll be supervising the drill, but I have to clear out the card room first. There are some people who'd keep playing even if we hit an iceberg."

Three tremendous, belly-quivering toots from the *Normandie*'s main whistle got everyone's attention. Then the loudspeakers squawked, and the captain's voice echoed through the ship.

"Attention, passengers and crew members. In compliance with international maritime regulations, we shall hold a lifeboat drill in one half hour. This drill is strictly routine, but in these troubled times, I am sure I do not have to tell you that it is important to the safety of everyone on board this ship. Please be calm, be careful, and follow instructions. Thank you for your cooperation."

The speaker squawked off.

"According to the instructions on the back of the door," Victor said, "our lifeboat number is the same as the first number of our dining room table."

Tina looked at Nathan and waited.

"I remember it," he protested. "Three."

"Very good. You get an A."

"And the life jackets," Victor went on, "are under the beds."

He got down on his hands and knees and pulled out three puffy tan life vests, shaped like horse collars. He kept one for himself and handed the other two to Tina and David Nathan.

"Ugly," Tina said, slipping it over her sundress. "Do I have to wear it?"

"Only if you want to float," Victor told her.

"Everybody ready?" Nathan asked.

The *Normandie* tooted her whistle again, three times.

Nathan opened the door and came face-to-face with Maurice Cosset, their friendly young steward, who was about to knock on the door.

"You're all ready?" he asked, surprised.

"I had a hunch there'd be a drill," Nathan said.

Cosset was still a little taken aback. "You're the only ones in my service who have your life jackets on already. But let me check to see if you've done it correctly." He examined the three life jackets. "Just fine. You know your boat number?"

"Three," Tina said proudly.

"Good. That's on the starboard side, amidships. Take the little stairway near the entrance to the Smoking Room. I have to see to the rest of my passengers—the unprepared ones."

He gave them a cheery wave and went on his way.

In the corridor, they soon met other passengers nervously making their way to the Boat Deck. Stewards and pages were everywhere, courteous and imperturbable, giving directions, offering reassurance, providing a sense of order and competence.

Up on the open promenade of the Boat Deck, however, there was considerable confusion.

An elderly woman simply couldn't remember her lifeboat number. She wasn't even sure which of her several married names she was using on this voyage.

A Chicago banker insisted on changing his seat, to a lifeboat on the forward port side, which he insisted was safer than the one to which he'd been assigned.

A man and wife who had been only too happy to park their children in the playroom for the entire voyage now insisted that they get their own family lifeboat.

Marlene Dietrich arrived on the Boat Deck with a young Japanese female servant, two chinchilla coats, a mink jacket, a cosmetics bag, a jewelry case, and a hatbox, all of which she wanted to take aboard her lifeboat.

A doddering old man slipped and fell against a deck chair and had to be taken to the infirmary.

The Countess de Chambord's dog hopped out of the woman's enormous handbag, ran across the deck and, before he could be retrieved, piddled on a pile of life jackets.

A group of Polish refugees, dragging all of their shabby belongings with them, claimed that they were not notified of any emergency and that there was a conspiracy to keep them away from the lifeboats.

Mrs. Phipps Ogden Stewart demanded to be assigned to another lifeboat, any other lifeboat, so long as she did not have to "risk being shipwrecked" with Mrs. James Brown Bigelow, who she insisted was her social inferior.

Any one of these or a score of other minor problems could have mushroomed into major disturbances and these disturbances could have escalated into pandemonium, but the detachment of ship's officers overseen by Deputy Captain Martel handled each incident with dignity and aplomb.

Soon, practically all the passengers—film stars and refugees, stockbrokers and schoolteachers, the displaced and the dowagers—were assembled on the open promenade of the Boat Deck, along with most of the ship's non-essential crew members.

A long row of thirty-foot mahogany lifeboats was suspended above the passengers' heads. Each could carry as many as eighty-eight passengers and each was equipped with a Lutetia-Echard mechanical screw, which, when properly turned, could propel the vessel at about three knots.

The lifeboats were cradled in Glasgow-built gravity davits and suspended from a network of steel cables. Powerful electric winches could lower all the boats simultaneously, sliding them down steel tracks to the open promenade level, for passenger boarding. Once the passengers were aboard, the lifeboats would be swung out from the ship — far enough so they wouldn't crash into the hull — and lowered, by cable, to the ocean's surface.

Now Deputy Captain Martel blew sharply on the little silver whistle he wore around his neck. A junior officer threw the switch controlling the electric winches. All of the lifeboats began a grinding, shuddering descent to the open promenade level, where the passengers were assembled.

When the boats were in position, an army of deck hands ran down the line, removing canvas covers, making minor adjustments, checking to see that each vessel was properly equipped with emergency rations and medical supplies. The entire task was completed in less than three minutes.

Then Martel blew his whistle again. All along the lifeboat line, deck officers began instructing people to take their seats. "Step lively, step gently, step into the boat as if you were descending a stair. Do not leap, do not jump, do not hop." The instructions were repeated again and again, up and down the length of the Boat Deck.

Nathan watched as Tina and Victor took seats at the lifeboat bow. He settled in on the bench right behind them, a little confused. None of the other lifeboat drills he'd witnessed involved an actual lowering of the boats, much less passenger loading. Barthou was really taking this seriously. He was both pleased and disturbed. It made the danger that much more real.

The lifeboat filled rapidly, swaying slightly from side to side with each addition, hanging precariously from its cables. "Step lively, step gently, step into the boat as if you were descending a stair. Do not leap, do not jump, do not hop," a deck officer repeated mechanically.

The Stickney sisters, Claire and Daphne, fluttering like birds, took seats at the other end of the boat. Arthur Shepard, after a futile attempt to push through the crowd toward Tina, settled for a seat in the middle of the boat, next to Count

Cherbatoff and his young lady friend. And a couple of rows from them, Wallace Westbrook took one of the few remaining seats. He was looking a little green, perhaps because the lifeboat was swaying so much.

"Excuse me."

Nathan looked up. It was Rothmann, the silent young Viennese gentleman with the tragic history. He stepped into the boat and took a seat on Nathan's bench, to his right, almost directly behind Tina but facing in the opposite direction. That left a single vacancy in the boat — on Nathan's bench, to his immediate left.

"Hold the lifeboats!"

Someone was running across the deck.

"Wait for me!"

Karla Kirkland was sprinting toward the lifeboat, shouting and waving her hands frantically, her athlete's body making a very pretty picture indeed.

Half the ship's company watched her approach, entranced. One deck steward, however, managed to recover himself sufficiently to sing out the melody of the moment: "Step lively, step gently . . ."

"David!" she cried out, spotting him near the bow. "Save me the seat!" She launched herself off the deck in Nathan's direction, perhaps expecting to be caught in midair or, if she'd aimed right, to fall into his lap.

Nathan saw her coming across the deck. He did not, however, anticipate her bold and reckless swan dive. He had only a moment to prepare for the impact. It wasn't enough.

Karla Kirkland's nicely muscled one hundred twenty-two-pound body hit David Nathan about mid-chest. The impact hurtled him against the gunwale and knocked the breath out of him.

With the sudden shift in its center of gravity, the lifeboat swung violently away from the ship, davit cables twanging at the sudden strain. At the apogee of the swing, the forward cable rolled up the side of the pulley flange, then, with a loud crack, slipped free.

The lifeboat instantly dropped three feet at the bow. Then the safety mechanism took hold and the vessel's descent halted abruptly. All the boat's inhabitants were flung forward against one another. And Victor and Tina Meisner were catapulted out of the vessel, toward the ocean ninety feet below.

Victor somehow managed to stick out a hand and grab the lifeboat rail as he tumbled over it. Tina didn't do as well. She snagged the davit cable, then began to slide downward, her green eyes wide with shock and fear.

Nathan couldn't see what had happened to Tina, but he somehow managed to squirm out from under Karla Kirkland and seize Victor's hand. That little bit of help allowed Victor to fling his other arm up and get his fingers around the gunwale. Nathan then pulled him back aboard. The moment Victor was safe, he turned to try to help Tina, but she was far beyond his reach. She was not beyond the reach of Kurt Jaekcl, however.

Jaekel had reacted instinctively when the boat fell. The moment he saw the girl tumble out, he'd somersaulted over the rail himself, wrapping his legs around the davit cable. Using commando school techniques, he shinnied down toward Tina, twenty feet below him and slipping fast.

Suddenly, Jaekel hit a greasy spot on the cable. He fell toward Tina, out of control. Arms flailing, he desperately tried to catch himself, aware that if he collided with the girl, both of them would be knocked off the cable and into the sea. Barely ten feet above her, he finally got a grip on the cable and managed to break his descent.

Meanwhile, a horrified deck officer, seeing what had happened to lifeboat #3, raced toward the winch control, to bring the craft up to an even keel again, so the passengers could get off. Deputy Captain Martel, however, realized that no one inside the boat was still in danger. Although they'd all been violently tossed about, each passenger had found a way to hang on. He also realized that if the deck officer activated the winch, the cable would give a jerk and the girl hanging from it would fall sixty feet into the icy Atlantic. The chance she would survive the impact was very small.

"Stop!" he shouted. "Don't touch the winch!" Martel vaulted over a pair of deck chairs and dashed toward the winch control, determined to prevent the deck officer from pulling the lever.

The deck officer, his hand on the winch lever now, looked up at the onrushing deputy captain uncertainly and tried to understand what he was shouting. Was the man telling him to hurry? "I'm getting it!" he shouted back.

Martel threw a ferocious body block at the startled deck officer, knocking the man off his feet. They rolled across the Boat Deck in an unlikely tangle, finally crashing against the rail. The deck officer stared at his superior in shock and incomprehension.

Tina had slid another ten feet down the greasy cable by the time Jaekel reached her and she was on the verge of losing her grip. By now, everyone in the port lifeboats—especially those in boat number 3, and particularly Victor Meisner and David Nathan—was transfixed by the drama below them, by the attractive young woman who had such a fragile hold on life and by the handsome young man who was risking everything to save her.

The lifeboat's occupants gasped with relief when Jaekel got hold of Tina's life jacket, then gave another gasp—this one of surprise—when he made no attempt to pull her up, instead using his grip on her jacket as a kind of fulcrum to swing his body past her, to the section of cable immediately below her, between her and the sea.

He fastened himself to the cable as though he were a part of it. An instant later, Tina slipped again, but this time Jaekel's body halted her slide. Then, slowly and deliberately, in a breathtaking display of strength and balance, he began pulling himself upward, with Tina sitting on his shoulders.

No longer fearful of falling into the sea, no longer solely

responsible for her body weight, Tina was able to help now, pulling herself upward on the cable while Jaekel pushed from below.

Then they hit the greasy patch on the cable. For all of his strength, Jaekel was unable to maintain his hand hold. He abruptly slid toward the ocean, his arms and legs wrapped around the cable in a death grip. Suddenly unsupported, Tina held her place for a moment, then hurtled toward him.

The collision took place about fifty feet above the waterline. Everyone on board the lifeboats watched in horror, imagining the two figures wrenched away from the cable, picturing them tumbling toward the surface of the sea, toward death.

Jaekel held on despite the impact, but Tina couldn't maintain her grip. Jaekel shot out one strong arm and grabbed her by the waist. Then he managed to lift her just high enough so she could take hold of the cable once more and pull herself above him again.

After a few minutes rest, Jaekel again started to climb, Tina back on his shoulders. They came to the greasy spot again, but this time, Jaekel picked his way past it and continued upward.

Finally, after what seemed like hours — it was actually about ten minutes — Tina was within Victor and Nathan's reach. They each took an arm and lifted her into the boat. Then Nathan reached back down and gave Jaekel a hand. When the handsome, dark-haired young man at last tumbled back into the boat, there was silence for a moment or two, then the applause began from those sitting in the lifeboats, those who had seen everything. It was thin and scattered at first, then swelling, then clamorous.

"Now," Deputy Captain Martel instructed the deck officer, pointing to the winch control. The deck officer threw the lever and the bow of lifeboat number 3 rose until it was once more level with the open promenade.

Martel and a dozen deck officers scurried to help Tina and the others back onto the deck. Martel himself plucked her out of the boat and set her down on the Boat Deck, the closest thing to *terra firma* that the *Normandie* could offer. She stood there, trembling, eyes overflowing with tears, while Nathan and Victor scrambled out of the lifeboat and Martel helped Jaekel onto the deck.

"You're all right?" Jaekel asked Tina with unguarded concern.

She nodded, tears streaming down her cheeks. Then she lifted her head. Their eyes met and held. Then, surprising even herself, Tina threw her arms around him and kissed him full on the lips. It was Jaekel who finally broke the embrace.

Now other passengers and crew members surrounded Tina and smothered her with sympathy, Victor and David Nathan taking the lead. Were her hands all right? Yes, the grease had safeguarded them. Did she have any cuts and bruises? No, the life jacket had protected her. Did she want to go back to the cabin and rest? No, she was all right. Yes, she was sure.

At the same time, other passengers and crew members inundated Jaekel with praise and admiration. "So brave . . . unselfish . . . amazingly strong . . . risked your life . . . acrobatic talent . . . authentic hero . . ."

Jaekel received the compliments with what the complimenters thought was becoming modesty. Actually, it was nothing more than an intense desire to be elsewhere, to be out of the public eye, to be anonymous once more. He couldn't let the others see it, of course, but he was furious with himself. For most of the voyage, he'd had but a single duty: to remain inconspicuous. And he had failed.

When Tina regained her composure, she went looking for the man she knew as Simon Rothmann. To her puzzlement and consternation, he was nowhere to be found. He had slipped away. What was the matter with him? What was the matter with her? Maybe she would find out at dinner.

It was at this moment that someone found her, someone who had been looking for her ever since the rescue: Karla Kirkland.

"Lilly, I don't know what to say. . . ." she began apologetically.

"That was a pretty stupid stunt," Victor told her.

Karla was thoroughly subdued. "I didn't realize what would happen."

Now that it was all over, Nathan saw no reason to be cruel. "You couldn't have known," he told the pretty brunette. "You were just playing around. Anyhow, it all turned out all right."

The woman looked at Tina, tears in her eyes. "Lilly?"

Tina touched the woman's hand reassuringly. "It's all right, Karla," she said with a little toss of her head. "I'm just fine."

"I was so frightened," Karla said, crying now.

"You were frightened?" Victor said. "After what you did?"

"That's enough, Victor," Tina snapped. The fire was back.

The ship's loudspeakers crackled, then squawked. "Attention, ladies and gentlemen," a voice announced, "There has been a change in the afternoon programme. The afternoon cinema presentation, formerly scheduled for three o'clock P.M., will instead be shown an hour earlier — that is, in fifteen minutes, in the theater on the Promenade Deck. All classes are welcome to attend."

"That's all we need," Victor said sarcastically. "A movie."

"No," Tina said, "it's a good idea. It would take my mind off what happened."

Nathan was not pleased. He wanted both Victor and Tina back in the room, where they'd be safe. He wanted to talk with the security chief, to make sure the accident had actually been an accident. On the other hand, maybe Tina did need a little pampering.

"And I think I'd like Karla to come with us," Tina said. "We tablemates have to stick together, isn't that right, Uncle David?"

Karla smiled, first at Tina, then at Nathan. "I'd love that," she said.

Nathan accepted his fate as graciously as he could. And after all, how bad was it? Karla Kirkland was a very appealing woman, although a little too flirtatious for his taste. Anyhow, as long as they were all going to be cooped up on this ship for the next few days . . .

They found a stairway, descended one level, then walked forward, toward the theater, Karla Kirkland on David Nathan's arm. Then they went through a pair of doors decorated with the gilded masks of comedy and drama, entering the only room on the ship where it wasn't the passengers who invented the dialogue and plot, but rather dramatists and scriptwriters.

This was the first permanent theater ever installed in an ocean liner, an auditorium that would have been perfectly acceptable on Broadway, a lushly carpeted, indirectly lit chamber with silver plaster of paris walls, an acoustic ceiling of concentric grooves, and three hundred eighty plush red velvet theater seats.

Nathan and his companions were the first to arrive . . . almost. Seven men were sitting in the back row of the theater on one side. Nathan recognized three of them—the gangster Barzinni and his two bodyguards. The other four were scruffy, dangerous-looking types, definitely not first-class passengers.

It was clear that they'd been there for some time, that they hadn't bothered to attend the lifeboat drill. It was equally clear that they were discussing something of great urgency.

As soon as Barzinni realized he and his people were no longer alone in the theater, he manufactured some specious laughter. His group joined in, with obvious discomfort. The little play lasted for a couple of minutes, then the meeting—if that's what it had been—adjourned. Barzinni and his men left the theater, running awkwardly into a flock of passengers coming in to see the film.

Tina, Victor, Karla, and David took seats in mid-theater, in that order, Tina on the aisle. Soon they were surrounded by others, including several of the celebrities on board: Jack Benny, Fred Allen, and their wives, together with Edward G.

Robinson, Arthur Murray, Ramon Novarro, Marlene Dietrich, and Erich von Stroheim, who upon seeing Tina, took a seat directly across the aisle from her.

"I heard about the accident," he said. "I am so very glad you are safe."

Tina had seen von Stroheim take his seat and had made up her mind not to look in his direction. But he seemed genuinely concerned and she couldn't bring herself to be impolite. "It was a scare, but I'm fine, thank you."

He stared at her, his eyes incredibly intense. "I could not bear to have lost you."

Tina didn't know how to respond.

At that moment, the theater lights began to dim.

"I was there this afternoon," von Stroheim went on, as the auditorium grew dark. "I saw your courage and composure."

The music started.

"You were magnificent. You *are* the horsewoman," von Stroheim went on.

Tina concentrated on the screen.

For the next one hundred and five minutes, Tina and the rest of the audience were diverted and entertained by the athletic adventures of Errol Flynn, in skintight green leggings and open-chested jerkin, as he pursued a luminous Olivia de Havilland and, with the help of Alan Hale, fought off the villainous Claude Rains and Basil Rathbone, in *The Adventures of Robin Hood*.

During this time, everyone in the *Normandie*'s theater forgot not only their troubles and misadventures, but also the world's. And as Robin happily carried Maid Marian away from the castle hall, Karla reached over and took David Nathan's hand. "I love happy endings, don't you?" she said.

The theater lights gradually came on while the titles were still rolling. Tina, on the aisle, got up and found herself face-to-face with von Stroheim. He spoke to her in his mesmerizing whisper. "Miss de Havilland is beautiful, isn't she? But you are far more beautiful."

Tina turned up the aisle in an attempt to get away from him. He followed close on her heels, cutting her off from her brother, who lost sight of her in the crowd. David Nathan, waiting for Karla Kirkland to begin moving toward the aisle, saw nothing.

"My offer was a serious one," von Stroheim continued hypnotically as they walked up the aisle together. "It will make you the most celebrated actress of the age."

Tina anxiously looked for a way to get away from him, to push through the crowd in the theater aisle. While she was searching for an opening, von Stroheim slid an arm around her waist.

"Millions of people will see you," he confided, eyes glittering. "Millions will admire you. Millions will *desire* you. Millions will experience your body and your soul. You will have fame and fortune — and unimaginable ecstasy."

Tina looked over her shoulder for Victor or David, who were hopelessly lost in the crush of people. And she was being irresistibly enveloped in some horrible yet fascinating spell.

"I will transform you from what you are into a woman of surpassing beauty and knowledge," von Stroheim said, his voice almost a chant. "There will be no pleasure which you have not experienced, even the pleasure of pain. You will be born anew."

"Let go," Tina protested in a tiny voice.

"Come with me," von Stroheim whispered.

At the head of the aisle, they ran into Marlene Dietrich and her entourage of alluring women and handsome men. "Ah, von Stroheim," Dietrich said, "I see you've found her, the fluff who fell off the ship."

"Is she not as lovely as I said?" von Stroheim asked, as if seeking Dietrich's approval.

The sloe-eyed film star looked at Tina, her eyes slowly trailing over the girl's body, then rising again, until their eyes met. "Yes. She is a miracle," Dietrich concluded.

Tina smiled uncertainly.

Dietrich took her hand. "Come back to the suite with us, darling child. We wish to know you better."

"No, I —"

"You see," von Stroheim whispered, "already it begins."

Now David Nathan finally caught up to Tina, Victor at his side. "Well, what do you know," Nathan said. "If it isn't the sharpshooter. I'm a little surprised they let you out of your cage."

Von Stroheim stiffened and bowed. "My compliments, sir. And again, my apologies."

"Let's go, Lilly. We have things to talk about."

Von Stroheim was taken aback. "You know this man?" he asked Tina, evidently forgetting exactly what had happened in the Cafe Grill.

"My uncle," she said, pulling free of von Stroheim's arm and moving toward Nathan. "And this is my brother."

"Hello," Victor said pleasantly.

Marlene Dietrich's eyes were still on Tina. "Another time then, darling child?" She suddenly bent over and pressed her red heart-shaped lips against Tina's. Then she took von Stroheim's arm and floated out of the theater, leaving Tina in shock.

"What was *that* all about?" Karla Kirkland asked, finally catching up with them. "Do you know Marlene Dietrich?"

"I was just introduced," Tina answered, still a little stunned.

"I think it would be a good idea to keep your distance from those people," Nathan said, annoyed. "You can pursue your acting career when you get to New York."

"I didn't . . . I wasn't . . . he tried to . . . oh, forget it!"

"Let's go back to the cabin," Nathan said. "We have things to talk about."

"See you at dinner?" Karla asked.

"Of course."

Nathan locked the door behind them. He sat the Meisners

199

down and looked at them, Tina radiant and charming, Victor the serious young professor. He felt terribly responsible for both of them.

"How are you feeling, Tina?" he asked.

"Just fine," she said, still sulking.

"Good. Now, I want you both to listen to me. Some things have happened that you should know about."

That got their attention.

"Trouble?" Victor prompted.

"A little. Maybe more on the way."

"Are we in danger?" Tina asked. Her pout was gone.

"I'm not sure. Maybe."

He told them about the murder of the cargo supervisor.

"You think the murderer was after us?" Victor asked thoughtfully.

"Who knows? Maybe he's after something else altogether."

Then Nathan told them about the gold.

Victor was quite surprised. "That does change things."

"It's puzzling, actually," Nathan said. "I mean, how could someone steal fourteen tons of gold with a company of French soldiers guarding it? It would take hours to carry it away, even with a dozen longshoremen. Besides, where could the thieves put it, except where it is already?"

Victor considered the question. "What if the thieves removed it from the ship entirely?"

Nathan chuckled. "Removed it? How? A mid-ocean stickup by a couple of German battleships, maybe?"

Victor didn't even smile. "No, that wouldn't work. The *Normandie* could radio for help, and US or British planes would be here almost before the Germans could start transferring it."

Victor began doodling, apparently, in a small notebook.

"I'm sure the Nazis would love to steal the gold, assuming they know it's here," Nathan said. "That would certainly finish off French morale. They could even torpedo the ship and send the gold to the bottom. But I think Hitler is too greedy for that."

"The Nazis won't order the *Normandie* torpedoed," Victor told him. He slipped on a pair of eyeglasses, which made him look even more professorial than usual.

"Why not?"

"Because it would be an act of war. And when the survivors told the story, the world would be outraged — especially America. It would be a disaster for Germany. And, because they don't have to."

"I think Victor is right," Tina said drowsily. "He's always right."

Nathan glanced over at her. She'd curled up on one of the beds. That pleased him. She'd been through quite an ordeal, no matter what she said.

"So the ship is safe," Nathan said.

Victor was startled. "Wait a minute. I didn't say any such thing."

"But . . . yes you did." Nathan couldn't understand why Victor was so surprised. "A German warship is no good. You said so yourself. Same goes for a submarine attack."

Victor drew a long line on his notepad, connecting a box to a circle. "That's true, but it doesn't mean the ship is safe."

"Well, where's the threat? You think the Nazis will send out a squadron of Heinkels and blow us out of the water?"

Victor shook his head. "That's not what I'm suggesting."

"Then what?" Nathan went on. "A bomb on board? That wouldn't work either — even if a single bomb could sink the *Normandie*, which I doubt. It would just send the gold to the bottom of the Atlantic, out of reach."

Victor tore one sheet of paper out of the notebook and started on another, writing furiously. "You're wrong about that," he said.

"What?"

Tina whimpered a little, then changed position on the bed.

"I said you're mistaken," Victor repeated. "Here . . . look." He showed Nathan his notebook. It was an incomprehensible mishmash of calculations, diagrams, and formulae. "What is all this supposed to be?" Nathan asked in consternation.

Victor was genuinely apologetic. "I'm sorry. I forgot who I was talking to. And I don't mean anything by that, just that you're not a scientist."

Nathan couldn't help smiling. Even when Victor was trying to be polite, he sounded insulting. "Okay, why am I wrong about the ship being safe?"

"Well, I've calculated the *Normandie*'s volume, structural rigidity, the tensile strength of the frame and the plating. It's all right here." He pointed to some numbers. "It's really quite obvious."

"What is?" Nathan was starting to feel out of his depth.

"That a bomb could sink the ship, of course."

"One bomb?"

"A fairly small one, in fact."

"How small?"

"Depends on the explosive. It would take about three hundred thirty-four pounds of cyclotol. Or about ninety-six pounds of PETN — but that's still experimental."

Nathan thought of the bearded man and his big wooden box. Was the box full of PETN? Then another idea occurred to him. "The bomb won't work. It would leave witnesses, just like submarines or warships or airplanes."

"Not necessarily," Victor came right back. "If you put it in the right place, the bomb could blow out the ship's bottom. She'd go down so fast there'd be no time to launch the lifeboats. There wouldn't be any survivors."

Nathan suddenly realized that he and Victor were actually having a civil conversation, their very first. Until now, all he'd gotten from the boy wonder was insults and scarcely concealed contempt. Now he was getting respect — and good sense. Fortunately, he saw a flaw in what Victor was now suggesting.

"Even if a bomb could sink the ship, Hitler wouldn't do it,"

202

Nathan told the young man.

"Why is that?" Victor was feeling comfortable for the first time since he'd left the Institute. His mind was fully engaged.

"Because of the gold," Nathan said. "It wouldn't do Hitler much good lying at the bottom."

Victor nodded. "Which bottom is that?"

"The bottom of the Atlantic," Nathan said impatiently. "Thousands of feet below the surface. Davy Jones's locker."

Victor drew a jagged wavy line with a sudden rise at one end and a small plateau. "Take a look at this." He pointed to his pad, as though teaching a child.

"I see it. What is it?"

"It's the continental shelf. Runs down almost the entire Atlantic coast of Canada and United States, sometimes more than a hundred miles wide and as shallow as ninety meters, if I remember correctly."

"I'll bet you do." Nathan was trying to understand what Victor was saying, and he was feeling stupid. "But why — ?"

"If the *Normandie* went down in shallow waters on the continental shelf, the gold could easily be recovered by normal salvage techniques."

Nathan wasn't sure he got it. "Normal salvage techniques?"

"Yes. You know, a salvage ship, divers, a crane, a sling. I think the gold could be raised in a matter of hours."

Tina gave a sharp snort, then a soft little snore, distracting them both. She was sound asleep, which was just as well.

"Well, that's a nice theory, Victor," Nathan admitted, "but I think it's full of holes."

Victor was genuinely enjoying himself. "Okay, name them."

"The bomb, for instance. This ship is tightly guarded in port. I doubt anyone could have smuggled a bomb aboard, then gotten away. Let's see if you have an answer for that, professor."

Victor hardly paused for thought. "What if the saboteur were a passenger — and the bomb was stashed in his luggage?"

"Aha," Nathan said, springing a trap. "That means the man

would be committing suicide. No, some Nazis are fanatics, but isn't that asking a little too much?"

"You're assuming the man *knows* he's carrying a bomb," Victor said.

Nathan was insistent. "He'd have to know. Otherwise, how could he put it in the right place and set the fuse for the right time?"

For a moment, Victor seemed stymied. Then he had the answer. "Why does our man have to go down with the ship?"

"What's he supposed to do?" Nathan asked caustically. "Swim to New York?"

"No, but he could swim to the salvage ship."

Now Nathan pounced. "That's another hole in your theory, Victor . . . that salvage ship. Just how would it find the *Normandie?* It's an awfully big ocean out there. If the salvage ship isn't johnny-on-the-spot when the ship sinks, the gold will be lost forever."

This was turning into a momentous conversation, Nathan realized. The safety of the ship and the lives of all aboard might depend on its outcome, but he was having a good time anyhow. He was engaged in the kind of chess game he'd played so often with his colleagues, a game that had almost always ended in the thwarting of a racketeer or an assassin or someone else with evil intent.

No, not always, he thought. Sometimes, all the theorizing and analyzing in the world wasn't enough. Sometimes, a fair amount of luck was also needed. Sometimes, that was all that prevented disaster.

He remembered one of those times. It was in the middle of February 1933. He'd been with FDR, then president-elect, due to take office in a little more than a month. Roosevelt had been in Miami, just back from a carefree cruise off the Florida coast on Vincent Astor's yacht, the *Nourmahal*. A motorcade had taken him to a reception at the Bay Front Park just as dusk had begun to fall.

Nathan had spent the previous evening with the Secret

Service men detailed to guard FDR, going over the list of local lunatics and debating ways to protect the president-elect as he rode in an open motor car along the crowded city streets.

They had talked long into the night — just as he and Victor were doing now — theorizing about how a potential assassin might approach the motorcade, what positions he might take up in a tall building on the route, what kind of weapon he might use, how he could be spotted in the crowd.

Nathan had been very impressed by the Secret Service men. They understood the dangers and they had developed brilliant ways to deal with them — most of them. But some dangers, they'd said, were impossible to protect against. For instance, they'd found no way to nullify an assassin who was willing to risk his own life.

"In the end," one of the Secret Service agents had said, "there's only one sure way to deal with a man like that: Get your body between him and his target." It had been a grim thought.

Sitting on top of the back seat of his open car, the tanned and ebullient president-elect had given a short speech to the twenty thousand or so who had pressed close to his motorcade. The Secret Service men were spread out around the limousine, Nathan at the rear fender.

When Roosevelt finished his speech, the newsreel people had asked him to repeat it for them. He'd politely declined. Just then, Mayor Anton Cermak of Chicago had come forward to speak to Roosevelt, to request political favors. At the same time, a man with a long telegram had appeared. As he started to explain it, Roosevelt had leaned forward to listen.

Just then, there'd been the sound of a firecracker explosion, followed immediately by several more sharp cracks. Nathan had instinctively moved toward FDR at the first explosion and thrown up his hands in front of the man. To his total astonishment, a small bloody hole had suddenly appeared in the center of his left wrist.

He'd looked up to see two of the Secret Service men struggling with a short, swarthy curly-haired man standing on a park bench scarcely thirty-five feet from the president-elect. A roar of fear and horror had begun to rise from the crowd, but Roosevelt's strong voice had rung out above the panic. "I'm all right! I'm all right!"

FDR had been all right, but Mayor Anton Cermak had been fatally wounded from a bullet fired by Joseph Zangara, a thirty-three-year-old Italian immigrant who'd later testified that he "did not hate Roosevelt personally, but hated all presidents and all officials and everyone who is rich."

Roosevelt had been saved, all right, not by theorizing or analysis, but by pure dumb luck. Nathan still had the scar to prove it. And he was beginning to think they might need some more of that luck right now, on the *Normandie*.

Victor had strolled over to the balcony and was gazing out to sea. The ocean was remarkably calm, the ship's motion smooth and steady. There were no ships on the horizon. After a few moments, he turned back toward Nathan.

"You asked how the salvage ship would know where the *Normandie* was. Well, there are two ways," he said. "First, the saboteur could regularly radio the salvage ship—directly or through Berlin—relaying the *Normandie*'s position, route, and speed. He could get that information easily. Second, the Germans could visually track the *Normandie,* with a series of picket ships."

This time, Nathan couldn't find any flaw in Victor's reasoning. "That makes sense," he said at last. He realized, as he said it, that he wasn't simply admitting Victor was probably right, he was also admitting the ship was in serious danger. "You know," he added, "you'd make a hell of a detective."

Victor practically blushed. "Thank you. I take that as a real compliment."

"What if we've invented this whole idea, Victor? What if this whole theory is just a figment of our imagination?"

"Was the murder a figment of someone's imagination?"

"No."

"Do you genuinely believe a Nazi agent was behind it?"

"That's the only explanation that makes any sense," Nathan said. He glanced at Tina, who was still asleep.

"Well, I agree with you."

"If we're right," Nathan said, "we have a job to do. We have to find this man—and his bomb—before we reach the continental shelf."

Victor was suddenly very silent. "My God," he said quietly. "What now?"

"I just realized what could happen if we don't find the man." The thought occurred to him that if the saboteur succeeded, Hitler's enemies would lose something even more valuable than the bullion or the lives of the thousands of innocent people aboard this ship. They'd lose what he knew about Germany's atomic bomb and what he could contribute to building an American version. And that might be the difference between victory and defeat.

Two months ago, Victor had smuggled a letter to his old teacher, begging him for help in getting out of Germany. Einstein had understood the danger his protege was facing— and the importance of what he knew—and had somehow convinced Roosevelt to send this brave and resourceful man to help him.

A couple of times—especially in Berlin—Victor had been almost tempted to tell Nathan why it was so important for him to get to America, why Roosevelt had sent David to bring him back. There had been no good opportunity, however. And after they boarded the *Normandie,* it hadn't seemed necessary. Besides, it was not in his nature to confide such things. And now Victor once again decided to say nothing. The gold, along with all the people traveling on the ship, was pressure enough for any man, even a man such as David Nathan.

"How long do we have, Victor?" Nathan asked, interrupting the young scientist's reverie. "When are we going to reach the continental shelf?"

Victor checked his watch and did some mental calculations.

"About sixty-five hours, I'd say."

"Good God," Nathan said, shaking his head. "We're going to need help." He picked up the phone. "Give me the room of Jean-Louis Segonzak," he said.

Victor watched Nathan go into action. The man was very good, he told himself, but was he good enough? Was anyone?

Kurt Jaekel changed into a blue blazer and white pants, giving him the appearance, more or less, of a ship's officer. Then he took an alternate route toward the cargo hold, going down a back stairway behind the swimming pool. He had to avoid being seen if at all possible, but on the other hand, he had to move the automobile.

This time, no one spotted him. So he decided to detour slightly, past the chock closet, to see if it was still locked. The longer the cargo supervisor's body remained undiscovered, the better his chances of successfully accomplishing his mission.

There it was ahead of him, still locked. He smiled. Now if he could just move the motor car, his mission would be half done. Then, as he walked by the closet, something caught his eye—a reflection, a glint of light.

He walked a few more paces, not really sure anything was different. Then he turned around and went back to examine the closet door. He squatted down and took a close look at the lock. It was brand-new. Had the lock he'd put on the closet yesterday been brand-new? He tried to remember. He recalled taking the lock from the hasp. He remembered twisting the shackle and clicking it closed.

The shackle. It hadn't moved smoothly. In fact, it had made a little squeaking noise when he'd twisted it. It had been corroded. He studied the lock in front of him. This one practically sparkled. The shackle, in particular, looked chrome-plated. No corrosion, anyway.

Jaekel felt the sweat in his armpits.

At some time since he had last been in the cargo hold, sometime during the last twenty-four hours, the chock closet had been opened, then reclosed. Somebody knew about the body. The captain, the crew, the security force knew. But just what did they know? They knew a man had been murdered.

Why had they relocked the door? Why had they chosen a new lock? Were they trying to set a trap? Were they trying to get him to react, to panic, maybe to break into the closet to see if the body was gone, to see if his memory about the lock was correct. Well, he didn't need to do that. He knew his memory was correct.

He looked around in near panic. Could they be watching him right now, waiting for him to try to open the closet? He released the lock as though it were red-hot.

Jaekel fought back his panic. They may have realized the cargo supervisor hadn't been killed in a simple quarrel. They'd shown that when they had relocked the chock closet. Still, they could not know who had killed the cargo supervisor or why. Nonetheless, it was time to go, time to get out of here, to return to his cabin and think. He backed away from the chock closet and headed up the little stairway.

EVENING

For forty-five solid minutes, Lt. Jean-Louis Segonzak, senior intelligence officer of the *Service de Documentation Extérieure et de Contra-Espionage* — the renowned SDECE — grilled Dr. Victor Meisner. David Nathan and Tina Meisner listened and occasionally made comments.

Segonzak was polite. He never once raised his voice. He was respectful. He never questioned Victor's intelligence, motives, or his sanity. And he was considerate. When the young man asked for a drink of water, Segonzak poured it himself. At the same time, he was unrelenting, subjecting Victor to the fiercest, most thorough, most exacting interrogation the young man had ever experienced, even at the Institute, even in the heat of scientific debate. Finally, Lieutenant Segonzak was convinced.

"It seems that we have some police work to do, David," the soft-spoken, sandy-haired intelligence man said.

"My thought exactly, Jean-Louis."

"Where do we start?"

"Not by telling Barthou — not yet."

"Agreed. Not until we can present him with a list of suspects."

The Frenchman looked at his watch. "Let's give ourselves a deadline, David. It's five-thirty now. Shall we say eleven P.M.?"

"Suspect list by eleven P.M.?" Nathan was skeptical. "Well, if you say so." He didn't like other people making promises for him, but this was a promise they both had to keep.

"We'll tell him everything then. And maybe we'll have at least the beginning of an answer for him. Shall I call him and make an appointment?"

Nathan sighed. "Might as well."

Segonzak made the call.

Victor was incredulous. "You two don't really expect to figure out who the agent is by eleven o'clock tonight, do you?"

"Maybe, maybe not," Nathan said. "But we should be able to narrow it down by then."

"You've helped us a lot, Dr. Meisner, but now it's our turn," Segonzak added.

Tina sat down beside David Nathan. "You know," she said pensively, "I think I'm starting to get a little scared."

"I know. But it's going to be all right."

Segonzak also comforted her. "Never fear, little one. We're not going to let anything happen to you — or anyone else. Isn't that right, David?"

"Of course," Nathan said. He was trying not to think about the harm that would come to Tina and Victor — and everyone else on board this magnificent vessel — if he and Segonzak failed.

There was a knock on the door. "Come in," Nathan said.

Maurice Cosset, the friendly young steward, entered the cabin carrying a flower display almost as big as he was. "Flowers for someone," he said, peering out from behind them mischievously. "Flowers for someone very pretty."

"Who in the world could you be talking about?" Victor asked innocently.

"Next time I bring flowers for you, Monsieur Jack. These are for Mademoiselle Lilly." He handed them to her with a gallant Gallic flourish.

Tina instantly brightened. "Why, thank you, Maurice. You shouldn't have."

"Oh, but I didn't, Mademoiselle Lilly." He handed her a cream-colored envelope.

Tina opened the envelope and read the card. She blushed very becomingly and handed it to Victor.

"Please accept this floral offering as a tribute to a very brave passenger," Victor read. "And please accept my apologies for the accident that made it necessary for you to display that courage," he went on. "It's signed 'Pierre Barthou, Captain.' "

"That's very sweet," Tina said, "especially considering I haven't even met him."

"Oh, it was the talk of the ship, Mademoiselle Lilly," Cosset said. "I mean, the accident. I saw the whole thing, you know. It was terrifying. But you and Herr Rothmann . . . well, you were both . . . wonderful!"

"Did you ever get an opportunity to thank Rothmann?" Victor asked.

"He disappeared before I had a chance to talk to him," Tina said, frowning. "I guess he was embarrassed or something."

"Well, you'll see him tonight at dinner," Victor said.

"Can I be of service to you in any other way?" Cosset asked.

"No, Maurice," Tina told him. "But thank you for bringing the flowers. You are very considerate."

Cosset smiled a pixie grin, then left.

"Listen, Jean-Louis and I are going to go back to his cabin

211

and do some work," Nathan said. "Why don't the two of you go to dinner without us."

Tina feigned astonishment. "What! You're letting us off the leash?"

"Just promise me you'll keep an eye on each other and come right back here after dinner."

"Of course," Victor said smoothly.

"And I'd appreciate it if you kept away from those movie types, Tina. Okay?" Nathan was doing his best to be gentle but firm, and he thought he'd hit just the right tone.

"And what would you like me to tell Karla Kirkland, Mr. Cameron?" Tina responded, smiling dangerously.

The second night in the first-class dining room was almost as glittering as the first. The men all looked the same, one tux being more or less like all the others, but the women had reappeared in entirely new plumage. The seasons are short on a transatlantic voyage.

Tina wore a flowing, sleeveless pale blue chiffon evening dress that encircled her like a second skin, displaying every perfect curve. She looked like a prettier version of Ginger Rogers, ready to be swept away by an elegant Fred Astaire. Every eye followed her as she and Victor descended the staircase and made their way to table #34.

Sitting there already were Claire and Daphne Stickney, Karla Kirkland, and Wallace Westbrook. Each was pleased to see Tina and Victor take their places.

"How are you feeling, dear?" Daphne Stickney asked Tina, suppressing her giggling for once.

"Just fine."

"Well, you certainly look lovely," Claire Stickney observed with an inoffensive little tee-hee. She and her sister were dressed in identical pink and silver moire dresses, with pink uncurled ostrich boas.

"Will David be here soon?" Karla put the question shyly

and charmingly. She was a stunning figure, in a strapless red silk crepe evening gown that emphasized her firm bosom and contrasted beautifully with her shining brown hair and creamy complexion.

"I'm afraid he's gotten himself occupied with an old fraternity friend," Tina told her.

Karla was downhearted.

"But he said to say hello and he hopes to see you tomorrow," Victor added.

"Thank you," Karla said.

"Has Mr. Rothmann been here yet?" Tina asked.

"Haven't seen him," Claire Stickney told her. "But I'm sure he'll be here soon."

"He's a very handsome young man," Daphne Stickney chimed in, flashing Tina a knowing look.

"As men go," she allowed.

Wallace Westbrook had been listening without bothering to hide it. He'd been looking forward to seeing Cameron and quizzing him again, having gotten nowhere in his shipboard inquiries about the man. But maybe this was better. Surely he ought to be able to pump some information out of this girl and her brother.

"You know, your uncle isn't with some fraternity friend," Westbrook told Tina confidentially.

"He isn't?"

"He's in conference with the captain again. I saw them together." He shook his head grimly; this was very serious business.

Victor realized the man was talking to his sister. "Who's with the captain?" he asked.

"Uncle David . . . so he says."

Westbrook baited the hook. "They were meeting about the problem."

Tina couldn't resist a nibble. "What problem?"

"You know, the same one they were talking about the other night. The one involving the ship."

"Oh," she said wisely, "that one."

"Then you know about it."

"Nope."

Westbrook tried another approach. "I know he told you to say nothing about it, but it's all right. The captain has asked my help, too."

Tina flashed him a winsome smile. "Oh, you must be talking about the leak, then."

"Yes . . . the what? Leak? What leak?"

"Why, the one on the side of the boat, of course," Victor said, joining the fun.

Westbrook's face darkened. "You think you're pretty smart, don't you? Well, I'll tell you something: I have important friends on this ship, and if there's something funny going on — and I'm sure there is — you can bet I'm going to find out about it."

Tina was disappointed. "Oh, pooh," she said. "I thought you were going to go help the captain plug the leak. With your head, maybe."

Westbrook glared at her. Then he opened his menu, sweating and furious, his heart pounding. She's going to pay for that, he told himself. I'm going to nail that uncle of hers. This afternoon, I'll radio New York and get my bulldogs working on it. I smell something here, and my nose is never wrong.

"After all, it *is* a charitable function, Mr. Heifetz," Mrs. Hearst said, selling hard.

"I would consider it a personal favor," added a dignified man with gray hair. He was Thomas Watson, president of the International Business Machine Company.

The celebrated violinist looked around the Captain's Table, at the famous and powerful faces that were studying him expectantly. He was trapped and he knew it.

"Well," he said graciously, "perhaps I could perform a few

214

short, popular pieces—a Gershwin prelude, a little bit of Brahms, maybe some Mozart."

"I do so love Jerome Kern," Mrs. Hearst told him.

"Well, yes, maybe I could play 'Make Believe,' especially for you, Mrs. Hearst."

She beamed.

"That's really very unselfish of you," Chief Purser Freppel told the violinist. "I'm sure you'll draw a big crowd, and they'll give generously."

Captain Barthou offered a little toast. "The orphaned children of French sailors salute you."

The persuasion successfully concluded, the captain's guests returned to their meals and their individual conversations.

"What were you saying about Howard Aiken?" asked Cameron Rockefeller.

Thomas Watson scowled. "I can't stand him. He's arrogant, he's stubborn, and he's temperamental. But I've decided to give him the five hundred thousand dollars he's been asking for, anyway." Watson popped a bite of steak into his mouth.

"You're giving half a million dollars to a man you detest?" Rockefeller asked, marveling. "Why in the world are you going to do that?"

Watson leaned toward him and spoke confidentially. "He and a man named Eckert are working on this immensely complicated machine they call the Automatic Sequence Controlled Calculator. My man Lake says it could revolutionize computation in both business and government. Someday, it may even replace tabulators, accounting machines, and punch card sorters."

"That would just about wipe out your business," Rockfeller observed. He downed a forkful of parsley potatoes.

Watson shook his head. "Not if we put it on the market before anyone else," he said.

A few seats down from Captain Barthou, Joseph P. Kennedy, lately the American Ambassador to Great Britain, was engaged in an intense conversation with José Ribero, the

Mexican Envoy to Germany.

"If it does come to the worst—war between England and Germany—who, in your opinion, will be the victor?" Ribero asked.

"The British are still living in the nineteenth century, Ambassador Ribero," Kennedy said. "You know, 'the sun never sets on the British empire' . . . that sort of thing. But Germany is a twentieth-century nation, with twentieth-century organization and ideas. It is vital, England is effete. It is ambitious, England is fat and lazy. I hope England doesn't pick a fight with Hitler, but if she does, I'm afraid she'll be destroyed."

"But let's say that England and Germany do go to war," the Mexican said. "Will America come to England's aid?"

"In the end, I don't think so. I think America will just sit by watch."

"It's my impression that there's a great deal of pro-English sentiment in the United States. Am I wrong?"

Kennedy snorted. "I wish you were. There are too many weak-minded sentimentalists in America, ready to do anything to save England—even go to war. Furthermore, some groups loathe Herr Hitler. I'm sure I don't have to tell you who they are. But most Americans don't give a damn about what happens in Europe, let me assure you."

"I see," Ribero said thoughtfully. "But what of President Roosevelt? He's definitely an Anglophile, isn't he?"

"Of the very worst kind," Kennedy agreed. "He's doing everything he can to drag us into war. But a presidential election is coming next year, and after that, if I have anything to do with it, Mr. Franklin Delano two-terms-is-more-than-enough Roosevelt will be out of a job."

The Mexican raised an eyebrow. "Do you have presidential ambitions of your own?"

Kennedy waited silently while a waiter put a plate of roast beef in front of him, gave Ambassador Ribero some braised sweetbreads, then went back to his tray to get more food.

"No," Kennedy said modestly. "I'm not interested in high office myself. But a group of us are thinking of asking Charles Lindbergh to make a run for it. He's spent a lot of time in Germany, you know, and he has a deep understanding of the European issue."

A messenger approached the Captain's Table with two telegrams. He handed the first one to Captain Barthou and the other to Chief Purser Freppel.

Barthou's telegram was marked "for the Captain only," in the handwriting of Rene Champeaux, the ship's chief wireless operator. This cannot be good news, the captain told himself. He finished his champagne and opened the envelope. As he read the message, his blood ran cold.

Private to Barthou:

Urgent warning! French government says its analysis of German radio signals indicates the *Normandie* is being tracked across the Atlantic by German ships. Purpose of tracking unclear. Government has issued you the following orders:

1. Put shipboard troops on highest alert
2. Immediately break off visual contact with any German vessels
3. Radio news of such contacts to Paris
4. Establish all-quarters, round-the-clock U-boat watch.

Have complete confidence in your judgment.
Good luck. Signed Henri Cangardel

Barthou folded the telegram neatly and replaced it in the envelope. He signaled to the wine steward to refill his glass. Then he looked around the table at his self-important guests, watching them conduct their business — and their pleasure — with great verve and impressive skill. How would they be

217

acting if they knew U-boats were following the ship?

Across the table from the captain, Chief Purser Freppel was intently absorbed in his own telegram. "Bad news, Henri?" Barthou asked, noticing his troubled expression.

Freppel was startled. "What? Oh, no, no. Good news. My wife tells me I am a grandfather again. I have another grandson."

"Well, that is very good news," Barthou said. "Congratulations."

"And yours?" Freppel said, pointing at the envelope.

"Not so pleasant." He handed the telegram to his chief purser. "See for yourself. And then ask the deputy captain to meet me in my quarters in fifteen minutes."

"Where do you start in the SDECE, with elimination or selection?"

"In groups under a hundred," Segonzak said, "we begin with selection. Anything larger, we eliminate first."

"Okay," Nathan said, "let's eliminate." This was the long way around, he thought, the opposite of American practice. But he liked Segonzak and didn't see the need to push him, not yet.

They studied their passenger lists for a few moments.

"Here's a category," Nathan said helpfully. "Parents with children."

"Basis?"

"No professional uses kids as a cover. Too unpredictable."

Segonzak thought a moment. "Okay, I buy that."

They went through their passenger lists, crossing out names here and there.

"My turn," the Frenchman said. "Go ahead."

"Big stars."

"But wouldn't that be an excellent cover?" Nathan suggested. "Who would suspect them?"

"It would be a good cover for someone gathering information, yes, but not for a saboteur," Segonzak replied. "Stars are noticed everywhere they go. Saboteurs need anonymity."

Nathan was convinced. "You're right. Cross out the big stars."

They studied their passenger lists again.

"Now here's a big one," Nathan said. "Everyone in tourist or third class."

"*Everyone?* What makes you say that?"

"Well, isn't it true that first-class passengers have access to the entire ship, while tourist and third-class passengers are confined to their own areas?

The Frenchman was noncommittal. "Yes, of course."

"Well, what professional would want to worry about getting caught in the wrong class? He'd demand maximum freedom of action."

"Good point," Segonzak said. He wished that some of his colleagues were as sharp as this American. "I think you're right, David. And it really helps us a lot. How many do we lose?"

"Let's see . . . three hundred thirty in third, six hundred nineteen in tourist. That leaves the seven hundred thirty-four in first class. Plus the crew, of course."

"Why of course?" Segonzak asked. *Of course* was not a phrase that had much value in police work.

"Well, it could be anyone in the crew. . . ." Nathan suddenly stopped. "Wait a minute, Jean-Louis, that's not true. The Nazis wouldn't put a first-class agent in the crew and just leave him here in place, doing nothing. He'd have to have a specific assignment."

"Isn't stealing the gold specific enough, David?"

Nathan laughed. "It sure is. But how could the Nazis know — in advance — that it would be shipped aboard the *Normandie?* Why not the *Ile de France* or some other ship?"

Segonzak thought about what the American had said. "Okay, I agree with you. The crew members aren't good suspects. It would be a waste of manpower to permanently assign a top agent to the crew. But what about the floaters . . . the journeymen who signed up for the voyage after the French government decided to ship the gold to America?"

Nathan hadn't considered that angle. His respect for Segonzak went up a notch. "When was the decision made, Jean-Louis? Do you know?"

"It was a week before we left Le Havre. I know. I was involved."

Nathan scribbled some numbers on the edge of the passenger list. "No more than a dozen crew members could have joined up that late. We'll get a list from Nadeau."

"Nadeau?" Segonzak said with distaste. "I don't know about that. The man is a real pain."

Nathan thought about it a moment. "You're right. He's a *schmuck*. We'll ask Martel."

Segonzak laughed. He liked this American, this broad-shouldered New Yorker whose directness and rough good looks reminded him of the movie actor John Garfield.

Nathan was also enjoying the give-and-take. It was almost as though he had a partner again, although except for a sense of humor, Segonzak didn't have much in common with Paddy O'Neil.

Paddy certainly wouldn't have attacked the problem the way they had. He would have spent a couple of hours in the dining room, watching everyone eat, then picked out about ten suspects—one of which, sure enough, would have been their saboteur. The man's instincts had been uncanny.

Except for once.

They'd been on the track of something pretty nasty—a federal judge who'd sold out to the mob and was about to let one of the kingpins slip away from a bribery charge.

There'd been the inevitable confrontation in the judge's chambers and the expected arrest. Then something had happened that neither of them had anticipated: The bailiff turned out to be the bagman. Nathan had missed it, and in this case, Paddy's famous sixth sense had failed him.

Anyhow, the bailiff had walked in on the arrest and started shooting. Paddy had caught one in the temple before Nathan had gotten his gun out. He'd shot the gun out of the bailiff's hand, but it had been too late for Paddy by then.

After that, for almost six years, he'd had no partners. Until now.

"Let's see," Nathan said, coming back to the subject. "That leaves us with a suspect list of about seven hundred fifty. Can we do any more eliminating?"

"Yes, I think so," the Frenchman said. "We should cross off anyone over the age of seventy and anyone less than eighteen."

"Right. We'll ask Martel about that, too. How about eliminating all the women?"

"No, no, no," Segonzak protested. "I've worked with some women who could rip off your arm and hand it to you. I once got pretty badly beaten up by a Dutch woman, a smuggler."

"Got past all the *tae kwon do* moves? How?"

"An elbow to the balls."

"Ouch."

"So let's not eliminate the women, David—at least not yet."

Nathan had a sudden chilling idea. "We haven't been considering one thing, Jean-Louis: What if the agent we're looking for is a *team* of agents?"

"That, thank God, is something I don't think we have to worry about," Segonzak said.

Nathan was skeptical. "What makes you so sure?"

"Three reasons," Segonzak replied. "First, in six years of fighting Nazi agents, I have yet to run across a single team. Characteristically, they pick the best possible man for the job and make him completely responsible."

"Yep, my experience, too. But you said three reasons."

"Second, it would be too risky to put a team aboard the ship. It would be too easy to discover. But the third reason is the clincher, I think: It's a one-man job if ever there was one. More would just get in the way."

"All right," Nathan said, "I'm convinced. But I think another Nazi agent may be on board, on a different mission entirely."

"You're thinking of the bearded man."

"Right."

"Well, David, I just don't believe Nazi intelligence could have mounted an operation quickly enough to get a man on board the *Normandie* after you escaped from Berlin. But even if they did, I think our elimination process will uncover him."

"I hope so."

There was a knock on Segonzak's door. The French agent was instantly alert. The knock was repeated. "Your dinner, sir," came a voice through the door.

Segonzak opened the door and the steward entered, pushing an elegant dinner cart ahead of him.

For a few minutes they suspended their work, while the steward turned the cart into a sparkling table for two, complete with fine china, stemware, silver, and linens. He held out a chair, first for Segonzak, then for Nathan. Then he busied himself at removing platter domes.

"The truffed terrine of *foie gras?*"

"Mine," Segonzak said.

"The pumpkins *à la maintenon?*"

"Mine also."

"The asparagus tip *salade?*"

"Right here," Segonzak said with a laugh.

"The Dom Perignon?"

Segonzak nodded again.

"And this must be yours, sir," the steward said.

"That's right," Nathan replied. "Corned beef on rye, potato *latkes* . . ."

The Frenchman shook his head sadly.

"Do you take sour cream or the applesauce with your *latkes?*" the steward asked.

"Sour cream, thanks," Nathan said. He grinned at Segonzak.

"And the root beer?"

"Guilty," Nathan said.

"The desserts are in the cold compartment, underneath. The coffee is in the pot."

"That's fine, steward," Segonzak said. "We'll serve ourselves."

"As you wish." He bowed and took his leave.

"So, Jean-Louis, how did you happen to get into this business, anyhow?" Nathan asked, taking a bite of his sandwich.

The French agent swallowed down a forkful of pumpkin. "It was an inherited position."

"Inherited? How so?"

"My father was an inspector for the Paris police—homicide division. I always knew I'd follow him into the force."

"So how did you get to Indochina and learn *tae kwon do?*"

"I served in Army intelligence for a while. They posted me to Cochin China—Phnom Penh. That was back in '26. They were having some problems with an insurgent group, the followers of the former emperor, Duy Tan."

"You joined the Paris police after you came back?"

"For a couple of years. Then the SDECE recruited me. I guess they wanted someone with experience in Southeast Asia."

Nathan nodded and took a swallow of his root beer.

"What about you, David?" Segonzak took another forkful of pumpkin. "How did you happen to get involved with this impossible profession?"

"Same way you did, I guess. My dad was also a cop—a Bronx detective. Worked in the racketeering unit."

"The Mafia? Murder, Incorporated . . . that sort of thing?"

"He went after the big-time bootleggers."

"Sounds dangerous, David."

"Dangerous? He was wounded six times, and I was kidnapped twice."

Segonzak whistled softly. "So I guess you also inherited your position."

"Not exactly." Nathan paused for another bite of corned beef sandwich. "My folks put me through law school. Columbia University."

"Oh, so you're a lawyer, are you?" Segonzak was grinning broadly now.

"Well, I passed the bar," Nathan admitted. "But, no, I never went into practice. My father convinced me to become a police lawyer."

Segonzak groaned. "They're the worst kind."

"Yeah, I know. But I got myself out of the legal department pretty quickly. They put me in charge of a unit that set up security for visiting dignitaries."

The sandy-haired Frenchman took a sip of champagne. "How in the world did you get from there to here, David?"

"It's odd the way life turns out," Nathan said, half to himself. "I got the job of setting up the security for the Governor of New York. FDR. And one day, he and I got to talking about postage stamps. Turned out we're both collectors."

A uniquely Gallic expression of amusement passed over Segonzak's face. "Somehow, I have trouble imagining you and Franklin Delano Roosevelt looking through albums of postage stamps."

"Well, that's exactly what we did," Nathan said a little defensively.

Segonzak decided to tease him a little. "So you and Mr. Governor of New York FDR became—how do you say it—buddies?"

"Yes, I guess you could say that. We ate some meals together, bought stamps for each other. Went to a couple of baseball games. He even got to know my father before he died."

"And that was when you started working for him?"

The American agent shrugged. "Wasn't much work at first—investigating some of the people he was thinking of appointing to office, tracking down a fugitive or two, baby-sitting some dignitaries, that sort of thing. Then he was elected President. Since then, he's had me traveling all over the world, doing things that couldn't be handled officially."

"What kind of things are you talking about?"

Nathan shook his head. "I'm not sure you'd believe me if I told you. He's had me up against spies, assassins, gangsters, corrupt politicians . . . you know, the scum of the earth."

"Alas, I know them only too well," Segonzak said. "I've been dealing with the same sort of citizens in the last few years. It's lots of fun."

Nathan laughed ruefully. "Oh, yes, lots."

They both paused to eat for a while.

"So, who pays you?" Segonzak asked.

"Believe it or not, the New York City Police Department. I'm on something called 'detached duty.' "

"Sounds pretty detached to me."

"Yup."

"Well, what do you think, my friend? Are we going to prevail this time?"

"We goddamn better."

"Right."

Nathan cut himself a chunk of potato *latke*, smeared some sour cream on it, and popped it into his mouth. "So tell me, Jean-Louis, why did you get yourself involved in this gold transfer operation? You seem a little overqualified for the job."

"It is pretty ridiculous, isn't it? Soldiers, for God's sake. If they hadn't bribed me, I wouldn't have done it."

"Bribed you?"

"A week in New York, expenses paid. I've never been there."

"I see."

"But what about you? Victor must be awfully valuable to your government if the President himself has sent you to get him."

"I'm sure you're right, but Roosevelt didn't share the details with me."

"Maybe the sister is the valuable one," Segonzak suggested

coyly.

"She is something, isn't she?"

The fox-faced Frenchman nodded thoughtfully. "I'm just glad that I'm happily married and I don't have to worry about such things anymore. But what about you?"

"Never got around to it."

Segonzak ate some of his asparagus. "You better watch yourself, then."

"Me?!" Nathan protested. "She's not my type."

"I see," Segonzak said, amused and skeptical. "Not your type. I should have guessed that."

Nathan just shook his head. "Well, be that as it may, what do you say we get back to business."

Segonzak was still smiling. "Of course, David. Whatever you like."

The *Normandie* thundered westward across the Atlantic, toward the New World. Up ahead, on the far horizon, the setting sun finally winked out. A moment later the stars blinked on, like thousands of tiny streetlights. Capt. Pierre Barthou stood on the starboard bridge wing, watching it all, as he had countless times before. But this time was different from all the others. This time he was frightened.

The meeting with Martel had helped some. His deputy captain, his friend and colleague, had promised to carry out all the security measures the telegram called for—the troop alert, the U-boat watch, everything. That was reassuring. He knew he could trust Martel to do the job well.

Martel had also reassured Barthou by telling him he was sure that the Germans would not be foolish enough to sink the ship "and send all that gold to the bottom of the ocean, where it would benefit no one."

All this had helped. For a while. Then he'd come out here and started to think—about Clouzot's murder, about the American agent, about Segonzak and the mysterious eleven

226

P.M. appointment, about the telegram, about the New Order in Germany.

Barthou had faced dangers before, many times, and he'd brought his ships and passengers through all of them safely: fogs and storms and groundings and engine problems and fires. But he had never before confronted war.

As he gazed out to sea, a ship slowly steamed over the horizon and came into view. She was a luxury liner, headed toward Europe, her porthole lights brilliant pinpoints against the night sea. It was a comforting sight, like logs ablaze in a fireplace on a snowy night. And it was heartening, the thought that some Americans were still willing to risk a voyage to Europe. It made him feel better.

Barthou watched the vessel draw nearer. It wasn't uncommon for two liners to pass each other at night, at least in spring and summer, and it was a lovely sight for both. But it was rare in late August, when eastbound ships usually took the southerly track toward Europe, to take advantage of the mid-Atlantic's stronger currents and winds.

Why was it then, Barthou wondered, that this liner was traveling so far north? She was certainly burning more fuel than necessary. Perhaps she was trying to avoid an unusual August storm, although that seemed unlikely, since the *Normandie* had encountered nothing but calm since she'd left England.

Barthou considered the question as the gap between the two ships steadily shrank. He wished he had his binoculars. As it was, all he could be sure of was that the other ship had two funnels. What ship was she? the captain wondered. The *Nieuw Amsterdam?* The *Mauretania?* The *Conte di Savoia?* She was fast, whoever she was.

Then he knew. He knew the identity of the ship and he knew why she had taken such a northerly route, and the knowledge took his breath away.

Pierre Barthou, Captain of the *Normandie,* was looking across the dark ocean at the onrushing Norddeutscher Lloyd express steamer *Europa*, twin sister to the *Bremen*, the powerful German liner his vessel had eluded earlier in the trip. At this very moment, if that telegram had been correct, she was radioing Berlin with news of the *Normandie*'s speed and position. Soon, a U-boat somewhere ahead of them would know exactly when to expect them.

"Okay," Nathan said, taking one last bite of his corned beef sandwich. "Any other categories of people we can eliminate?"

"I can think of one," Segonzak said. "All the passengers who booked cabins before the decision to ship the gold."

Nathan shook his head in amazement. "I can't believe I didn't think of that one myself, Jean-Louis."

"I'm sure you would have, David—if you were more accustomed to traveling on ocean liners."

"You saying I ain't got no culture?"

"I don't think a man with a glass of root beer in his hand should be asking questions like that."

Nathan grinned and put the root beer down. "Do you think anyone has that information, Jean-Louis?"

"But, of course. We French keep excellent records, although we are not quite as meticulous as our German friends, I suppose. Martel should be able to find out for us."

"And what do you think that does to our total?" Nathan asked.

"Not as much as I'd like, I imagine," Segonzak said. "In recent years, people have become notoriously late about booking their cabins."

"Why is that?"

Segonzak sighed. "It's because there's usually plenty of space on board, even if you arrive just before the ship casts off."

Nathan was puzzled. "Was it always this way?"

"The ships were always crowded in the 1920's," Segonzak explained. "Then there was the Depression. Then, Herr

228

Hitler. Tourist traffic dropped off pretty quickly after he came into power, likewise business traffic."

"But I would think that a famous ship like the *Normandie* . . ."

"Even the *Normandie*," said Segonzak. "Even on this voyage, we're three hundred short of capacity."

"Well, at least that gives us fewer people to check out."

"You're right, David . . . but more people who made reservations just before sailing time."

"So what do you think our suspect total is now?" Nathan asked.

"That depends on what we find out about the late crew hirings and passenger bookings," the Frenchman said. "But I'd guess about four hundred or so."

Nathan nodded. He was thinking along the same lines himself. "Yeah, it must be something like that. Almost too many for us to interview individually, even with Martel's help."

"I wish we had SDECE background checks on all of them."

"Yeah, or FBI."

"Of course, we could get them."

Nathan looked at Segonzak as if the Frenchman had just lost his sanity. "Get them? How?"

"By wireless," Segonzak said.

"Damn it!" Nathan exclaimed. "Why didn't *I* think of that?"

"Too much time in the field," Segonzak said generously. "Not enough time at the desk."

Nathan laughed.

Segonzak called Deputy Captain Martel and asked him to come over immediately, bringing with him the crew hiring roll and the cabin bookings chart.

"What's this all about?" Martel asked. "Can't it wait until morning?"

"I wish we had it yesterday, Marius," Segonzak replied.

Grand Admiral Raeder sat at his desk, shuffling wireless

messages and waiting. He checked his watch, then shuffled the papers again, looking through them as if he'd missed something important, which he knew he hadn't.

He looked at his watch again, then at his door, silently commanding it to open, trying to summon the message by the force of will. So much was riding on this single radi gram — his career, possibly even his life, not to mention the future of the Third Reich. But the door remained closed. He shrugged, opened his humidor, and selected a Montecristo cigar. The knock came just as he struck a match.

"Enter," said the admiral.

It was Hansel, the taller of the two blond gods who served as aides. "Wireless message, just arrived."

Somehow Raeder managed to restrain himself from tearing the paper out of Hansel's hands. Instead, he received it calmly and read it with composure, all the while his heart threatening to beat its way right through his sternum. As he had hoped and prayed, it was a message from the *Europa:*

> *Normandie* sighted at 7:13 Greenwich mean time at 45 degrees 18 minutes north latitude, 37 degrees 28 minutes west longitude. Estimated speed 28.56 knots.
>
> Klaus von Bluecher, commanding.

Raeder grinned foolishly, almost overwhelmed by his sense of elation. The message was all that he had hoped for. The *Normandie* was on course, holding at about a half hour ahead of schedule. More importantly, he could now be certain that earlier wireless reports from the *Bremen,* the tanker *Prins Willem IV,* the freighter *Waldemar Kophamel,* and the fishing trawler *Bacchus* were absolutely correct. The luxury liner he was tracking had not deviated a mile from the northern steamer track French ships had used every August since the old *La Savoi* first crossed the Atlantic in '01.

In a little more than sixty-two hours, the *Normandie* would reach the rendezvous point, exactly as he had planned, exactly as he had anticipated. In less than three days, he would be a hero of the Third Reich. What would that fat fool Goering have to say then?

But this was not the time to gloat. It was the time to strike the first blow against the French.

"Corporal, I wish the wireless room to send out a telegram."

Hansel produced a pad. "Yes, Admiral," he said, pencil ready.

"The recipient is Herr — no, *Mr.* — Simon Rothmann, on board the *Normandie*. The message is: All is well here. Don't forget to cable us when you get to New York. Sign it 'Uncle Erich.' And have it sent through Vienna."

Hansel scribbled it all down with typical Teutonic efficiency. When he finished, he looked up at his commanding officer, ready for the next order.

"Next, send a coded radiogram to Kommandant Zentner in the U-42. He should be surfacing for a communications check in about fifteen minutes. The message: Proceed as planned."

"That's all, sir . . . 'Proceed as planned'?"

"He will understand." Even if you don't, Corporal, Raeder added silently.

"Yes, sir."

"The Rothmann message should be sent the instant you leave my office, Corporal. The Zentner message should be sent in response to his communications check."

"It will be done, sir."

Hansel swiveled on his heel, as he had been taught, and strode out of Raeder's office. He passed his slightly shorter bookend, Gretel, heading for Raeder's office.

"Sir?"

"Come in, Corporal," Raeder said expansively, so pleased with himself that he was willing to treat underlings as equals, at least for a moment. "What can I do for you?"

"This has just arrived for you from Abwehr radio intelligence."

The corporal handed the admiral an envelope. Inside were

two pieces of paper, a short handwritten note and a message typed on a single sheet of onionskin. The admiral read the note. "Erich — Thought this might be of interest — Canaris." Unlikely, thought the admiral, but let's see.

He unfolded the onionskin sheet, and his euphoria suddenly turned to shock and fury. "I'll be goddamned to hell!" he said aloud.

"I beg your pardon, sir?"

"Oh, sorry, Corporal. That will be all."

He couldn't believe it. After all that careful planning, with everything happening according to plan . . . then this! The damned French government! He'd underestimated them. He'd been positive they'd never notice what he was doing, not with all the troop mobilizations and war scares. But they had — and they'd warned the *Normandie!*

Was his entire plan a shambles?

He read the message again, carefully. Troops — no problem. Break off contact with German ships — didn't matter anymore. Radio news — there wouldn't be any. U-boat watch — that wouldn't make any difference. And, of course, this was the last warning the *Normandie* would ever receive.

He took a deep breath. This wasn't so bad after all. Maybe there was nothing to worry about, as long as the *Normandie's* captain didn't exceed his orders. Yes, that was the key: So long as the captain didn't panic, so long as he didn't change course or speed, there was nothing to worry about — at least nothing more than before.

Now, if the *Normandie's* captain had been a German, there wouldn't have been any question of exceeding orders or panicking. The sort of people who acted that way never became commanders in the German merchant marine. But French ship captains were notorious for their independence and unpredictability.

Raeder opened a drawer and pulled out the *Normandie* file. He quickly found the paragraph on the ship's captain:

Captain Pierre Barthou, 63. Joined CGT at age 19 as common seaman, quickly rose in ranks. Has commanded many passenger ships on many routes, from the Channel to the Orient to South America. Has demonstrated calmness and competence in several emergency situations. Given command of *Normandie* after his ship, the *Paris,* burned at Le Havre. Considered very steady, but dull and plodding.

Dull and plodding, eh? Well, he certainly hoped so. Everything now depended on the poverty of Captain Barthou's imagination.

Maurice Cosset walked down the corridor, whistling, a spring in his step and a smile on his face, the picture of a man who'd found his life's calling and couldn't have been happier about it. In one hand he carried a small silver tray, in the other a yellow envelope. Stopping in front of the door to cabin number 235, he put the envelope on the tray and knocked.

"Who's there?" a voice said from within.

"Steward Cosset, with a radiogram for Mr. Rothmann."

The door opened a few inches and a hand reached out. Cosset looked at the hand and raised an eyebrow. Man undressed? Lady inside? He put the telegram into the outstretched hand, which then withdrew, the door closing quickly behind it. No tip. Cosset tucked the silver tray under an arm, shrugged, and continued on down the corridor.

Inside, Jaekel tore open the envelope. He was not surprised by the message; indeed, he had been expecting it, he was ready for it.

Burrowing into a side pocket of the smaller of his two suitcases, Jaekel felt around for a moment, then pulled out the pistol Admiral Raeder had given him. His father's pistol. The silencer came out of another pocket. He screwed the two of them together quickly and easily, the act of a man thoroughly familiar with handguns. Tucking the weapon into his waist-band, he listened briefly at his cabin door. When he was reasonably sure no one was in there, he opened the door, stepped out, and quickly walked down the corridor.

Jaekel was anxious to avoid being observed by other passengers, so he took a series of back stairways instead of an elevator. The Sun Deck was four flights up, but he wasn't even winded when he got there. He was in absolutely splendid condition.

When he reached the Sun Deck, he spotted a couple strolling under the stars, nuzzling each other. He quickly stepped into the shadows at the base of the *Normandie*'s middle funnel, and they walked right past him, totally unaware of his presence. They continued along the deck for a while, then found a door and went inside, evidently chilled by the night air.

Alone now, Jaekel turn his eyes toward the sky. Up above him, stretched out between the ship's second and third funnels, the radio antenna grid shimmered in the moonlight.

Jaekel fired five quick shots toward the antenna grid, none of them louder than a cough. The slender antenna wires, anchored no longer, slid off the ship and disappeared into the sea.

The initial problem had been to convince Deputy Captain Marius Martel. It wasn't easy. At first, he thought they were kidding. When they finally persuaded him they were serious, he was absolutely certain that they'd lost their minds.

So they ran through the reasoning point by point. Nathan took the first shot at it, telling him how he and Victor had arrived at the theory in the first place. Then Segonzak took over, describing his interrogation of the young scientist.

"You still haven't proved a saboteur is aboard and he intends to sink her," Martel said.

Nathan agreed. "You're absolutely right. We haven't proved it. But we have proved that it is quite possible to steal the gold and that one single agent, a skilled professional, could do the job."

"And we already know that there is such a man aboard this ship," Segonzak added.

Martel finally surrendered. "Okay, okay. So what do we do about it?"

"We figure out who the saboteur is," Nathan said. And he and his French colleague told the deputy captain what they'd accomplished so far and what they needed from him. Then they all paid a visit to the radio-telephone room.

Unfortunately, they now found themselves facing new problems — for instance, raising the night operations chief at the SDECE in Paris. No less than four different people came on the phone to ask Segonzak who he was, where he was, why he was calling, and what he wanted.

Finally, he got hold of someone he knew and he explained what he had in mind — an SDECE background check on every one of the three hundred ninety-two *Normandie* passengers in first class and the eighteen crew members who'd survived the elimination process.

Then there were more time-consuming arguments: Can't it wait until morning? What makes you suspect them? What kind of evidence do you have? What does the captain say? Aren't you exceeding your authority?

After that, someone decided that nothing at all could be done without the permission of the Director himself, who was at the opera.

"They've sent someone to the opera to talk to the director," Segonzak told Nathan and Deputy Captain Martel, who were standing by, listening to the whole thing. "I'm glad you weren't so hard to convince, Marius."

"Bureaucrats are always a problem," the deputy captain said sympathetically.

"Maybe we should have tried Washington first," Segonzak said in exasperation. "Maybe we still should."

"Not a good idea," Nathan told him. He'd had his own run-ins with the Bureau and knew that they could be at least as dense as the SDECE.

Finally, Segonzak's friend came back on the line. "The Director wasn't pleased to be interrupted," he said. "But I convinced him you were on to something."

"Many thanks."

"So why don't you give us the names?"

Segonzak read the names into the phone, with Nathan checking them off, one by one.

They'd transmitted nearly two hundred fifty names before the radio-telephone went dead.

At one moment, the surface of the sea was quiet and undisturbed, the swells gentle under the night sky. The only other object in view was the awkward bulk of the salvage ship *Otto Wunsche,* riding at anchor half a mile away.

At the next moment, there was a tiny ripple, a wake no larger or more prominent than a feather. Then an ominous shape rose beneath the feather and pushed it aside, the shape's metal sides catching the moonlight and reflecting it across the water. The phantom rolled uneasily.

"Antenna up," Zentner said.

"Up, sir," came the response.

"Send the call and ready the recorder."

The wireless operator turned a knob, activating the reels, then tapped out a signal and waited. For a moment, there was no response, then the little vessel was filled with a high-pitched squeal. The sound lasted less than five seconds.

"You have it?"

"Yes, sir."

"Then run it back at normal speed."

The wireless operator adjusted his machine, then turned it on again, the reels revolving much more slowly this time. What had been an earsplitting squeal was transformed into a coherent series of dots and dashes, which the radio man transcribed and decoded with ease. When he finished, he looked up at his captain in surprise and confusion.

"What does it say?"

"It says 'Proceed as planned'."

"That's it? Proceed as planned?"

"Yes, sir."

Horst Bibermann, the 1st watch officer and Zentner's second in command, who had watched the entire operation, was puzzled. "What does it mean?"

It was, Zentner knew, a question he was not allowed to answer, which galled him no end, since he had long followed a policy of sharing every detail of his orders with his second in command. "It means what it says . . . proceed as planned."

"And that's the message we surfaced to get?"

"It seems so."

Bibermann knew better than to argue. He changed the subject. "Kommandant, permission to open the hatch?"

"Of course."

Bibermann spun the wheel and put a shoulder to the heavy round steel door. Fresh air flooded into the hull, mixing with the dank, stale stench of the U-boat, the obnoxious mixture of sweat, grease, diesel fumes, and rotting food.

During the fifteen minutes the hatch remained open, practically every crew member on board took the opportunity to steal a few minutes to look at the stars and fill his lungs with clean, fresh air.

Zentner waited until everyone else had taken his turn, then went outside himself. When he returned, he spoke to his 1st watch officer again. "Bibermann, we will proceed on the surface until the first rays of dawn. See to it, please."

"Yes, sir."

The 1st watch officer gave the necessary commands.

They proceeded westward with one diesel full ahead, while the other recharged the U-42's exhausted batteries.

* * *

Nathan, Segonzak, and Martel walked into the captain's suite at a few minutes after eleven P.M.

"Where have you been, Marius?" Barthou asked rather sharply, his ruddy face redder than usual. He rose from his piano bench and began pacing around the suite. "We've been looking for you."

The deputy captain was taken aback by Barthou's tone of voice. Very rarely had the captain expressed any irritation toward him — toward anyone, for that matter. He seldom raised his voice.

"I was with Lieutenant Segonzak and Mr. Nathan. . . ."

"We needed you here. We have a problem."

"I know. We've been trying to solve it."

"Solve it?" Barthou was surprised, then annoyed. "You don't even know about it."

Now Martel was amazed. The captain was actually angry. "What are you talking about?"

Barthou gestured to Freppel, who handed the telegram to the deputy captain. Martel read it, shook his head in dismay, then passed it on to Nathan and Segonzak.

"That's not the worst of it," Barthou told them. "About twenty minutes ago, we crossed paths with the *Europa,* headed east."

Martel was surprised again. "What? The *Europa?* What was it doing so far north?"

"What is the *Europa?*" Nathan asked.

"A big German liner," Martel told him. "The *Bremen*'s sister ship."

"I can think of only one logical explanation for the deviation," Barthou told them. "She was looking for *us.*"

At that moment, Security Chief Nadeau burst into the captain's private suite, his uniform misbuttoned and his cap askew. "Sorry I took so long to get here, sir," he told Barthou. "I was bathing." Segonzak handed him the telegram, partly to inform him, partly to shut him up.

"We just crossed paths with the *Europa,*" Martel said after

Nadeau finished reading. "The captain believes she radioed our position to Berlin."

"I think the captain is being a little alarmist," Freppel said, "but in view of the telegram . . ."

"I don't think he's being alarmist at all," Nathan interrupted. "In fact, the situation may be worse than you think."

Barthou's eyes narrowed. "I remember now . . . you and the lieutenant wanted to see me at eleven P.M. What was that all about?"

Nathan took a deep breath. It was time to tell Barthou and the others about Victor's theory, and he didn't relish the job. But Segonzak launched into the story before Nathan could even open his mouth. He told them about the bomb, the continental shelf, the salvage ship, the winnowing down of the suspects, everything.

Barthou didn't argue. He'd seen the telegrams, he'd had a member of his crew murdered, and he'd been on the bridge when the *Europa* steamed by. He was prepared to believe the worst—and Victor's theory was merely a confirmation of what he already feared.

Security Chief Nadeau and Chief Purser Freppel didn't react the same way.

"That's just about the most preposterous idea I've ever heard," Nadeau proclaimed in his stentorian voice. "It's a ridiculous mishmash of guesswork and assumption."

For some reason, Freppel decided to play defense attorney, taking Nadeau for his client. "Where's your evidence, gentlemen? Where's your proof?"

"We don't have any actual proof," Martel said, "but we don't need—"

"Exactly," Nadeau snapped. "All you have is the airy theorizing of some spoiled intellectual, still wet behind the ears. A German, no less. And for some unknown reason, you expect us to believe him."

"Everything you've said is hearsay," Freppel put in. "Not only that, but conjecture and supposition. If I were a judge,

I'd laugh the case right out of court."

Segonzak had trouble containing his contempt for this pop-injay. "This is no courtroom, Purser. We're not debating some obscure legal point. We're talking about life and death—yours, among others."

"Who the hell are you and what do you know about this ship?" Nadeau broke in angrily. "And who asked you, anyway?"

"Bernard . . ." the captain began, intending to calm the man.

The chief purser had not concluded his opening statement. "Just as a point of order, let's remember that the company has seen fit to entrust Monsieur Nadeau with the security on this vessel. Lieutenant Segonzak is here merely to oversee the gold guard detail. And as for Mr. Nathan, well . . ." He shrugged his deprecating little shrug.

That was all the encouragement Nadeau needed. "That's right," he thundered. "*I* am the security chief on this ship—not some hoity-toity government agent from Paris who's never even gotten his hands dirty."

Perhaps unwisely, David Nathan stepped into the fray. "Listen, Bernard, if you can find a flaw in our reasoning . . ."

Nadeau's eyes narrowed. "And you . . . who the hell are you? I'll tell you what you are: You're a baby-sitter. So why don't you go back to your cabin and make sure the children are in bed?"

"That is quite enough, Bernard!" Martel said sharply. "These men are just trying to help us. . . ."

"Well, who asked them? Who needs them? And as for you, Mr. High-and-Mighty *Deputy* Captain, what do you know about police work? Have you ever caught a saboteur? Have you ever even *seen* a bomb?"

"Have you ever used your brain instead of your mouth?" Martel asked acidly.

The lanky ex-cop suddenly boiled over. He took two steps toward Martel, grabbed him by the lapels, and lifted him off

240

the floor. "Why, you stuck-up pretty-boy son of a bitch, I'll teach you to—"

"Bernard!" Captain Barthou was actually shouting—the first time anyone had ever heard him do that. "Sit down and take your hands off the deputy captain!"

Nadeau was torn between rage and duty.

"I said sit down! Now! And let Martel go!"

Nadeau shoved Martel away in disgust, the deputy captain crashing against one wall of the captain's suite. He picked himself up, shaken but unhurt.

"I said sit!"

Nadeau somehow managed to contain his fury. He plopped down on Barthou's piano bench.

"The next time you touch one of my officers," Barthou said, his ruddy face now blazing red, "I will personally throw you in the brig and toss the key into the ocean. And if you think I can't handle someone like you, just try me. Do you understand what I am saying?"

Nadeau hung his head. He was being disciplined by a superior officer. "Yes, sir. I understand, sir."

"Consider yourself on report and relieved of your duties. Mr. Martel will assume your post until the voyage is over."

Nadeau looked up at the captain with huge, wounded eyes. "I'm very sorry, sir. I didn't mean any harm to—"

"Your behavior has been absolutely inexcusable, Nadeau."

"Yes, sir, I know. But I'm only trying to protect the ship. Surely *you* don't believe this insane nonsense about a bomb?"

"Believe!" Barthou exclaimed angrily. "You're asking me what I believe? I don't know what I believe. But I am convinced there damn well *could* be a bomb . . . and a saboteur . . . and a submarine waiting to pick him up. I am convinced that this ship and everyone aboard it *could* be in the gravest possible danger, and until I am certain that is not true, I intend to act on that possibility."

Nadeau was now thoroughly deflated. And as for Freppel, he realized that his client had been convicted, and he decided not to put himself on trial as well.

"Are you all right, Marius?" Barthou was struggling to regain his composure.

"Yes, Captain. I'm fine."

"Good. Now, Bernard, I want you to go to your cabin and cool off."

"But I could help . . ."

"We'll see about that later."

Nadeau accepted his fate. "I'm sorry, sir, I truly am." He reluctantly got up and left the room.

The captain sat down on his piano bench. He was totally in control again. "Now, Lieutenant Segonzak, is that the whole story or do you have more to tell me?"

Segonzak was anxious to get back to business. "I'm afraid we have one more problem. While we were in the midst of transmitting our suspect list to the SDECE, the ship's wireless failed."

The captain blanched. "What do you mean, failed?"

"It just went dead, sir," Martel told him.

The chief purser was puzzled. "The transmission broke up?"

Segonzak described what had happened. "We were just cut off. One moment, everything was very clear. The next, we could hear no sound at all. We tried to restore the circuit several times without any luck."

Barthou turned to Deputy Captain Martel. "Marius, could you check with Champeaux? We need that radio."

"Yes, sir. Of course." Martel saluted briskly and hurried out of the room.

"All right, gentlemen," Barthou said. "Does anyone have any suggestions about saving my ship?"

The question hung in the air like a guillotine.

Nathan waited for someone, anyone, to say something. But when no one volunteered any advice, he spoke up. "I think we should immediately change our speed and course," Nathan told him.

242

"We can't do that, Mr. Nathan," the chief purser said. If we go south, we risk running into other ships, and to the north, there are icebergs. I'm sure you agree that one *Titanic* is enough."

Nathan nodded. This ocean liner business was more complicated than he realized.

"The chief purser is right about our course," Barthou put in, "but, if it would help, we could certainly alter our speed."

Now Segonzak spoke up. "It could help a lot, Captain Barthou. That way, at least we wouldn't get to the continental shelf when the Nazis expect us."

Freppel shook his head. Obviously, he disagreed completely. "That just wouldn't work. The agent would immediately radio Berlin and inform them of our new speed."

"Not if our radio is dead — which it actually appears to be," Nathan came back quickly.,

Now it was Segonzak who had an inspiration. "Even if we get the radio fixed, let's make it off-limits for all passengers."

"Good idea," Nathan said.

Barthou raised a strong, callused hand. "We were talking about changing speed. Faster or slower, gentlemen . . . your recommendations?"

Nathan had been watching the captain carefully. He was not a young man and he was no doubt set in his ways. He had just learned that his ship and all of the nearly three thousand people aboard were in terrible danger, and he had just relieved his security chief after a horrendous argument. Yet here he was, calmly asking for suggestions about saving his ship and weighing the alternatives. Would I be doing so well, Nathan wondered, if I were responsible for this ship?

Segonzak had a quick answer to Barthou's question. "We should speed up. That will get us to the continental shelf before they're set up, before they're ready for us."

"Makes sense to me, Barthou said. "Anyone disagree?"

He looked at Chief Purser Freppel, then at David Nathan.

Both shook their heads.

"Let's do it now," Nathan suggested. "The more we can alter our schedule, the better."

"I agree," Barthou said. He called the engine room and spoke quietly to Chief Engineer Gaston LeBrun for several minutes. He wasn't happy when he hung up.

"What's the matter?" Freppel asked.

"LeBrun has been having some boiler problems," Barthou said. "He promised to raise our speed to at least thirty-two knots, possibly even more, but he couldn't guarantee how long he could maintain it."

"How fast are we going now?" Nathan asked.

"Just over twenty-eight and a half knots," the captain replied.

Nathan did some mental calculations. Let's say we improve our speed by four knots an hour, he thought. That means we'd reach the continental shelf in . . . damn. Victor could have figured it out in an instant, but he didn't even know how to start. "How fast is a knot?" Nathan asked.

"It's 1.15 miles an hour," Freppel said, having answered that question for approximately 43,126 American tourists over the course of his eighteen-year career.

"So we're doing . . ."

"Just short of thirty-three miles an hour," Martel said, calculating the number in his head. "And at thirty-two and a half knots, our speed will be just over thirty-seven miles an hour."

Barthou went to his desk and spent a few moments examining a navigation chart. "We're now about 1,980 miles from the edge of the continental shelf," he said. "At our current speed, we'll be there in about 60 hours. But at 32 ½ knots, we could make it in about 53 ½ hours."

"Six hours and thirty minutes before they expect us," Nathan said. Maybe it will be enough, he thought.

It was the slender French intelligence agent who broke the spell. "Listen, gentlemen, I hate to say it, but that only solves half the problem — the easy half. We still have to catch the

244

saboteur and find the bomb. And if we don't, speed changes won't help us a bit."

The air had been filled with hope for a few minutes. Now the gloom returned full force. Barthou walked to a porthole and searched the sea, as if hoping the Atlantic would provide reassurance.

At that moment, Martel returned. "I'm sorry, my friends. More bad news. The wireless is completely dead."

"Even the emergency circuits?" Barthou asked.

"All dead. We can't receive and we can't send."

Nathan glanced at the captain, whose ruddy face was now a bit gray. For a moment, he seemed about to speak, then he apparently thought better of it. Nathan knew what he must be thinking — that nobody in Europe knew what was happening aboard the *Normandie* and nobody aboard the ship knew what might be happening in Europe. It was not a pleasant thought.

"When will it be fixed?" Segonzak asked.

Martel shrugged dejectedly. "There's no way of knowing, Jean-Louis. Champeaux doesn't even know what's wrong. Everything is working, but all we can hear is static."

"Well," Barthou said quietly, "either we save ourselves somehow, or no one will ever hear from us again."

"We're going to increase our speed, Marius," Nathan told the deputy captain. "We hope to hit the continental shelf before they're ready for us. It looks like we can gain six hours or so."

"That might help," Martel said.

Nathan looked around at his cast of characters. There was, he realized, a new player in the group: himself. Was he playing the savior or the voice of doom? He didn't know yet.

The chief purser suddenly got to his feet and began pacing. "Our change of speed isn't going to make a bit of difference, you know. They'll know exactly when we're coming."

"How will they know?" Segonzak asked.

"They're tracking us with ships — the *Bremen,* the *Europa,* and who knows what else," Freppel said. "And we can't shut

245

down their wireless sets. They'll see us and radio our position back to Germany."

Barthou nodded heavily. "Henri does have a point."

Nathan didn't like this at all. Every time we get a good idea, he thought, something turns up to make it impossible. It was frustrating. More than that, it was frightening.

"We can do one more thing," Martel said. "We can hide."

Nathan didn't have the faintest idea what the handsome deputy captain was talking about. "Hide?"

"That's right," Martel said. "Black out the ship. Cover the portholes and the windows. We'll be practically invisible, at least at night. Maybe they'd lose track of us then."

Freppel was shaking his head in disapproval. "That would terrify the passengers. The European news has them edgy and scared. A blackout will convince them we're in serious trouble."

"But we *are* in serious trouble, Henri," Barthou observed. "I know a blackout might upset the passengers, but it could also help save their lives. Would you take care of it? We need heavy curtains, maybe even some black paint."

Freppel wasn't about to contest this one. "Certainly, sir."

There was a knock on the door. "Enter," Barthou said wearily.

An assistant purser—a thin, sallow-faced fellow about twenty-two years old—came into the captain's quarters, upset and disturbed.

"What's wrong, Charette?" Martel asked.

"You asked me to report anything unusual, sir."

"That's right," Martel said. "What do you have?"

"It's a passenger, sir. He offered me a bribe."

"A bribe? What did he want from you?"

"He wanted me to give him course and speed information."

Segonzak was flabbergasted. "Are you serious? Who was it?"

"The count. You know, the one with the pretty little girlfriend."

246

"Cherbatoff," Freppel said, supplying the name.

"Yes, that's it.

Nathan and Segonzak exchanged hopeful glances. Maybe the search for the saboteur wouldn't be as hard as they thought.

"How much was he willing to pay?" Martel asked the young officer.

"Fifty francs."

Freppel snorted. "To win two or three hundred? Probably just trying to impress his paramour."

"Is Cherbatoff on your list?" Barthou asked Segonzak.

"He is indeed. David has been suspicious of him from the beginning."

"Then maybe you or Mr. Nathan should have a conversation with him."

"The problem is we have more than four hundred people on that list. We may have to question them all."

"Or at least all the ones we can't eliminate in some other way," Nathan added.

"I see," Barthou said reflectively. "Well, I want you to question as few as possible. Spend the night eliminating as many as you can. Then start your questioning in the morning."

Segonzak had his doubts. "In the morning?"

"We just can't start rousting passengers from their beds at this hour. We'll have a panic," the silver-haired captain told him.

"I think the captain is right," Freppel said.

You would, Nathan thought uncharitably. But the captain did have a point.

"Shall we meet here at seven o'clock tomorrow morning?" the captain asked. "I'll have breakfast waiting."

"That will give us about two and a half days to find the saboteur," Segonzak said. "I guess that will be time enough — if we can do it at all."

"But of course you must," Barthou said

"We will, sir," Nathan said, trying to reassure him. "I promise you." He liked this strong, stolid man. He wanted very much not to disappoint him.

"He's not coming, Tina."

"Just a little longer, Victor."

Victor sighed. "We've been here for almost two and a half hours. It's starting to get a little embarrassing."

"But nobody knows *why* we're still here."

"The Stickney sisters knew, and Karla Kirkwood."

"But they're gone."

"We should be gone, too," Victor told her.

"I suppose you're right," Tina said. She got up reluctantly, and Victor escorted her out of the dining room, which was nearly deserted.

"Good night, mademoiselle, good night, monsieur," the maitre d' said. He gave a go-ahead nod to the cleaning crew, which had been standing off to one side with their buckets and mops, waiting.

"Do you suppose they're running a movie tonight, Victor?"

"I'm sure are, but we're not going. Besides, if he didn't come for dinner, he probably won't be at the movies."

"Why must you always be so logical, Victor?"

"It's a family curse—which seems to have skipped you."

Out in the hallway, they waited for an elevator.

"Maybe he went to the Cafe Grill for dinner," Tina suggested.

"You know," Victor replied agreeably, "that's a pretty good possibility."

"So maybe we could just stop in there for a few minutes? You know, for coffee."

"Not a chance."

Tina pouted. "Why are you always so mean to me, Victor?"

"I'm not being mean, little sister. I'm just keeping my promise to David Nathan."

The elevator door opened and they got in, telling the young

red-jacketed page what deck they wanted. They were silent during the short ride. Then, as they walked down the corridor toward their stateroom, the conversation resumed.

"What's your opinion of David Nathan, Victor?"

"I dunno. What do you think of him?"

"I think he's sweet."

"Sweet? That's an odd word to use, Tina, especially after the way he's been treating you."

"What do you mean, the way he's been treating me? How has he been treating me?"

"Like a disapproving parent, I'd say."

"Oh, that's just his way. He doesn't mean anything by it. He just does it because I tease him all the time."

"So, stop teasing him."

"Stop? Oh, I couldn't do that. He likes it."

Victor sighed. "I give up."

"Seriously, Victor, what do you think of him — not as a man, I mean as a detective?"

Victor's expression grew serious. "I wasn't very impressed when we first met, Tina. But now that I've gotten to know him, I've changed my mind. He's a smart man, smarter than I thought. I like that Segonzak, too. They make a good team."

"Yes, but will they able to find the man with the bomb?"

"I think so, Tina. I hope so."

"Victor, I'm getting a little frightened."

The young scientist put his arm around his sister. "I understand. I wish I could be more reassuring."

They were at their stateroom now. Victor unlocked the door and they went in.

"I think I may not be able to sleep tonight," Tina announced.

Victor had a naughty thought. "Try dreaming about Simon Rothmann. Maybe that will help."

Tina punched her brother in the shoulder, not altogether playfully.

"Cut it out, Tina."

he punched him again.

"You're acting like a baby."

"You'd better watch what you say," she told him. "If you don't, I just might start tickling."

Victor was getting annoyed now. "Tickling? Don't you think we're both a little too old for tickling, Tina?"

"And maybe a little too old for you to constantly tease me about the men I'm attracted to," Tina shot back.

"I'm just being protective," Victor protested.

"You're being a pain in the ass, Victor."

"I'm sorry," he said sincerely. "I really don't have anything against Rothmann. If you're interested in him, I wish you well — although he doesn't seem to return your interest."

Tina sat up on her bed, cross-legged. She was suddenly perplexed. "I know. And it bothers me. I just can't understand why he's avoiding me."

"I doubt he's avoiding you. He's probably just a little embarrassed. Or maybe he's a little intimidated by you. A lot of men are, you know."

"I don't think that's it," Tina said. "He had all the confidence in the world yesterday, when I fell."

"That was an act of genuine heroism," Victor reflected.

"It certainly was," Tina said, remembering the strong arms. "I want to thank him."

"Of course. I understand."

"He's such a tragic figure, you know." Tina said.

"Yes, and so handsome."

"I suppose so." There was a note of warning in her voice.

"Needs comforting, I'd say," Victor went on, undaunted.

Tina swung a fist toward Victor's shoulder, but this time he sidestepped the blow.

Day Five

MORNING

Barthou was on the bridge by six A.M., as usual, peering out to sea, getting a feel for the day ahead. He didn't like what he saw. It was gray and threatening, more like October than August. The seas were a little rough and getting worse. We're heading toward a major thunderstorm, Barthou thought—and in more ways than one.

"Captain?"

Barthou turned to find Rene Champeaux, the chief wireless operator, standing at his elbow. "Yes, Rene. Have you discovered the source of the problem?"

"I have, Captain," the tall young man said. "It's the ship's antenna grid. It's gone."

"Gone?" Barthou was dumbfounded. "That can't be."

"Nevertheless it is, sir. Not a single wire is left."

"I don't understand," Barthou said blankly.

"Neither do I, sir. I mean, we have a wire snap from time to time, usually because of salt water corrosion. But I've never seen anything like this."

"Corrosion? That's what caused the problem?"

"No, sir, I don't think so. I haven't climbed up to see, but I have examined the mountings with binoculars. The anchor cables have been severed."

Barthou had a sinking feeling in his heart. Ever since he'd gotten up, he'd been trying to dismiss the threat to his ship as the fantasy of two intelligence agents overreacting— understandably—to their weighty responsibilities. He had half convinced himself, until this. "What do you mean, severed?"

"Well, from what I can see," the chief wireless operator said, "all five anchor points are cleanly broken."

"What could do that?"

"I don't know, sir. A blow from an axe?"

"How could someone with an axe get up that high?"

The wireless operator shrugged. "Maybe someone shot off the antenna."

Barthou immediately thought of von Stroheim and the rifles in the skeet shooting gallery. Could he be the agent they were looking for? That didn't seem very likely, and yet . . . and yet he'd bring it up at the meeting this morning. "Can the antenna be fixed, Rene?"

"Of course, but not at sea. We don't carry spare antenna cable. Even if we did, mounting it high on the stacks—in mid-ocean, at twenty-eight knots or so—would be a difficult and dangerous business."

"See if you can rig something, Rene. It's essential that we regain contact with Paris. It's a matter of the ship's safety."

Champeaux was startled. "The safety of the ship?"

Barthou sighed deeply. "I'm afraid so, Rene."

The wireless operator did not ask the captain what he meant. That would have been presumptuous. Besides, he knew his duty. "I will do my best, sir."

"I know you will."

* * *

Hans Hatzfeld listened at his door. It was imperative that he not be seen—especially by a crew member. That's why he'd arisen at six-thirty A.M. Hearing no one, he opened the door quickly, slipped out into the corridor, and disappeared into a nearby stairway.

Three flights down, Hatzfeld repeated his precautions. He could hear a vacuum cleaner in the distance and the tinkle of a meal cart being trundled down a corridor, but no one was in view. He darted across the hall into the radio-telephone room.

Hatzfeld quickly closed the door behind him and blocked it with a chair. Then he checked his watch—he was three minutes early. Klaus might already be there, but it was better not to take any chances. He didn't dare make one more call than he had to, not since he'd almost been recognized. He had to be extraordinarily cautious now.

It took what seemed like a half hour for the three minutes to pass. Then, finally, it was time. In a matter of moments, he'd have the vital information he needed, the information he didn't have time to get in the rush to board the ship.

Hatzfeld picked up the radio-telephone receiver. Nothing. He clicked the hook a few times but nothing happened, nothing at all. Was it possible that the ship's radio-telephone operators were not yet on duty? No, he knew better. The system was automatic. He hung up the receiver, waited a few moments, and tried again. Still nothing.

What would Klaus be thinking now? Would he conclude he'd been abandoned? Would he think Hatzfeld had been caught? Hatzfeld looked at his watch. Five minutes after. Klaus would be gone by now; he never lingered—that was the procedure—and it had saved them both more times than he cared to remember. Still, he had to try one last time. He lifted the receiver and waited. Nothing, not even static. This was something they hadn't anticipated, something they hadn't planned for. He would be completely on his own now.

Someone rattled the door. . . . God, that was all he needed. But at least he hadn't been overheard talking to Klaus. He pulled the chair away from the door and opened it. A man was standing there, and Hatzfeld recognized him immediately. It was the bantamweight American newspaper reporter, Westbrook.

"Why was the door locked?" Westbrook said, annoyed.

"Stuck, not locked. I had the same problem."

"Yeah, well, excuse me, I have to make a call."

"It's not working," Hatzfeld said.

"Whadda you mean, not working. It was working fine yesterday."

Hatzfeld just shook his head. "Your guess is as good as mine. It's just . . . I don't know, dead."

"I can't believe it, the radio-telephone out of order at a time like this," Westbrook said, working toward a tantrum. "The captain's gonna hear about this, you can bet on that."

"It isn't *my* fault, you know," Hatzfeld said.

Westbrook was confused for a moment. "No, of course not. But it's someone's fault, and he's going to answer for it." Then he had a sudden thought: Could it be that the radio had been shut down so he couldn't make inquiries about Cameron? Could the meeting have been *that* important?

"Fine by me," Hatzfeld said, but Westbrook was already storming away, murder in his eye.

Chief Purser Freppel looked out at his illustrious audience and smiled his most engaging smile. "Ladies and gentlemen," he began, "I want first of all to thank you for joining me here in the Winter Garden at the ungodly hour of eight-thirty A.M. Many of you, I know, have not had a full night's sleep. Some of you haven't slept at all — and those people have my greatest admiration."

The audience tittered mildly.

"But you all know me very well and I think you know that I wouldn't have summoned you to this meeting—and risked my gratuities for this entire voyage—for any trivial reason."

This time, the laughter was a little more spirited. Freppel acknowledged it with his famous little shrug.

"I've convened this assembly," he went on in high good humor, "because I need your help. I know that sounds truly incredible, the chief purser of the *Normandie* needing help from his passengers, but it is, alas, the truth."

Freppel paused for effect. His audience, he was happy to see, was pleasantly attentive and interested, just as he had expected. He was, he had to admit, very skilled at handling people, either singly or in groups.

"With your kind permission," he went on, eyes twinkling, "I wish to introduce the man who will explain exactly what I mean. He is a very old and dear friend of mine, Inspector Jean-Louis, of the Paris police, detective *extraordinaire.*"

There was a smattering of applause, mingled with whispers of confusion and concern. Freppel yielded the stool on which he'd been standing to Lieutenant Segonzak.

"Good morning, ladies and gentlemen," Segonzak began in a cheery voice. "Of course, it is not the chief purser who needs your assistance, it is I. Or, rather, it is the greatest museum in all of the world, the Louvre."

Segonzak paused and studied the faces before him. There were about fifty in all. A number were instantly recognizable—the movie stars and performing artists.

Then there were those whose faces were unfamiliar to him but whose names he knew, people Freppel told him he was inviting: the President of IBM, the Grand Duchess Marie, Mrs. William Randolph Hearst, the writer Ludwig Bemelmans, Walter P. Chrysler, and Carl Loeb, among others.

And, he knew, there were still more whose names would

have meant nothing to him, although Freppel had insisted they were—or had been—Persons of Consequence, sometimes considerable consequence, with wide circles of acquaintances.

All the people in this room had been selected because they were personally known to Chief Purser Henri Freppel, who had served them on at least one other voyage and could testify that they were, without question, exactly who they said they were. They had been summoned here as a result of the staff meeting in the captain's quarters earlier that morning, to help narrow the field of sabotage suspects—a fact that he was now about to hide from them.

"On Monday morning, when the guards opened the doors of the Louvre, they discovered that one of the world's most famous antiquities had been stolen." Segonzak stopped for a moment, to let his words sink in. "It is an object which you have all, no doubt, seen and admired for yourselves—the incomparable *Tablet Of Urnansche,* from ancient Ur. It dates back to 2630 B.C., and it is one of the greatest treasures of ancient times."

Segonzak was gratified by his audience's expressions of shock and disbelief, whether genuine or pretended. Three quarters of them, he was sure, had never heard of the *Tablet of Urnansche,* but no matter. The stolen artifact had been a far better idea than the bank theft idea or the escaped political assassin. It was a surprising and somewhat disturbing event, but it was certainly not frightening. Art thieves might be dastardly criminals, but they were rarely dangerous.

"I know that museum," Edward G. Robinson said, appalled. "And I know how well guarded it is. How could the tablet have been stolen?"

"We suspect collusion," Segonzak told him. "But, of course, that is not why I am here. I am on board the *Normandie* because I have tracked the criminal to this very ship."

There were gasps from the audience. "Surely you do not suspect any of us," said Lilly Daché, the clothing designer. "Many of us collect art, but we do not steal it. We just try to buy it cheaply."

Segonzak chuckled along with everyone else. "Of course I do not suspect any of the people in this room. That, in fact, is why you are here. The chief purser has told me he personally knows and trusts every one of you. But I have reason to believe that the thief is on this ship, traveling in first class, using a false name."

Segonzak watched his audience very carefully. Here was the critical moment. Either they would believe his story and lend their assistance, or they would guess the ship had a serious problem, and spread rumors and fear.

A matronly lady near one of the bird cages raised a hand, and Segonzak nodded in her direction. "I'm Mrs. William Randolph Hearst," she said. "Could you tell us why there's been no word of this theft in the newspapers? I mean, for heaven's sake, the *Tablet of Urnansche!* Wouldn't the people who visited the Louvre on Monday have noticed that it was missing?"

Damn, Segonzak thought. Well, here we go. "What they saw was a sign apologizing for the fact that the *Tablet of Urnansche* was on loan to the Prado, madam. But, of course, you are right. We cannot expect to keep this theft secret much longer. That's why we must act quickly. In fact, that's why I had the chief purser arrange this early meeting."

"I don't . . . uh . . . see what we can do to help," said Jimmy Stewart, "but . . . uh . . . I'd sure be willing to do whatever I can, so long as you don't . . . uh . . . make me go back to the Louvre again. My feet are still hurting from last time."

Whatever tension there had been instantly disappeared in an outburst of laughter.

"What we need from all of you is really very simple,"

257

Segonzak said after the merriment had died down. "We need you to help us narrow our suspect list. We'd like you to identify every first-class passenger you know personally, and not just from this trip."

"What, exactly, do you mean *know*, darling?" Marlene Dietrich asked slyly.

Segonzak ignored the innuendo. "What we're looking for is someone who isn't who he says he is. So if any one of you knows someone—for sure—and that person is traveling under his right name, we can cross that name off our suspect list."

"Man or woman, darling?" Dietrich inquired.

"Since when has it mattered to you?" came a voice from the crowd.

Once more, the room dissolved in laughter. Segonzak waited until it had subsided. "It could be either a man or a woman." His remark provoked a new outburst of mirth.

"I mean—" Segonzak began, when he could be heard again.

"It's all right, darling," Dietrich interjected in that familiar, insinuating accent. "All of us know what you mean."

"Anyhow, we're going to give each of you a copy of the first-class passenger list," Segonzak went on. "Please circle the names of everyone you know—personally—and initial the circles. If you're not absolutely positive, or if it's someone you've just met, please don't circle the name. Is this all right with everyone?" He looked at his audience expectantly.

"As I always say, I'm happy to cooperate with the cops," said George Raft, playacting the gangster's role.

Sensing general agreement in the room, Segonzak glanced over at Freppel, who signaled to a pair of pages. The pages passed through the group, handing out copies of the passenger list, noting the names of the recipients, and distributing pens and pencils. Soon, the celebrities were soberly pouring over their lists and marking them up with great care.

"One more thing," Segonzak said. "As part of our effort to find this unspeakable felon, this crook, we are going to conduct a general search of the ship."

A man sitting near one of the Winter Garden's burbling fountains got to his feet. He was an Indian gentlemen, attired in classic Hindu robes. "Excuse me, sir," he said. "Does that mean you or your men intend to examine *our* quarters?"

Freppel was ready for this one. "Not only your quarters, but your luggage, Maharajah. There's no telling where the perpetrator may have hidden the *Tablet of Urnansche*. It could even be in your steamer trunk, Highness."

"In my steamer trunk!"

"But let me assure you, if that is the case, you will not be implicated in the theft. You will have played a part in the recovery of one of our greatest national treasures."

"Listen, is there any reward in this?" George Raft asked. "I mean, maybe I could help you search."

"The reward," Freppel said haughtily, "will be to see that the *Tablet of Urnansche* is returned to its rightful place on the first floor of our wonderful Louvre."

"Of course, buddy," Raft said. "And that'd be enough reward for any of us. Right, guys?"

At that moment, shouting erupted in the hallway outside of the Winter Garden, and despite the guards Freppel had posted at the doors, a man burst into the room. It was Wallace Westbrook, Jr.

"Well, whadda ya know," he said to Freppel. "I finally tracked you down."

"I'm sorry, Mr. Westbrook, you were looking for me?" Butter would not have melted in Freppel's mouth.

"Damn right!" Westbrook looked around the room, and his eyes narrowed. "What's going on here, anyhow? Another meeting."

"It's a private party, Mr. Westbrook," Freppel said

smoothly. "How can I help you?"

"Whadda ya mean, a private party? This early in the morning? Where's the champagne? Where's the crackers and cheese — excuse me, the crackers and caviar?"

Before either Freppel or Segonzak could answer, a formidable-looking woman in her late sixties rose from her seat near the forward windows. The ocean was visible behind her.

"Young man," she said with undisguised disdain, "do you know who I am?"

"Sorry, lady. The face isn't familiar."

"I am pleased. I have never wished to have a familiar face, or at least a face that would be familiar to you. But I will tell you who I am. I am the Grand Duchess Marie, and these ladies and gentlemen are my friends. They are here to honor me on my sixty-ninth birthday."

"A birthday party at eight A.M.? Without a cake?"

"I've been an early riser since my youth, as if it's any business of yours," the woman said. "The Czar's entire household rose at six-thirty. It is a good habit. I recommend it to you. As for the missing cake, you have merely had the misfortune to arrive in advance of the refreshments. You have also had the misfortune not to be invited at all. I trust I am making myself clear."

"Okay, lady. I hear you and I'm leaving. But I got a question first for Freppel here."

"Yes, sir," the chief purser said with enough civility to freeze the Red Sea. "How can I be of service?"

"You can tell me what the hell is wrong with the wireless," Westbrook demanded.

"Beg pardon?"

"The radio-telephone is dead," Westbrook went on. "Why is that? And when will it be fixed?"

"A simple malfunction, I'm sure. I'll report it to the main wireless room."

"I've already reported it to the wireless room. They told

260

me to see you."

"Their standing instructions are to refer all passenger complaints to me, Mr. Westbrook. But all I can tell you is that we've had a wireless malfunction and that it's being repaired right now. Shall I have you notified when the equipment is working again?"

"Damn right. I have important questions to ask my research staff, if you know what I mean." He looked at Freppel as though he knew the man had an important secret and he wasn't going to rest until he discovered what it was.

Freppel merely shrugged his celebrated shrug.

The first thought was to use the troops guarding the gold to search the ship. After all, they were sitting around, essentially doing nothing. But that idea proved impractical for several reasons.

First, the detail was under fixed orders never to leave its assigned position for any reason. Second, it was completely unfamiliar with the ship and its thousands of nooks and crannies. The third and deciding reason: Practically every man in the detail had been seasick from the moment the *Normandie* left port.

"Believe me, it wasn't my idea to bring them on board," Segonzak told Martel. "But it's government regulations. Whenever substantial quantities of gold are moved, armed guards must go along."

"So what good are seasick troops?" Martel asked.

Segonzak considered the question. "Well," he said finally, "if Captain Kidd stopped us in mid-ocean and his men tried to board us, they might be able to repel the boarding party."

Eventually, they decided to leave the search to men who knew the ship. Altogether they selected seventy-five crew members, all trusted senior staff: junior officers, departmental supervisors (baggage, cargo, plumbing, electrical, mechanical, engine room, carpentry, etc.), first-class stewards, tourist and third-class stewards, and assistant pursers.

At Martel's suggestion, the men were assembled in the steward's common room, in the ship's peak on D Deck, where they probably wouldn't be noticed, even by the other crew members. When everyone was present, Martel gave them the pitch about the missing work of art and the search, Nathan and Victor looking on.

A few of the men were interested, and many were willing to cooperate. But there was plenty of grumbling, too, a lot more than Nathan would have preferred. Motivating these people was going to be a problem, he realized.

"Are you absolutely sure this thing is on the ship?" one of the supervisors asked.

"As sure as we are that *you're* on the ship," Deputy Captain Martel told him.

"What about our regular work?" asked one of the assistant pursers.

"You'll have to do it, of course," Martel replied.

"In addition to searching the area you've assigned to us?"

"That's right."

A few of the men started to protest.

"Of course, the man who finds the tablet will get a month's bonus," Martel added.

One of the chief electricians spoke up. "That means we have one chance out of seventy-five of making a few extra francs out of this."

Martel sighed. "And the rest of you will all get fifty francs extra in your pay envelope—unless the object isn't found at all."

There were murmurs of approval now.

"And we'll have a party in the crew quarters afterward—with free beer for everyone."

"Now you're talking," said one of the chief mechanics.

"How big is this thing, this tablet?" one of the security men asked, getting back to business.

Martel gestured toward Victor Meisner, who was wearing a dark business suit, complete with vest. "This is the famous art historian, Dr. Sigfried Krakow. He can tell you all about the piece."

"It's hard to say exactly how big the package will be," Victor told him. "The object itself is approximately a foot and a half square. Depending on how it's packed, however, it could be quite a bit larger."

"Well, then, how heavy is it?" The question came from one of the senior stewards.

"That also depends on how the tablet is packed," Victor said. "But it will weigh at least one hundred pounds—maybe much more."

Martel looked at Nathan. "Gentlemen, this is David Cameron, of Continental Insurance. His firm is responsible for the piece. Do you have anything to add, Mr. Cameron?"

Nathan addressed the group. "I just wanted to say that the piece could be packed in a wooden crate, or maybe a wooden box with a rope handle." He was thinking about his bearded man.

"Why would it be crated?" the carpentry supervisor asked.

"Because it could break so easily," Nathan told him. "It's quite fragile." What he really wanted to say—but what they knew they could not tell the men—was that the package might be booby-trapped.

"That's correct," Victor said. "Because of its age, it's very, very fragile. But it's also very heavy, since it's made of solid limestone."

"So what do we do when we find it?" a security man asked.

"You don't pick it up. You don't even touch it," Nathan told him. "We don't want it damaged. Whoever finds it calls the deputy captain, and he calls me. Everybody got that?"

Toward the back of the room, a steward stood up. "What

do I say if I'm searching a cabin and its occupants return?"

"You tell them the truth," Martel replied. "You tell them that a shipwide search is being conducted for a stolen art treasure. If that's not enough, ask the passenger to check with the deputy captain or the chief purser."

"What if we find something that might be the thing, but we're not sure?" The question came from a burly mechanic in the front row.

"You still don't touch it, and you call us anyhow. I won't care if you're wrong—I'll admire your initiative." Somehow, someone had to rouse these fellows, Nathan thought. He wanted them to do their damndest to find the thing. That was their only chance. But he couldn't be the one to deliver the pep talk.

Deputy Captain Martel rose to address the men, as if he'd been reading Nathan's mind. "Gentlemen, I know you have more than enough work to do without spending your time searching for a stolen art treasure. I am as annoyed as you are. But the bastard who stole this treasure has seen fit to involve the *Normandie* in his evil deed. If we do not find the tablet, our good name will be smeared. But if we do find it, if we rescue this treasure from the hands of the son of a bitch who stole it, we will all be heroes."

"And what good is that?" a man in the back called out.

"What good is being a hero?" Martel repeated thoughtfully. "That's a very good question, my friend. The way I see it, there are three benefits.

"First, there's the actual result. Something good happens. In this case, the treasure gets returned to the Louvre and the thief is punished. Second, there's the recognition. Heroes get their pictures in the paper. Heroes' names are mentioned with respect."

"I don't mind the picture in the paper," an engine room mechanic called out. "But what good is the respect going to do me?"

"Maybe it will make your girlfriend forget how dumb you

are," another man said.

Martel waited until the laughter had subsided. "Actually, what he said is true, you know. When you're a hero, that makes up for a lot."

"You'd better be the one to find the thief, Giraud," one of the stewards said to a friend. "You've got a hell of a lot to make up for."

Once more, Martel waited until the laughter had died down. "There's one more thing about being a hero," he said. "When you do something heroic, you feel big inside. Just think about it. Hundreds of policeman have been chasing this crook across the French countryside and they haven't been able to catch him. He's slipped by all kinds of big shot cops. Just think of how you'll feel if you're the one to put the finger on him."

The room was silent for a moment as the men considered Martel's words.

"And just think about how your girlfriend will feel about you," Nathan said.

"Jesus Christ," the chief carpenter said, "if finding this thing can do anything to warm up Olga, lead me to it."

His remarks provoked an outburst of catcalls and hooting, which Martel let continue for a while. Then he put a hand up.

"All right, men, you have your assigned areas. Let's search the ship like it's never been searched before. Let's find this thing and make ourselves some money — and some fame. Let's show that bastard what it means to try to take advantage of the *Normandie!* Go to it!"

The men roared out their approval and pored out of the room like sharks scenting blood.

The captain sat at his piano, playing Liszt's "Hungarian Rhapsody #12." Meanwhile, Segonzak and Nathan poured over the passenger lists provided by the people at Freppel's meeting, transferring the information to their own master list. The chief purser sat at the dining room table, listening to the music and the conversation.

"That's it," Segonzak said, putting the last of the passenger lists on the pile on top of Barthou's piano.

Then, everyone waited for the captain to conclude the piece, which he did in short order. "All right," he said, looking at Segonzak, "how many do we have left?"

Segonzak counted up the names. "By my count, one hundred and fifty-seven."

The chief purser was pleased. "That's better than we expected. We managed to cut the list by more than half."

"Including Salvatore Barzinni — one of my best suspects," Nathan said ruefully.

"When do you begin the questioning?" the captain asked.

"We begin immediately," Segonzak told him.

"If you like, you can conduct the questioning right here, in my quarters."

Nathan was pleased. "That's a good idea."

"I agree," Segonzak said. "It takes them away from the security of their own rooms, and it adds the captain's authority to the proceedings. Could you bring us the people, Purser, one by one, say every fifteen minutes or so?"

"Of course."

"That's fine," Nathan said. "About one every fifteen minutes."

"Let's do it alphabetically," Nathan suggested, looking at his list. "Beginning with Samuel Abrahamson."

"I'll find him and bring him to you," Freppel said.

Barthou waited until Freppel had left the captain's suite. "I'm worried about time. Are you going to have enough time to interview everyone on the list? Do you want me to help . . . or Martel? Maybe even Nadeau could be useful."

Segonzak shook his head. "I think we'd better handle it, sir. We both know what we're looking for."

Barthou understood.

"You know, the first person we talk to could turn out to be our man," Nathan added.

"You feel fairly sure of finding him, then?" the captain asked.

Segonzak put a reassuring hand on the man's shoulder. "I think we have an excellent chance."

"Well, I am depending on you. We all are."

Deputy Captain Martel suddenly burst into the room. "Captain . . . problem on the bridge."

"Coming." Barthou slipped on his uniform jacket and went after Martel, who was already heading forward. "Good luck, gentlemen."

David Nathan and Lt. Jean-Louis Segonzak were alone in the captain's quarters now.

"How do you want to handle this?"

"Oh, it doesn't matter," Nathan replied absently. "You be the good guy, I'll be the bastard for a while, then we'll switch."

Nathan's mind wasn't really focused on the interrogation process, which he knew as well as any man alive. He was struggling with his doubts. It was a struggle that so often plagued him at this stage of the game, a struggle between ego and id that weakened him and made his work even harder than it was.

Have we been working too fast, too carelessly? he asked himself. Maybe the guy has slipped through our fingers somehow. Maybe our assumptions about tourist and third-class passengers—and even about the crew—are all wrong. Maybe I should be worrying more about protecting Victor and less about protecting the ship.

The more he struggled with his doubts, the stronger they got. This, too, was part of the pattern. Maybe the whole thing is the product of our overheated imaginations. Maybe all we're really doing is scaring ourselves out of our wits. Or maybe we're absolutely right about the bomb but we'll never find it, even if we somehow manage to identify the

Nazi agent.

"Thinking?" Segonzak asked.

"Yeah."

"About whether our man is on the list?"

"Yeah, about that. And some other things."

Segonzak sighed sympathetically. "It is — how do you Americans say it — an occupational disease."

Nathan managed a halfhearted smile. "Guess you're right."

There was a knock on the door.

"Come in," Segonzak called.

Freppel entered, accompanying a stout, balding man in his mid-fifties. "Gentlemen, this is Samuel Abrahamson."

The captain caught up with his deputy. "What's the emergency, Martel?"

"Maybe it's nothing, sir, but a crew member claims he saw something off the port bow."

"Something? What?"

"He says it was a periscope."

"Oh, God. Well, let's have a look."

The captain walked through the navigating bridge, glancing out toward the ocean. They were much closer to the storm now. The seas were starting to pick up, and spray was crashing against the *Normandie*'s forepeak and pounding the bridge windows.

The captain took his accustomed position on the bridge, steadied his feet against the ship's increasing pitching and rolling, and peered forward, through one of the Kent Clear-View Screens. Its thirteen-inch glass disk, driven at high speed like a phonograph record, threw off the ocean spray as it hit, providing him with a blur-free look at the sea.

He saw nothing but foamy wave tops and glassy troughs. If there is a submarine out there at periscope depth, he told himself, every member of the crew must be thoroughly sea-sick. "I don't see anything," he told Martel.

"Me neither, Captain, but a crew member swears he did."

"Which crew member?"

"One of the deck machinery boys, an old-timer."

The captain took a deep breath and let it out slowly. "Okay, I guess we can't take any chances. Put the radio detection equipment into operation and keep a man at the listening gear until we reach New York's outer harbor."

Here was their one advantage, Barthou thought. It was something that even Nazi intelligence, in all likelihood, knew nothing about: The *Normandie* was the first Atlantic passenger liner to be equipped with a radio detection device. A transmitter on the ship's bridge sent low-band radio waves out to sea in all directions. If the radio waves encountered a solid object, they bounced back toward the *Normandie*, where they were picked up by a receiving antenna adjacent to the transmitter. These signals were sent down to telephonelike listening gear on the bridge, where they registered as a series of clicks. In tests, this equipment had demonstrated it could detect a floating ten-foot log at a distance of up to four miles. Its only shortcoming—and it wasn't all that serious—was that it could not pinpoint the precise direction of the returning signal.

"Yes, sir," Martel said. "I'll put Lieutenant Lebarre on it."

"Any word from the searchers yet, Marius?"

"Not yet. They're just starting to spread out and begin looking. How about Lieutenant Segonzak and the American?"

"They're just beginning to question people."

Martel paused a moment, apparently reluctant to bring up what was really bothering him. The captain looked at him expectantly, until the young man finally spoke his piece.

"Do you think they'll find the saboteur, Captain?"

"I think they're both excellent men, Marius. I think if

anyone can do it, they can."

Martel nodded thoughtfully. "Do you think there *is* a saboteur? Are we really in danger or is this just—"

"Imagination? I've been asking myself that question again and again ever since I heard Victor Meisner's theory. I just don't know. It is both completely preposterous and completely logical. But we simply cannot afford to assume Meisner is wrong."

On the upper deck, not far from the *Normandie*'s little shopping center—which included the hair-dressing salons, a bookstore, a florist's shop, and a novelty shop that sold postcards and souvenirs—was the ship's printing plant.

Normally, the printing plant turned out menus, race card programs, entertainment schedules, and the ship's daily newspaper. On this day, however, there was no newspaper, because there was no radio communication with Europe or America.

If there had been an edition for Friday, August 25, 1939, however, it would have contained a number of troubling items.

In Poland, one and a half million men had been called to arms. And the Polish government had accepted Roosevelt's plea for direct negotiations with Germany.

In Germany, Hitler had demanded the unconditional return of Danzig before he would attend any parley.

In Britain, Parliament had rushed through a bill conferring emergency powers on the Prime Minister. Preparations for a blackout of London were now under way.

In France, Premier Daladier had announced that he was forming a national government to deal with the crisis. French authorities had confirmed that one and a half million soldiers had been mobilized and were standing guard along the Franco-German border from the North Sea to the Mediterranean. The concrete fortresses of the Maginot

Line, it was said, were fully manned and operational.

Not all the news, of course, would have related to the instabilities of Europe. The ship's paper no doubt would have carried the news that mobster Louis Lekpe had surrendered directly to FBI Director J. Edgar Hoover last night, after an intensive manhunt.

It might also have noted that the league-leading New York Yankees had won their fifth straight, beating the St. Louis Browns 11–5, with Joltin' Joe DiMaggio getting three singles in five at bats, raising his batting average, the best in either circuit, to an even .400.

But the passengers learned none of this. Cut off from the news, they were forced to imagine what must be happening on the Continent and elsewhere. And what they imagined scared them half to death.

AFTERNOON

Maurice Cosset knocked politely at the door of 233. As he had expected, no one answered him. He turned the key in the lock, stepped inside, and flipped on the lights. He found a large steamer trunk in the vestibule and three suitcases in the closet. No strange boxes, no suspicious packages.

Feeling a little like a customs inspector, Cosset opened the drawers of the steamer trunk and inspected their contents, then felt through the clothing in the hanging compartment. Nothing unusual here. Next, he fumbled around in the suitcases, checking the corners as he'd seen the customs agents do, feeling for false bottoms or hidden pockets. Just ordinary suitcases, full of ordinary clothing.

It was the eighth cabin he'd checked out of the fifty he'd been assigned to, and it was the eighth time he hadn't found a thing. No, that wasn't exactly true. He'd found quite a lot: lingerie, syringes, bags of gold coins, a military sword in a scabbard, several sets of elevator shoes, a number of objects whose purpose he could not divine, and some photographs that made him blush.

Cosset wasn't comfortable with what he was doing. He enjoyed helping all the beautiful passengers, assisting them as they selected their outfits, bringing them food and drink, comforting them when, inevitably, they were afflicted with *mal de mer,* answering their questions . . . *serving* them in every way he could, with a smile and a happy thought. But he did not like pawing through their dirty laundry, even in hopes of catching a thief.

He backed out of 233, locking the door behind him, and knocked on the door of 235.

Jaekel had decided to delay going back down to the cargo hold to move the automobile. He wanted to let them puzzle over the cargo supervisor's body and give them a chance to let down their guard. Then, when the time was right, when the time *felt* right, he'd take care of the motor car.

Meanwhile, he would spend his time in his cabin. At least that had been his intention. But, in the end, Jaekel hadn't been able to stand being cooped up so long. He'd taken dinner in his cabin, spent the evening there, slept there, then eaten breakfast there.

Now he was almost unbearably restless. He needed physical activity of some kind. Where could he go, yet stay out of the public eye? According to his map of the ship, there was one place that would satisfy both needs—the gymnasium, on D Deck. Few passengers would be there, he was sure. For the great majority of them, exercise was too much like work.

He slipped on the baggy athletic trousers and white V-neck sweater he'd found in his luggage—a striking change from the elegant blue blazer he'd worn the day before, when he'd rescued the girl—and took a back stairway down to the gym, running into few passengers and fewer crewmen.

The place was surprisingly large and well equipped, considering it was on a ship. It contained a leather-covered pommel horse, a set of parallel bars, a large rowing machine mounted on a cushioned table, a set of weights attached to the wall by cables, and several barbells.

In addition, a wall rack contained pairs of foils, épées, and sabers. Hanging from the ceiling were a set of rings and two punching bags, one large, one small. Murals of skiers, golfers, and tennis players covered the walls. Except for the attendant, a young man in gym clothes sitting in a corner and reading a copy of *L'Illustration*, the room was unoccupied.

"Got any boxing gloves?" Jaekel asked the fellow.

"Some ten-ouncers."

"I'd like to give them a try."

The gym attendant found the boxing gloves in a closet and helped Jaekel put them on. Jaekel gave the smaller of the two punching bags a few tentative taps. The attendant, who was watching and hoping to be entertained, concluded that there was nothing of any special interest here and went back to his chair and his magazine.

Jaekel started slowly, as he always did. And, as he always did, he let his thoughts drift back over the events of the last few days: the meeting with Raeder, the long drive to Le Havre, the motor car being loaded aboard the ship, his awkward and forced attempts to blend in with the other first-class passengers, the wealthy, the famous, and the merely beautiful. Too much had happened in too short a time; he was having trouble grasping it all.

He increased his punching pace, seeking a rhythm. He had to clear his mind. He had to concentrate on what really mattered, on the reason he was on this voyage, on the single crucial task he had in front of him, on which he must focus all of his energies: the destruction of the ship.

His hands began to find their tempo, and the punching

bag started to bounce back and forth in time with his crisp, powerful blows. His mission was a simple, straightforward one, he thought — or at least it should have been. But he'd come up against unexpected complications.

He unleashed a brief flurry of punches, his thoughts picking up speed at the same time. There was the Delahaye in the place he'd been instructed to park the Mercedes. There was the stupid cargo handler who had forced him to kill again.

Jaekel increased the tempo once more. The punching bag struggled to keep up, to return blow for blow. His mind kept pace with his fists. There was the new lock on the chock closet door. There was the very good chance that the ship's security force was looking for him right now.

His fists flailed away against the punching bag until it was very nearly a blur. The adrenaline set his mind whirling with ideas and thoughts and fears. There was the desperate need to keep pretending, to maintain the false identity with which he was so uncomfortable, and the simultaneous and contradictory need to remain as inconspicuous as possible, which he had totally forgotten yesterday in the misguided urge to be a hero. And there was the pretty girl he had rescued, who was trying so hard to get him to notice her, whose face he couldn't get out of his mind.

All these thoughts swirled through his mind, seeking an outlet. They did not find one, however. As if in an attempt to expel them by force, Jaekel's gloved fists accelerated to a ferocious, machine-gun staccato. The punching bag, his captive opponent, bobbed and weaved in a desperate and futile attempt to escape the terrible punishment. Suddenly, the anchor chain snapped and the bag flew into the air, banging into one wall and ricocheting against another.

"What the shit!" the gym attendant yelled, eyes wide. "How the hell did you do that? You broke the damn bag."

Jaekel looked blankly at the punching bag, which was still spinning on the rubber tile floor. Then his cold eyes met the attendant's. The attendant quickly looked away.

While walking back to his quarters to see how Nathan and Segonzak were doing, Captain Barthou was stopped by a fat, tough looking man in a gray silk suit and a black shirt.

"Listen, Captain, I wanna tell you something."

"Yes, sir. How can I be of assistance?"

"Naw, it's how can *we* help *you?*"

"We?"

"Yeah, me and my friends. We heard you got problems."

Barthou's eyes narrowed. "I'm not sure I know what you mean."

"I mean the guy that stole that thing from the museum."

"Oh, yes. That has us all very concerned. How did you hear about it?"

"I have friends in the crew."

"I see."

"Anyway, I just wanted ya to know we're ready to help if you need us."

"Help? How?"

"Listen, I got two of the best shooters in Chicago on board this boat."

"I don't understand," the captain said. "Shooters?"

"Y'know . . . hit men."

"Hit men?"

"That's right. And if that lousy thief tries anything, you just let me know and we'll take care of him for you."

"I see. Well, I'm not sure we'll need your help, but I do appreciate the offer."

The captain extended his hand and the fat man shook it vigorously. "Remember, if you need us, just let me know. Won't cost you a thing, neither."

* * *

Cosset unlocked 235, stepped inside, and closed the door behind him. This one should go quickly, he thought. The man who occupies this stateroom has only two fairly small leather suitcases, if he remembered correctly.

He found the first suitcase in the closet. Laying it on the floor, he unsnapped the catches and opened it up. Just clothing—dirty clothing on one side, clean clothing on the other. He poked a hand beneath the clean clothing. Something hard—shoes. He dug down through the dirty clothing. Nothing at all. Well, one down.

Cosset relocked the suitcase, put it back in place, and looked around for the other one. It wasn't in the closet, and he couldn't see it anywhere else in the room. But that wasn't really so strange. Passengers often concealed a suitcase somewhere in the cabin, in hopes of protecting their valuables from the stewards they imagined were eager to rob them at the first opportunity. It was insulting in a way, although he'd learned long ago not to take it personally. It would never have occurred to him to steal from a passenger, even if the passenger had left cash lying on the dresser top, but he knew that some stewards, even aboard the *Normandie*, were not strong enough to resist such temptations. Every barrel had its bad apples.

If this passenger had hidden a suitcase, then, that was completely understandable. But on this voyage, a hidden suitcase could mean something else altogether. It could be concealing the artwork everyone was searching for, which was all the more reason to find it and inspect it carefully.

Whistling absently, Cosset peered into the bathroom, checking behind the shower curtain. For some reason, passengers thought bathtubs were a good place to hide their valuables. Did it never occur to them that the maids cleaned the bathtubs? But this time, there was no suitcase in the bathroom. Where then?

The friendly little steward walked back into the cabin and scratched his head. Well, of course. The suitcase must be in the most obvious hiding place of all, the place any real thief would be sure to look—under the bed. Cosset dropped to his hands and knees and lifted the bedspread. *Violà!*

He had to struggle to get the suitcase out from under the bed—it was quite a bit larger and heavier than the one in the closet—but he finally succeeded. He unsnapped the latches and opened it up. Now what in the world, he asked himself, was that?

Lying on top of everything was what looked like a black rubber sheet. No, Cosset thought, it couldn't be a sheet. It was too thick, and it had a zipper. He picked the thing up and began to examine it. It felt sticky, almost slimy, and it had arms and legs. It was a suit of some kind, the strangest suit he'd ever seen. He dropped it back into the suitcase and quickly wiped his hands on his pants, wishing he hadn't found the thing in the first place.

It wouldn't be right to close the suitcase now, however. Not yet. Shutting his eyes, he probed beneath the black thing, searching for whatever else the suitcase might be concealing. Just clothing. No, wait, there were pockets along the sides of the suitcase, and something hard in one of the pockets. He reached in and pulled out the biggest, blackest, most terrifying pistol he had ever seen.

At that moment, Cosset heard a key in the lock, then the cabin door swung open. Simon Rothmann, the Viennese businessman, walked in, shut the door behind him, then stopped dead as he saw the steward kneeling over the suitcase, the Luger in his hand.

Cosset dropped the gun and scrambled to his feet. "Good afternoon, Herr Rothmann," he said with a smile. "I was just—"

"Stay where you are, thief," Jaekel snarled.

"I'm sorry, sir, I'm not stealing anything. All I was doing was—"

Jaekel glanced down at his suitcase. The steward had not only found his gun, he'd also discovered the wet suit.

277

"I'm calling security and having you arrested," he said.

"No, no, no, you don't understand," Cosset told him. "I'm not a thief at all. A search is being conducted throughout the ship, and this is one of the cabins I've been assigned to."

"What do you mean, search?" Jaekel asked, shaken. "What are you searching for? My jewelry and my money?"

Cosset was also getting rattled. "*Non,* monsieur. A thief is hiding aboard the ship and we're trying to find the art treasure he's stolen. You can call the purser or the deputy captain if you don't believe me."

"I don't believe you," Jaekel said flatly. "There's no thief and no art treasure. You're searching for something else. What is it?"

"I assure you, Herr Rothmann," Cosset said solemnly, "I am telling you the God's honest truth."

Rothmann shoved the little man into a chair and smacked him once across the face, hard. "What are you searching for?" he repeated.

Cosset was shocked by the blow. "Please, call the purser. He'll tell you. We're looking for an ancient stone tablet."

Jaekel snickered contemptuously. "A tablet? Like Moses brought down from Mount Sinai?"

"Yes, that's it . . . well, something like that, from the museum, the Louvre. . . ."

Could this chipmunk be telling the truth? Jaekel asked himself. Could a thief actually be hiding aboard the *Normandie,* and could the crew really be searching for stolen artwork? Not likely. But he had to be positive. He smacked the young man once more, this time hard enough to draw blood. "The truth, steward," he said coldly, "not more of your horseshit."

"I *am* telling you the truth, Monsieur Rothmann. I swear it on my mother's grave." He put a hand to his mouth and was unnerved to feel the blood.

"Why were you sent to this cabin?" Jaekel demanded.

"I wasn't sent here . . . I mean, I was, but I was given fifty cabins to search."

"Who's in charge of this search?" Jaekel asked.

For a moment, Cosset couldn't remember. "It is . . . the deputy captain."

The answer sent chills down Jaekel's spine. The operation was being led by the second highest-ranking officer on the ship. That's it, he thought. They are searching the ship, all right, but they are not searching for some ancient tablet. They are searching for me or for the bomb or both. God knows how they found out, but they have. No other explanation makes any sense.

Cosset shook his head, trying to think straight. He struggled to his feet. "Excuse me, sir, I have to be going. More rooms to check."

Jaekel pushed him back into the chair. "And I have more questions to ask."

"Yes, sir. But please don't hit me anymore. I'll tell you whatever I know."

"What parts of the ship are being searched?"

"The entire ship."

"Machinery spaces, cargo areas, crew quarters?"

"Yes, Herr Rothmann, everything. But there's no reason for you to be excited about it, sir. They're looking for a thief and an art treasure. That doesn't have anything to do with you, does it?"

Jaekel laughed sardonically. "No. No, I'm not a thief."

"Can I go now?" Cosset sounded as timid as a mouse.

"Another question first. Describe the object you're looking for. How big is it? How heavy?"

Cosset tried to think. "They didn't know exactly. They said it would be very heavy—a hundred pounds or more. And at least a foot and a half square."

"Who are you supposed to bring it to if you find it?"

"No one. I'm supposed to call the deputy captain. I'm not supposed to touch it. It could break. It's very fragile, they said."

Fragile, eh? Well, that's one way to put it. It's so fragile that if it's mishandled, it just might blow the entire ship to smithereens. "How many people are in on this search?" Jaekel asked.

"I don't know exactly, maybe sixty or seventy," Cossett said, his head finally beginning to clear. Until this encounter, the gentleman had been very polite to him. What could have caused him to go berserk like this? he wondered. Was it the personal tragedy Rothmann had suffered so recently? Yes, that must be it, and it was a very, very sad business. But it didn't matter now. This physical attack must be reported to the deputy captain immediately. "Now I really must go," he said. "I have many more staterooms to inspect."

Jaekel allowed the steward to get up. He stood aside so Cossett could pass. He permitted him to walk toward the door. Then, coming up from behind, he slipped both of his powerful arms around the little steward's neck and, before Cosset could utter a single sound, snapped his neck as easily as if it were a chicken bone. Then he tossed the body on the bed.

Of course, he'd had to kill the steward. What choice did he have? If he'd let him live, the young man would have gone directly to the deputy captain and reported the gun and the wet suit. And that would have ended everything.

But now what? Now he had a dead body to dispose of, another one, the body of a man who had been assigned to search *his* stateroom, among others, a man who would be missed quickly, who would be the object of an intensive search.

Yes, he'd staved off immediate disaster, but now, unless he could get rid of the body in a way that didn't draw suspicion, he would be chased down and trapped, and his mission would be a total failure.

Jaekel had to think. Yes, that was it, think. He had to

figure out a way to save himself. He picked up the steward's small, limp, lifeless body and deposited it in the stateroom closet, hiding it behind some clothing, then he closed up the suitcase Cosset had been searching and slid it back under the bed.

Satisfied that the cabin would pass a cursory inspection, at least, Jaekel decided that he had to get out of the room. He needed to clear his head, to give his panic a chance to subside and let reason take over.

The decision made, Jaekel slipped on the golf jacket and cap Admiral Raeder had seen fit to include in his luggage. Then he left the cabin, locking the door behind him.

"Coming into the home stretch, it's Bold Venture!" called out a young man in a red uniform. "Running a close second is Gallant Fox. Coming up on the outside, Man-o'-War. And bringing up the rear, it's Omaha and War Admiral, closing fast. *Time to roll again.*"

The crowd cried out in delight and woe.

"Come on, War Admiral!" Tina called out.

"Get going, Man-o'-War!" yelled Karla.

The red-jacketed page spun the metal cage, and the three huge dice tumbled over one another in random disarray, while nearly two hundred passengers held their breath and watched. Even more passengers had been present for the earlier races, but the *Normandie* was beginning to roll now as she headed into choppy seas and a number of delicate souls had gone back to their rooms to be miserable in private.

Finally, the spinning cage stopped and the dice came to a rest. The page began moving the horse models over the felt track that had been unrolled on the floor of the Grand Lounge over what the ship brochures claimed was the world's largest Aubusson carpet.

"It's Man-o'-War taking second from Gallant Fox, and

War Admiral moving up a furlong on Omaha," the page said, shifting the models. "And . . . ladies and gentlemen, I do believe we have a winner. Yes, it's Bold Venture—that's the *great* Bold Venture—crossing the finish line in record time and taking the Gulf Stream Steeplechase in the closest and most exciting race of the afternoon. My sincerest congratulations to the winners and my sympathies to the losers." He picked up one horse model and set it down on the other side of the finish line.

"Damn," said a distinguished-looking man in the back of the huge ballroom, standing up dramatically. "That's the fifth race you've run and the fifth race I've lost." He waved his losing tickets in the air for all to see, and the crowd burst into laughter. To his credit, the man joined in.

The man pushed his way through the Art Deco armchairs and statue-sized glass lighting fixtures, reaching Victor Meisner, who was sitting beside his sister and Karla Kirkland.

"Now I understand losing," he said, still playing to the crowd. "I've done plenty of that in my time. What truly mystifies me is how this particular young man has managed to take my money every time."

"Beginner's luck," Tina said, batting her eyelashes at the man and drawing even more laughter from the crowd. She was, as usual, the most fetching figure in view, in her cream-colored Turkish-cut flannel slacks, pastel-striped weskit, and blue bolero jacket.

"Probability theory," Victor explained quite seriously, jotting some figures in his notebook and accepting the wad of cash the man handed him.

"Young man, that's just about as clear to me as the theory of relativity."

"Actually," Victor told him, "it's quite a lot simpler than that."

"All right, ladies and gentlemen," said the red-jacketed page. "The Atlantic Handicap is coming up. Place your

282

bets."

"I don't think I'm going to bet anymore," the distinguished man told everyone. "I'm just going to will all my possessions to this young man here. Much less anguish that way."

When the frivolity finally began to fade and the page started spinning the cage again, Karla Kirkland turned to Tina. One was moonlight, the other sunshine. "Where is he? The races are almost over."

"He's gotten himself caught up with that fraternity brother of his, Karla. Maybe for dinner. Do you want me to tell him you've been asking after him?"

Karla smiled ruefully, her red lips, olive complexion, and dark hair making a very pretty combination. "Yes. That would be nice—if you think it would do any good."

Jackel opened the stairway door and came out on the Sun Deck, not far from the aft funnel. He liked this deck, with its wide teak flooring, its rows of covered lifeboats, its ventilation grills. Here, more than anywhere else on this mammoth vessel, he felt as though he were aboard a ship.

Despite its size, this place reminded him of the destroyer deck where he'd spent so many hours on watch, in all kinds of weather, alone with his thoughts. In some ways, those had been the best hours of his Navy training, a time when he could find solutions to the problems that had been plaguing him.

That's why he had come up here now. He desperately needed a solution, this time to a problem of his own making—the body in his stateroom closet. What could he do with it? How could he get rid of it without pointing a finger at himself?

If this had been a wrestling ring, he would have been confident, even fearless. But in this situation, his ferocity, his physical strength, his remarkable reflexes, did him no good. He had no opponent to intimidate and crush.

Instead, he was confronted with a situation that called for skills he had never been able to demonstrate, especially to himself: the ability to calculate and manipulate, to understand others' motives, to remain composed no matter what happened.

He turned aft, toward the turbulent wake that trailed behind the ship for miles, the only evidence of her remarkable speed. Now that was strange, he thought. The wake seemed wider than before. Had the *Normandie* picked up speed? Come to think of it, that wouldn't be so surprising. She might very well be under orders to make port in New York as fast as possible because of the war scare.

Oh, no! Jaekel thought. If the *Normandie* has actually picked up speed, my entire mission could be in danger! She'll pass the rendezvous point before the U-boat and the salvage ship get there, and she'll explode God knows how many miles away. The gold will be lost forever, and I'll be swimming toward a U-boat that will never come. But maybe I'm wrong. Maybe nothing has changed.

Jaekel looked around. A junior ship's officer was strolling in his direction. Here was a chance to determine the truth.

"Good afternoon, sir," the officer said. "Getting a little rough, isn't it?"

How could he draw the man out? "Just a little."

"We're serving bouillon and biscuits on the Promenade Deck now, sir."

"Bouillon," Jaekel said, trying to be casual. "Yes, well, that would be very bracing. Maybe I'll try some."

"Yes, sir."

"Looks like we've picked up some speed," Jaekel observed casually, gesturing toward the wake.

"You're very observant, sir. Yes, I understand the cold boilers have all been brought back on line."

"Why is that?"

The officer shrugged. "I don't really know, sir. Probably

making an attempt to win back the Blue Ribbon from the *Queen Mary,* I'd say."

"Any idea of our present speed?"

"Yes, sir. I was just on the bridge. We're traveling at better than thirty-two knots now."

Jaekel suppressed his shock. They were racing across the Atlantic at nearly four knots faster than normal cruising speed. At that rate, they'd pass the rendezvous point *hours* ahead of schedule. "Very impressive," he told the young man.

The officer beamed with pride. "Faster than most destroyers," he said. "Well, enjoy the voyage." He gave Jaekel a little wave and walked on.

Jaekel stared fixedly at the ship's wake, thinking. The problems were beginning to overwhelm him. Not only did he have to dispose of a body, he also had to somehow get the ship to slow down. Impossible!

Then, in a moment of inspiration, the solution occurred to him.

David Nathan looked at himself in the bathroom mirror. The beard was growing again. The black hair needed combing. As for that crooked nose of his . . . there was, he could do nothing about that.

They'd been at it for only three hours, and he was already starting to fade. Well, he knew the cure for that. He let the water run in the sink until it was as cold as it got, then gave his face a thorough splashing, drying himself with one of the captain's thick white towels.

There was a knock on the door of the captain's suite. "He's back already," Segonzak called.

Nathan returned to the captain's private dining room and took his seat. "God, that Freppel is fast. Doesn't he ever have to empty his bladder?"

Segonzak laughed. "Pursers develop very special talents along those lines, I'm told."

"Well, who's next?" Nathan asked, returning to his seat at the table.

"As a matter of fact," Segonzak said, consulting his list, "it is one of our leading suspects: Count Cherbatoff."

Nathan sat up, erect and alert. "Tell me what you have on him."

Segonzak looked at his notes. "Outside of that attempted bribe the other night, very little. All we really know is who he represents himself to be—a White Russian, a minor noble of some kind, independently wealthy, with a taste for spring chicken. But he's been on your suspect list for a long time, David. I don't really know why."

"I watched him board the ship with his young lady and I had a chance to study them a while at dinner the other night, Jean-Louis," Nathan said. "And all I can really tell you is that there's something about the two of them that doesn't ring true."

"Not much to go on," Segonzak said dryly. "But I'm not one to dismiss instinct."

Nathan had a thought. "A little odd that the Grand Duchess Marie didn't check him off on her passenger list."

"I hadn't thought of that. It is odd."

"Well, let's see what we can do with him."

"Please come in," Segonzak called.

The door opened and Chief Purser Freppel entered, escorting the tall, thin, aristocratic-looking man. He was haggard but noble, a kind of Russian Don Quixote, not exactly seedy but beginning to fray.

"Count Cherbatoff," the chief purser said, "these are the men I was telling you about—Dr. Jean-Louis and Mr. Cameron. I'll be leaving you with them." He departed.

"I object to these entire proceedings," the count announced with contempt. He inserted a brown Turkish cigarette in a gold holder, lit it, and took a deep drag.

"What proceedings are those, Count Cherbatoff?" Segonzak asked politely. "We'd just like to have a conversation with you."

"I stand on my rights as a citizen of France," the man stated.

"France?" Nathan asked in surprise. "I thought you were Russian."

"I was granted French citizenship after the Bolshevik uprising," he said. "Many others of my countrymen have also received that benefit."

"What is your real name, sir?"

Cherbatoff turned white. "Sir?"

"Your name," Nathan repeated implacably. "It certainly isn't Count Cherbatoff."

The man clicked his heels and bowed from the waist. "Count Andre Sergeyevich Cherbatoff at your service, sir. That is my real name, I assure you. You can check my passport if you are so inclined."

It was Segonzak's turn. "As a Russian nobleman, I assume you are some distant relative of the late Czar Nicholas?"

"I have the honor to be his second cousin, once removed."

Nathan pounced. "Then how is it that you are totally unknown to the Grand Duchess Marie, who I believe is also one of the Czar's second cousins?"

"I, ah . . ."

"What is the source of your funds, sir?" Segonzak demanded. "I don't imagine the Bolsheviks let you smuggle cash out of Russia?"

"Well, I . . ."

"What is your relationship with the young woman you have brought aboard?" Nathan asked.

"Is she of legal age?" Segonzak demanded, keeping the interrogation rhythm going.

"Yes, she . . ."

Nathan interrupted. "What is the real purpose of your trip to America?"

They did not give Cherbatoff time to reply.

"Why have you been lying about yourself?" Segonzak persisted.

"And what kind of drugs have you been giving the girl?" Nathan asked, recalling what he had seen at dinner that first night.

Cherbatoff staggered backward, battered by the questioning, retreating to one of the captain's armchairs. Then, to Nathan's and Segonzak's surprise, he began to weep.

Nathan darted a hand into the count's coat pocket and pulled out a handful of small paper-covered packets. "This," he said accusingly, shaking the packets in front of the man's face, "this is what I mean."

Nathan tossed a packet to Segonzak, who tore it open and tasted it delicately. "Sugar," he said in surprise.

"Sugar?" Nathan repeated. He tore open one of the packets and tasted it for himself. Then he looked up at Cherbatoff. "Sugar?"

"Yes, sugar," the man said, tears welling up in his eyes. "Alexandra is a diabetic. She requires sugar when she feels faint or weak."

"Alexandra . . . that's her name?" Segonzak asked. "Wasn't that the name of the Czarina?"

"Is she related to the Czarina?" Nathan asked, resuming the grilling. "Is she one of her children?"

The man refused to answer, and it was his refusal that inspired Segonzak's next question. "Do you expect us to believe that this girl survived the Bolshevik slaughter in 1918?"

"I don't expect you to believe anything," the man said bitterly.

Nathan and Segonzak exchanged puzzled glances. They had uncovered something, all right, but not what they expected.

"The truth now," Nathan demanded. "It always comes out in the end, you know."

The man began crying again. "I have kept the secret too

long," he said, surrendering.

Segonzak gave him one more push. "Your name, sir."

"My name is Fyodor Alekseyevich Volkov. I am a physician."

"And Alexandra?"

"She is Alexandra Petrovna Romanov, the Czar's only living grandniece, the illegitimate child of the Czarina's younger sister and the heir to the throne of the Romanovs. She was born three months before her mother was slaughtered by Lenin's cutthroats. I attended the birth, and I have cared for her ever since."

"Unbelievable," Segonzak said, stunned.

"She is terribly ill now. I am taking her to Toronto, Canada, to see Dr. Frederick Banting, who has saved the lives of many diabetics by injecting them with a substance called zinc protamine insulin."

"What is your relationship with her?" Nathan asked quictly.

"It is the relationship of physician to patient."

Nathan was skeptical. "No more?"

"She is physically and emotionally dependent on me," the doctor said. "And I suppose that during these last twenty-one years, I have become emotionally and financially dependent on her as well."

"And you have kept this secret all this time?"

The man started crying again. "I have signed her death warrant by revealing the truth to you." He buried his face in his hand.

"Nonsense," Nathan told him.

"He's right, David. If Stalin and his men learn that a member of the Romanov dynasty has survived, they will come after her. They will not rest until they have killed her."

Nathan put a hand on the doctor's shoulder. "They will not learn about Alexandra from us, sir," he said.

"We have no reason to repeat the story to anyone," Segonzak added. "In fact, we have no reason to remember it ourselves."

Fyodor Alekseyevich Volkov looked up at them, a glimmer of hope in his eyes. "What are you going to do with me?"

"We're going to send you on your way," Segonzak replied.

"And ask you to forget that this interview ever took place."

Volkov wiped his eyes with an initialed handkerchief and slowly rose from his seat. "That is most kind of you," he said. "Most kind." He shook Nathan's hand, then Segonzak's.

"I hope you enjoy the rest of the voyage, Count Cherbatoff," Segonzak told him. "And I hope your stay in the New World is all you wish it to be."

Volkov bowed from the waist and left.

After a moment, Nathan looked at Segonzak. "And that, my friend, was one of our very best suspects."

Jaekel cautiously unlocked the door to his cabin and peered inside. Everything was exactly as he had left it. He locked the door behind him, got the steward's body out of the closet, and dropped it into a chair beside the porthole.

He'd been concerned about the porthole, but that turned out to be no problem at all. *Normandie* portholes weren't the typical small round windows found on most ships. They were Ducroux pivoting sidelights—openings large enough for all but the fattest passenger to squeeze through if, for instance, the stateroom door was blocked by fire.

Jaekel unlatched the porthole window. Then, in one quick motion, he picked up Cosset's slender body and shoved it through the opening, out into the sea. He counted to five and picked up his stateroom telephone. "My God!" he cried. "A man has jumped into the ocean! Man overboard! Stop the ship!" A few moments later, the ship's alarm Klaxon began sounding.

"You cannot do this, Captain."

Barthou was firm. "I *must* do it, Lieutenant Segonzak. I have a duty to the victim of this terrible accident. Besides, it is the law of the sea."

"The man is dead already," Nathan insisted, "and if we circle back to pick up his body, we may also die, every last one of us."

Barthou shook his head stubbornly. "I have no choice."

"Captain, if we try to retrieve the man who has fallen overboard, we could lose three or four hours," Segonzak continued. "We will be squandering most of the advantage we've gained by increasing our speed."

"And we will arrive at the continental shelf almost exactly when they expect us," Nathan said, finishing the thought.

Barthou stared into the sea, refusing to meet their eyes. "I cannot and will not cancel the recovery operations."

At that moment, Deputy Captain Martel dashed through the door of the wheelhouse, breathing hard. "I have the report from the crow's nest, sir."

"Yes, Marius. Tell us."

"The man in the sea is wearing a steward's uniform. He is floating facedown."

"My God," Barthou said softly. "One of my stewards."

"I am sorry, Captain." Segonzak put a hand on the man's shoulder. "It is a terrible thing to lose a shipmate. I understand what it must mean to you, because I have also lost colleagues. But I ask you this: Would that steward want you to go back for his body if it meant putting every passenger and every crew member on the ship in danger?"

Barthou struggled with the dilemma. "We don't even know who it is," he said.

"I can do a roll call in a matter of minutes, Captain," Martel told him.

"Chief Purser, what do you think?"

291

"The man may be a corpse," Freppel said, "but even in the heat of battle, soldiers retrieve their dead and bury them."

"Martel?"

"The sea will claim him for her own, Captain," Martel responded. "I don't think any seaman could hope for a better resting place. But now we have to think of the living."

For almost a minute, Barthou said nothing at all. Everyone on the bridge watched him, aware of the battle he was fighting within himself. Then, in a rare display of anger and frustration, he slammed a hand against the bulkhead. "Cancel all recovery operations," he told Martel abruptly. "Resume our former speed immediately."

"Yes, sir."

"And I want that steward's name in fifteen minutes or less, Marius."

"You will have it." Deputy Captain Martel left the bridge immediately.

The chief purser had one more comment to make. "You know, sir, this entire episode is certain to scare the passengers — as if they're not upset enough already."

The captain thought a moment. "Make a loudspeaker announcement, Henri," he said glumly. "Tell the passengers that it was a false alarm. Tell them that everyone has been accounted for. Tell them that it was a prank, that someone threw a bag of laundry overboard."

"As you wish." Freppel went off to do as he had been told.

"We have something else to talk about, Captain," Segonzak told Barthou.

"What's that?"

"We think the man may not have fallen overboard accidentally," Nathan said.

"That possibility had already occurred to me."

"It's my belief," said Segonzak, "that he discovered something suspicious during the search and got himself killed because of it."

Nathan shook his head. "I have another theory. I think our saboteur realized that we'd put on speed and was looking for a way to slow us down."

"If you're right," Barthou observed, "he came very close to finding it."

Deputy Captain Martel returned. "Captain, I've identified the missing steward. It's Maurice Cosset."

For a few moments, no one was able to say anything.

"You're sure it's Cosset?" The captain's eyes were filled with tears.

"I'm afraid so, Captain. No one has seen him since the search began."

"Cosset is one of my favorites," Barthou said sadly. "I've never seen him without a smile on his face."

"I know the man," Nathan said. "He was my steward."

Barthou was startled. "*Your* steward? Do you think he was murdered because he was your steward?"

"I don't think so. That doesn't really make any sense. But I do have a question about Cosset, Martel: Was he one of the searchers?"

"As a matter of fact, he was."

"What was his assigned area?"

"He had about fifty first-class staterooms, most of them on the Promenade Deck, aft and the Main Deck, amidships."

"May help us, may not," Segonzak said.

The light dawned in Martel's eyes. "You think the saboteur is staying in one of those cabins?"

"Could be," Nathan said. "On the other hand, Cosset could just as easily have surprised him doing something suspicious practically anywhere else in the ship."

Martel was completely frustrated. "So we're right back where we started."

Segonzak nodded. "I'm afraid so."

"Except for Cosset," Barthou said. "Except for Cosset."

It had begun exactly as he expected. The Klaxon had sounded, and the huge vessel had begun to slow. But then it had all gone wrong. Instead of turning back to retrieve the man who had fallen overboard, the *Normandie* began to pick up speed once more. Soon, it was barreling through the ocean just as fast as it had been before the alarm. Obviously, the ship wasn't going to make any rescue attempt. But that was a violation of every man-overboard procedure in the book, a violation of one of the oldest rules of the sea. What was going on here?

Then the purser came on the public address system. It was a mistake, it was a prank, no one had fallen overboard, it was a bag of laundry, for God's sake. We will be proceeding on schedule, sorry for any inconvenience.

Jaekel threw up his hands in disgust. The plan hadn't worked, or at least half of it hadn't worked. True, he was rid of the steward and the body couldn't be connected with him, but he had failed to slow down the ship. She would still arrive far ahead of schedule.

Damn.

Had the captain been ordered to proceed at top speed, no matter what? No, that didn't make sense. If those were the captain's orders, he wouldn't have slowed down at all. No, he had started emergency procedures, then he'd abandoned them. Someone had changed his mind, someone had recognized that the ship was in danger, no doubt the very same someone who'd inspired the search for him.

Well, anyhow, the man-overboard stunt hadn't worked. That simply meant he had to find another way to delay the ship or cut her speed. Unfortunately, that would have to wait. He still had very nearly two full days before rendezvous. Tonight, Jaekel had something else to do. He had orders to follow. He had a cover to maintain and a command appearance to make, by the direct and specific mandate of Grand Admiral Erich Raeder, Commander in Chief of the German Navy.

Three P.M., Greenwich mean time. The U-42 broached the surface for routine radio communications. It emitted a brief signal: Proceeding to rendezvous point in tandem *Otto Wunsche* and expect to arrive at least an hour ahead of schedule. Any further instructions?

After two minutes, a return signal came in, complete in two words: Follow orders.

The U-boat retracted its antenna and sank beneath the waters of the North Atlantic once again.

EVENING

Just before dusk, Chief Purser Freppel assembled his ten assistant pursers and told them about the blackout. His announcement was greeted with nervous discomfort.

"Chief Purser," one of his assistants said, taking his life in his hands, "could you explain why we have to do this? Some of the passengers may have questions."

Freppel was inclined to cut the man off at the knees—he despised giving explanations to his inferiors—but he realized the assistant might be right.

"If a passenger asks why we're covering the windows and the portholes," Freppel replied, "we laugh and we shrug off the blackout as bureaucratic stupidity. God knows there's plenty of that."

"I don't understand," another assistant purser said.

"It's really very simple, Paul," Freppel said a little unpleasantly. "But I'll spell it out for you. The French government sent out an order to black out ship windows and portholes. They meant battleships and cruisers, of course, but some moron in the Merchant Marine got the idea it was meant for passenger liners as well."

"But why are we obeying this order if it's so stupid?"

Freppel glared at the man. "Because we always humor the bureaucrats. We wouldn't want to endanger our subsidy, would we?"

The chief purser waited for other questions, but no one else was willing to risk one. "We'll begin in the public rooms, with the drapes. Then you will visit each of the staterooms to which you have been assigned and instruct passengers to turn off the overhead lights and close the porthole drapes. Make it clear this is not a request. It is an order."

One of the assistant pursers timidly raised a hand. "Yes?"

"Third class, too?"

"Yes, third class and tourist class and crew quarters as well. Any more questions?"

There were none.

David Nathan made his way down to B Deck, Victor and Tina in tow. For once, all three of them were conservatively dressed—dark suits for the men, a modest hat and a black dress for Tina, adorned by nothing more than a single strand of pearls.

Nathan hadn't intended to come. As of six P.M., he and Segonzak had questioned—and eliminated—only fifty-two passengers, less than a third of their remaining suspects. So far, all the people interviewed had turned out to be exactly who they said they were. There were no ringers, no one traveling under a false identity.

Nathan had planned to continue working with the Frenchman all through the night, questioning additional suspects, but he'd made the mistake of asking Freppel if the ship had Friday night services.

"I didn't know you were a religious man, David," Segonzak had said.

"I'm not. But I have been saying *Kaddish*."

"What?"

"The mourning ceremony. My father died six weeks ago—July 12. According to Hebraic law, the son is supposed to mourn for a year."

"And say—"

"*Kaddish.* Yes. It's not much, really, just a few lines of ancient Aramaic. But it helps."

They'd interrogated two more passengers before Segonzak brought up the subject again.

"Why don't you go to your religious services tonight," Segonzak suggested. "I can handle the questioning for a few hours."

Nathan had put him off the first time, but when Segonzak brought it up again after another couple of interviews, he gave in. He'd wanted to give in all along. He'd wanted to say *Kaddish,* to think of his father, to remember the man who meant so much to him.

The synagogue on board the *Normandie* was modest but pleasant. There had been no such facility on the ship when it made its debut, but many had requested one, including some People of Consequence. So, just before the beginning of the ship's second season, CGT had stripped one of the larger private dining rooms on B Deck and installed an ark with filigreed doors, a handsome eternal light, a pulpit, and ten small pews. The Torah had been blessed by Cantor Herschel Katz, his first official act as the ship's rabbi.

Tonight, the temple was filling up rapidly, perhaps because an unusual number of Jews were on board, escaping the spreading Nazi contagion at what might be the last possible moment, perhaps because, given the events in Europe, prayer seemed appropriate, even necessary. Those who showed up were an odd combination of refugees, stockbrokers, show people, businessmen, doctors, and lawyers.

Nathan and his charges stopped at the door. While Tina waited, the men picked out *yarmulkes* and prayer books, and Nathan chose a delicately fringed *tallith,* draping it around his shoulders. Then they took seats in a front pew. It was apparently a Reform Synagogue; the men and women were allowed to sit together.

After a few minutes, they were amazed to see Erich von Stroheim walk in, don a *yarmulke* and *tallith*, and sit down on the other side of the room, without casting so much as a glance toward Tina.

Tina bent over and whispered to Nathan. "He's Jewish?"

"It appears so," Nathan said.

Shortly afterward, Kurt Jaekel—Simon Rothmann as he was known on this vessel—entered the tiny synagogue. He was wearing a dark suit, as instructed. Never had he felt so distant from the farm on which he'd been raised. Even in the Navy, he'd been surrounded by young men very much like himself. But here, he felt as though he'd stumbled into a meeting of alien beings.

Rabbi Katz, an owlish-looking man with thick glasses who was standing at the door, handed Jaekel a black *yarmulke* and a prayer book. Jaekel looked at the *yarmulke* as though it were a strange handkerchief of some sort. Then, realizing its purpose, he placed it on the crown of his head, as the others had. He found a seat across the aisle from Nathan and his companions.

After the little *shul* was almost full, Rabbi Katz closed the door and took his place at the pulpit. He then proceeded to deliver a short service—a few psalms, a little responsive reading in the prayer book, a *kiddush* over a cup of red wine to celebrate the coming of the Sabbath, then a prayer over the lighting of the Sabbath candles, followed by the breaking of the bread.

Jaekel participated as he had been told. When the others mumbled their prayers, he also mumbled. When the others read the verses in the prayer book, he joined in. He found the service queer and unsettling, but he realized that participating established his Rothmann identity as nothing else could. Who but a Jew would be here tonight? Who but a

Jew would wear the little hat and utter the mysterious ancient words?

As the prayers went on, Jaekel stole a glance around the room. They had accepted him. As far as they were concerned, he was one of them, a *landsman,* to use their word. No doubt, those among them who'd heard the story Raeder had planted deeply sympathized with him over the brutal death of his family. What would they have said if they'd known the truth?

The rabbi delivered a brief sermon. He spoke of the darkness that was falling over the world and offered a prayer to God, asking that He protect the people of Abraham, Jacob, and Isaac. He begged God to save the world from the horrors of another war. He prayed that the rest of the world would recognize the evil Hitler was perpetrating and come to the rescue of the people of Israel.

Then the rabbi paused to indicate that the evening's sermon had come to an end. After a moment, he spoke again. "Would those who wish to say *Kaddish* please rise."

David Nathan stood, as did Erich von Stroheim and several obvious refugees.

"Any others?" the rabbi asked.

After a moment, Jaekel realized that the pretty girl from the lifeboat was staring at him . . . and so was the young man beside her . . . and an older man in the pew in front of him . . . and a couple across the aisle. What have I done? he asked himself. Why are they looking at me? He felt a rising sense of panic. Something was expected of him now and he had no idea what.

"*Kaddish,*" muttered the man next to him, under his breath, trying to be helpful.

"Kidrush?" Jaekel asked, confused. The gaze of his fellow worshipers, originally merely inquisitive, was hardening into suspicion.

Jaekel's mind exploded with a million thoughts, a million ideas, a million instructions to himself, none of them useful. He did not know what to do. He did not know what was being asked of him or why. He'd known this was going to happen. He'd warned Raeder that he was unfamiliar with Jews and their habits. Now, his presence here, instead of helping him blend in, was proving to everyone that he was an outsider, a stranger to these peculiar people and their faith.

He was, he realized, not only about to dishonor himself and his great friend Raeder and the entire *Kriegsmarine,* but he was also about to dishonor the memory of his beloved father.

What would his father say now, his father who had wanted so much for him but who had died so painfully, long before his hopes could be fulfilled? He remembered that sturdy, smiling face looking down at him, telling him how proud he was of his little Kurt, telling him that someday his little boy would grow into a wonderful man and he would be even prouder then. What would his father say now?

"Are you all right?" his neighbor asked.

"He's just overcome," he heard someone whisper.

Could that be a clue? Was it a reasonable question under the circumstances? Maybe he shouldn't be all right. Maybe he should be overcome. Maybe that was it. And maybe that offered him his very last chance to cloak his differences with these people.

Jaekel buried his face in his hands and began to cry, softly at first, then more loudly, then in great wrenching sobs. The tears came easily. They were not an act. He felt a comforting hand on his shoulder and heard murmurs of sympathy from his fellow worshipers. Strong arms, understanding, helped him to his feet and supported him when he let his knees buckle. And the rabbi continued the religious ceremony, half singing, half chanting, the others joining in.

Yitbm-rah v'yishtabah v'yitpa'ar v'yitroman v'yitnasei, v'yithadar v'yit'aleh v'yit-ha-lal sh'mei d'kud-sho, b'rikh hu; l'elo min kol birhata v'shirata, tushb'hata v'nehemata da-amiran b'almo, vi'imru o-mayn.

When the odd but powerful chanting came to an end, the strong arms that had helped him remain on his feet assisted him as he took his seat once more. Gentle hands remained on his shoulder, letting him know that he was not alone. Compassionate words were whispered in his ear. His sobbing eased.

Now Jaekel realized what this ceremony was. Perhaps he had known all along somewhere inside of himself; perhaps that was why the tears had come so naturally, perhaps that was why he felt such uncontrollable grief. It was the prayer for the dead.

At the pulpit, Rabbi Katz waited for the young man to regain control of himself. He then poured a cup of wine, lit a candle, and said the *havdalah,* the short benediction that noted the distinction between the Sabbath and a weekday. When he finished, he looked up at the congregation with a smile. "*Gut Shabbes,*" he said, wishing them well, "Good Sabbath to you all."

In the pews, worshipers turned to each other, shook hands, and murmured the same words to each other: *Gut Shabbes . . . Gut Shabbes . . . Gut Shabbes.* Jaekel felt his hand clasped again and again in this same greeting, and he even managed to repeat it to his well-wishers: *Gut Shabbes.*

The congregation began to file out of the tiny synagogue, but Jaekel remained seated. He had decided to stay until all the rest were gone, to minimize further contact with these people. But when he finally rose to leave, he found himself face-to-face with the beautiful young girl from the lifeboat. Her lovely eyes were filled with tears.

"I didn't realize how terrible it was for you," she said tenderly. She put her arms around him before he had a chance to resist or pull away, and she drew him toward her.

Jaekel was almost overcome by her kindness, by her car-

301

ing and compassionate words, by the silky hair against his face, by the perfume, and by the intensely erotic sensation of the woman's firm young body against his own.

"Thank you, I . . ."

"Now I understand why you've kept to yourself. . . ."

"It's just that . . ."

"You've simply been overwhelmed by grief."

He felt himself responding to her—to her words, to her kindness, to her warmth, and especially to her womanliness. "My family . . ."

She put a finger to his lips. "I also lost my parents," she said. "They were taken away from us almost four years ago. They knew they were in danger and they asked us not to grieve if something happened to them, but to live our lives to the fullest, for them and for ourselves."

Jaekel did nothing to break their embrace. He could not; he did not want to. "And have you lived your life that way?"

She smiled up at him, a beam of sunlight suddenly breaking through the blackness. "I've tried very hard," she said. "Now I wonder, could you do the same?"

He looked at her lovely face, so concerned, so caring. He felt her slender body against him, unashamed, unself-conscious. In her compassionate kindness, she was offering herself to him, he realized. It was a unique moment in his life. For once, he did not feel the overpowering awkwardness and reticence that inevitably unnerved him when he spoke with an attractive woman. Here was a woman he did not need to woo or impress. "I could try, Miss Cameron," he said timidly. "I could try."

"Lilly," Tina said, taking his arm. "And I would like that."

They walked out of the synagogue together.

A few yards behind them, Nathan was disconcerted by Tina's reaction to Rothmann. "Where are you going?"

She smiled and shrugged.

"When will you be back?"

"Don't worry about me," Tina said. "I'll be fine."

Nathan reached for her, but Victor waved him off. "She'll be all right," he said. "She loves tending the wounded."

Nathan watched Tina and Simon Rothmann head down the corridor, arm in arm. It bothered him a great deal, although he knew it should not. After all, she was a free agent. She could do whatever she wanted. If she liked this man . . . well, what business was it of his? And why did it disturb him so much?

NIGHT

She had never met anyone quite like him. He was a combination of opposites — strong and handsome, yet disarmingly defenseless; hesitant and tentative with her, yet self-confident and assured; physically powerful, as he had demonstrated when the lifeboat fell, yet so gentle in the way he had held her in the synagogue.

They headed toward the upper decks, talking and holding hands. Tina thanked him for rescuing her. He told her how he'd almost dropped her. She told him about going to the movie afterward. He asked her how she liked the food and if she'd been seasick. They began to get comfortable with each other.

They took an elevator to the Promenade Deck, meandered past the rows of empty deck chairs and, from the safe island that was the *Normandie,* silently surveyed the dark and turbulent ocean as they traveled across it toward America. Then she kissed him. It was a long, moist, loving kiss, tender but passionate.

He accepted the kiss because it came as a complete surprise, because it was heartfelt and real, because her lips were astonishingly soft, and because what else could he do.

She broke it off and turned away from him, but he caught her from behind, turned her back around toward him, and took her in his arms and returned the kiss. And for the very first time in his life, he felt it all fall away — the

303

hesitancy, the awkwardness, the failures, the humiliations, the fear.

They held each other for a long time, their eyes closed, she feeling protected by his strength, he protective of her frailty. After a couple of minutes, they broke apart and walked a few more steps. Then they came together again.

At the aft end of the enclosed promenade, they found a door leading to the Upper Deck and to his cabin. He guided her through it and took her to his room, number 235. She waited patiently while he unlocked the door, as if coming back here was completely natural, a foregone conclusion.

Inside, they scarcely closed the door before they fell into each other's arms once more, hugging, kissing, and touching. For Tina, it was as though he'd tapped her deepest emotions. She was in the arms of a remarkable man who needed her and obviously wanted her. For Kurt Jaekel, it was a new world. He was holding the most beautiful girl in the world and she was showering him with love.

She slipped off his suit jacket and began to unbutton his shirt. Reciprocating, he found the catches at the back of her black dress. From time to time, they simply stopped and looked at each other in the dim light of the table lamp, amazed. She touched his chest, hard and muscular. He ran the side of a finger down her arm, feeling her warm, satiny skin.

They were naked to the waist now, still touching and still looking, each astonished by the other, each unable to think of anything except what their senses told them.

Many times in the past, Tina had imagined such a moment. And many times in the past, it had almost happened. Almost, but not quite. It had never happened because it had never been exactly right, not until now.

It was not quite so new an experience for Kurt. There had been women in Hamburg during his training days, women who hung out near the docks, waiting for sailors.

But he'd never known a woman or a time such as this.

It started, as such things always do, as a pinhole.

"Chief Engineer, I hear something," said Jean Gaspard, the first assistant.

"I hear nothing," the tiny chief engineer Gaston LeBrun responded. "What are you talking about?"

"I hear a hissing noise."

"A hissing? I don't hear it. Where is it?"

Gaspard ran a hand along a steam line, head down, listening. "I'm not sure. Somewhere near here."

LeBrun followed the steam line in the other direction. He came to an elbow and traced it around the corner, listening carefully, which was not an easy task since the sounds of throbbing machinery filled the engine room.

Then, just as LeBrun finished checking one section, a small quarter-sized chunk of the pipe abruptly broke away and a stream of superheated steam shot out of the hole like a geyser, hitting him squarely in one ear. He leaped away from the pipe, screaming and holding his head. And at that moment, another piece of pipe broke away, a section as big as a man's hand. Steam began to flood the engine room.

"Mechanics to the control panel!" the first assistant yelled out. "Someone bring a stretcher!"

The chief engineer lay on the floor near the pipe, writhing in pain and trying to cover his ear, which was already red and blistered. Gaspard bent over him. "How bad is it, sir?"

"I'll be all right," the chief engineer gasped. "You get the men on the steam pipe. . . . We're losing pressure fast."

Half a dozen mechanics gathered at the control panel. One of them had brought a canvas stretcher.

"Pierre and Jacques, you take the chief engineer to the infirmary," First Assistant Gaspard ordered.

"It's all right, Jean," the chief engineer moaned. "I'm okay."

The men looked at Gaspard uncertainly.

"Do what I told you. Now!"

The two mechanics lifted LeBrun onto the litter and carried him away. He did not protest again.

Gaspard, meanwhile, busied himself turning valve wheels. Slowly, the stream of superheated steam shooting out of the broken pipe began to diminish. Eventually, it ceased altogether.

At the same time, the throb of the engine machinery took on a new and more leisurely note. The whirling dynamos slowed, the rotation of the propeller shafts became more and more deliberate.

The engine room phone rang and Gaspard picked it up. It was Captain Barthou.

"LeBrun will be all right, Captain, but we've lost a main steam line, sir," Gaspard told him. "Six boilers are down."

"We need that speed, Gaspard," the captain said. "When can you get those boilers back on line?"

"I don't know if we can do it at all, sir. The entire steam line seems to be shot. I'll try to jerry-rig something, but it could be several hours."

The captain sighed. "Do your best, Gaspard. The safety of the ship may depend on your success."

"The safety of the ship? Are we running from something?"

"It's too complicated to explain, Gaspard. But we need every last fraction of a knot you can give us."

"I understand, sir."

He was amazed by his boldness.

He'd fumbled his way persistently through all kinds of feminine paraphernalia — garter belts and snaps and garments with hooks — and now she lay naked on the bed, his daydreams brought to life. And he stood before her in nothing more than his trousers.

"You are so lovely."

She smiled at him with such warmth that he could barely stand it.

"I wish to make love to you."

"You don't need to ask permission, Simon," she replied in the smallest and sweetest voice he had ever heard.

He reached for his belt buckle, feeling crude and awkward, but her hands intercepted his. Her slender fingers struggled with the heavy buckle until it finally opened. Then she unbuttoned his trousers, which slipped down to his ankles. He stood there and let her do all this, like a man being attended to by a tailor, except that no tailor's touch had ever thrilled a man this much.

"Left foot."

He lifted it and she pulled off the corresponding trouser leg. Then they cooperated on the other one. He was wearing only boxer trunks now, and he was more erect and more aroused than he had ever been in his entire life.

"Come to bed," she said, and he did. They pressed the entire lengths of their bodies against one another, oak against velvet. But for his growing passion, he might have been hesitant, even fearful. As it was, he was impelled by need and desire. For her part, she was neither bold nor timid, but to his joy, welcoming.

He sat up and slipped off his boxers in one swift, smooth motion, his eyes locked with hers. Then he touched her everywhere, with the care and reverence of someone making a flower arrangement. She touched him, too, more intimately than any woman had ever touched him, even the girls in Hamburg.

Then she stopped suddenly, frozen.

He knew why she had stopped, and the knowledge touched him deeply. She was frightened of his manhood. Despite her easy manner and the depth of her affection, she had never gone this far before, and she was apprehensive about what was going to happen and perhaps how it was going to feel.

"Do not be afraid, my dear little girl. I will not hurt you." He enfolded her in his powerful arms and comforted her.

She had to be sure, so she touched him again. It just couldn't be, she thought. But, nevertheless, it was. When their embrace at last dissolved, she looked at him. My God, my God, my God. He looked exactly like the Dutch boys she'd seen at the border, only larger and fully aroused.

He was not circumcised.

She looked into his eyes searchingly, confused. He took it for the sort of fear many innocent girls feel the very first time. But it was much more than that.

Tina knew. She knew he was not Simon Rothmann, the Viennese businessman, the tragic figure, the man who had lost his family to Nazi brutality. He was not even Jewish. The sliver of suspicion she'd felt during the service now returned, magnified to towering proportions, bringing anger and accusation.

He was lying about his religion and about his identity, and that could mean only one thing: This man, Simon Rothmann — or whatever his real name was — was the Nazi agent Nathan and Segonzak had been searching for, the saboteur, the man who intended to murder them all.

And he was about to make love to her.

"I will go slowly. I will be very careful with you, you will see," he said. This tender feeling was unfamiliar to him, almost strange. But how could he treat this lovely creature in any other way?

"I am afraid." What could she do? She could think of no way to get away from him, not now. If she betrayed the slightest hint that she knew who he was . . . she thought of the cargo supervisor. She remembered the fate of the friendly little steward, Maurice Cosset.

"I know you are afraid, but do not worry. You are safe with me."

Tina looked at this strong and handsome man, so attrac-

308

tive, so appealing, so dangerous, so evil. I am an actress, she told herself. And if I expect to walk out of here alive and to save the others, I had better act.

She put her arms around his neck. "Please do not hurt me."

"Of course not. I will love you."

And fighting back panic and revulsion, she let him do just that. She did what she could to respond, to control her fear and her pain, to make him feel she returned his passion and his love, and it was enough.

Strangely enough, it was her pain and fear that helped her most. It was, at least, a genuine feeling. And, perceiving it not for the anguish and suffering that it was, but instead as ardor, it made him that much more tender . . . and masterful.

Exactly how long it all lasted, she did not know. But she did know that she could not have stood it if it had lasted another minute. And after it was finally over, she told him she was very tired, and she rolled over, feigned sleep, and tried to deal with what had just happened to her. Tomorrow morning could not come quickly enough. Tomorrow morning, she would tell David Nathan, and he and Jean-Louis would kill this evil creature.

Jaekel watched her slow, regular breathing. She was even more beautiful asleep than awake, if that were possible. She was a vision and what had just happened could not have been real. Nothing like this could have happened to him.

Then he had a disturbing thought: It had *not* happened to him, not at all, not to Kurt Jaekel, Raeder's man, the Nazi agent who was going to blow up this ship and everyone on it in less than two days. It had happened to Simon Rothmann, a man who did not exist.

Something else caught his attention. Something had changed, something was different. He tried to figure out what it was and finally it came to him: The ship's engine vibrations had changed pitch. They were lower, less frenzied. For some reason, he realized, the ship had lost speed. He listened more closely now. The engine note was significantly lower. It was what he would have expected if the ship were coming into port. This was not the sort of vibration the *Normandie* produced at thirty-two knots. It sounded and felt more like twenty-two knots.

Jaekel lay there, awake and listening, waiting for the vibrations to pick up again. What was going on here? Why had the *Normandie* slowed down? What new stratagem was this? Had his adversaries found some new way to confound him?

Whatever it was, it looked as though some higher power had come to the aid of his cause. At this rate, the ship would soon lose all the time she'd gained traveling at thirty-two knots. It was practically miraculous.

But what if the ship continued to crawl along, well below her normal cruising speed? At this speed, the *Normandie* could be *late* for the rendezvous, maybe hours late. What would happen then? How long would the U-boat and the salvage ship be able to keep station?

Had his enemies somehow guessed what awaited them and was this their way to frustrate Raeder's plan? Were they heading toward some rendezvous of their own, perhaps with British or American warships?

Jaekel had trouble sleeping. He had too much on his mind—the girl, the ship, the job he had to do. It was just about dawn when the pulsing sounds rose once more to their former pitch. Jaekel did the calculations in his head. If he was right, the *Normandie* had lost at least two hours, maybe more. That just might be enough. Evidently, whoever was searching for him had not guessed the plan after all. Evidently, the slowdown had just been a mechanical problem.

The girl beside him stirred and made a little snoring

sound. He still felt an almost overpowering tenderness toward her, but he no longer had any illusions. He had remembered who he was, and his sense of duty had returned. He had to dispose of the girl now and go move the motor car into position. But she looked so innocent, so peaceful. He could not bring himself to harm her, not here, not now. She would die soon enough, along with everyone else on the ship.

Jaekel made up his mind about the automobile. He would not attempt to move it now. He would make a single visit to the cargo hold on Sunday morning, move the vehicle into the proper parking spot, and set the fuse. If anyone tried to stop him . . . well, by then, he could handle the situation as he wished without worrying about arousing suspicion.

Until then? He looked at the lovely woman lying next to him. Until then, he could continue to live in this beautiful daydream.

Day Six

EARLY MORNING

It was very boring duty.

It was hours of sitting and staring at a thousand little lights that never went on.

It was trying to stay awake and trying not to think of home and counting the minutes until your relief arrived.

But not this morning. This morning, it was seeing an alarm light blink on and wondering what in the world it was, then seeing two more appear and starting to get scared.

The watch officer tapped the bulbs, hoping they would go out. Nothing happened. Reluctantly, he picked up the emergency phone that connected him directly with the fire brigade and with the brigade chief.

"What is it, Paul," the chief said, annoyed. "Don't you know it's six A.M.? I've been in bed for less than two hours."

"We have three lights on E Deck aft."

"Probably loose bulbs. Happens pretty often. Give 'em a

312

tap."

"Already did. Didn't even flicker."

Merde.

"All right, sound the Klaxon."

"The passengers aren't going to like it, Chief. It's been a pretty rough voyage."

"I imagine they'd rather be rudely awakened than incinerated in their beds."

"Well, if those are your orders . . ." The watch officer hit a button and the fire alarm Klaxon began sounding throughout the ship.

One second before the Klaxon sounded, the vast mass of humanity aboard the *Normandie* had been sound asleep, except for small crews in the engine room, the kitchen, and on the bridge. A second later, all 2,935 passengers and crew members were wide awake, and most of them were either angry or terrified.

At Freppel's orders, stewards filtered through the ship, rousting sleepy passengers from their beds, explaining that a fire drill was in progress and herding them out into the corridors.

The Klaxon had come as a total surprise to David Nathan, who'd been lying in bed wide awake, waiting for Tina to return. He'd been in their cabin since about two A.M., when he and Segonzak had decided to suspend their interrogations until morning.

Nathan had no idea what the alarm meant, but he was determined to find out. He called Martel, who told him it was a fire, probably a minor fire, on E Deck. Then he called Segonzak and asked him to come to the fire site. No telling what they'd find.

"I'm going, too," Victor said, climbing out of bed.

"No you're not," Nathan told him. "You're staying here in case Tina comes back. I'll return soon."

Victor accepted his fate without any special grace.

Nathan headed down the stairway toward E Deck. He

was almost there before he caught even the faintest whiff of smoke. Maybe there's a fire here, he thought, but it wasn't much of a fire.

He saw several members of the fire brigade standing near the third-class dining room, outside of a large portside supply room. Segonzak was already on the scene.

"What's up?"

"A stowaway's cooking fire," Segonzak explained. "It set some sheets ablaze. But it's already out."

At that moment, the fire chief and one of his assistants brought the stowaway out of the supply room. The man, who was incongruously attired in a brown felt hat and a brown herringbone-tweed overcoat, was wringing his hands and apologizing profusely.

"My God . . . you!" Nathan exclaimed. "Hold that man!"

Segonzak was astounded. "You know him?"

"He is the bearded man I saw boarding the ship. And unless I'm very much mistaken, we'll find the bomb in the wooden box he was carrying."

The man was incredulous. "Bomb? No bomb!"

Nathan pushed past the man without a word, leading Segonzak into the storeroom. A large, rough pine box was leaning against a wall. The words *Salesmen's Samples* were stenciled on the long side.

Somehow, the bearded man pulled away from the fire chief and darted into the supply room. He grabbed the wooden box before Nathan could touch it and clutched it to his chest protectively.

"Give me the box," Nathan demanded.

The stowaway was wild-eyed. "I will not! I will defend it with my life."

"Then you will die." Nathan pulled the gun out of his sock.

The fire chief seized the stowaway's arms and pinioned them behind his back. Terrified that there would be an ex-

314

plosion, Segonzak caught the wooden box before it hit the floor.

"Open it," Nathan said.

Segonzak pointed at the small steel padlock. "It's locked."

"No problem." Nathan pointed his pistol at the lock and fired a single shot, smashing it to pieces.

"No! No!" the bearded man cried, as though he himself had been wounded by the shot. "Don't harm it!"

Segonzak opened the box.

Beneath the lid was a chamber sumptuously lined and cushioned in blue velvet, interwoven with gold threads. Inside, like an infant in swaddling clothes, rested a strip of yellowed parchment rolled up on two scroll pins and tied together with silk ribbons.

The stowaway wrested free from the fire chief once more, seized the scroll, and clutched it to his chest. Nathan, Segonzak, and the fire chief stared at him, totally bewildered.

"Go ahead," the bearded man said defiantly, "kill me! Shoot me! That's the only way you'll get the manuscript from me."

"The artwork!" cried the fire chief. "We've found the stolen artwork! And he's the thief!"

Segonzak shook his head. "That's not it."

"What do you mean? There it is! We've caught the thief red-handed." The fire chief was utterly convinced.

"Does that look like a stone tablet to you, Chief?" the dark-haired American agent asked.

The fire chief seemed confused

"Don't worry," Segonzak told the bearded man. "No one is going to shoot you." Whoever this man was, he was no threat to anyone.

"Who are you?" Nathan demanded. "And what are you holding?"

"I am Casimir Sulkowski," said the bearded man. "And this—"

315

Segonzak interrupted. "Just tell us the truth," he said wearily. "Nothing's going to happen to you. I promise."

"My name is Reb Pinchas Nachman," the bearded man said defiantly. "I am from Prague. And this treasure is the original handwritten manuscript of the *Mishna Torah*, by Maimonides. I am carrying it to Rabbi Herzberg in Brooklyn, USA."

David Nathan and Jean-Louis Segonzak exchanged glances. The bearded man was just one more dead end, and a bizarre one at that. Every road they'd taken had been a dead end. Two telegrams from France, two murders, the sabotage of the ship's wireless, and almost one hundred passengers questioned, and they were no nearer to finding a suspect than they had been when they started.

"Give him back his box and put him in a third-class cabin," Nathan told the fire chief.

"I don't know who you are, sir, but you have no authority on this ship as far as stowaways are concerned. . . ."

"I am not a stowaway," Nachman protested. "I paid twenty-five American dollars for my passage."

"You paid twenty-five dollars?"

"We have some dishonest crewmen," the fire chief explained. "They are preying on refugees, taking money in return for smuggling them aboard the ship."

"Well, put him in a third-class room," Nathan repeated.

The fire chief objected again. "I don't have any authority to do that."

"Do what he says," Segonzak said wearily. "If you need more authority, call Martel or Freppel or the captain."

The fire chief puffed out his chest. "I'm going to do just that."

Segonzak ignored him. "Ready to start questioning people again, David?"

"Yes. But I've got to go back to my cabin for a moment, Jean-Louis. I promised to tell Victor what was going on. Care to join me?"

316

"Let's go."

Ever since they'd made love, Tina's mind had been focused on getting away from this monster somehow, on escaping from him without arousing his suspicion. The fire alarm provided the perfect opportunity.

"I've got to go back to my cabin," she told him as they stood together in the hallway with the other passengers. "My brother and my uncle will be worried about me."

Jaekel was very tender with her. "I don't want you to go, Lilly."

She squeezed his hand. "I don't want to go either, Simon. But I must. I'll come back as soon as I can."

He took her in his arms and kissed her deeply, and she responded passionately, as she knew she must. "Please hurry," he said.

She hurried. She hurried away from him, her revulsion and fear barely under control. She hurried back to her brother and to David Nathan.

"So all we succeeded in doing was eliminating one suspect," Segonzak concluded.

Victor nodded. "How many do we have left to question?"

"Fifty-nine," Nathan told him.

Victor thought a moment. "At fifteen minutes apiece, that's just a little under fifteen hours. You should be finished by midnight, assuming you have your meals brought to you."

"Assuming we have to interview everyone," Segonzak said.

"Assuming the saboteur is on our list at all," Nathan added grimly.

There was a frantic knocking on the door. Victor

opened it and Tina burst into the stateroom, sobbing. She flung herself into her brother's arms.

"My God, Tina," cried Nathan, "what's wrong?"

"I've found him!" she blurted out. "I know who he is!"

"What?" Segonzak asked urgently. "Who?"

"Him. The Nazi. I spent the night with him. I slept with him, God help me, I slept with that animal!"

"Who, Tina?" Victor pressed on, sick with dawning realization. "Who are you talking about?"

"Simon Rothmann . . . only that's not his name."

Nathan could not mask his distress. It had been disturbing enough to see her go off with Rothmann last night. He'd tortured himself with speculation. But this was beyond all imagining. He should have stopped her. He should have protected her somehow. "Tina, I'm so sorry."

"It wasn't your fault."

The fox-faced Frenchman was confused. "Who's Rothmann?"

Nathan explained. "He's the man who rescued Tina when the lifeboat fell."

"You can't be serious."

Tina took a seat. She was struggling for composure. "Look, you said that when we find the man who *isn't* who he says he is, the person who's lying about his identity, then we'll have the saboteur."

Nathan spoke to her with pained deliberation. "Yes, that's true. But what makes you think Rothmann isn't . . . well, Rothmann?"

Tina sighed. "Okay, remember those Dutch boys at the border?"

"Of course."

"Well, he looked just like them."

"What do you mean?" Nathan asked.

"I know what she means," said Victor. "I know *exactly* what she means."

The light dawned in Nathan's eyes.

Segonzak was exasperated. "Would anybody care to tell me what this discussion is about?"

Nathan volunteered. "We saw a Nazi patrol at the border stop some Dutch boys and make them pull down their pants to prove they weren't Jews."

"Ah. And this Rothmann?"

"He could have passed the test," Tina said.

"Bingo," Nathan said softly.

The Frenchman was still a little puzzled. "Why bingo?"

"Because he was at the synagogue last night, wearing a *yarmulke* and evidently pretending to mourn for his family — a famous Jewish merchant family," Nathan told him. "He's planted the rumor that the Nazis killed them."

Victor drew the conclusion. "And that means he is lying about his identity."

Segonzak finally understood. "As you say, bin-go."

"I want you to kill him," Tina said flatly.

Nathan put a hand on hers. "Wait a minute, I have to know something first. Does he have *any* idea you've guessed who he is?"

"None."

"You're sure?" Segonzak said. "It's crucial."

Tina turned to the French agent, her green eyes filled with tears. "I made love with that monster last night and would have had to do it again this morning if it hadn't been for the fire alarm."

Segonzak shook his head, shocked and upset, sorry he'd had to ask the question.

"That must have been . . ." Nathan couldn't find words to describe what he was feeling. He was sick at heart and he was enraged — at Rothmann and at himself for letting this terrible thing happen. Of course, Tina was a sassy little thing, but underneath all that she was vulnerable and basically innocent, a lot like his own little sister. He'd come to feel very protective of her. And it was almost impossible for him to bear the thought of what she'd been through.

319

"There wasn't any choice . . . if he'd guessed I knew . . . the little steward . . . I thought about the steward . . . he killed them, you know . . . I was afraid he would . . . I just had to pretend . . . I had to act as though . . ." She was crying openly again, the explanations she'd clung to all night finally tumbling out in fractured sentences.

"Tina, I'm so sorry. . . ." Nathan started. He tried to put his arms around her, but she refused to be comforted.

"He seemed so *wounded*. . . . But that's all a monstrous lie. . . . The worst thing of it is, it was the first time for me. . . ."

"Jesus, Tina." Nathan bit his lips helplessly. "I had no idea. I can't tell you how sorry I am."

"I don't know what to say, little one," Segonzak told her. He was just as shocked and upset as Nathan. "God, I wish we could have caught him first. I'm so sorry we didn't."

Victor put his arm around her. "It's over now, Tina. You're safe."

"I want you to kill him," she ordered Nathan flatly. "I want you to shoot him in the head."

Nathan understood her impulse perfectly. He had the same feeling himself. "That's just what I want to do, Tina. I want to kill him in the most painful way possible. I want him to suffer. But I can't do that—not yet."

Tina was furious. "If you can't do it, then I will. Just give me your gun and I'll kill him myself, I swear it."

"He will die, little one," Segonzak said kindly. "I promise you that. It just can't happen yet."

"You? You're a coward, too? What's the matter with you, both of you? Is it all right with you what he did to me?"

Nathan did his best to calm her. "If it were just a matter of courage, we'd both be at his door right now, Tina. And I guarantee you, he will be punished. But we have the ship to consider, remember that."

Tina was momentarily confused. "The ship?"

"Remember who he is, Tina," Victor said. "Remember why he is aboard the ship."

For a moment, that made sense to her. Then it didn't make any sense at all. "I don't understand. If you kill him, then the ship will be safe."

"I only wish that were so," Nathan told her. He knew where this conversation was going, and it made him even more furious at the German and at himself, for getting Tina into this terrible situation. "It's just not that simple."

"What are you talking about?" Tina demanded. It was more an accusation of cowardice than a simple question.

Nathan and Segonzak looked at one another. The Frenchman took it upon himself to explain what they both knew. He spoke to Tina in the tones an adult uses to tell a child that something very bad has happened. "We need to locate and disarm the bomb, little one. If we arrest him or tip our hand somehow, we'll never find it, and he may succeed in blowing up the ship—even if he's dead or in the brig."

Tina was stupefied. "You can't let him remain free!"

"We have to. We don't have any more choice than you did." Nathan was speaking sternly and deliberately now. "We have to let him lead us to the bomb. He's the only one who knows where it is. Remember, we've searched the ship thoroughly and no one's come up with it. He has some hiding place that we haven't been able to find."

"It makes sense to trail him—at least if he hasn't set the timing mechanism," Victor said thoughtfully. "But what if he already has? Then we don't gain a thing if we let him go free. We should seize him and force him to tell us where it is."

"If we try to force him to talk," Nathan said, "we won't get anywhere. He'll deny everything—if he speaks at all. You don't know the way these men are trained. They'd rather die."

Segonzak backed him up. "David is right. I've captured

six Nazi agents myself, and I haven't been able to get a word out of any one of them. And that isn't because we were nice to them. Four died during questioning."

Nathan whistled softly.

"But if the timing mechanism is set, and he doesn't have to go back to the bomb, how *do* we find it, then?" Victor asked, truly puzzled.

"Fortunately," Segonzac told him, "Rothmann *must* go back to the bomb, even if he's already set the timer."

"Why in the world would he have to do that?" Victor asked stubbornly. "It just doesn't make sense."

For a change, Nathan noted with a certain amount of relish, he'd come across something the young scientist didn't know. "It's a matter of standard procedure, Victor. The book."

Segonzac agreed. "That's right. You see, German agents are trained to do things by the book and only by the book. Deviations just aren't tolerated. And the book on explosives says saboteurs must recheck—or set—the timer no more than sixty minutes before a scheduled detonation."

"But why?" Victor asked, grilling Segonzac as the Frenchman had once grilled him. "That only increases the agent's jeopardy."

"It certainly does," Segonzac admitted. "But timing mechanisms are notoriously unreliable. I guess the rule is an attempt to compensate. Our people are trained the same way."

"Ours, too," Nathan said.

"Interesting," Victor said.

"So Rothmann will be going back to the bomb one way or another," Segonzac said.

Victor did some brief mental calculations. "That should happen sometime late tomorrow morning."

Nathan contradicted him. "It could be earlier. He may have to retrieve the device from a hiding place or assemble something. The parts may be scattered. Maybe that's why we haven't been able to find the thing."

"So we trail him," Victor said, following their logic. "And he leads us to the bomb. What then?"

Nathan shrugged. "Then we grab him, and we disarm the bomb."

Everyone had the same thought, but no one said it: Grabbing Rothmann and disarming the bomb might not be anywhere near as easy as Nathan had made it sound.

Tina spoke up again, fear in her voice. "What will Rothmann do until Sunday morning?"

"Enjoy himself, I suppose," Segonzak told her.

"What do you mean by that?"

This time, it was Nathan who volunteered to explain the obvious. "I'm sure he's going to want to see you, Tina."

The stateroom was suddenly very quiet again.

"And how do you expect me to treat him?"

No one answered her question, but that was answer enough. "Oh, no," she protested. "I'm not going back to him. You can't make me do that."

"Tina . . ." Nathan began, then stopped. He didn't know what to say to her.

"Just forget it. You'll have to find some other way. If he touches me again, I'll kill him myself. I'll strangle him if I have to."

"What will he conclude if you shun him, little one?" Segonzak asked.

Tina looked at her brother desperately. "Stop them, Victor! Tell them they can't do this."

Victor Meisner refused to meet his sister's eyes.

"A day and a half, Tina," Nathan said. "That's all."

"That's a lifetime."

"I know it's asking a great deal," Segonzak said. "I wish I knew some other way."

"A great deal?" Tina snapped. "Would *you* do what you are asking me to do?"

Segonzak paused for a moment, thoughtful. "I have,

little one. I have."

"Maybe so, but you're a trained agent."

Nathan dropped the gentle tone. "Listen, you're trained, too — you're an *actress,* right? Now you're going to find out if you're any good at it."

"You've already played the part once," Segonzak observed. "And evidently with great skill."

"The man is right, Tina," her brother told her.

"I just don't know if I can do it again."

"I think you can," Nathan said, "if you accept him for what he appears to be, for what he wants you to think he is."

"Do you want me to do this, David?" She looked at him searchingly. If this really was his wish, she couldn't refuse him. She realized that now, for the first time.

"Do I want you to?" Nathan retorted. "Of course I don't. I despise the whole thing. But there's no choice." If there'd been any way, *he* would have gone back to Rothmann's room rather than sending Tina. If there had been any way.

Tina thought about what Nathan had said.

Segonzak tried to encourage her. "Both of you will be playing roles, you know."

Victor joined in. "He's right, Tina. And if you reinforce him in his role, if you *help* him play it, he'll help you play yours."

The men waited for Tina's reaction.

"If I do this," she demanded icily, "I want one of you near me all the time — within sight, or at least within shouting distance. *If* I do this."

"Of course," Nathan assured her. "Either Jean-Louis or I or both of us. Wherever the two of you go, we will be nearby. You will not be alone with him — that's a promise."

"Except in his cabin," Segonzak pointed out.

They all knew what that meant.

"Even then, we'll be in the hallway, within view of the

door," Nathan pledged. "If you call out, we'll hear you and we'll come for you."

"Just remember who he is, Tina," Victor said.

"How could I ever forget?"

Victor shook his head. "That's not what I meant."

"He is Simon Rothmann, Tina," her brother told her. "A Viennese businessman whose family was murdered by the Nazis. Just keep your mind riveted on that."

"Yes," she said hesitantly.

"He is in great pain and he needs your sympathy, your compassion, and your love," Victor went on.

Tina listened intently, as though hearing the playwright talk about his intentions, as though taking direction.

Seeing her mood begin to change, Victor continued instructing her. "He needs an opportunity to express his love, Tina. Maybe his sadness, too. Remember how he cried in the synagogue? He is in genuine pain. He's feeling very real grief of some kind. He needs you to be kind to him, because he's very fragile now."

"He did seem to genuinely care about me," she reflected. "He was very concerned about frightening me."

Nathan reinforced the thought. "Maybe you've caught him off guard, Tina. Maybe you've touched the real man." He hoped desperately that he was right.

"Maybe."

"You must make him believe you think he's Simon Rothmann, little one," Segonzak added. "As long as he's convinced you do, you will be safe."

"I see." Tina was sarcastic. "If I give a convincing performance, I get to live."

"If you give a convincing performance, Tina," Nathan said, "we all get to live."

Once again, no newspaper was printed aboard the *Normandie,* to the intense distress of the passengers, who rightly felt they'd been cut off from the outside world. They yearned for news from Europe almost as much as they yearned for the safety of New York.

But if the ship's printing plant had published a paper on this day, Saturday, August 26, 1939, it might have contained the following bulletins:

*Hitler and the British Ambassador to Berlin met last night and renewed hope that the current German-Polish dispute might be settled short of war. Hitler was said to be ready to agree to a "compromise" providing for the return of Danzig, the Polish Corridor, and parts of the former German province of Pozen.

*In France, Premier Daladier said in his radio broadcast that whatever Hitler demanded or threatened this time, there would be no "Munich."

*On the Rhine, French engineers cut all eight of the bridges between Basel and Strasbourg, severing the links between Germany and France. The permanent railroad bridges, the only other means of communication across the Rhine, were mined and made ready to be blown up at a moment's notice.

*On the stock exchanges, the British pound and French franc fell sharply as their countries withdrew support, apparently forced to do so by the rush to convert both of these currencies into dollars.

*In Paris, the art treasures in the Louvre and Versailles were packed up and transferred to the safety of the vaults of the Bank of France or other secret security centers in the provinces. Scaffolds were also erected around the Chartres Cathedral for the removal of the famous stained glass windows.

The passengers of the *Normandie* might also have learned, had their newspaper been published as usual, that their ship was not the only one at sea caught in a risky position. Many other famous liners, packed with passengers, were also in mid-ocean, half of them heading to America, the other half returning to Europe. They included the *Aquitania,* the *Georgic,* the *Britannic,* the *Queen Mary,* the *De Grasse,* the *Ile de France,* and the two German giants the *Normandie* had already encountered, the *Bremen* and the *Europa.*

At any moment, however, a few well-aimed torpedoes could sever the broad transatlantic highway that carried all of this traffic and that connected the civilization of the Old World with the civilization of the New World.

AFTERNOON

When compared to other man-made objects, the *Normandie* was a behemoth. Stood on end, she would have surpassed the Eiffel Tower by forty-five feet and fallen just seventeen feet short of the tip of the pointed spire that topped the Chrysler Building. She was built of more than sixty-seven thousand tons of wood and glass and marble and steel. On the surface of the mighty Atlantic, however, she was just another toothpick.

And now, in the midst of a driving rain and fairly heavy seas, she was starting to pitch and roll noticeably. She would fall forward, into a wave trough, then lift herself up, out and over the crest, and then do it all over again. At the same time, she would slowly oscillate from side to side like a windshield wiper.

Actually, big express steamers don't pitch much. Their vast length bridges the distance between most wave tops. But every passenger liner rolls plenty, no matter how large it is.

Some liners—the *Queen Mary,* for instance—roll lazily from one side to another. This can be quite suspenseful. At the far point of the roll, passengers wonder if she'll recover or simply keep going this time and turn turtle. They ask themselves how long she can steam this way, lying almost on her side. Then, slowly, she'll right herself. And just when the passengers are congratulating each other on the ship's miraculous survival, she'll gradually roll just as far in the other direction. Four or five days of that gives most people a greatly heightened appreciation of *terra firma*.

The *Normandie* rolled in a somewhat different manner. She flipped quickly to one side, then back to an even keel, then to the other side, and so forth. This was nowhere near as terrifying as the sluggish rolling—and righting—of the *Queen Mary*, but for about half the people on board, passengers and crew members alike, it meant intense and continuing bouts of *mal de mer* and trips to the rail or the lavatory, rather than to the dining room. So, while *Queen Mary* passengers prayed to be saved from what they thought was certain death, many a *Normandie* passenger longed for exactly that.

But the seas weren't high enough for that yet. The pitching and rolling was still reasonable. Only the most susceptible were retiring to their staterooms to curl up in a ball and moan. Some of the others were queasy but still able to carry on, which is exactly what they did, as the adrenaline of the fire drill faded and the safety of America grew closer.

A fair number of first-class passengers, uninterested in sitting on the enclosed promenade and watching the rain or sick of watching movies, donned bathing suits and robes and descended to D Deck, the location of the *Normandie's* *piscine des premieres classes*—her first-class swimming pool. A few of them even intended to get wet.

The envy of many a YMCA, the *Normandie piscine* was seventy-five feet long, eighteen feet wide, two decks high, and completely surrounded by a four-foot tiled platform. That made it the largest swimming pool ever installed in an ocean liner.

The walls and ceilings of the chamber were covered by pale blue enameled tiles and set off by a decorative mosaic frieze. At the pool's stern end was a gilded bronze circular bar. Indirect lighting gave the entire area—pool and bar—the glow of a pale, balmy day.

If you were inclined to queasiness, the swimming pool was a good place to go in rough weather. The pitching and rolling weren't so prominent there, because the room was so low in the ship and right on the centerline. And if you were a little drunk, which was an extremely common affliction on a transatlantic liner, you could almost mistake the sloshing for beach waves.

David Nathan and Jean-Louis Segonzak stood at the bar with a number of other passengers, wearing their bathing suits. They were sipping Scotches and idly watching Simon Rothmann doing laps, with a pretty, powerful stroke that barely rippled the water.

Tina was wrapped in a pale blue one-piece suit that made all kinds of promises without really keeping any of them. She'd found a perch on the edge of the pool and was attracting the usual attention from most of the men in the room. From time to time, Rothmann would teasingly splash her or swim over to touch her hand and say something romantic. She'd smile and giggle, then look a little embarrassed and warn him that people were watching.

"Well, what do you know?" It was Karla Kirkland, sheathed in something red and shiny that, in a pinch, could have served as an anatomical chart.

"Oh, hello, Karla."

"And I suppose this is the fraternity brother who's been taking up so much of your time?"

Segonzak, whose eyebrows were already elevated, tried to crank them up another notch. "Beg pardon?"

"Oh, yes," Nathan said. "Liberty, equality, fraternity, and all that."

He made the introductions. Karla shook Segonzak's

hand and draped a slender, perfectly tapered arm over Nathan's broad shoulder. "You look terrific in a bathing suit," she told him. "I didn't realize how muscular you are."

Nathan tried to pass it off. "Well, I—"

"I didn't even know you swam."

"I'm really not much of a swimmer."

"Well, let's just see about that."

Karla grabbed his hand and pulled him off the bar stool, toward the water. Nathan looked back toward Segonzak, imploring him for help.

"It's all right," the Frenchman taunted him. "Enjoy yourself."

Karla dragged Nathan to the edge of the pool, pushed him in, then jumped in herself. For the next quarter of an hour or so, she chased him around the pool, splashing him, trying to dunk him and literally swimming circles around him. He hadn't the faintest idea what to do with her. Despite her circumstances, Tina found herself laughing at the scene.

At one point, Karla swam over to Tina. "Looks like you're making some progress," Tina said. To her surprise, the thought troubled her a little. Was she feeling jealous?

Karla shrugged. "Can't tell yet. But I'm persistent. I see you're doing pretty well. Must be pretty nice."

Tina smiled ironically. "Kind of like swallowing cyanide."

"What did you say?"

"Just a joke. Hey, good luck with David."

"Thanks. I need it."

She swam off, displaying beautiful legs and a practically perfect rear end.

At the bar, Segonzak ate some pretzels and watched the scene, apparently without a care in the world. After a few minutes, the lifeguard sat down beside him and ordered a soft drink.

"Quite a swimmer," Segonzak said, making idle conversation.

"He was the German champion at one time."

"I was referring to the girl in the red bathing suit."

"Oh, her. No, I was talking about the guy doing laps."

"A champion?"

"Not only that, a channel swimmer," the lifeguard said. His eyes narrowed briefly as he tried to remember something. "Broke the record in '34. Or was it '33? I don't remember exactly."

"He's not a Viennese businessman named Rothmann?" Segonzak asked, very interested now.

"Nope. Not him. I swam against the guy once, and he beat the hell out of me."

"You're sure?"

"Seems to me he was a German Navy officer," the lifeguard recalled. "But I don't remember for sure. What I do remember is those arms and shoulders."

"Looks pretty strong to me."

"Unbelievable endurance," the lifeguard said.

"What's his name?"

"Jaguar? Yokel? Something like that. It's been a long time."

"But not Rothmann?"

"No, I'm sure that wasn't it. Started with a *J* or maybe a *Y?*"

If Segonzak had had any lingering doubt, that ended it. Who was better for an assignment that called for swimming to a submarine than a channel swimmer? He couldn't wait to tell Nathan. The captain would also be pleased by this final confirmation.

Just then, Rothmann hopped out of the pool and started toward a doorway. Segonzak slid off his stool and went after him, following him into the men's room. They stood at adjacent urinals and did what they had to do.

"I was watching you in the pool," Segonzak said. "You're quite a swimmer."

"My parents had a summer home on Lake Neusiedler,"

331

Jaekel said, quoting the background paper Raeder had made him memorize. "Used to swim there a lot when I was a boy."

He pulled the flush lever and walked back into the pool area. Segonzak was three steps behind him. He joined Nathan, who had returned to the bar.

"Where did he go?" Nathan asked.

"Pee break."

"I see."

"Having a good time?"

"Not exactly. I can't figure out how to get rid of her." Nathan gestured over his shoulder. Karla had climbed out of the pool, at the far end, and was confidently striding toward them, her lithe body glistening wetly.

"Terrible problem."

"I mean, at another moment . . ."

"Of course. Well, what do you have in mind, David? A fight?"

"Too messy."

"How about a hand on the knee and a soulful gaze?"

Nathan rolled his eyes.

"A crude remark?"

"Tried it. She's impervious."

"What then?"

"Never mind," Nathan said. "She's almost here."

"I have an idea, David. Just play along with me."

Nathan looked at him skeptically. "She isn't easy to discourage."

"This will work."

Karla plopped down on the seat next to Nathan's and ordered a martini.

"It's really nice to see David with a woman again," Segonzak mentioned casually.

"What do you mean?" Karla asked.

"Well, it's . . . how long, David, four years?"

"Closer to five," Nathan said. He didn't have any idea

where Segonzak was going, but it sounded promising.

"Right. Ever since the injury."

Now Karla was concerned. "What injury?"

"He doesn't like to discuss it," Segonzak told her confidentially. "But that's understandable."

"What is he talking about, David?"

Nathan shook his head and refused to answer. What could he have said, anyhow?

Segonzak grew quite serious. "He was gored, Karla."

She winced. "Gored? What do you mean?"

"It happened at Pamplona, just before the Spanish Civil War."

"You went to the running of the bulls?" Karla was surprised.

"He and Hemingway are friends," Segonzak explained. "In fact, Hemingway modeled a character after him. Wasn't that in *The Sun Also Rises*, David?"

"That's right."

"But I don't see any scar. Oh, he's kidding . . . isn't he, David?"

Nathan looked her square in the eye. "I wish he were."

"Oh, my God, David! I didn't know."

"I'm all right now," David said. "More or less."

"Just listen to him," Segonzak said with admiration. "In a strange way, he's more of a man now than he was before."

Karla stared at David in horror.

"Maybe I should have told you," he said. "But it doesn't really matter, does it?"

Karla suddenly seemed ill at ease. "No, of course not. Listen, I'm getting a chill. I think I'm going to go upstairs and get some clothes on."

"Karla, I—"

"Listen, I'll see you at dinner, David."

She practically ran out of the room.

"Oh, bartender," Nathan called out, "would you bring

my friend a . . . what'll you have, Jean-Louis?"

"Scotch and soda would be fine."

At that moment, Tina laughed, and both Nathan and Segonzak turned toward her, suddenly remembering why they were here and what was really going on between the girl and her companion.

"She's quite a soldier, that one," Segonzak observed.

"I just hope we're not asking too much of her."

The Young Lovers continued to flirt and frolic in the pool until mid-afternoon, Tina several times putting off Rothmann's suggestion that they go back to his cabin. Finally, at about three-thirty she gave in, and they playfully dried each other off with the big Turkish towels the ship provided.

"Kinda nice to see that sort of thing," the bartender told Nathan and Segonzak.

"Looks like a typical shipboard romance to me," Segonzak said.

"I'd say it was more than that," the bartender replied. "They really seem to like each other."

The Young Lovers slipped on their robes and headed toward the elevator, Nathan and Segonzak close behind. They rode up together, along with a number of other passengers. Rothmann was too involved with nuzzling Tina to notice anyone else, but in the midst of a hug, Tina managed to make a face at Nathan.

The elevator doors opened and the Young Lovers slowly strolled down the corridor, arms around each other. Their watchdogs followed at a discreet distance until the Twosome disappeared inside Rothmann's room.

"What now?" the Frenchman asked.

Nathan looked around. Almost directly across the hall was a linen closet. "I wait in there, in case she needs me."

"Doesn't look like she's going to need you, David."

Nathan nodded glumly.

"I'll get changed for dinner and relieve you," Segonzak

334

told him.

"Two fast knocks, two slow knocks."

"Right."

Segonzak walked off, and Nathan shut himself inside the closet, leaving the door open just a crack. He looked at the closed door across the hall and did his best not to imagine what was going on behind it. She's really doing very well, he told himself. I think she's actually going to pull it off. So what is it that's troubling me so much?

EVENING

Tina Meisner and Simon Rothmann ate dinner at the Cafe Grill that evening. They sat at a table for two overlooking the ocean waves, holding hands between courses. David Nathan and his French colleague watched them from a table on the other side of the room, partially hidden from the Twosome by a marble pillar.

The Cafe Grill was half empty, the inclement weather forcing some of its usual patrons to remain in their cabins, close to their bathrooms. Erich von Stroheim was there, however. He was sitting alone, his chair positioned so he could watch Tina as he ate. And against the back wall sat Hans Hatzfeld, also alone. He was watching von Stroheim.

"A bird of prey," Segonzak said.

"Yes," Nathan agreed. "Observing another of his kind."

"Was he on the list?"

"Yes, he was. And if Tina hadn't found out about Rothmann, we would have questioned him this morning."

"Still something about him I don't trust," Segonzak told the husky, dark-haired American.

"Same here. Maybe I'll ask Martel to talk to him."

The Young Lovers were in the midst of dessert — pistachio ice cream for Tina, pudding *Martiniquais* for Rothmann — when von Stroheim pushed himself away from his table and went over to them.

"Good evening, Miss Cameron," von Stroheim said with a small formal bow.

"Good evening," she replied. A lick of dry ice would have been warmer.

Rothmann's expression changed, from a silly grin of love, into puzzlement, then suspicion.

"I have been thinking about you and about the part," von Stroheim said. "I think it would be a good idea for you to read the script."

"Funny," Tina said, puzzled, "you must have laryngitis. I didn't hear a word you said."

Von Stroheim persisted. "The script will change your mind. About *everything*."

Rothmann spoke. "The lady said she wasn't interested."

"Also, I have sketches of the costumes back in my cabin," von Stroheim went on. "I have been looking at them and imagining you in them. You will look unbelievably erotic."

Rothmann got to his feet.

"We better get over there and stop that before it gets started," Nathan said, rising.

"Wait a minute. We may not have to do anything." Segonzak gestured toward Hans Hatzfeld, who was walking toward von Stroheim.

"Ah, Herr von Stroheim," Hatzfeld said cheerily. "I've been looking for a chance to talk to you."

"Sir?"

"That's right," Hatzfeld went on. "I understand you play poker quite well, and I wonder if you'd be willing to play a hand or two with me."

Von Stroheim stared at the man as though passing a death sentence. "You wish to play poker with me, sir? You've come over here and interrupted my conversation with this beautiful lady to ask me to play poker with you?"

"Not to ask you, Herr von Stroheim, not exactly. I've

come to challenge you. Because I play poker pretty well myself."

Tina spoke up unexpectedly. "You're not going to ignore his challenge, are you?"

"Not if you'll witness the game," von Stroheim replied, locking his eyes with hers.

"Let's leave this place, Lilly," Rothmann said earnestly. "Let's go back to my cabin."

Tina gave his hand an affectionate squeeze. "Oh, don't be such a stick-in-the-mud, Simon. We won't stay long."

"When do you propose to play this match?" von Stroheim asked Hatzfeld.

"Well, if you're finished with dinner, now is as good a time as any. We can play in the Smoking Room."

"Fine."

Joined by other diners who'd heard the challenge—and by Nathan and Segonzak—the group now left the Cafe Grill, descended the Grand Stairway, en masse, and entered the Smoking Room, the vast hall with the gilded wooden walls. A fair number of card players were already in combat.

Hatzfeld found a table near the middle of the room and invited von Stroheim to take a seat. While the spectators—the Young Lovers, David Nathan, Jean-Louis Segonzak, and others—took their places around the table, a page brought several fresh decks of cards and a case of chips.

"Shall we start with a thousand dollars?" Hatzfeld asked von Stroheim. The German actor merely shrugged. Both men purchased the requisite number of chips, and the page closed the case. Each man put down a single white chip as a blind.

Then they cut for the deal, von Stroheim turning over a ten of spades, Hatzfeld a queen of diamonds. Hatzfeld shuffled absently, then von Stroheim cut the cards. Hatzfeld left the cut portion of the pack on the table and picked up the rest. Off to the side of the table, Segonzak jabbed

337

Nathan in the ribs. Nathan nodded.

They played six hands in about forty minutes. Hatzfeld won four, von Stroheim two. Von Stroheim's margins were large—a flush over two pairs, four of a kind over a straight. Hatzfeld's were small—a flush over a straight, two pairs over one, three queens over three tens. Nevertheless, all the chips ended up in front of Hatzfeld.

Von Stroheim signaled the page, who brought over the chip case, and he bought another two thousand dollars' worth. Half an hour later, those were also neatly stacked in front of Hatzfeld. He did it with nothing more than a full house.

"He's a very good player, isn't he?" Tina whispered to Rothmann.

"Just lucky, I think," Rothmann said. He pulled her closer to him and spoke into her ear, very quietly. "I'm having a terrible time keeping my hands off of you. Let's go back to my stateroom."

"I think we'd better stay here for a while," Tina said. "We don't want people to start gossiping about us, do we?"

Rothmann was disappointed, but he agreed.

In the midst of the poker game, Chief Purser Henri Freppel walked into the room and started doing his social duties, stopping to charm one group of elderly card players, chatting with a large woman who had some kind of complaint, and instructing a page to straighten his jacket. Then, attracted by the crowd, he strolled over to the table where Hatzfeld and von Stroheim were playing. After watching them for a few minutes, he suddenly summoned a page and whispered to him briefly. The page hurried off.

Hatzfeld and von Stroheim played two more hands, both of which von Stroheim lost. They were in the middle of a third when one of the Smoking Room pages returned to the room, bringing with him some security officers. Freppel edged his way through the crowd that had gathered around Hatzfeld and von Stroheim, the security men behind him.

"Sorry, gentlemen," he said. "Game over."

Freppel pushed all the chips back to von Stroheim. Both players looked at him in astonishment. "What are you doing?" von Stroheim asked.

"I'm stopping the game and returning your losings to you, sir," Freppel said. "And I am detaining Mr. Norman Hartman for questioning." He motioned to a security man, who grabbed Hatzfeld by the arm.

"I am Hans Hatzfeld," the man protested. "You have the wrong man. I will tell the captain about this insult."

"Please come with me, sir," the senior security officer said, ignoring the outburst.

"This is an outrage!" von Stroheim complained. "We're just having a friendly game of poker."

"I'm afraid the friendliness is quite one-sided, sir," Freppel explained. "You see, this is no friendly game of poker for Mr. Hartman. It is a matter of practicing his trade, which is that of professional gambler."

Von Stroheim turned his rage on Hatzfeld. "So that's why you won. You are a cheat and a thief!" He raised his arm and smashed Hatzfeld in the face full force, backhand, drawing blood. "That will teach you to trifle with me."

Freppel interposed himself between the two men. "Mr. von Stroheim, I suggest you cash in your chips, go back to your cabin, and compose yourself."

Von Stroheim was still sputtering. "I have been humiliated and I demand satisfaction."

"You will have your satisfaction, sir," Freppel told him. "Mr. Hartman will be immediately arrested when we get to New York and sent off to jail for quite a number of years. Meanwhile, I want to point out to you that you have not lost anything at all."

"I have been humiliated by a thief," von Stroheim said bitterly. "Isn't that loss enough?"

Freppel shrugged his charming shrug.

"Cash me in and bring the money to my room," von Stroheim commanded. He shoved his way through the crowd and out the door.

"Imagine that," Tina said, as innocent as a high school freshman. "A professional gambler right here on the *Normandie!*"

"Those things happen," Rothmann said. He was intoxicated by her nearness and increasingly desperate to get her back to his stateroom.

"Ladies and gentlemen," Chief Purser Freppel announced, trying to get the attention of the buzzing crowd, "I hope you are not too terribly upset by what has happened here. It is, unfortunately, a common hazard on transatlantic liners, even the best of them. As you can see, we will do everything in our power to protect you, but we ask you, in your own interest, not to gamble with strangers."

The security officers led a sullen Hatzfeld through the crowd and out of the room.

"And now, on a much happier subject, I have a wonderful announcement to make," Freppel went on. "Our customary Gala Charity Benefit is just about to begin in the Grand Lounge, right next door. As part of the program, the eminent violinist Jascha Heifetz has consented to play a few numbers for us. You are all invited."

Tina turned her eyes toward Rothmann and smiled winningly. "I love violin music, Simon. Could we go to the benefit?"

Jaekel could not bring himself to tamper with the daydream, even to pursue his own urgent needs. "Of course, Lilly. For a little while."

The *Normandie* was pitching and rolling, but not severely, certainly not severely enough to keep any large number of first-class passengers away from the Charity Gala, even those who were mildly seasick. The reason was simple enough. The Charity Gala was the most important social event of the voyage, with the possible exception of the Captain's Dinner.

To prepare for the event, the ship's staff had decorated the room with brightly colored balloons and crepe paper streamers—as if further ornamentation were needed—and rolled up the huge Aubusson carpet that covered the central part of the Grand Lounge, revealing a handsome parquet dance floor.

The kitchen had also done its part, preparing dozens of trays of exotic and delicious *hors d'oeuvres,* including crabmeat cocktail, caviar and crackers, and enough sugary confections to provide a college education for the offspring of a dozen dentists.

Neither were alcoholic beverages ignored. There was punch; there was a wine list that Maxim's would have been proud of. And for those with more complicated tastes, a detachment of bartenders stood ready to mix anything from a Cuba Libre to a mint julep.

But the entertainment was meant to be the evening's high point. Tonight's program included José and Carmelita, the flamenco dancers; Miss Marilyn McConnell, the nightclub singer with the notable bosom; Signor Ignacio, Sicily's greatest juggler; Miltie Korngold, "comedian to the stars," fresh from a stint at the Palace Theater; bandleader Sy Ramone and his Merry Men, and of course, Jascha Heifetz.

Sometime in the middle of the festivities, Chief Purser Freppel planned to interrupt the proceedings and collect contributions to the Fund for Orphaned Seamen's Children.

While the crowd drifted in, Sy Ramone and his band provided some dancing music, "to get everyone in the mood," as he put it. They began with a fine rendition of Kay Kyser's hit "You Go to My Head."

"Shall we dance?" Tina asked her escort.

Rothmann demurred. "I've never been much of a dancer."

"Maybe you've never danced with the right person before." She put her arms around him and whirled him away.

Nathan and Segonzak stood near the back of the room, keeping an eye on Tina and watching everything else as well.

"They look good together," the Frenchman told his American counterpart.

"She's making a pretty fair show of it," Nathan admitted. He almost wished she weren't doing so well.

Tina's head was resting on Rothmann's shoulder and her eyes were closed. She seemed to be dreaming wonderful dreams. More likely, though, she was imagining herself far away from this entire scene.

"He's a very good-looking fellow," Segonzak remarked.

"For a Nazi."

"I hope she remembers that, David."

"If I recall correctly, Jean-Louis, that's exactly what we told her to forget."

They watched for a while, Jean-Louis pleased at what was going on, Nathan struggling with mixed emotions.

"Look," said Segonzak, "over there."

Nathan peered through the dancing couples. There, on the far side of the room, was Karla Kirkland. She was dancing with Tina's college boy admirer, Arthur Shepard.

"Who is he?"

"A tablemate. He preferred Tina, but —"

"But they both have settled for second prize," the Frenchman observed with a droll smile.

Nathan laughed. "Second prize, eh? Well, that's a very nice compliment, Jean-Louis. Thank you very much."

The dance number finally came to an end.

Across the floor, the formidable woman with the face like Roquefort cheese approached the Young Lovers, like a man-o'-war under full sail. Her Pekinese peeped out of the enormous handbag that dangled from her shoulder.

"Ah, child," she said, "I see you've found him."

Tina curtsied nicely. Rothmann stood by like a butler.

"Yes, Countess," Tina said, forcing a happy smile. "Countess, I'd like you to meet my friend Simon Rothmann, of Vienna."

Rothmann bowed, took the old lady's hand rather gallantly, and kissed it. The countess was enchanted. "I saw you rescue this dear child the other day, and I want to thank you personally for your heroic deed."

Rothmann bowed again, a little awkwardly.

"Simon, this is my friend the Countess de Chambord."

"Madam."

"And this," said the countess, indicating her Pekinese, "is Pichou."

Rothmann reached out a hand to pet the little beast, which sniffed him once, then came frighteningly close to biting off his index finger.

"Pichou!" the countess said sharply, upbraiding her pet. "I am so sorry, Mr. Rothmann. Pichou is usually very well behaved. I don't know what got into him."

Rothman was gracious. "Perfectly all right, Madam. I must have frightened him."

"I hardly think so," the countess told him haughtily. Then she softened. "But I just wanted to tell you both how happy I am that you have found each other and what a handsome couple you make. You almost make me feel young again, which is truly miraculous."

"Thank you, Countess." Tina beamed with pleasure.

"And I want you to know that I hope the association between the two of you continues long after the ship docks. Long after." She winked ponderously at Tina, who smiled conspiratorially.

"Thank you, Madam," Rothmann told her.

The dance band struck up another tune.

"Well, there's the music again," the countess said, practi-

343

cally twinkling. "Go ahead and dance. You don't want to spend the whole evening jabbering away with an old lady. Go, go, go."

Tina kissed the veined and furrowed cheek and danced away in Rothmann's arms.

"Let's go back to the stateroom, Lilly," Rothmann said as they glided around the dance floor. "We don't have all that much more time together, you know."

"Not on the ship, I suppose. But once we get to New York, we have all the time in the world . . . right?"

"Yes, of course," Rothmann said. "But the ship is a very special place. . . ."

"Well, all right," Tina said brightly. "But first I have to dance with my uncle just once. I promised him."

Rothmann was a little annoyed. "You're not putting me off, are you?"

"What? I hope you're kidding."

"It's just that it's getting late. . . ."

"Please," she said, giving him one of her best smiles, "just one short dance?"

"Okay, if it's a short one."

Tina kissed him fondly, then went looking for Nathan. He frowned when he saw her coming. "What's wrong?"

"Nothing's wrong," she said. "I told him I promised this dance to my uncle."

The music started again, "Begin the Beguine," very much as Artie Shaw would have played it. Nathan put an arm around Tina and took her hand. It was the first time he had ever touched her. He was surprised, first by the warmth and softness of her hand, then by the slenderness of her waist.

"He took me back to his room this afternoon."

"I know. I was in the linen closet across the hall." He didn't want to think about it.

"Well, I guess you'll be going back there soon," Tina informed him. "We're returning to his room right after this dance. I can't put him off any longer."

"Are you all right, Tina?"

"Right as rain." For the moment, anyhow, that was the truth. She felt safe in Nathan's strong arms. She felt as though she were really dancing, not just pretending to dance.

"You're sure?"

"You don't have to worry about me. I'm giving the performance of my life."

"I know that. I can see that. But I'm worried about you, anyway."

She looked up at him, melting him with her huge green eyes. She wanted to tell him she knew he cared. She wanted him to know that as long as he was looking out for her, she'd be all right. But that wasn't how they talked to each other. "I'm an actress, remember? All I require is applause."

Nathan briefly released her and clapped a few times. She rewarded him with a broad smile, then slipped back into his arms and danced away with him.

"We know a little more about Rothmann now, Tina," he told her. "He's a champion swimmer. The lifeguard remembered him. Says he broke the Channel crossing record."

"A swimmer. That fits, doesn't it."

He could feel the small bones in her back with the arm he had wrapped around her. Her body was pressed against him, and for some reason, he was having a little trouble breathing.

"Can I do anything for you, Tina? Anything that could make it any easier?"

"Besides shooting him dead? No, I guess not. I'll be all right, David. Just stay close." Why couldn't she just dance the evening away with this man?

"I promise I'll stay close — if you promise to be careful."

Nathan felt a tap on his shoulder. Rothmann.

345

"My turn," the impatient young man announced.

Nathan yielded politely, his hand lingering on hers for just a moment. "Enjoy yourselves." He'd hated to make the remark, but he hoped it was convincing.

No sooner had Tina and Rothmann danced away than Nathan found Wallace Westbrook standing at his side. "Hullo, Cameron."

"Oh, Westbrook. Hello."

"Why don't you introduce me to your friend."

The fox-faced Frenchman extended a hand. "We met in the captain's quarters the other night."

Westbrook wasn't satisfied. "We didn't exactly meet. I never got your name."

"It's Louis," Segonzak said. "Jean-Louis."

Nathan smiled. "I know what you're thinking, but no, he's not related to the prize-fighter."

"What?"

"Nothing."

"Tell me, Mr. Louis, what do you do for a living?"

"Well, I don't know why you're interested, but I'm a landlord, not that it matters. I own a couple of apartment buildings near Philadelphia."

Westbrook frowned.

Nathan put a strong but friendly hand on Westbrook's shoulder. "You see, Wally, that's how we met. At a party for landlords."

Westbrook pushed his hand away. "Just you wait until the radio is fixed. Then you won't be laughing anymore."

He strode away, not bothering to hide his anger.

The Young Lovers did not remain on the floor for the whole dance. They took a couple of turns around the room, then headed aft, toward the Smoking Room and the stairways near the stern.

David Nathan and Jean-Louis Segonzak walked after them, keeping them just barely in sight. They did not need to hurry. Both men knew exactly where the Twosome

346

was going.

Victor hadn't wanted to go to the Gala. He didn't much like the idea of watching Tina dance with a Nazi agent. On the other hand, he wasn't interested in another night alone in the stateroom.

"A movie is playing in the theater," Nathan had said. "Why don't you go? I'd just as soon you stayed out of the line of fire."

"Line of fire?"

"A metaphor," Nathan said. "But we'll have enough on our hands taking care of Tina. It would be better if you kept your distance from her—and us."

"A movie might help make the time pass quickly," Segonzak told the young scientist.

It was as good a suggestion as any.

And so Victor made his way to the theater. To his surprise, it was packed—not with first-class passengers, they were all at the Gala—but with business travelers and shop owners from tourist class, along with teachers, students, and refugees from the bowels of the ship. Knowing that the *corps d'élite* would be otherwise occupied, Chief Purser Freppel had designated it an "all-classes" evening.

Victor arrived in the middle of the first show and found a seat toward the front of the auditorium, next to a shabbily dressed young refugee couple with a sleeping baby.

He sat down and looked at the screen. Several men and a woman, all of them evidently worried or upset about something, were standing, sitting, or pacing about in a large bedroom of vaguely classical design. They appeared to be American or British, but they were dressed in Indian or perhaps Tibetan outfits—high-necked embroidered jackets, floor-length silk skirts, and slippers.

Looks like a comedy, Victor thought. He liked the idea. One of the men, a stout fellow with an expressive Irish

347

face, spoke to the apparent leader of the group, a handsome fellow who looked like a British sportsman, calling him Conway. He asked if it were true that they had been kidnapped.

Conway, pacing, refused to answer.

The Irish fellow asked the same question again, more insistently.

Instead of answering, Conway went to the bedroom door and called out into the hall, asking for a Mr. Chang.

The camera angle changed, revealing a wide, impressive hallway with marble pillars and filigreed screens. An aesthetic-looking older man, wearing eyeglasses and monks' robes, was hurrying toward the bedroom.

Conway asked the man if he would mind stepping into the room for a moment.

Mr. Chang complied. Once he was inside, Conway locked the door and pocketed the key. He politely invited the man to sit down.

Beside Victor, the baby started to cry. His mother adjusted her position and her clothing and, to Victor's surprise and embarrassment, put him to her breast. The crying came to an instant stop.

Sitting down, Chang mentioned that it was very, very strange Conway had summoned him, because he had been on his way to see Conway. He had what he called "the most amazing news."

The others in the room bent forward to hear what it was.

Chang told Conway that the High Lama wished to see him.

High Lama? What was this? Some kind of religious picture? Maybe he would have been better off at the Charity Gala.

Conway rose to go, telling his friends to wait until he returned. By then, it should be clear where they stood.

Chang led Conway up a wide and majestic stairway,

while the sound track swelled with orchestral music that was mysterious, yet moving.

Conway passed through a hexagonal door at the top of the stairway into a dimly lit two-story chamber filled with plants and bookshelves. Motionless against a bare back wall sat a small, pale old man. A candle was on a table beside him, casting a glow on the wall that illuminated his head like a halo. The old man seemed to emanate dignity and peace.

Victor felt himself being drawn into the world portrayed on the screen. He was wondering who this Conway was, what the old man would tell him, and why it mattered. He was, at least at this moment, not thinking about Tina or Rothmann or bombs.

Conway gazed at the ancient creature sitting next to the candle and asked if he was the High Lama.

The man said he was. He had the face of a shriveled prune, framed with a fringe of snowy white hair. He asked Conway if he'd been comfortable at Shangri-La since his arrival.

Conway said that personally he'd been enjoying the community very much, but his friends did not care for this mystery and were determined to leave as soon as they could.

Then his voice trailed off. Something had surprised him profoundly. The view shifted to the corner of the old man's chair. Leaning against it was a single crutch, simple and well-worn. Conway looked down toward the bottom edge of the High Lama's robe. A single foot protruded.

Conway mumbled, half to himself, how astonishing and incredible this was.

The High Lama asked what he was saying.

Conway could not contain himself. He told the High Lama that he must be the man Chang had spoken about, the first man who had come to Shangri-La . . . *two hundred years ago!* He was greatly astonished to find him still alive

. . . the Father Perreault he had heard about.

Two hundred years ago? Now, that was asking a lot from the audience, Victor thought. Still, he looks old enough. But what is the point of all this?

The High Lama was talking now, saying he'd wanted to meet the Conway who, in one of his books, had said, 'There are moments in every man's life when he glimpses the eternal.' He said that this Conway seemed to belong here, that, in fact, it was suggested someone be sent to bring him here.

A very large man in the row in front of Victor got up and made his way to the aisle. Victor missed several of Conway's lines.

The High Lama was entreating Conway to stay, saying they needed men like him there to be sure the community continued to thrive. In return, the High Lama went on, Shangri-La had much to give him. He was still, the High Lama noted, a youngish man, by the standards of the day. Yet, in the normal course of existence, he could expect twenty or thirty years of gradually diminishing activity. Here, however, in Shangri-La, by the community's standards, Conway's life had just begun. And it might go on and on.

Conway was skeptical. He said that, to be candid, he wasn't excited by a prolonged future. It would have to have a point. He sometimes doubted whether life itself had any, he told the High Lama. If that was so, he added, then long life must be even more pointless. He concluded that he would need a much more definite reason for going on and on.

Father Perreault paused. Something in his manner conveyed profound wisdom and infinite understanding. Even Victor, skeptical and worldly, a man of science and mathematics, was intrigued by the sense of mystery and peace.

The High Lama told Conway, simply and without guile, that they had the reason, that it was the entire meaning and purpose of Shangri-La. It was something that had come to the old man in a vision, long, long ago. He had seen all the nations strengthening—not in wisdom, but in the will to destroy. He had foreseen a time when man would rage so hotly over the world that every book, every treasure, would be doomed to destruction. This vision, he said, had been so vivid and so moving that he had decided to gather together all things of beauty and culture that he was able to and preserve them here against the doom toward which the world was thrashing.

Beside Victor, the baby started crying again. He strained to hear the High Lama's words. The mother shifted the baby to the other breast, and it quieted down. Up on the screen, the old monk was still speaking.

The High Lama told Conway that the time must come when this orgy had spent itself, when brutality and the lust for power had perished by its own sword. That, he said, was why he had avoided death, why he had stayed here, and why Conway had been brought here. For when that day came, he said, the world must begin to look for a new life.

With Conway listening in awe, the High Lama told him it was his hope that the world might find that new life in Shangri-La, for here we shall be with their books and their music and a way of life based on one simple rule: *be kind*. When that day comes, the High Lama said, it is our hope that the brotherly love of Shangri-La will spread throughout the world. When the strong have devoured each other, the High Lama solemnly intoned, the Christian ethic may at last be fulfilled, and the meek shall inherit the earth.

The theater was absolutely quiet now.

Conway had surrendered to the beauty and power of the old man's words. He told the High Lama that he understood him. Then he bent down and kissed the High Lama's hand.

In a voice that was barely audible, the old man told

351

Conway to come again and bade him good night

The movie went on, but Victor no longer followed it. His mind echoed with Father Perreault's words. Someone had foreseen the future—not the actor playing the old man, of course, but the person who had written that speech. Someone understood the great danger civilization faced. Someone knew that in its deepest heart, humanity yearned for a real Shangri-La.

Victor looked not at the screen, but at the audience. Here they sat, a reasonable sampling of the humanity that populated the globe, a few hundred worn and ragged souls fleeing the approaching deluge on board a modern Noah's ark, hoping to find their Shangri-La on the other side of the ocean, far from trouble, far from danger.

And here he sat in their midst, no Robert Conway. He was not transporting a great treasure to this new land, like the stowaway with the manuscript. He was not contributing anything of beauty or culture. He was bringing the key to—how did Father Perreault put it—"techniques of murder." Would his contribution be used to save civilization or destroy it? Would it help the meek inherit the earth or obliterate them?

But there was no Shangri-La, no Father Perreault, no Robert Conway, he told himself. There was only good and evil, and they were poised to begin a battle to the death. The best he could hope to do was tip the scales.

He looked up at the screen again. Conway was now in a European hat and coat, up at the edge of a mountain pass, looking back toward Shangri-La, tears in his eyes. A pretty girl in a white dress was desperately chasing him and calling after him. He turned and left before he saw her.

Victor thought about Tina, dancing away with Rothmann at the Gala, getting deeper and deeper into danger—while he watched a movie. What would his father say to this? Would he say that his son was keeping his promise?

He got up and found his way out of the theater. He headed toward the music and laughter that was pouring out of the Grand Lounge not far away.

Inside, in the center of the parquet dance floor, surrounded by attentive and appreciative first-class passengers, a haughty man in an embroidered jacket and clinging tights was stamping out a frenzied staccato in tandem with an equally arrogant woman in a lacy, low-cut black dress that revealed the upper three quarters of her breasts.

There was no sign of Tina or the German. Nathan and Segonzak were also gone. Victor knew they'd want him to go back to the cabin and wait, but he couldn't do that and still keep his promise. He had to find a way to watch over his sister, to protect her. It was his duty.

NIGHT

Each night during the voyage, after dinner or after the evening's festivities, the Stickney sisters indulged themselves with a stroll down the enclosed promenade.

They used the time to relive the events of the day, to dissect the people they had met, and to generally reinforce each other's opinions.

This night was no exception.

When the Charity Gala finally broke up at about one A.M., most passengers headed back to their cabins or to one of the many bars scattered around the ship. But the Stickney girls, as they liked to call themselves ("Hello, we're the Stickney girls"), drifted out through the big glass doors of the Grand Lounge and perambulated forward, past rows of deserted deck chairs, toward the Winter Garden, a pair of pink flamingos on the loose.

"That was really very sweet, what Mr. Heifetz said," Claire remarked.

"It certainly was," Daphne responded, "dedicating a song

to the young lovers."

"And isn't it a shame that they weren't there to enjoy it?" asked Claire.

"A great shame," Daphne agreed. "I saw them dancing together for a while. Didn't they make a beautiful couple?"

"Perfectly lovely."

"It's so romantic, him saving her and all," Daphne said. "Just like in the movies."

"Where do you think they went, Claire?"

Daphne started to giggle. It was a wonder she'd been able to hold back until now. "I think I know," she said.

"Tell."

"I shouldn't. It's private."

"Come on, Daphne. Tell, tell, tell."

"Well, okay. I heard them talking. He was asking her to go back to his room."

"His room?" Claire was scandalized but thrilled. "I don't believe you."

"It's true, Claire. I heard him say it."

"What did she say, Daphne? Did she want to?"

"What do you think?"

They both broke into giggles.

Then Daphne stopped abruptly. She pointed ahead. A man—a young crewman—was furtively running across the deck.

"What do you suppose . . ." Claire began.

Daphne shushed her. They tiptoed forward, keeping to the shadows.

The running man reached his goal: a ship's officer standing at the rail. He snapped his arm up into the air in the familiar Nazi salute.

The Stickney girls couldn't hear the officer's reply, but they got the drift. The officer was angry with the other man for some reason. The crewman was giving some kind of report. The two of them conferred in whispers for a few minutes, then the younger man walked away, briskly. His meeting over, the officer left the rail and hurried down the Promenade Deck toward the Stickney girls. They crouched behind a ventilating pipe and held their breaths.

The officer rushed past them, oblivious to their presence. It was Chief Purser Henri Freppel.

"Admiral Raeder?"

He stirred and opened an eye. "Yes?"

"Another message from the U-42."

"Yes, what?"

"Proceeding as planned with *Otto Wunsche*. Expect to reach rendezvous approximately two hours ahead of schedule."

"Good. Notify me immediately when the next message comes in."

Raeder turned over and tried to go back to sleep, hoping to make the hours go faster. But his thoughts prevented him. They were a whirlwind of anxiety and expectation.

Day Seven

EARLY MORNING

Fog.

Billowing clouds of it.

Few maritime hazards are more frightening, even in the wide open ocean, because the ocean is never as wide open as it seems, because ships travel surprisingly close together in the sea-lanes — the shortest and fastest routes between ports — and because even in the middle of the Atlantic the chances of collision are immense.

On the morning of August 27, 1939, fog covered the North Atlantic like cotton batting. And yet the *Normandie* continued to steam ahead, full speed.

Capt. Pierre Barthou didn't like driving the ship this hard through fog. But he believed that the threat to his ship and her passengers from the Germans was greater than the threat from the weather.

Neither did he like waiting, while Nathan and Segonzak tried to flush the saboteur and find the bomb. Nevertheless, he trusted them. He trusted them partly because he had no choice. He couldn't very well put Bernard Nadeau in charge of the investigation.

Lt. Claude Lebarre, a baby-faced blond, joined the *Normandie* crew just after Barthou had signed on, now approached his commanding officer. "Captain, we have a signal from the radio detection equipment."

Barthou's mouth went dry. "A signal?"

"Yes, sir. A strong one."

Were Nathan and Segonzak too late? Had the Germans anticipated their speed change? "Give me a distance and direction estimate, Claude."

"Isn't available yet, sir.

"Well, get it for me as soon as possible," Barthou ordered. "Also, alert the crow's nest and order the helmsman Ameil to prepare to commence zigzag pattern A."

"Yes, sir." Lieutenant Lebarre left to carry out his orders.

A moment later, Deputy Captain Martel entered the wheelhouse, looking handsome as a movie star in his fresh uniform. Barthou told him about the report.

"You think it's the Germans?"

Barthou shook his head. "I don't know, Marius. We lost nearly three hours when the steam line broke and we're still quite a distance from the continental shelf. Still . . ."

Lebarre reappeared. "I have some more information on the signal, sir. The object is about four miles away and maybe thirty degrees west."

"Right in our path," Barthou said grimly.

"Or near it," Martel agreed. "Anything else, Claude?"

"Yes, sir. The object is stationary."

Barthou was surprised. "Stationary?"

"Yes, sir. It hasn't moved in the fifteen minutes or so we've been tracking it."

"*Mon Dieu,*" the captain said softly, "they're waiting for us."

The deputy captain put his binoculars to his eyes and tried to stare right through the fog.

"See anything, Marius?"

"No objects, sir. But I think we're coming to a break."

At that moment, the bridge phone rang. The captain

357

picked it up. "Barthou here."

"Crow's nest, Captain. I have a sighting. Iceberg about four miles ahead. We should miss it by about a half mile."

"An iceberg?"

"That's right, sir."

Barthou managed a weak smile. "You hear that, Marius? An iceberg."

Then their eyes met. Each knew what the other was thinking. It was within two hundred miles of this spot, only twenty-seven years ago, that the *Titanic* hit an iceberg and sank.

"Thank God we have a device to warn us of such things," Martel said.

"Yes," Barthou replied. "We are protected against Acts of God. I wish we were as well protected against the acts of man."

Within half an hour, the *Normandie* had broken out of the fog. But she had run smack into the thunderstorm that had been brewing for days. The seas, which had been quite turbulent, now began to churn and seethe. Before long, giant waves were slamming into the ship's superstructure.

Unlike almost every one of his passengers and a fair proportion of his crew, Captain Barthou liked rough weather. He liked the crashing waves, the high winds, the pelting rain. He liked fighting the elements.

He especially liked piloting the *Normandie* at times like these. She was magnificent in calm weather and sunny skies. But in stormy weather, she was nothing less than spectacular. There was no need to reduce speed or to seek out smoother waters. All in all, he thought, this is the finest ship ever built.

An enormous breaker smashed against the whaleback that covered the ship's forward deck and splattered against the wheelhouse windows, momentarily blinding everyone. The *Normandie* slid down its trough and climbed back up over the

358

crest of the next wave like a roller coaster, tilting back and forth from side to side at the same time. But she did not lose a fraction of a knot in forward speed.

Chief Purser Freppel entered the wheelhouse. "Captain, the furniture . . ."

"Oh, yes, Henri. Have it all bolted down, as usual, and rig lines in the public rooms."

"How about the swimming pool?"

Barthou hated the idea of closing the swimming pool or putting any other part of the ship off-limits. "How bad is it?"

"The entire bar area is wet."

"Okay, drain it by a quarter. But keep it open."

"Yes, sir."

"And send the stewards through the public rooms. Have them suggest to the older passengers that they might be more comfortable in their staterooms. I want to avoid broken arms, legs, and especially hips."

"Yes, sir."

On his way out of the wheelhouse, Freppel ran directly into the Stickney sisters. "I'm sorry, ladies," he told them. "Beyond this point, it's crew only."

"We must see the captain," Claire Stickney said.

"Immediately," her sister added. Like Donald Duck's nephews, Huey, Dewey, and Louie, the Stickney sisters habitually finished each other's sentences.

"In private."

Barthou had overheard the conversation. "Can I be of some assistance, ladies?"

"Could we talk to you in private?" Daphne Stickney asked.

"I'm sure the purser . . ."

"No," said Claire Stickney. "We need to talk to you, only you."

"It's very important," Daphne added.

Claire almost pleaded with him. "It won't take five minutes."

Barthou sighed. Many times over the years, passengers

had waylaid him, demanding private conversations. And in these private conversations, he'd been propositioned, offered bribes, asked for loans, chewed out over imagined insults, and begged for introductions. But never once had a passenger told him anything he needed to know, anything important to the safety and comfort of the ship and its passengers.

Now these giraffes were demanding an audience, God knows why. Unfortunately, he had no choice. "Yes, of course," he said, as graciously as he could. He escorted them to his office, which was directly behind the wheelhouse.

"Now, what's this all about?"

"You start, Daphne."

"No, you, Claire."

The silver-haired captain stopped them. "You go first," he said, pointing to the twin with the slightly larger Adam's apple.

"Well, all right. Captain, there's a Nazi agent aboard the ship!"

"What!?" Barthou was flabbergasted. Had they also somehow discovered the man Nathan and Segonzak had identified? Or was this just as it appeared to be, the silly imaginings of a pair of birdbrains?

"She's right, Captain," Daphne said. "We saw him last night on the Promenade Deck. And he has a confederate."

"A confederate?" This was getting worse.

"Yes, Captain. We saw them both."

"How do you know they're Nazis?"

"One of them gave the other the *Heil* Hitler salute," Claire told him.

"You saw this?"

Daphne nodded vigorously. "Yes, we did, with our own eyes."

"And who were these people?" Barthou asked.

"We don't know the one who saluted, except that he was a crew member. . . ."

Barthou found that hard to credit. "A member of my

360

crew? No!"

"But we do know the other one," Claire went on. "In fact, we saw him just a minute ago. He is your chief purser, Henri Freppel."

"No! Impossible!"

"Yes he is, Captain," Daphne said. "We saw him."

"With our own eyes."

This could not be as it seemed, Barthou thought. These cuckoo clocks have totally misinterpreted something. Freppel was foolish about politics, and they must have overheard one of his more cockeyed statements. "Tell me exactly what you saw and heard."

They told him about the crewman running across the deck, about the unmistakable Nazi salute, and about the urgent whispered conversation—not a word of which they could repeat, unfortunately.

Barthou understood, or thought he had. "Ladies, I know why you came to the conclusion you did. I would have thought the same thing, I'm sure. But the explanation is really very simple."

"What explanation?" said Daphne Stickney. "We saw what we saw."

"You certainly did. But that was not a Nazi salute. It was the salute of the *Francistes,* a veterans' organization."

"I've never heard of it," Daphne said.

"Well, it has thousands of members in France," Barthou explained. "They just sit around and talk politics. Totally harmless."

"What about the other crew member?" Claire Stickney asked.

"A member of Freppel's chapter, no doubt," Barthou explained. He would have to talk with Freppel. When the passengers started noticing things, that was going too far.

"Well, I don't know," Daphne said doubtfully.

"I'll tell you what," Barthou said. "Just so that you'll feel better, I'll keep an eye on him. Okay?"

They agreed, not fully convinced.

"Now, why don't you two go back to your cabins? They're much more comfortable than the public rooms in a storm like this."

Daphne looked at Claire, Claire looked at Daphne, and they shrugged in unison. "Thank you for listening to us, Captain," Claire said.

The *Normandie* rolled sharply to starboard, then abruptly righted herself, then rolled again, this time to port. Daphne Stickney was the first to turn green. "Captain, I . . ." She put a hand to her mouth.

Barthou, having seen the gesture ten million times or so, knew what was troubling her. He pointed at a door. "The lavatory is in there," he said. Both of the women bolted toward it.

Segonzak knocked twice rapidly, then twice more slowly. The linen closet door opened. Nathan was sitting on a pile of bed linen. "Seven A.M. already?" he asked.

"Yup. Time for me to take over and you to get some sleep." He braced himself against the wall as the ship rolled sharply to port.

"I'm not that tired."

"You've had about three hours sleep out of the last thirty-six. When the action begins here, I want you at your best."

"We don't know when he's going to make his move, Jean-Louis. I want to be on the scene when that happens."

"It's going to be at least a couple of hours, David. Go get some sleep."

The ship righted herself very quickly, then began heeling over in the other direction. Both men leaned with it.

"All right . . . an hour."

"Good," Segonzak said. "Now tell me, anything going on over there?"

"They're asleep. I listened at the door for a while. Not a

362

sound."

"Fine. Then I should have an easy time of it."

Nathan awkwardly pulled himself out of the pile of sheets and Segonzak took his place. "I'll be back no later than nine A.M.," Nathan told his friend.

"That's fine. Just get some sleep, okay?"

Nathan agreed. But the last thing he was thinking of was sleep. He was worried, and he knew Segonzak shared his fears. They thought they knew when the rendezvous—and the explosion—was supposed to happen, but what if they were off somehow?

As the day broke, the storm intensified. Rolling and pitching continuously now, the *Normandie* proceeded across the ocean in a kind of corkscrew motion. Captain Barthou reluctantly had the pool closed and ordered the public rooms cleared.

Chief Purser Freppel reappeared on the bridge.

"Problems, Henri?"

"I'm having trouble with the cooks. They've walked off the job."

"What? Why?"

"The main china closet door broke open, sir."

"Oh, God. How bad is it?"

"The entire kitchen is awash in broken crockery. I have a crew trying to clean it up now."

"I understand. But why have the cooks walked off the job?"

"They say it's too dangerous—until all the shards have been picked up."

"How long will it be before it's clean?"

"At least a half hour, assuming we don't break any more. That will mean breakfast is late."

"Okay," Barthou told him, "I'll talk to the head cook. Anything else?"

"Yes," the chief purser said with disgust. "Wallace

Westbrook. Fell down and hit his chin against the bar in the Cafe Grill. Knocked him cold."

"Westbrook? I don't believe it. Is he all right?"

"Just bruised. But he's threatening to sue."

Barthou nodded. "Did the accident occur before or after the passengers were warned about the weather?"

"Afterward."

"Let him sue, then."

"Well, he doesn't have a case, of course, but he's also threatening to write a column in the newspaper."

"Saying what?" the captain inquired.

"That the *Normandie* is unsteady in a storm—and that we have been negligent about repairing the wireless."

"I see. What would you like me to do about it, Henri?"

The chief purser shrugged his characteristic little shrug. "Well, I've sent him the usual basket of fruit and a card in your name. But I think it might be a good idea to have him to dinner tonight in your suite."

Barthou winced. "You think we really have to go that far?"

"His column is read by fifty million people, he told me. It would be very bad publicity."

"Okay," the captain said. "But invite some others, too—the Countess de Chambord, and those American comedians and their wives."

The chief purser cocked an eyebrow.

"Don't look at me like that, Henri," Barthou said. "I need all the cheering up I can get."

"As you wish."

The chief purser left the wheelhouse, bracing himself first against one bulkhead, then another, as the huge liner heeled heavily to port, then to starboard, then back again.

The deputy captain approached Barthou. "Captain, I think we have to reduce speed."

Barthou was surprised. "Why? The ship is riding well. We're in no danger from the weather."

"The waves are running at twenty-five to thirty feet, sir,"

Martel told him. "One or two have even hit the funnels. And I'm getting worried about the windows in the Grand Lounge."

"Have we taken on any water?"

"Not yet, but it could happen at any moment. Besides, international regulations require us to reduce speed to twenty-five knots in storms this severe."

Barthou took a deep breath. "Marius, if we reduce speed to twenty-five knots, we'll arrive at the continental shelf exactly when they expect us."

"I know, sir," Martel said, "but three quarters of the ship is sick, crew included. I'm having trouble finding enough men to handle essential operations."

"But what about the saboteur? We'll be playing into his hands if we cut our speed."

The deputy captain thought a moment. "I understand what you're saying, sir, believe me. But I think Segonzak and the American are on top of that situation."

"You're absolutely sure they can handle it?" Barthou asked. "You can guarantee it?"

"No," Martel admitted. "But I can guarantee we'll have trouble if we keep up this speed."

At that moment, the bridge phone rang. Barthou picked it up.

"Sir, it's Assistant Purser Furneau, in third class. I just wanted to tell you we have a woman who broke a leg falling out of her bunk."

"I see."

"We've taken her to the infirmary."

"Have a card sent in my name, Furneau. Any other injuries?"

"Plenty of cuts and bruises, sir. Nothing more serious."

"I see. Thank you, Furneau. Let me know if you have any more problems."

Barthou hung up the phone and turned to Martel, who was looking at him expectantly. "Reduce speed to twenty-seven knots, Marius."

"Just twenty-seven?"

"Yes. At least that will give us forty-five minutes or an hour."

"Yes, sir."

Victor stopped at his cabin and messed up his bed. When Nathan gets back, he thought, he'll think I've gotten up and gone to breakfast. It's better that way. That way, Nathan won't worry about me — or interfere with me.

The young man relocked the door and found his way to Rothmann's corridor. He avoided walking past the closet he knew Nathan and Segonzak were using as a lookout, instead finding a spot under a dark stairway. Here, he could watch Rothmann's stateroom for himself. And if something went wrong, if Tina needed him, he would not hear about it later. He would be there to help, to keep his promise.

Rothmann stretched and looked down at Tina, who was nestled in the crook of his arm. She was as pretty as fresh-cut flowers. But this daydream must come to an end.

He tried to rise, but she threw a leg over him and briefly pinned him to the bed. "Hey," he said, "I have to get up."

"But why? Why can't we just lie here or something?"

"Lilly, I have something to do."

Without warning, she started tickling him, fiercely but playfully. For a while, he tickled her back in the same spirit. Then he tired of the game. He gently removed her, stood up, and began dressing.

"Why are you getting dressed?" she asked.

"I . . . ah . . . have to do my morning calisthenics."

She knew immediately that he was lying. "Come back to bed." She smiled beguilingly and held out her arms.

He bent down and kissed her, then resumed dressing.

"Later."

He is a very handsome man, she thought. And he has been genuinely gentle and loving toward me. I know he cares about me. Maybe, just maybe, I can divert him. Maybe I can make him forget why he is here.

"I can't wait until we get to New York," she said. "Won't it be wonderful to explore it together."

"Yes," Rothmann replied absently, buttoning his shirt, "very nice." And what a shame it would never happen, he thought.

"I want you to take me to the top of the Empire State Building," Tina said, standing, putting her arms around him, and preventing him from fastening a button.

"Whatever you say." The ship rolled heavily and they clung to each other to avoid falling. Then he detached himself and reached for his pants.

"And we'll go shopping at . . . what's the name of that big store in New York?"

Rothmann thought for an instant. It had been in his briefing sheet, the sort of information Raeder had thought a Viennese department store owner should know. "Macy's," he remembered.

"Yes."

She hugged him again. He hugged her back, letting his pants drop to his ankles. It felt wonderful to hold her delicate, perfect body. He would always treasure the memory, assuming he survived this mission.

"Listen," she said, "why don't you stay here? Why don't you come back to bed? You can do your errand some other time."

Why was she pushing so hard? he wondered. Last night, she hadn't been so eager. In fact, he'd had trouble dragging her away from that ridiculous party.

He pulled up his pants and buttoned them, fighting the tilt of the floor as the ship listed first to port, then to starboard.

"There's a big, beautiful park in New York," she said. "I've seen pictures of it. Couples ride through it in the moonlight,

367

in horse-drawn buggies. Wouldn't that be romantic?"

"Yes, it would," Rothmann said. But they would never see it together, not in this lifetime, not in this world. He had miraculously found this beautiful girl, and they had loved each other. But now . . .

This time, he was the one to hold out his arms. She came to him without hesitation. But now, he told himself, completing the thought, he must give her up. He must give her up and he must complete his mission, even though it meant her death.

It was almost too much to bear. He'd dreamed of a woman like this. He'd prayed for her. He'd imagined what it would be like, all the while knowing it would never happen, not to him. Yet it had. She cared for him and he cared for her.

"Stay with me, Simon. Forget about the exercising."

One word stopped him. The word was *Simon*. It reminded him of how much of a daydream this was. She didn't love him—she loved Simon Rothmann. And he—he did not love her. Simon Rothmann loved her. Unfortunately, he was not Simon Rothmann. He was Kurt Jaekel. And if she knew that, she would not love him at all. She would loathe him.

"I must do my calisthenics. I never miss them, not for any reason. But do not worry. I will not be long."

"Please don't go," she said.

Why was she being so insistent? She had never acted this way before. It was . . . strange.

He fastened his belt. "I have to," he said.

"I don't understand about these calisthenics of yours. Why are they so important?"

"I told you, Lilly. They're a part of my morning routine. They help give my life order. And they won't wait."

Tina threw her arms around him just as the floor tilted crazily once more. "Don't," she implored. "Don't go. Please."

Jaekel pulled away and looked at her. What was this? Something was odd here. "Why are you so anxious to keep me here, Lilly? I'll be back in a few moments."

Suddenly, Tina realized she may have gone too far. "Well, it's just that we have such a short time left on the ship, and I wanted us to spend every moment together."

"I said the same thing to you last night, Lilly, and you said we had all the time in the world, once we got to New York. Then you went off to dance with your uncle."

"I know," Tina said, "but after the night we've just spent together . . ."

Jaekel looked at the woman, appraising her. He didn't understand why she was acting this way. She almost seemed to be begging him to stay.

Then he knew.

"You know, don't you?"

Tina felt the color drain from her face. "Know what?"

"You know where I'm going."

"I don't," she said innocently. "I have no idea. And I don't know why your exercises are more important to you than I am."

"How could anything be more important to me than you?" Jaekel said. He held out his arms and she snuggled into them, the rolling of the ship pressing them together. Her body was trembling.

Jaekel held the girl at arm's length and gazed at her. She was smiling lovingly, but he saw fear in her eyes. He turned her around, then drew her to him again, wrapping one powerful arm across her chest and around her neck.

"What's the matter?" she asked, her voice quivering ever so slightly.

"We both know what's the matter," he said. "No more pretending, okay?"

"What do you mean?"

He tightened his arm around her neck. "I said no more pretending."

Tina tried to push his arm away. "I'm not pretending," she said. "I just don't want you to go."

Jaekel braced his feet against the rolling of the ship and

369

tightened his grip a bit more. "Why? Why not?"

She had to give him something, she had to say something that would make him stop before he choked her. "Because I think you're going to do something bad."

"Bad? What do you mean?"

"I don't know. I just have a bad feeling. You've given it to me, you know."

"Oh yes? How?"

"Well, you're so serious and so secretive about this errand of yours. Are you going to steal something? Are you going to get in a fight with someone?"

"What in the world would make you think that?"

"You seem so . . . I don't know . . . determined. And now you're questioning me, like a criminal. I can tell that something is wrong."

So she doesn't know, Jaekel thought. But she suspects something, which is almost as bad. He should kill her here and now. That was the right thing to do. But he could not bring himself to commit the deed, not after all that had happened between them.

If he left her here, she might tell someone about her suspicions and people might come looking for him. The same thing might happen if he killed her and left her body here. He could just picture that uncle of hers, wondering where she was and getting a steward to look in this cabin. Killing her and throwing the body out the window was a bad idea, too. If anybody identified her, they'd come looking for him — and practically the whole ship knew what she looked like and that they'd been together.

But the solution was simple. He'd take her with him to the cargo hold. Somewhere along the way, he'd find a place to leave her. He might not even have to kill her, or at least watch her die. Locking her up might do the job, if he could find some out of-the-way place where she'd remain undiscovered until his deed was done. He released his grip around her neck.

"I'm afraid you're going to have to come with me," he said.

"I have to? What happens if I don't?"

"Please don't make me answer that. Just get dressed. Now."

"Okay, Simon," Tina said. "If it's that important to you."

She slipped back into her clothing, still frightened but at the same time relieved. David was out there waiting for just this, or Jean-Louis, or maybe both of them. They would take care of her. They would take care of him.

Jaekel got the wet suit out of his suitcase. "Okay," he said. "Let's go."

"What's that thing?"

"Has to do with my calisthenics."

"What if I run away from you once we leave the room?"

"I'm sure you won't go far," Jaekel said. He took Tina by the arm and pushed her out the door. The *Normandie* rolled sharply and she stumbled, but his grip prevented her from falling.

From his hideout in the closet, the door opened just a crack, Segonzak saw Rothmann leave his room, pushing Tina in front of him. This, he knew, was it. But why was Rothmann taking Tina with him? Either she had not been able to keep up the act, or Rothmann just wasn't taking any chances with her.

He let them walk along the corridor and head down a set of stairs, then he went after them, hanging back far enough so that Rothmann did not see him.

Crouched underneath the stairs, Victor watched Rothmann come down the corridor, leading Tina in front of him, occasionally bracing himself against a wall as the ship rolled. Victor could see how frightened Tina was and how valiantly she was trying to hide it. Shortly after the two of them started down the stairs, Segonzak appeared, trailing them as he and Nathan had previously discussed.

"Where are we going?" Tina asked. That would be the natural question, she thought. Rothmann would expect it.

"Down a few decks. Don't you worry yourself about it."

They were on F deck, not far from cargo hold #1, when Rothmann came to a dead stop. He put a hand over Tina's mouth, listening carefully. Then he pulled her into an alcove and waited.

The *Normandie* heeled sharply to starboard, hovered there a moment, then snapped back to an even keel. After that, she proceeded to tilt just as far in the other direction. In the struggle to maintain his balance, Rothmann was forced to grab for a nearby plumbing line, momentarily taking his hand away from Tina's mouth.

"Watch out!" she shouted.

It was too late.

Segonzak came around a corner at just that moment.

Jaekel abandoned Tina and leaped out at the Frenchman, knocking him off his feet, but Segonzak instantly scrambled up again and faced his attacker with poise and confidence.

The blood pounding in his temples now, Jaekel heard the crowd once more, shouting, cheering, gasping in surprise. He sprang at Segonzak again but was neatly knocked aside with a *tae kwon do* move. The crowd roared. Jaekel rolled once, then was on his feet again.

Segonzak kicked mightily and caught Jaekel in the chest. The German's vision dimmed for a moment and he stumbled backward, just as the ship rolled. He smashed into a bulkhead but rebounded almost at once.

Watching the two of them, Tina had almost forgotten to breathe. Jean-Louis had hit the German twice, hard, but he'd recovered each time. Could Segonzak win this battle? And where was David?

Segonzak lashed out again, catching Jaekel in the throat

372

with his fist. The German was shocked by the sudden, sharp pain. The crowd was yelling for blood now — for *his* blood, the way Jaekel heard it. He knew he was up against an extraordinarily dangerous foe this time, a man who wrestled in a way that was totally foreign to him. But he was sure it would not matter in the end. He assumed the crouch and made ready to grapple.

Once more, Jaekel sprang. This time, he was beaten back by two ferocious fist blows, one to the chest, one to the stomach. But even though he was partially doubled over, he managed to get in a blow of his own, a hard, closed-fist smash to Segonzak's temple. The Frenchman gasped in pain and stumbled backward several steps.

It had been years since Segonzak had felt fear during hand-to-hand combat, but he felt it now. He'd hit this man hard enough to put him down and out, not once but several times. And yet the German kept coming on, relentlessly.

Again, they faced each other, both men breathing hard, the roar of the crowd surging in Jaekel's ears. Once more, the German carried the fight to the Frenchman. Just as they began to grapple, however, the ship listed sharply, throwing the two of them off balance and sending them sprawling.

Segonzak struggled to get up as quickly as possible, to attack his foe before he could rise. But the German rose at almost the same instant he did and came at him once more. Segonzak felt himself beginning to panic. Somehow, he must find a way to beat this man, because he knew all too well what would happen if he did not.

As the German approached, Segonzak wickedly flung a foot toward his opponent's head. It was a blow vicious enough to fracture a man's skull, but the *Normandie* rolled at exactly the moment Segonzak unleashed it. The foot thrust, which almost certainly would have ended the battle, turned out to be nothing more than a clean miss.

Even worse, the miss left Segonzak slightly off balance for just an instant, and in that instant Jaekel got his brawny arms around his enemy. He spun the Frenchman around until they were front to back, then wrapped one powerful arm around his opponent's throat.

Knowing what was coming and terrified of it, Segonzak heaved the upper half of his body toward the floor with all of his might, trying to fling the German over his head and break the man's grip. Sidestepping slightly, Jaekel managed to keep both feet on the ground and maintain the arm-lock. Segonzak pounded his fists against the German's forearm, again without result. As a last resort, the Frenchman desperately stabbed his fingers backward into his foe's rib cage. A single sharp gasp escaped the German's throat, but his grip around Segonzak's throat actually tightened.

"Run, Tina!" Segonzak called out somehow, choking. "Run!"

Tina, hypnotized by the life-and-death struggle in front of her, couldn't move a muscle.

Even as Segonzak was struggling to get free, the German tensed his arm around his opponent's throat and gave a mighty jerk, lifting the little Frenchman off the floor entirely. There was a sharp crack. Segonzak went limp. Jaekel released him and he slid to the floor, lifeless.

Tina stared at Segonzak in disbelief, frozen to the spot. But before she recovered, Jaekel recovered himself, grabbed her by the arm, and propelled her down the corridor. The crowd was cheering its lungs out now. He had won a stunning victory.

Nathan had been mildly surprised that Victor wasn't in the stateroom, but he didn't think much about it. Apparently, his charge had just gotten up and gone down for breakfast. Given the *Normandie*'s forceful pitching and rolling, that was admirable.

Exhausted, the stern-faced New Yorker had slipped off his shoes and lain down on his bed, fully clothed. He intended to get a few minutes sleep, then go back down to the linen closet to join Jean-Louis on watch. It would all be happening pretty soon now, if they were right, and he wasn't sure Segonzak could handle the German by himself.

Victor came around the corner cautiously, alert to every sound, determined to sacrifice himself on behalf of his sister if it came to that. In the dimly lit corridor, he almost stumbled over Segonzak's body, recoiling in disbelief when he saw who it was. He fell to his knees. "Jean-Louis? Are you all right?" Jean-Louis was not all right.

Victor lightly slapped Segonzak on the face, and the Frenchman's head lolled sickeningly to one side. The young scientist knew that there would be no reviving him. That meant Tina was alone with the German and that she was in terrible danger.

A gun. Where was Segonzak's gun? Victor felt around for it and found it in a shoulder holster. Then he continued down the corridor, armed and dangerous, determined to find Jean-Louis's assassin and kill him if necessary.

The ship lurched violently and Nathan awoke with a start. He glanced at his watch. He'd been sound asleep for nearly forty-five minutes. He jumped up, got back into his shoes, splashed some water on his face — no time to shave his heavy beard, of course — and rushed out of the stateroom, struggling to maintain his balance as the *Normandie* canted first to one side, then to the other.

In a few minutes, he was standing outside the linen closet. He knocked twice slowly, twice quickly. There was no response. He pushed the door open. Segonzak was gone. And that meant . . .

Nathan bolted down to Rothmann's door, pressed an ear against it, and listened for a few moments. Nothing. He knocked. No answer. He tried the door, but it was locked. He raised a foot and kicked it open. Like the linen closet, Rothmann's room was empty. He felt the panic wash over him.

Jaekel shoved Tina along the corridor in front of him, pushing her around a bend, both of them bouncing off the bulkheads as the ship rolled giddily. Suddenly, he stopped. He thought he heard footsteps. Was there another one of them? Ah, yes, the uncle. That's who it must be. He pulled Tina into a doorway, clamped a hand over her mouth, and waited.

Victor came charging around the bend, Segonzak's revolver in his hand. When Jaekel saw who it was, he spun Tina about and snaked a strong arm around her neck, using her body as a shield.

"Stop right there," he told Victor.

"Shoot him, Victor, kill him!" Tina shouted.

The slender young man halted, keeping the gun pointed in Jaekel's direction. Because of Tina, however, he could not get a clear shot at the man. "Let her go," he warned.

"Drop the gun . . . now!" Jaekel ordered with a cold smile. "If you don't, I'll break her neck."

"You let her go," Victor said defiantly, "or I'll kill you where you stand! I have the gun, not you."

His arm locked around Tina's throat, Jaekel lifted her off the floor slightly. Tina pulled at his arm helplessly, gasping for air. She looked at Victor imploringly.

"What's it going to be, little boy? Are you going to drop the gun or must I kill your sister? You choose." The German's voice was totally emotionless.

For about ten seconds, they just stood there, as Victor tried to think of an option, a way to free his sister from this man's death grip so that he could attack him. This time, he came up with no answers at all. Having no choice, he dropped the gun.

In one smooth motion, Jaekel released Tina and scooped up the weapon. "Neither of you move," he said. "I am expert with revolvers, and you know that I can and will kill both of you if you so much as take a step."

They stood there in the corridor, the three of them, Victor filled with hatred but helpless to do anything, Tina terrified about what the German would do next. Only Jaekel's mind was clear and in complete control. He had no intention of killing either of them. The gunfire might summon help and ruin everything.

"Walk ahead of me," he commanded, poking the barrel of the revolver into Victor's back. "And please don't try to attack me. You wouldn't have a chance."

He forced them to go down the corridor, all three of them staggering and swaying as the ship careened wildly from port to starboard and back again. Then he spotted the entrance to a small sleeping room.

"I'm afraid I cannot tolerate any further interference from either of you," Jaekel said. He gave Victor a shove that carried him through the door and sent him crashing against a chest of drawers.

Then he let his gaze fall one last time on Tina. "You will never know how much it has meant to me to know you," he said. "I wish with all of my heart that I could change our fates, but that is utterly impossible."

Tina pleaded with him. "Please, Simon, it is still not too late."

"You say that even after you have seen me kill a man?"

"Yes, yes . . . he attacked you, didn't he? You had to defend yourself. Please let us go and—"

"And what, Lilly? Turn myself in? Forget who I am and why I am here?"

She tried one last time. "Why are you here, Simon? Why are you doing this? Don't you know that I love you?"

"You love Simon Rothmann, perhaps," Jaekel said, "but

you do not love me. You could not love me."

The actress in Tina was desperate to convince this murderer that she cared for him and that it could still be all right. The real woman was terrified. It was the actress, however, who made the last gesture.

"Simon, please," she said, her voice aching with love. She held out her arms to him.

"Good-bye, Lilly." Jaekel's eyes were glistening with tears. He shut her inside the cabin, wedging the door closed with a wooden doorstop.

"Please don't wear yourselves out shouting for help," he called to them. "No one will hear you."

Nathan was in a quandary. Obviously, the German was making his move and Segonzak was following him. But where was Tina? Was Rothmann forcing her to come along with him? Had he seen through her act?

This was something he and Jean-Louis had not anticipated, although they probably should have. They'd thought they'd be following a man secure in his false identity and confident that no one suspected him of anything. They thought they'd simply be tracking the German to the bomb, where they could then deal with both problems. But Tina's absence told him that was no longer the situation. Rothmann might have forced her to tell him what they knew about him and his mission. Or he might be using her as a hostage. In either case, he knew his danger — and was therefore far more dangerous himself.

There was one other possibility, which Nathan was completely unwilling to consider. He would have avoided the thought altogether if it had given him any advance notice: Tina might be dead already. Rothmann might have questioned her, killed her, and shoved her out of his porthole, as he had the young steward.

Nathan knew they must be found and they must be found

immediately. He ran toward the bridge now, in search of Martel, the captain, even Freppel. He had to get search parties going, even if it meant using the troops.

Sprinting down a corridor, Nathan turned a corner and almost collided with Wallace Westbrook, who was now wearing a large bandage on his chin.

"Well, well, well . . . Cameron. What's the big hurry, buddy? Where are you going?"

Nathan tried to move around the scrappy reporter, but Westbrook blocked his path.

"Let me by, Westbrook."

"You tell me where you're going, and I'll step aside."

That was it for Nathan. He grabbed the little man by an arm and, in one quick motion, tossed him over his head. Westbrook landed on his back, astonished but not hurt. Nathan continued down the corridor at top speed, not even looking back to see if he'd done any damage.

"Damn you, Cameron!" Westbrook shouted at the departing figure. "Just you wait until we get to New York!"

Jaekel glanced at his watch. It was going to be tight, but he should make it. He kicked the chocks out from under the Delahaye's wheels and climbed in. The keys were still in the ignition lock. He started the motor and began to back the car out of its space.

Just then, the *Normandie* rolled sharply to starboard. The red and white Delahaye suddenly slipped backward, toward the outside bulkhead. Jaekel slammed on the brakes, but still it slid. He was reaching for the emergency brake when the ship rolled in the other direction and the Delahaye abruptly reversed course, heading now toward the port bulkhead. Once more, Jaekel barely managed to regain control.

Fortunately, the ship now held an even keel for a few moments, long enough for the German to steer the vehicle into its new parking place. He set the emergency brake, hopped out, and put chocks under the wheels. Even if someone managed to trace him here, he wanted everything to look normal.

Now Jaekel removed the chocks that engaged the wheels of the lustrous black Mercedes-Benz typ 770 he'd driven from Berlin to Le Havre, the motor car he'd come so close to losing during the loading process.

He carefully backed the huge vehicle out of its spot, fighting the constant rolling of the ship, and drove it past two rows of parked cars, toward the place Raeder's experts had determined was the *Normandie*'s weakest point.

Just as he was about to make the final turn, the ship suddenly leaned sideways. The Mercedes, whose wheels were now parallel to the ship's beam instead of her length, looked down on the starboard bulkhead as though it were a wall at the bottom of a tall hill. All of her enormous weight urged her forward. Without restraint, she would have crashed into that outer bulkhead, either exploding or going right through it or both.

As the list increased, the motor car began to move. Using all of his considerable strength, Jaekel mashed a foot down on the brake pedal. The Mercedes hesitated slightly. He pulled on the emergency brake until his arm muscles were bulging. He could not hold it. The giant car headed for disaster.

Then the *Normandie* changed her mind and decided to careen toward port. For a few seconds, the Mercedes continued forward, on momentum alone. It stopped just six inches short of the bulkhead. Jaekel, his heart pounding, prepared for what he knew was coming—a sharp tilt in the opposite direction. But it never happened. This swing of the pendulum turned out to be far short of the previous one.

Going with it this time instead of against it, Jaekel backed up a few feet, then before it happened all over again, he whisked the motor car into the parking place once occupied by the Delahaye. He shut off the ignition, set the emergency break, hopped out, and shoved wooden chocks against the

380

tires.

Jaekel checked his watch. *Gott in himmel!* There was very, very little time to spare. He was going to make it, but just barely. Getting into the automobile once more, Jaekel flipped open the dashboard clock, moved the hands back, and set it. Fifteen minutes. Fifteen minutes and it would all be over, the daydream, the nightmare, the mission. Fifteen minutes and his father would be avenged and his benefactor repaid.

There was only one thing to worry about now: his personal survival. He'd been trying not to think about it, but he knew he was going to have trouble with the huge waves that awaited him in the Atlantic. He'd faced conditions like this once during a channel swim and had almost drowned. But that was merely athletic competition. This was a mission for his country and it would make him a hero. Nothing, he told himself, not even the highest waves in the ocean, would stop him from reaching that submarine.

Somewhere, she knew, Rothmann — or whatever his name was — was doing what they had all tried so hard to prevent. He was getting the bomb ready, setting the timing mechanism. Before long, a titanic explosion would rock the ship, seawater would pour into the staterooms, and everyone on board would die.

It didn't seem real. It was more like a distant dream. Was she really here, trapped in a crew member's room with her brother? Was Jean-Louis really lying in a corridor not far away, dead? Were they really about to die? And where was David?

Victor had given up struggling with the cabin door. He hadn't been able to budge it an inch. Instead, he sat on the bed, lost in thought. Then, suddenly, he looked up at the ceiling, at a small fixture adjacent to the overhead light.

"Victor," Tina began.

"Do you have any matches?" he interrupted.

"Matches?" She couldn't believe the question. "What do you want with matches?"

"If we're going to do anything, we've got to get out of here," he said. He pointed toward the odd ceiling fixture. "That's a fire detector," he said. "Every room on this ship has one. If we can trigger it, help will arrive in no time. I could do that with a matchbook."

"I don't have any matches," Tina said plaintively.

"Me neither," Victor admitted. "But there must be a pack in this room somewhere." He pointed to an ashtray that contained a couple of cigarette butts.

Working together, they frantically searched the room, dumping out dresser drawers full of rough seaman's clothing, crawling under the bed, going through a nightstand, which yielded only a paperback copy of Henry Miller's *Tropic of Capricorn*. No matches.

It was Tina's idea to look behind the nightstand. Victor pulled it away from the wall and found half a book of paper matches with a picture of the *Normandie* on the cover.

He hopped up on an unfinished wooden chair, lit the pack — after a couple of tries — and held it up against the fire detector.

"Nothing happened." Tina was distraught.

"Nothing would happen down here," Victor explained. "If the thing works, a light will flash at the central fire alarm station."

"If?" Tina said.

"If. We won't know until someone comes to get us. I just hope it's soon."

The captain was on the bridge phone when Nathan reached the wheelhouse.

"Only one alarm light?"

"What is it?" Nathan asked.

"A small fire, evidently."

382

"Where?"

The captain repeated the question into the phone and repeated the answer. "It's in the cargo supervisor's room."

"The cargo supervisor?" Nathan was astonished. "Not the man who was murdered."

Barthou's expression changed dramatically. "My God, you're right!" Then he spoke into the phone. "Send a fire team — fast!"

"We'd better get down there," Nathan told him.

They took the crew elevator, picking up Martel along the way. Nathan told them what he knew — and what he guessed.

"So what is this fire?" Martel asked.

"Maybe it's a signal, or maybe someone's in trouble. But I'll bet it involves our people."

The elevator door opened, and they rushed down the service passage that led to the cargo supervisor's room, the ship's rolling repeatedly tossing them against bulkheads and partitions.

They got there — Nathan with his gun drawn — just as three members of the fire brigade had begun battering down the door. Leading them was none other than Security Chief Bernard Nadeau, who had evidently heard that there was trouble and was determined to redeem himself.

As the door collapsed, Tina burst through the opening and flung herself into Nathan's arms.

"Oh, David," she sobbed, "he killed Jean-Louis. He broke his neck."

Nathan was staggered. "Killed Jean-Louis?"

Victor had come out of the cabin. "Yes. His body's down the hall about a hundred feet, around a corner."

"Where's Rothmann?" Nadeau asked.

Victor shook his head. "I'm not sure. But I heard automobile engines and the sound of squealing brakes."

Nathan looked at Captain Barthou. "This way," the silver-haired captain said, leading them toward cargo hold #1.

The men rushed forward, looking frantically among the

crates and boxes and between the motor cars. But it was Tina who spotted Rothmann. He was standing almost as far forward as possible, beside an open porthole, zipping up his black rubber wet suit.

"No!" she shouted, running toward him. "Don't jump!"

"Stop, Rothmann!" Nadeau shouted. "Stop right where you are!"

Nathan crouched and aimed his pistol in Rothmann's direction. It was going to be a tough shot, he knew. He had to hit the man but not kill him. They needed him. But just as Nathan pulled the trigger, the ship abruptly tipped toward starboard. The bullet ricocheted harmlessly off the outer hull plating.

Jaekel smiled at his pursuers, dropped his street clothing through the open porthole, then lifted himself up and climbed out. Tina reached him just before he slid through the opening. She clutched at a slippery black foot, but it easily slid free of her grasp and disappeared through the porthole.

She stuck her head through the porthole just as the huge vessel careened back toward starboard. A moment before, Jaekel would have had a clear drop to the ocean's surface, but now, because of the roll, it was the *Normandie*'s slab-sided hull that lay directly beneath him. Evidently, he realized the problem. As he fell, he flailed his arms in an attempt to hit the ship's side feet first. He failed.

Jaekel's head clanged into the half-inch-high tensile steel plating, and he dropped into the heaving ocean as inanimate as a bag of garbage. He sank at once and did not reappear on the surface.

"No, no!" Tina screamed. "My God, no!" She pulled back from the porthole, her face dead white. After a moment, the tears began rolling down her cheeks. Catching up with her, David Nathan held out his arms and she buried herself against his chest, sobbing wildly, unsure whether she was feeling grief or relief.

384

Victor, who had replaced Tina at the porthole, looked back at Nathan, Barthou, and the others. He shook his head no.

"What about the bomb?" Martel asked.

There was a sudden silence as everyone simultaneously realized that the German's death had not eased their peril in the least.

Victor checked his watch. "David, the way I figure it, we're only minutes away from the rendezvous point."

"Then I guess we'll just have to find the bomb ourselves," Nathan said. The ship rolled sharply to port, everyone bracing himself against a wall or a pillar.

Nadeau just shook his head. "We've already tried once and failed. What makes you think we can succeed this time?"

"Because we don't have any choice," Martel told him coldly.

The *Normandie* suddenly pitched forward. Then she violently rolled to port, snapped up to an even keel again, and rolled just as far to starboard.

Tina looked up at Nathan, her pretty face pale and anguished. "Did I fail, David? Have we lost?"

Nathan did not answer her. Then something occurred to him. "What did you say about motor cars, Victor?"

"I heard automobile engines when we were locked in the cargo supervisor's room."

"Were the motor cars searched, Bernard?" Captain Barthou asked his security chief.

"Yes, sir," Nadeau said, happy to be consulted. "The men checked the trunks and looked through the windows."

"Did they look under the hoods, under the fenders, under the seats?" Nathan asked.

"Well, no. We thought—"

"Do you believe the bomb is in an automobile, Monsieur Nathan?" the captain asked.

"I hope so."

Martel was confused. "Even if it is in a car, why was he moving it around?"

385

It was the young scientist — back on familiar ground now, the science of destruction — who understood why. "Captain, does the *Normandie* have a structural weak point somewhere in the cargo hold?"

Barthou shook his head. "I don't know. It may have. I've come late to this command. The original captain, Rene Pugnet, could have told you. He watched the ship being built. But—"

"I understand," Victor said. "But my guess is that Rothmann was moving an automobile into the parking place nearest the weak point."

They looked at the automobiles that filled the cargo hold — Dusenbergs, Packards, Bugattis, Rolls Royces, Austro-Daimlers, Panhards, Citroens. They had minutes, no more, minutes to find the bomb, minutes to disarm it.

"I'll start with this row," Martel said, pulling open the hood of a Panhard. The ship careened sharply to port and the Panhard's hood slammed shut, barely missing Martel's fingers.

"I know a better way, an old cop's trick," Nadeau said. "Feel the radiators. We want the one that's warm."

"Good idea," Nathan told the gaunt security chief.

Now Martel, Nadeau, Nathan, and even Captain Barthou darted from automobile to automobile, touching radiators.

"I've got one!" Martel shouted. He was standing in front of the red and white Delahaye Cabriolet, fumbling with the hood, then opening it.

"Anything?" Nathan asked.

"Nothing I can see."

"Check under the fenders and the seats."

While the others continued to feel radiators, Martel inspected the Delahaye. "Nothing," he said, crestfallen. "Nothing at all."

"That must be the automobile he had to move to put his own in the right spot," Victor said.

"His own car?" Tina asked, coming alive again. "He had

386

one, remember? He came in a big black Mercedes, the one that the crane almost dropped."

"Damnit, why didn't I think of that?" Nathan said. He glanced around, spotted the vehicle, and ran over to it. "Radiator's warm," he announced to the group.

Each of the men stood in place, hardly daring to breathe. Meanwhile, the big liner continued to roll from side to side, forcing them all to grab hold of car handles or something else stationary to avoid losing their balance.

On the Mercedes-Benz typ 770, big spare tires sit in fender wells on each side of the hood, blocking access to it. David Nathan removed the tire on the right side, undid the hood latch, and tugged. Nothing happened. He tugged again and this time the hood opened with a deafening bang, startling everyone in the room, Nathan included.

"Take a look at this, Victor," he said.

The young scientist peered inside. "There it is," he said softly.

In the meantime, Nathan was checking under the seats. "There's more in there."

Victor dropped to his knees and looked under the fenders. "Here, too."

The *Normandie* lurched to starboard, then back again, like a drunk maneuvering down the boulevard.

"Find the timer!" Martel called out.

Victor was already inside the automobile, prowling around. He stopped at the dashboard clock. "I think I already have," he said, peering at it. "Know anything about these things, David?"

"Not much. How about you?"

"Not my field," Victor admitted.

Deputy Captain Martel had a disturbing comment. "Could it be booby-trapped?"

"Quite likely," Victor said.

"What does the clock say?" asked Martel.

Victor took a look. "Five minutes to twelve."

Martel was shocked. "Does that mean we only have five minutes before the explosion?"

"I don't know," Victor said. "Probably."

"Wait a minute," Nathan said. "We don't have to worry about the timer. All we have to do is get rid of the vehicle."

"Get rid of it?" Security Chief Nadeau asked, puzzled.

Captain Barthou immediately grasped Nathan's idea. "Marius, get the cargo port open."

Now Martel also understood. He headed for the starboard cargo port, the giant door by which automobiles were loaded and unloaded at Pier 88 on New York's West Side. The *Normandie* chose that moment to lurch heavily to starboard. Martel, caught off guard, lost his balance, rolled across the floor of the cargo hold, and banged against the hull plates. For a moment, he did not move.

"Marius?" Barthou was concerned.

The deputy captain struggled to his feet. "I'm okay, Captain." He unfastened a latch on the cargo port door and gave a hard tug on a chain. The door slid sideways on its track, uncovering a huge, gaping hole in the hull. The churning, boiling ocean was plainly visible less than twenty feet below.

Nathan searched for the Mercedes's keys. "Damn! Rothmann must have taken the keys with him."

"Doesn't every policeman know how to start an automobile without its keys?" Victor asked.

"Sure, but the ignition could very easily be booby-trapped."

For a moment, no one said anything. Then Tina made a suggestion. "Why don't you push it out?"

It was the obvious solution.

"You steer," Nathan told Victor. "We'll push."

And so, Nathan, Martel, Nadeau, a couple of men from the fire brigade, and even Captain Pierre Barthou took positions around the massive automobile.

"Release the hand brake," Nathan instructed. "And put it in neutral."

Victor did as he was told, and the car began to move out of the parking place, half the men standing in front to get it going, the other half in back to stop it before it crashed into some other vehicle.

"Hard left," Nathan told Victor.

Victor steered as he was told, glancing at the clock. Four minutes left — if the clock was the timing mechanism for the bomb.

"Easy now," Martel instructed. "Wait for the right moment."

They held back until the ship rolled in the correct direction, then slowly pushed the motor car down the aisle. As the roll reversed itself, several of the men came around the back, to keep the vehicle from going in reverse.

"Hold it!" Martel shouted. "Hold it, hold it, get control of it! Good."

They held it for a few moments, waiting for the ship to roll in the other direction. When it did, they pushed again, briefly, then raced ahead to stop the vehicle before it rammed into a bulkhead.

Martel shouted out orders. "Watch out! Stop it! Hold it there!"

"I'm here, I'm here, I've got it!" Nadeau said, running around to the front of the motor car and pushing his huge frame against the mammoth vehicle, the others following.

The giant Mercedes was now aligned along the ship's center line, perpendicular to the direction of the roll but parallel to the ship's pitching — which was, fortunately, slight.

Victor looked at the clock once more. Three minutes now, maybe a little less.

"Okay," Martel said, "let's go. Easy now. No momentum, okay? Get ready. Now push!"

The men eased the vehicle past one row of parked cars. They had to pass one more row, then negotiate a sharp right turn, then it was a straight shot right out the cargo port and into the Atlantic.

"Keep it going, slowly. Easy, easy. Don't let it get away from us!"

The ship pitched forward slightly, and the pushers eased the vehicle past the last row of parked automobiles. "All right, Victor," Nathan instructed. "Give me a hard right."

Victor did as he was told and the men, perfectly timing the ship's roll, pushed the motor car around the turn, then held it when the ship rolled in the opposite direction.

"Just stop it there," Martel instructed. "Watch out for the roll! We gotta keep it under control."

Nadeau had all of his weight braced against the vehicle, and he was reinforced by the men from the fire brigade. "It's okay. We got it."

"Should I get out?" Victor asked. The clock, he noted, showed a little more than one minute to twelve.

"You can't," Nathan told him. "You've got to steer the thing. But if it starts to go too quickly, for God's sake, jump."

"Okay, here we go! Here comes the roll!" Martel yelled. "Make it slow and easy. . . . Don't let the thing get out of control!"

The *Normandie* inclined her tremendous bulk toward starboard and the vehicle began to roll toward the open cargo port, most of the men in front of it, straining mightily to prevent it from going out of control.

"Good, good," Martel grunted, helping the men in front. "We're getting it, we're stopping it."

Then the roll stopped and began to reverse itself. The pushers ran around to the rear end of the car to stop it from rolling all the way back. This time, however, all of their strength and weight was not enough. The explosive-laden vehicle slid backward, out of control.

Martel yelled out his orders. "Stop it, for God's sake! Hold it!"

"Can't stop it!"

"Watch out!"

"We're losing it!"

"Get out of the way!"

"Jesus Christ!"

"Crash it!" Nathan shouted. "Back it into something!"

Everyone in the cargo hold knew that was the only answer, yet everyone also knew it could trigger an explosion that would kill them all.

Victor understood what he had to do. He twisted the wheel sharply and the Mercedes's rear end swung to the left. Just as the ship regained an even keel, the automobile slammed into a pillar, the impact considerably reduced by the sudden dampening of the vehicle's momentum.

No explosion took place.

"For Christ's sake," Nadeau said in relief, wiping his brow. "Wait . . . watch out! Quick! Get it!"

"Hold it, hold it, hold it!" Martel yelled, almost in a panic.

The ship had suddenly tilted to starboard again, before any of the men had a chance to assume pushing or holding positions. The Mercedes shot toward the cargo opening, Victor at the wheel, Nathan, Barthou, and the others running after it, frantically. Inside, Victor glanced at the clock once more. The large hand was almost in line with the small hand, which was pointing directly at the twelve.

"Jump, Victor, jump!" Tina screamed.

"Get out!"

"Jump, damnit!"

When the Mercedes was just a few feet from the opening, the roll reversed itself once again. The automobile continued forward on momentum alone. When it reached the cargo port, it was barely crawling—and, at the very next roll, it would be more than ready to shoot backward into the cargo hold, totally out of control.

Victor leaped out of the driver's seat, hitting the cargo hold floor and rolling away from the vehicle. The Mercedes paused at the opening for an instant, stuck two wheels over the threshold like a swimmer testing the water, then plunged out of the ship and into the seething waters of the North Atlantic.

The men who had been struggling so hard to control it now stood at the edge of the cargo port, gazing openmouthed into the foamy Atlantic toward the spot where the car had disappeared, amazed at what they had done.

"Car overboard," David Nathan announced wryly.

Victor, picking himself up from the floor, broke out into loud whoops of triumph, drawing a look of total astonishment from Nathan, who had rarely even seen him smile.

Somewhere behind them, there was a muffled boom.

It took them several moments to realize that the phone in the cargo hold was ringing. Barthou picked it up.

"Captain speaking."

"Lieutenant Lebarre, sir. We have a radio detection sighting."

"A sighting?"

"Actually, two of them. One is apparently a vessel, about ten miles off our starboard bow. The other is . . . I don't know, it's barely big enough to be detected. It's about three miles away. I'm not sure what it is, maybe a log. We've had both objects on the radio detection gear for about ten minutes, but I couldn't find you."

"Are the objects moving, Claude?"

"Yes, sir—right toward us. The small object, whatever it is, is closing on our projected position at eight knots or so. It should intercept us in about ten minutes, I'd say. The other ship, which is approaching at twelve knots, will cross our path too late to intercept."

"Thank you, Claude. Please tell me immediately if you detect any change in their speed or direction."

He hung up the phone, disturbed.

"What is it, Captain?" Martel asked.

Barthou described the conversation.

"He thinks it's a log?" Martel said. "Making eight knots

392

and headed right for us? That's no log, that's a periscope!"

The room suddenly turned very still.

On board the U-42, which was rolling sickeningly just below the churning surface of the Atlantic, Kommandant Wolfgang Zentner glanced at his watch, then looked once more through the eyepiece of the attack periscope. The black speck in the distance was coming toward them at high speed, too far away to determine her identity.

"You look," he told Horst Bibermann, the bearded, pale-faced 1st watch officer, the U-boat's second in command.

Bibermann steadied himself against the U-boat's bobbing hull and put a sweaty eye to the periscope. "I don't see any evidence of the explosion described in our orders. All I see is a ship approaching us, making good progress — better than I would have expected in seas this rough."

"Those are my observations also." Zentner turned to his soundman. "Manfred, your report please."

"Propeller sounds approaching from the east at about twenty-eight knots," the soundman said.

"Any indication of an explosion or a ship breaking up?"

"None at all, sir."

Zentner and Bibermann exchanged glances. "Time for the sealed orders," the bearded officer prompted his kommandant.

Zentner nodded and opened the envelope. It contained a single sheet of paper, which was limp from the condensation inside the U-boat. He read it slowly, then showed it to Bibermann.

TOP SECRET — RAEDER TO ZENTNER:
If you have opened these orders, it means that no explosion has taken place at the appointed time and location. Approaching you now is the French passenger liner Normandie, *the target of this operation. She is carrying the bulk of France's gold reserve to*

America. Since our saboteur has failed in his mission, it is your duty to torpedo and sink this vessel so that the Otto Wunsche can recover the gold on behalf of Hitler and the Reich. You are hereby ordered to do so. You are also ordered to make sure no survivors live to describe what happened. The ship's radio system has been destroyed, so she will not be able to request help from French, British, or American military authorities, nor will she be able to radio an account of the incident. Germany is counting on your skill and efficiency. Signed Raeder.

Zentner showed the orders to Bibermann, then put the paper back in the envelope and stuck it into his pocket.

"Raeder is asking us to sink the *Normandie?*" Bibermann asked, dumbfounded. "*That* is the target he was unwilling to name in his original orders?"

"You read the orders just as I did, Horst. And I am just as surprised as you are."

"But an unarmed passenger ship? It's monstrous!"

Zentner transfixed his second in command with a cold glare. "We will, of course, follow our orders."

"Yes, of course."

"And we will not weep too long over the innocent civilians on the *Normandie.* Instead, we will think of the magnitude of the blow we are striking against our enemies and on behalf of the Reich."

"Yes, Kommandant." Bibermann was thoroughly cowed now.

"Ordinarily, I might feel some pangs myself, Horst. But the French government has been courteous enough to relieve me of such feelings. It did so when it took the cowardly step of loading France's wealth aboard the *Normandie* and sending it to America for safekeeping. So it is not we who will be responsible for the loss of life, it is the French government."

"I understand, sir."

"Perhaps," Zentner went on, in a rather philosophical tone, "we will be vilified in the decadent democracies—if they should ever discover what we have done. But we will be heroes at home."

"Yes, Kommandant. That is so."

Zentner allowed himself a single sigh. He was almost overcome by U-boat perfume—the stifling stench of oil, grease, sweat and decaying food, the result of too much time submerged. It was the kind of smell you never got used to. "Give me a recommended firing plan, Bibermann," he said, shaking it off.

Bibermann worked with a greasy slide rule for a few moments. "My recommendation is that we dive and take up position perpendicular to the *Normandie*'s projected path, at a distance of a thousand yards. Approximately ninety seconds before she crosses our line of fire, we discharge a simultaneous four-torpedo fan shot from the forward tubes."

"That sounds correct." Zentner sounded like a hospital chief of staff talking to an intern. "And what result would you expect from that course of action?"

Bibermann considered the question. "Unless the *Normandie* alters course—and she has no reason to do so—she should be hit by at least two and possibly all four of the torpedoes. She should sink within fifteen minutes, just as the *Lusitania* did in 1915."

"And if she does not?"

"If she does not sink, we fire our stern torpedoes—two more should be plenty."

"What then?" Zentner was getting annoyed with his second in command, who was too cautious to give the whole answer without prodding.

"Then we surface," Bibermann said. "If we find life rafts, we sink them with the anti-aircraft cannon or with machine gun fire."

"Very good, Bibermann. I accept your plan. Prepare the boat for firing."

Bibermann beamed. Usually, Zentner had corrections or niggling criticism. For once, however, the kommandant seemed satisfied.

"It's the submarine coming to pick up Rothmann," Nathan said.

"And the salvage ship approaching to retrieve the gold bullion," Victor added.

Deputy Captain Martel shook his head. "I don't think so. We've passed the rendezvous point. They must know there's been no explosion. But they're still coming at us."

"What are you suggesting, Marius?" Barthou asked.

"I think we're about to be attacked, sir," Martel said. "The U-boat is coming on at the fastest speed it can manage, submerged. It isn't headed for a point behind us, which it would do if it were picking up a swimmer. It is on an intersect pattern — a standard attack approach. I learned it myself, at the Naval Academy."

"The U-boat must be a backup to Rothmann," Nathan said.

Victor frowned. "Maybe that was always the plan — to torpedo us if the saboteur slipped up and the bomb failed to go off."

Barthou agreed. "It does look that way."

"So we're still in danger," Tina said, stunned, reeling from what had just happened.

"I'm afraid so," Martel told her.

She turned to ask Nathan a question, then her knees buckled. He caught her and held on. "It's okay," he said lamely, trying to comfort her. "You'll be all right."

Nathan helped Tina to a chair and crouched beside her. "Was it all for nothing?" she asked, recovering a bit.

"Not at all," he said. "You had to do what you did . . . and it will be all right, I'm sure of it."

"We do have one advantage," Martel told the group. "They don't know about our radio detection equipment. They don't know we've spotted them."

The captain picked up the phone and called the engine room. "Gaston," he said, "I need every last fraction of a knot you can give me—immediately!"

He hung up, then called the bridge. "Claude, tell Ameil to commence zigzag pattern A. Right now!"

He put the phone back on the hook. "Now we will see what we will see," he said.

Kommandant Zentner stared into the periscope eyepiece, looking directly at the black bulk of the onrushing ship. It was a spectacular sight—the largest, the most beautiful, and very nearly the fastest passenger liner in the world, slicing through the heavy seas of the North Atlantic at twenty-eight knots or so, heedlessly speeding toward her own destruction.

The little U-42, a mere minnow compared to the whale she was stalking, hovered just out of sight, barely beneath the surface of the boiling seas, pitching and rolling furiously, fighting to stay on the right heading.

"Helmsman, five degrees left."

The helmsman made the correction.

"No, two degrees right."

The helmsman moved the wheel a hair.

"Okay, now hold it!"

Zentner took a deep breath and peered through the periscope. The giant liner was coming into range. "Begin the count!" Zentner yelled.

"One hundred," Bibermann called out promptly.

Zentner's sweaty hands gripped the periscope handles hard enough to turn his knuckles white. He leaned toward the speaking tube and shouted into it, "Flood tubes one to four. Prepare for firing!"

After a short pause, a reply came back from the forward torpedo room. "Tubes flooded! Torpedoes ready!"

"Ninety-five," Bibermann said an instant later.

Zentner took a deep breath, almost gagging on the noxious air.

"Ninety-four."

"Ninety-three."

"Helmsman, hold the boat steady, damnit!" Zentner commanded sternly.

"Ninety-two."

"Ninety-one."

"Ninety!"

"Fire!" Zentner cried out. "Fire all forward torpedo tubes!"

A heavy shock indicated that the torpedoes had left their tubes. Moments later, a swishing sound came from the bow compartment, accompanied by an increase in air pressure. The compressed air, which had activated the large pin locks that expelled the torpedoes, was released into the boat instead of the water, thus avoiding the bubbly swell on the surface that had revealed the position of submerged U-boats during the Great War.

Four G7a torpedoes, each seven meters long, each driven by a star-shaped four-cylinder internal combustion engine and each carrying a three-hundred-eighty-kilogram warhead, burrowed through the cold Atlantic at approximately forty-four knots, leaving four tunnels of white water behind them.

The kommandant had fired the torpedoes not at the ship herself, of course, but at the spot where she would be, like a quarterback leading a downfield receiver. In ninety seconds, the torpedoes and the *Normandie* would arrive at the same ocean location.

"Report!?"

"All four forward torpedoes successfully away, sir," the bearded 1st watch officer told the kommandant.

On the *Normandie's* bridge, the helmsman, a round-faced little Parisian named Michel Ameil, spun the giant teak and brass wheel to the right as far as it could go, initiating the first leg of zigzag pattern A.

Suddenly, the immense vessel heeled over, quite violently, making a ninety-degree turn in mid-ocean—or as close to such a thing as a passenger liner of this size could manage.

From an airplane, it might have looked as though the ship had executed the maneuver with the ease of a slalom skier. She'd cut a graceful quarter-circle in the raging sea and smoothly changed direction from west southwest, to west northwest.

For those within the giant hull, however, the turn was anything but smooth or graceful. Everything not bolted down went flying—chairs, tables and lamps, paintings, silverware, dishes, the musicians' instruments, all the books in the library, the sides of beef hanging in the meat locker, innumerable vases of cut flowers, forty-three cartons full of metal napkin rings, a dozen shuffleboard sets, steamer trunks in at least a third of the first-class cabins, every single glass in the Cafe Grill bar, five hundred seventeen liters of *vin ordinaire*, which had not been locked into their racks—and plenty of human beings, passengers and crew members alike.

Chief Purser Henri Freppel, who had been circulating through the first-class staterooms, personally serving beef bouillon to some of the People of Consequence who were suffering from sea sickness, was flung into the bed of a very fat lady. The lady, who'd been practically comatose when he'd entered the room, was so startled by this sudden intrusion and so obviously not interested in pursuing its possibilities, that she sprang out of bed as if hit by lightning.

Erich von Stroheim had the opposite sort of experience. Prowling around the ship, by some quirk of fate immune to *mal de mer,* he had taken aim at Karla Kirkland, who, detecting his interest, had instantly detached herself from Arthur Shepard, the attentive young college student. Von Stroheim whisked her to his stateroom and, after her obligatory but mercifully brief show of reluctance, had personally fitted her with tight tan jodhpurs and demonstrated one of the positions he wanted her to assume in the filming of his next movie. They were enjoying themselves and each other, when the *Normandie* commenced zigzag pattern A. Von Stroheim was tossed out of the saddle without warning, landing on the cabin floor facedown, straining his favorite muscle.

Comparatively speaking, the purser, the fat lady, von Stroheim, and Karla Kirkland had had an easy time of it. They'd merely been inconvenienced — unexpectedly thrown together or torn asunder. They were angry, very angry. But many of the other passengers, tossed around like bowling pins by the ship's crash turn, were terrified. They were certain that the ship had been torpedoed, or that she'd hit a mine, or that she'd been struck by a monumental wave . . . a wave big enough to put her under. Many of them believed that she was going down and they were going to die.

But then the massive vessel righted herself. She was now plowing through the sea very nearly at a right angle to her former course . . . and still rolling and pitching in the fury of the storm. The frightened passengers waited for the inevitable — the cataclysmic explosion, the ocean water bursting through the stateroom door, the roaring gurgle as the sea poured into the funnels. But nothing much happened.

The absence of immediate catastrophe did not completely pacify those who had been terrified by the crash turn. They couldn't explain what had happened to the ship, but they were convinced that they were in immediate and extraordinary danger. Depending on their state of mind, they prayed, they cursed, or they fainted.

They had good reason.

Zigzag pattern A was one of three standard escape-and-evasion maneuvers for passenger ships, which had been worked out one hot summer afternoon in 1922 by a few junior officers at the French Merchant Marine Academy. Their instructor, a grizzled, barrel-chested old salt with a voice like a foghorn, who had commanded the dreadnought *Courbet* in the Great War, considered it a waste of time, an academic exercise. No passenger ship, he believed, would ever use such maneuvers. No passenger ship, if it were attacked by a warship or a submarine, would ever have the chance.

In general, Navy men had low opinions of passenger liners. In time of conflict, they felt, such vessels were nothing more than spectacularly inviting targets.

Unlike warships, which were protected by as much as a foot and a half of solid steel armor plating at the waterline, the shell plating of passenger liners was no more than half an inch thick.

Torpedoes often bounced off a warship's armor plating, exploding but leaving nothing more than a dent. But any torpedo that smashed into the delicate hull of a passenger liner would puncture it as easily as a pencil poking through a piece of wet toilet paper.

Even worse, the explosion would take place deep within the liner's hull, either blowing out half the ship's bottom or destroying most of its propulsion machinery or both. So even if the torpedo did not sink the ship within minutes, it would cripple her, leaving her dead in the water. And in that great veldt that was the Atlantic Ocean, she would then be like a gazelle with a broken leg—a feast for any passing lion.

In theory, zigzagging gave fast passenger ships a chance to outrun a pursuing warship, especially a slow-moving submarine. But there were several ifs in this equation. The passenger liner could escape destruction . . . *if* she spotted the submarine in time to begin zigzagging, *if* the submarine were approaching from an angle rather than lying in wait, *if* the submarine captain were stupid enough to rely on a single shot.

For the old salt at the Merchant Marine Academy, the ifs were so numerous that he was convinced zigzagging was essentially useless. As far as he was concerned, when a passenger ship was attacked by a sub or a warship, her best ally was lady luck.

Kommandant Zentner watched with satisfaction as the four torpedoes inscribed paths in the ocean, racing toward the eventual point of impact. In less than a minute and a half, the French express liner *Normandie* would be literally blown out of the water. He prepared himself for the remarkable spectacle.

And then, the incredible occurred. Instead of proceeding on the course she had been following ever since he'd sighted her, the *Normandie* abruptly turned out of the path of the onrushing torpedoes and toward . . . the U-42, her three huge funnels blending into one.

Zentner stared in total disbelief. For several moments, he was too dumbfounded to speak. Then it dawned on him that he was in great peril. The giant liner was now on a collision course with his tiny submarine, bearing down on her at a speed of twenty-eight knots.

Given the *Normandie's* immense size and her thirty-five-foot keel depth, he quickly realized, she would smash the U-boat into a thousand pieces if the impact actually took place. He and the other forty-seven men in his crew would be smashed into pulp.

Unfortunately, the U-42 had just been sitting in the water, waiting to see her torpedoes strike. She had no forward motion. She couldn't swing out of the *Normandie's* way, either to port or starboard. Her only chance of survival was to drop beneath the passenger ship, and it was a slim chance indeed.

Now Zentner heard the rhythmic thrashing of the *Normandie's* monstrous bronze propellers, growing louder and louder with each passing second. "Dive! Dive!" he screamed, coming out of it.

Bibermann stabbed a finger against a button, and the alarm bell shrieked throughout the boat. At the control center of the little vessel, machinists grabbed the handles of the leverage valves and hung from them, using their full weight to speed the opening of the ballast tanks. Others turned handwheels frantically.

With a loud roar, air escaped the tanks and water rushed in. But, amazingly, though the U-42 struggled violently to descend, huge swells held her in an iron grip, surface tension turning the ocean into a sea of glue.

Zentner stared into the periscope, hypnotized by the sight of the mammoth passenger ship thundering toward him. "Depth?" he demanded. "Depth!"

"Fifteen feet, Kommandant," Bibermann said, concerned at Zentner's unexplained display of anxiety.

"Down periscope!" Zentner ordered. "And keep calling out the depth!"

"Eighteen feet, Kommandant."

"All free hands to the forward torpedo room!" Zentner screamed.

A score of men, sweaty and pale-faced, stumbled along the steel floor plates toward the bow. Their additional weight slowly tilted the boat downward, while the menacing cadence of the *Normandie*'s propellers drew closer and closer. With maddening laziness, the U-42 churned toward the depths.

His mind working frantically, Zentner calculated their chances. At the speed the liner was traveling, he figured, she would ram them in less than thirty seconds.

"Depth?"

"Twenty feet."

How had she known? he wondered. What had made her change course? Surely, she could not have seen the torpedo wakes.

"Depth?"

"Twenty-five feet, Kommandant."

The U-42 tilted toward the depths, slowly drifting downward as her ballast tanks filled. By now, the entire vessel was vibrating in resonance with the ungodly rumble of the *Normandie*'s propellers.

"DEPTH?!"

"Thirty feet, sir," Bibermann shouted over the roaring propellers, panic in his voice. Now he, too, understood their danger.

Of course, Zentner could no longer see what was happening on the surface. But he could imagine it. He could imagine the huge black keel, towering over practically every other ship that had ever been built. He could imagine the "bone in her teeth"—the furious foaming wake she pushed in front of her as she powered her way through the ocean waters. She was hurtling toward them, her size and brute force wedging through tens of thousands of tons of sea water.

"Thirty-five feet, Captain!" It was a shout of terror as much as a report.

At that moment the world's largest express passenger liner, all seventy thousands tons of her, thundered over the U-42. No collision occurred. The little vessel's conning tower cleared the *Normandie's* double bottom by inches. But that didn't really matter. The passenger ship's gargantuan hull generated incalculable turbulence as it passed over the tiny submarine, creating underwater pressures far greater than the U-boat was designed to withstand.

Every valve and fitting inside the U-42 burst open, every gauge cracked, every pipe and tube split. Finally, the high tensile pressure hull itself ruptured along most of its length. The briny ocean rushed in to fill the tiny cavity that contained Kommandant Zentner and his crew.

How did they know? Zentner asked himself again. It was his last thought.

Before he was finished, helmsman Michel Ameil put the *Normandie* through five more gut-wrenching, crockery-breaking crash turns. During that time, Captain Barthou and the other veterans of the drama in the cargo hold—Nathan and his charges, Deputy Captain Martel, and Security Chief Nadeau managed to stumble through a service passageway and take the crew elevator to the bridge.

"Ah, Captain," Ameil said, calm and smiling, "do you wish me to continue pattern A or shift to the next pattern?"

"A moment, Michel. Marius, would you get me a radio detection reading?"

The deputy captain checked with Lieutenant Lebarre, who was monitoring the radio detection receiver. "We have only one signal, sir," the officer told him. "The slower of the two vessels . . . it's almost thirty miles off the stern and dropping back."

"What about the other one?"

"She was just about on top of us minutes ago, now she's gone."

Martel did some mental calculations, then approached the captain. "The way I figure it, sir, the submarine must be at least seven miles beyond us by now."

"What is our speed, Marius?"

The deputy captain checked the instruments and came away amazed. We're at almost thirty-three knots, sir!"

Barthou's stern visage was transformed into a rare grin. "You may cease zigzagging, Michel," he said. Then Barthou picked up the bridge phone, the direct line to engineering. "Gaston, this is Pierre," he said warmly. "I just wanted to give you my thanks."

"My pleasure, Captain. I hope it helped."

"It did indeed," Barthou said. "I think it may have saved our lives. We just left a U-boat struggling in our wake."

"I'm glad I didn't know that before," the chief engineer said. "I'm not accustomed to racing with U-boats."

The danger now past, the captain found himself feeling professional curiosity. "Tell me, Gaston, how many horsepower are we generating?"

"We're at one hundred ninety-seven thousand right now."

"Mon Dieu," Barthou breathed. "That's four thousand more than this ship has ever managed. How did you do that?"

"We reconnected the steam lines differently after the accident, and the new arrangement turned out to be something of an improvement. Frankly, I think we might even do a little bit better."

Barthou grinned again. "Sounds like you're ready for another run at the Blue Ribbon."

"Well, we never intended to let the *Queen Mary* keep it, did we?"

"Of course not."

"Give me a voyage or two, and we'll break thirty-three knots," the chief engineer said. "That ought to finish them off."

After what had just happened, the Blue Ribbon of the Atlantic, the mythical symbol of speed supremacy, so important in the normal course of events, seemed trivial indeed. "I agree, Gaston. I'll take it up with management when we get back."

Chief Purser Freppel burst through the wheelhouse door, waving his arms wildly, his face livid. He was a gourmet cook whose soufflé had fallen. "Would someone tell me what idiot . . . ah . . . Captain, you're here. What happened? Why did we do all that turning?"

"We had reason to think we were about to be attacked, Henri."

"Attacked? By whom? By what? There are no ships or airplanes in view. Whose overheated imagination—"

"By a submarine," Martel told him.

"A submarine! Don't be silly! That would be an act of war! Who would risk such a thing? Why even—"

"Even Adolf Hitler would not attack the *Normandie*, is that what you're saying?" Nathan said, finishing Freppel's sentence in a way that made the purser distinctly uncomfortable.

"Well, if it was a submarine—and I say *if*—it could have been anybody's submarine."

"Even one of ours?" Nathan inquired with interest.

"I don't know."

"A British submarine?" Martel suggested maliciously.

"Who knows. You're the expert, not me."

"That's true," Barthou put in.

"My job is to see to the comfort of the passengers," Freppel said, unwilling to let it die. "And do you know how they have reacted to these — these *maneuvers?*"

"Tell me," Barthou said mildly.

"They're terrified. They think we're in imminent danger of)sinking."

"I will reassure them."

"And the kitchen . . . Do you know what's happened there?"

"I'm sure you'll tell me."

"It's in an uproar," Freppel sputtered, "a total uproar. Pots and pans and broken crockery all over, food scattered everywhere. I don't know how we're going to put on a decent luncheon."

"I rely on your skills, Henri."

"You don't seem to care about what I'm saying, Captain. But the comfort of the passengers is really all that matters, isn't it?"

"I do care about the passengers, Henri. That's why we zig-zagged. I wanted to be sure they were alive to eat the lunch."

"I don't understand, Captain. First it's this imaginary bomb, then an imaginary submarine."

"We didn't imagine the submarine," Martel told him. "We spotted it on the radio detection device."

"Oh, that thing. Are you sure it wasn't a whale?"

"We also found the bomb," Nathan told him.

"What? You found it?"

"Yes. And disposed of it."

"Just in time," Martel added.

Freppel finally accepted reality. "Do you think we are safe now?"

The captain, his deputy, Nathan, and the security chief all looked at one another. They were of one mind. "We think so, yes."

"Well, thank God," Freppel said, his anger gone.

Barthou decided to placate the man. "Tell you what, Henri. I'll speak to the passengers on the public address system. I'll apologize and tell them we were avoiding some floating debris, but the danger is over and, in fact, that the maneuvers were just precautionary. I'll tell them that drinks will be on the house at dinner tonight. And I'll pay a personal visit to the kitchen. How's that?"

"That would help a great deal, Captain."

"And while I'm doing all that," Barthou went on, "I'd like you to set up a private luncheon in the Ritz for Mr. Nathan and his friends, Marius, myself, you — and Bernard, too. I think a celebration is in order."

Hearing his name, the security chief's eyes suddenly grew moist.

As for Freppel, his chest expanded by several inches. Here was an assignment he could handle like few others — a luncheon at the Ritz, the sumptuously decorated private dining room behind the wheelhouse. "Yes, sir. Of course."

"Too bad Jean-Louis cannot be there," Tina said, infinitely sad.

It was Barthou who comforted her. "Every war has its casualties, young lady," he said. "But I thank God Jean-Louis did not die in vain."

Nathan was very concerned about Tina. She'd been on the front lines, giving more of herself than anyone could have asked, taking risks that were not just physical, but emotional as well. She'd seen Jean-Louis die, then Rothmann. She'd barely escaped alive. And she had occupied his thoughts almost constantly for the last six days. He put his hand on hers. "Would you rather go back to the cabin, Tina?"

"No, David. It's all right, really. After all, we do have a pretty good reason to celebrate, don't we?" She looked into his eyes, asking him to let her stay, asking him to be gentle with her now, asking him . . . she didn't know what else.

"He was very proud of you, Tina."

"Thank you."

Barthou spoke up. "Let us remember what we have done. We have saved the lives of everyone on this vessel, nearly three thousand human beings. And we have prevented the wealth of France from falling into evil hands."

Victor listened without speaking. What the captain said was true, of course. But more had been preserved today than gold, more even than the lives of the passengers and the crew. That was something they might never know, something they did not need to know — Nathan, Barthou, and the others. And that was just fine with him.

"Please excuse me," Freppel said. "I have things to do."

Barthou sighed. "So do I. I must undertake the single most difficult task a ship's captain is called on to perform. I must deal with the kitchen staff."

If the *Normandie* had been publishing its daily newspaper, it would have been distributed at about this time of day, telling passengers what had happened in Europe and America during the night while they were eating, drinking, and partying.

In the August 27 edition of the ship's paper, passengers would have read that Hitler refused even to talk with Polish officials unless the Anglo-Polish alliance was dissolved. They would have learned that some British Army units had landed in France and were taking up positions in support of the French Army. They would have discovered that the German Army had begun commandeering civilian vehicles and restricting air and rail service. They would have read that the Polish government was nonetheless confident that no outbreak of hostilities would occur, at least "within the next twenty-four hours."

But with the radio still not functioning and no word of the outside world reaching the ship, no *Normandie* newspaper was published this Sunday. As a result, passengers were forced to imagine what might be happening in Europe. And their speculations, fueled by the ship's zigzagging and the radio silence, and stimulated by what they knew of modern warfare, were even worse than what was actually happening.

Ever since the Heinkel bombers of the Condor Legion had annihilated Guernica during the Spanish Civil War in April 1937, the residents of Europe's capitals had known what could happen to them if and when war broke out again. They knew that the skies over their cities would grow dark with bombers and that the planes' deadly droppings would turn everything they knew into rubble and kill tens of thousands of their friends, relatives, and neighbors.

And that is exactly what they thought might be happening now, those who let themselves think about it — London and Paris and Warsaw, and perhaps Berlin and Rome as well, consumed by flames, whole neighborhoods destroyed, great blocks of stores gutted, landmarks bombed out of existence, a thousand years of history obliterated, the orderliness and tranquillity of life gone forever.

During the early afternoon, the *Normandie* pushed through the western edge of the storm and into clearer skies and calmer waters, her troubles apparently behind her.

Soon afterward, the group responsible for assuring her safety reassembled in the Ritz. The men had showered and changed into fresh clothing or uniforms. Tina had done much more. She'd thrown out the clothing she'd worn with Rothmann, even the underwear and shoes, and found an outfit that she hadn't worn yet — a short-sleeved white rayon jersey ballerina playsuit with a short, full skirt and a tight elastic waistband. She took it into the cabin bathroom and came out wearing it.

"Wow," Nathan said.

She posed for him coquettishly. "You approve?"

It was a very silly question, so Nathan just laughed.

Victor tolerated all this for as long as he could, then he

spoke up. "Are you two ready to go to lunch, or would you rather just sit around and look at each other for a while?"

Tina smiled at her brother in exactly the way Billy the Kid smiled just before drawing on one of his victims. "Victor, is your underwear pulled up too tight again?"

Victor tried to think of a comeback. None came to mind.

Nathan offered Tina his arm. "Care for an escort to lunch?"

"Thank you, sir," she said.

The chief purser had outdone himself. The table was set with exquisite Lalique stemware, Puiforcat silver, and Haviland china. Where Freppel found enough intact pieces, he never revealed.

The chief cook also performed splendidly, providing a feast of lamb Richelieu, Long Island duckling, and a cold buffet that the maitre d' of the Waldorf Astoria would have admired, even envied.

Even the sommelier managed to deliver the *Normandie's* best — ten bottles of Dom Perignon plucked from the sopping shards that littered the floor of the wine cellar.

"I would like to make a toast," Captain Barthou said, standing. The color was back in his square-cut face now. He looked like a happy grandfather presiding over a family get-together.

"I raise my glass to this young lady," he said, lifting an arm in Tina's direction. "I will not repeat what we all know. But I do want to acknowledge her heroism, the sacrifices she made, and the risks she undertook on our behalf.

"Young lady," he said, "the passengers thank you, the crew thanks you, the company thanks you, the people of France thank you, and I thank you. You have my admiration, my respect, and my love."

Cries of "Hear, hear" erupted around the table, as everybody took a sip of champagne on Tina's behalf.

Tina stood, curtsied gracefully, and gave Barthou a big kiss on the cheek. "You know," she confided to the group, "I've always liked older men."

The captain's face turned an even deeper shade of red than usual. "Well, yes . . . um . . . thank you," he said, thoroughly discombobulated. "I would also . . . ah . . . like to propose a toast to all the rest of you, each of whom made a crucial contribution to our survival. If I can be of service to any of you in any way, I would be most happy to oblige."

To everyone's surprise, Victor spoke up. "As a matter of fact," he said thoughtfully, "there is something you could do for me. You could give me a tour of the engine room."

A grin spread over Barthou's squarish face. "I would be only too happy," he said. "I will come to your cabin after dinner and personally escort you through the engine room."

"Thank you, Captain Barthou. I would enjoy that very much."

"Finally, I would like to pay tribute to our beloved friends Maurice Cosset and Jean-Louis Segonzak. It saddens my heart that they cannot be here now to share our relief, for their contribution was greater than anyone else's. Jean-Louis, Maurice, we will never forget you." With tears in his eyes, the captain raised his glass and drank, in company with all the others in the room.

"I have a toast also, Captain," said the deputy captain, Marius Martel. "I would like to toast the freedom-loving peoples of the world and dedicate to them this great victory over our common enemy."

Once more, the glasses were raised and drained, this time quite solemnly.

"I share your sentiments, Marius," Captain Barthou said. "But I fear the victory we have won today is only a small skirmish in a vast conflict. I see a great struggle coming in which all of us, individuals and nations alike, will be tested to our limits. With God's help, we will meet that test and we will preserve the essence of our civilization."

The captain's words had their strongest effect on Victor, who was reminded of what the High Lama had said. He thought once again of the secrets he carried in his mind and how they could affect the survival of this civilization they all treasured.

At that moment, the dining room doors swung open and a covey of waiters entered carrying silver trays laden with desserts — *gâteau* Montpensier and other impossibly rich French pastries, Alsatian cream pie, *Chartreuse sorbet,* and many another wonderful sugary confection.

"Ah," said Captain Barthou, eyes twinkling. "Now the real feast can begin!"

After the luncheon, Pierre Barthou took a long, soaking bath, then put on a fresh uniform. Throughout most of the voyage, he had been feeling a little tired and, dare he admit it even to himself, a little old. But no more. He was refreshed and invigorated.

He sat down at his piano and began playing Sibelius's "Valse Triest," one of his favorite melodies. Tomorrow morning, he would bring the *Normandie* into New York Harbor, whole and undamaged, all of her irreplaceable cargo intact, human and otherwise, his responsibilities fulfilled.

On how many more crossings would he command this noble vessel? Not many. As Mathilde kept telling him, it was nearly time to make way for a younger man, a man who could bear the weight better than he. Perhaps this was the time.

Suddenly and unexpectedly, he made up his mind. After the *Normandie* made her return crossing, he would contact his employers and inform them that he wished to retire on January 1. He would tell them that Marius should succeed him.

He thought about Marius for a moment, imagining him on the bridge, giving commands, or in the first-class dining room, entertaining celebrities, or dealing with the kitchen staff or the engine room crew. Of course, there was much that the young man did not know, much that only experience could teach him. But he would learn.

Barthou felt a great deal of satisfaction in picturing Marius as his successor, for it was he who had taught the young man what it really meant to command a giant passenger ship like the *Normandie*. It was he who had showed him that being a captain meant more than merely mastering the technical skills of seamanship, or knowing everything there was to know about his vessel, or constantly exercising good judgment.

A certain quality was required from all captains, in direct proportion to their responsibilities, a quality that transcended anything that could be taught in the Merchant Marine Academy, a quality that in all his years at sea he had been unable to name.

It was this quality, Barthou believed, that he shared not only with the commanding officer of the *Europa* or the *Titanic*, but also with Magellan and Eric the Red and the man who'd commanded Cleopatra's barge.

It was something that descended on you when, through circumstance or choice, you found yourself accountable for the fate of so many other human beings. It raised you above the others—not in your own eyes, of course, but in theirs. And soon, Marius would feel it. It was in him already.

There was a knock at the door.

He lifted his hands from the keyboard. "Come in."

"Captain," said the chief purser, "I just wanted to remind you that you are dining this evening with Wallace Westbrook—in your own quarters."

Barthou groaned inwardly. "Of course, Henri," he said. "I remember. Bring him by at seven o'clock."

"Certainly—and, oh yes, I'm afraid the American comedians have begged off. Likewise the Countess de Chambord. *Mal de mer.*"

"You mean I am to dine alone with this man?"

"He has great influence, you know," Freppel said. "And he tells me he has many things he wishes to discuss with you."

Exactly what I am afraid of, Barthou thought. "Yes, of course. Well, thank you, Henri."

"Have a nice dinner, sir." Freppel closed the door behind him.

Barthou had already seen enough of Westbrook to want to avoid him if at all possible. The man was an obnoxious fool, a loudmouth who was willing to ask any question, no matter how personal, while regaling his captive audiences with tales of his own exploits for hours on end. Now, it looked as though he'd have to spend an evening with this hyena.

The captain picked up his phone. "Marius? It's the captain. Could you join me in my suite for dinner tonight?"

Tina, Victor, and David Nathan had a quiet dinner in their stateroom.

"I'm 'zhausted," Tina said. She leaned back from the table and closed her eyes.

"So I see," Nathan observed.

Victor looked over at his sister. "Why don't you get some sleep?"

Tina opened her eyes and got up. She rummaged around in her trunk for a few moments, then stopped.

"What's wrong?" Nathan asked.

"I only brought two nightgowns," she said, "and . . . ah . . . I disposed of them after—"

Nathan rummaged around in his suitcase and came up with a pair of pajamas. "Will these solve your problem?"

"That's very sweet of you," she said, "but I think all I'll need is the tops. They look long enough—you're a lot bigger than I am, after all."

Nathan frowned. "Please, if you don't mind, take the bottoms, too." He was sorry about the remark almost before it was out of his mouth. Why was he so stiff and distant toward

Tina? Was he stuck in this protector's role he'd taken on? God, he hoped not.

Tina was miffed by his comment. "Well, of course. I wouldn't want to offend you." She was surprised at how annoyed she sounded. She'd found his gesture charming, even intimate. Why didn't she respond in some way that would have conveyed her growing affection for this gruff and handsome man?

Nathan tossed the pajamas in her direction.

Tina caught them and held them up to her body. They were twice as large as she was. "They'll do very nicely, thank you."

Victor rolled his eyes.

At that moment, there was a knock on the door.

"Come on in," Nathan said. "We're finished."

But it was not a steward coming to remove the dinner dishes. It was a young officer.

"Dr. Meisner?"

"That's me."

"The captain has been detained by urgent business. He has asked me to escort you to the engine room. He'll meet you there."

Victor asked Nathan's permission with a glance. "Go ahead, Victor. I have a report to write, and I might as well get started on it now."

Victor slipped on a jacket and left with the officer. They walked forward, almost to the bridge, taking the service elevator down to F Deck—the same level where, earlier that day, Victor had guided a Mercedes-Benz out of a cargo port. But this time, instead of heading forward, toward the cargo hold, they turned aft.

They were met at the door of boiler room number 1 by Chief Purser Henri Freppel. "Ah, Dr. Meisner," he said. "The captain has asked me to send his regrets. He has been called away by an inconvenient social obligation. He requested that I give you a personal tour of the ship's engine rooms."

Victor had been looking forward to spending a few hours with Captain Barthou, whom he admired and respected. The same amount of time spent with this fussy, officious, and resolutely dapper little man would not be nearly as pleasurable, but he could do nothing about it.

"If I have questions about the machinery . . ."

"I can answer them. I've spent twenty-three years on the Atlantic, after all. Picked up a thing or two."

"Well," Victor said, "lead the way."

They entered an enormous room filled with rows and rows of giant steel boilers, each one the size of a detached garage, connected to one another by a jungle of pipes and tubes. Mammoth exhaust ducts led out of them at the top and into the ship's funnels.

This room was at least twenty degrees warmer than the rest of the ship, but aside from some hissing and gurgling, it was not particularly noisy. Furthermore, it was immaculately clean.

"This is where it all begins," Chief Purser Freppel said, as though repeating a memorized talk. "In this room and the three rooms aft of it, there are twenty-nine main boilers and four auxiliaries."

"I see." This wasn't the interesting section, as far as Victor was concerned.

"Each of the main boilers weighs just over one hundred tons, empty. It burns oil to heat water and produce steam at three hundred fifty degrees centigrade, at a pressure of twenty-eight kilograms."

Victor just nodded. The things were huge, but they were basically just teakettles.

The purser led Victor down the main aisle, between the boilers, and into the next boiler room.

"More of the same?"

"That's right."

They walked on, through two more boiler rooms.

"Where are the fuel tanks?"

"Two places," Freppel told him. "We keep fuel oil in the wing tanks on both sides of the hull and in the double bottom."

Something occurred to the young scientist. "So as the ship burns oil, her weight and stability changes."

"A very astute observation," Freppel noted. "Not many of the passengers who have toured these compartments have realized that. We compensate by shifting water ballast in the tanks reserved for that purpose."

"Very interesting."

Freppel continued to walk forward, leading Victor into the turbo-alternator room.

"Now, the steam produced by the boilers," the chief purser explained, "turns these four dynamos."

Victor surveyed the room. Bolted to the floor were four locomotive-sized semi-cylindrical cast steel casings, each fed by steam tubes coming from the boiler rooms. This room was cooler than the boiler rooms, and no hissing could be heard. Instead, there was the powerful, barely contained sound of something whirring.

"How much electricity do they produce?"

Freppel smiled. He knew he was about to amaze the young man. "In normal operation," he said, "about one hundred forty-six thousand kilowatts. In overload, as much as one hundred sixty-seven thousand. That's quite a bit when you consider that the entire metropolitan network of Paris uses about one hundred twenty thousand kilowatts."

"Pretty impressive," Victor allowed, still not very interested.

Freppel walked on, warming to his task. "Come, I have even more amazing things to show you."

They entered another huge compartment. Here were more mammoth cylinders — four of them.

"The dynamos power these motors," Freppel said. This is what Victor had really come to see — engines the likes of which simply did not exist on dry land. Two of them would have filled the average gymnasium, and this room had four. "If I were able to remove the metal casings," Freppel went on, "you would see the rotors and stators underneath."

"Tell me about the engines."

Freppel began to talk like a brochure once again. "The motors take in between five thousand and six thousand volts and put out about forty thousand horsepower. They are directly shafted to the propellers."

Victor nodded. "So the motors and the propellers turn at the same speed."

It was Freppel's turn to be impressed. "That's correct, Dr. Meisner. A maximum of two hundred forty-three rotations per minute."

"One question, Mr. Freppel," Victor said. "Why does the *Normandie* use this turbo-electric system, while almost every other passenger liner has steam turbines?"

"I was certain you would ask that question," Freppel said with a curious smile. "Everyone does. Anyhow, there are two main reasons. First, it's much quieter. And second—and this is the most remarkable thing of all—it gives us full power in reverse."

Victor found this interesting. "You mean that the *Normandie* can go backward as fast as it can go forward?"

"Except for hull shape, that's right. It gives us remarkable maneuverability in port or even at sea. But it's quite complex, technically speaking. Of course, I don't know if you're interested." Freppel waited confidently, like a tout who'd offered a tip to an addicted gambler.

Victor bit. "As a matter of fact, I am."

"Well," Freppel said in almost a teasing tone, "the reversing switch for the main propulsion motor circuit is in the electrical service corridor down this way. Care to look?"

"Please."

* * *

419

Barthou checked his watch. Almost nine p.m. He'd made a promise to the girl's brother, but this oaf was preventing him from keeping it.

"According to my information, Captain," Westbrook said, "the *Normandie* is slated to become an aircraft carrier in time of war. She was built with divided funnel uptakes to give her plenty of room for aircraft elevators. Isn't that right?"

"Ah . . . well, that's a question, isn't it?" Barthou replied. "I'm going to have to let my second in command answer it, I'm afraid. He's the expert on such matters."

Martel shot him a dirty look.

"In fact," Barthou said, "he's the expert on most matters around here. He's going to be the next captain of the *Normandie*, you see. As soon as I retire, that is."

Now Martel's eyes opened wide.

"I see," Westbrook said, shifting his focus to Martel. "What do you know about this aircraft carrier plan?"

Barthou stood. "Excuse me, gentlemen. I have a little work to do in preparation for our arrival tomorrow."

"It's no good denying it, Martel," Westbrook said. "I have it from authoritative sources in the French government itself."

Barthou slipped out of the room. Martel would have to handle this sort of thing when he was captain. No reason not to give him some practice.

He walked down the corridor toward David Nathan's stateroom. He was looking forward to showing Victor Meisner the engine room. The young man was shy and rather stiff, but it was a pleasure to watch that mind at work.

Barthou knocked on the door. Nathan opened it and invited him in, holding a finger to his lips and pointing to the bed. Tina was sound asleep, looking impossibly innocent and vulnerable in Nathan's enormous pajamas.

"She's had quite a time of it," the captain said quietly.

"Yes, indeed."

"I'm glad she's sleeping. I hope she'll sleep until tomorrow morning. Then I hope you'll take good care of her."

Nathan just smiled.

"All right," said the captain. "Where's Victor? I'm ready for that engine room tour."

"Victor? An officer came and got him about twenty minutes ago. Said you'd been detained by urgent business."

Barthou was confused. "Someone told you I'd been detained? Who?"

"I didn't recognize him. You weren't detained?"

"Not really—and I didn't send anyone."

"You're certain? Maybe someone got the idea you'd be delayed and thought they should tell Victor."

"No one even knew I was coming here—except the people at the luncheon."

"Then who—"

Something was very wrong here.

Their eyes met, understanding coming to both of them at the same moment.

Nathan felt his mouth go dry.

"Mon Dieu," said Barthou.

Nathan reached for his gun and stuffed it into his sock. "The officer said he was taking Victor to the engine room," he said. "I only hope that much was the truth."

"Come on, I'll show you the fastest route." On the way out, Barthou looked back at Tina.

"Don't worry about her. They're not after her."

Nathan double-locked the door anyway. Then he and the captain sprinted toward the engine room, neither talking about what they were afraid they'd find.

"How come there are so few crew members around?" Victor asked.

"Well, that's another one of the advantages of this system. It doesn't take many people to run it. And most of them just sit at the control panel, watching gauges. Not like the old days when passenger liners had hundreds of sooty, sweating

421

stokers in the holds, shoveling coal."

"Oil changed all that."

"That's right," Freppel said. "Here . . . this is the corridor where the reversing switch is located."

He led the young scientist between two ceiling-high banks of electrical switchboards, down the narrow hallway between them, to a steel rack about as high and wide as a garage door and perhaps two feet thick. On the rack were five large wooden handles.

"This is what does it?" Victor asked.

"Yes, you pull those handles and the ship literally goes into reverse. But of course you can't see much now, because the blow-out boxes cover the interior fittings."

Victor nodded. "What kind of voltage is involved?"

"About fifty-five hundred volts. Would you like to see the circuitry? It is quite unique, I'm told."

"Thank you," Victor said, "that would be very interesting."

Freppel unscrewed two fist-sized wing nuts at the top of one of the four blow-out boxes, the insulated shields designed to contain sparks or stray emissions from short circuits. Then he did the same with the two bottom wing nuts and lifted the blow-out box away from its fittings.

Visible now was a gleaming copper cable as thick as a man's forearm, fed by a complex network of smaller cables. In the center of the panel, there was a gap in the main cable. It was bridged by a pivoting copper switch, which was now in the up position. The switch had two other positions, a middle position in which the circuit was disengaged and a lower position in which the electrical flow was reversed.

"Do you understand the switch?" Freppel asked. "It's really beyond me." He shrugged theatrically, in that famous gesture of his.

"It's really not that complex," Victor said, peering into the electrical panel. "You see, the voltage comes through this cable here. . . ."

Freppel was standing beyond the young scientist, leaning

422

against a fire hose box. As Victor talked about the workings of the circuit, Freppel quickly and quietly opened the door and grasped the hose's brass nozzle.

David Nathan and Captain Pierre Barthou exited the service elevator and sprinted aft, into boiler room number one. Absolutely no one was in sight.

"Gaston!" Barthou shouted.

No answer.

"Why is the place deserted?" Nathan asked.

"They must be at the control station."

Once more they ran, the older man leading the way, his stride surprisingly strong and agile.

As they raced toward the ship's stern, Nathan peered among the boilers, desperate to spot Victor. How could I have forgotten? he asked himself. How could I have let down my guard? I got sidetracked on the gold business, which I should have let Jean-Louis handle, and I lost sight of the reason I was here. Ah, Jean-Louis, he thought. I truly need you now, my friend.

They burst into boiler room number two, Barthou shouting occasionally for Gaston LeBrun, the chief engineer — or anyone else who would answer his call. There was no response.

It had not been long, Nathan thought, but anything could have happened by now. Victor could have been killed outright, or simply tossed overboard, or locked in some compartment where he would never be found — at least not alive.

He'd botched it. He'd let himself get overconfident. He'd thought they all were safe when one of them, the very man he'd been sent to protect, had still been in grave danger. What would his father have thought of how he'd acted? And what would he tell Roosevelt when he got back? And Tina? . . . Tina! What could he say to her? How could he ever explain that his carelessness had cost her brother his life?

"Captain? Is that you?" It was Chief Engineer LeBrun, a tiny elfin-faced man with a heavily bandaged left ear. He came running toward the captain from an aft engine compartment.

"Gaston, I'm searching for a passenger. He'd be in company with one of our officers or someone dressed like an officer. Have you seen anyone like that?"

LeBrun shook his head. "I've been working with my crew on the broken steam line, making permanent our temporary repairs. So I haven't seen any passengers wandering around in the engine rooms, at least not tonight."

Nathan groaned. If Victor wasn't here, the chances are they'd never find him. He could be anywhere on the ship and literally anything might have happened to him. Or he might not even be on the ship anymore.

"I want you and your men to drop everything immediately and help us conduct a search of all the machinery spaces. I think the passenger's life may be in danger."

"Danger?" LeBrun said, surprised. "Captain, nothing down here is really very dangerous, so long as no one tampers with the valves, the covers, and the controls. . . ."

"Someone may want to murder this passenger," the captain interrupted.

The chief engineer was amazed. "Murder? Why?"

Nathan thought about Victor, so young and defenseless, such an easy mark, led down into this inferno like a mouse to a trap. "No time to explain."

The captain became insistent. "Gaston, I want you and your men to conduct an immediate search of the machinery spaces. We're looking for two men, maybe more. We must find them before it's too late."

"Yes, sir." He raced away to carry out Barthou's orders, while Nathan and the captain continued to comb the boiler rooms, finding no one.

* * *

424

"What puzzles me," Freppel said, "is what happens behind the main cable—where all those lesser wires go."

Victor took another half step forward, crouched down, and scrutinized the circuitry. The cables and wires looked totally inert, and yet he knew an incredible amount of electrical power was flowing through them at this very instant.

He could see exactly how the electro-mechanical device worked. It was, in essence, nothing more than a giant circuit breaker, the biggest he had ever seen. He wondered how often it was actually used.

Behind Victor, Freppel reached back into the fire hose box for an instant and opened the shut-off valve. Then he turned back toward Victor, pointed the hose nozzle at the young scientist, and twisted it open.

At that moment, Victor suddenly stood and looked back toward Freppel. "How often do you—?"

A thick, solid silvery stream of water shot out of the brass hose nozzle in Freppel's hands. The water stream missed Victor entirely but impacted, full force, against the main cable of the reversing switch.

A bright blue bolt of electricity instantaneously snaked back across the water stream into the hose nozzle. The chief purser, who realized too late what was happening, screamed once. It was a fearsome, high-pitched, blood-curdling shriek.

Strangely enough, however, Freppel did not move, not a muscle. He stood like a statue, totally paralyzed, his face frozen in terror, directing the water stream into the reversing switch as though it were his sole function in life, never to be interrupted.

For an instant, Victor just gaped at the chief purser. Then, realizing his peril, he clumsily backed away from the man, the water stream, and the growing puddle on the floor.

"Help!" he screamed in growing hysteria. "Someone help! My God, help!"

Nathan heard him. "Victor! I'm coming! Keep shouting!"

Victor continued screaming. "Help me! Oh, God, help

me!"

"Where are you?"

"Here! Near the reversing circuit. Help!"

LeBrun had caught up with Nathan. "This way!"

They raced toward the switching gear panels, Barthou close behind.

"Help me!" Victor kept screaming.

"We're coming!"

Victor stumbled out from between two giant electrical panels, shaken and dazed. He collapsed at Nathan's feet.

"Victor, are you all right?" Nathan bent down to help the young man, who sat up, then slowly got to his feet.

"Yes, I'm all right" he said. "But the purser . . . My God! Help the purser!"

"Where is he?" Barthou asked.

Victor pointed toward the narrow alleyway where he knew Freppel had gone. "Be careful!" he told them. "Stay out of the water."

"Water?" Puzzled by the warning, Nathan drew his gun and started down the corridor, Barthou at his side.

Rounding a corner, they saw Freppel, still holding the fire hose, still directing a thick stream of water into the reversing switch, still vibrating, his eyes wide open, bulging in fear.

"What the hell . . ."

It was Barthou who first understood what they were looking at. Carefully avoiding the water stream, he reached into the fire hose box and closed the shut-off valve.

The water stream slowed, fell away from the electrical cable, and died. Chief Purser Henri Freppel dropped the nozzle and slowly toppled over, falling face first into the gathering puddle on the floor. Steam rose from his back.

"Jesus H. Christ!" Nathan said.

Chief Engineer LeBrun joined them . . . and just stared.

Barthou cautiously poked a foot at the body. There wasn't the slightest sign of life.

"What happened?" LeBrun was amazed.

"I think I know," the captain told him. He pointed to the blow-out box cover lying nearby. "He must have showed Victor the inner workings of the reversing switch—"

"—and tried to electrocute him," Nathan said, full realization finally striking him.

"I don't understand," Lebrun said, looking at the still-smoldering body in shock. "Why would the chief purser do such a thing?"

Barthou answered. "I didn't take him seriously," he said. "I thought it was all foolish bluff and bluster. I never dreamed he would do anything like this."

Nathan was taken aback. "You knew he wanted to kill Victor?"

"No, no, not that," Barthou replied. "I knew he had some far right political ideas, but it all seemed like harmless blathering to me."

"Not so harmless," Nathan said.

"No," the captain agreed. "Not harmless at all."

They backed out of the corridor. Victor was leaning against one of the giant motors, shivering.

"I'm sorry, Victor," Nathan began.

"Sorry?"

"I shouldn't have let you go. . . ."

"How could you have known?"

Nathan shrugged. "It's my job to know."

"I still don't understand what happened," the chief engineer said. "Why did the chief purser want to kill this man?"

"That's really a very good question, Captain," Nathan said. "Who ordered him to kill Victor and—when?"

Barthou shook his head, then something occurred to him. "He got a telegram," he recalled. "It came during the Captain's Dinner, at the same time I got a warning message from the company."

"You remember it specifically?"

"Yes. I asked him about it, as I recall. He said it was news of the birth of another grandchild. Maybe it will turn up in

427

his quarters."

"Who was the telegram from?" LeBrun asked.

Nathan answered him. "Probably someone in Berlin."

"I don't think it really matters much anymore," Victor said.

"No," Captain Barthou agreed. "I think it's finally over."

Victor was very pensive. "Over?" he said at last, "I don't think so. I'm afraid it's just beginning, not for me so much, but for the world."

None of the others could argue with that.

"I'll see to it that everything is cleaned up down here, Captain," LeBrun said.

"Thank you."

"I'm completely wiped out," Victor said.

"I understand," Nathan said. "Let's go back to the cabin. There's someone I want to reassure."

Barthou walked them back to their stateroom, none of them saying very much. Then, as they reached the door, he finally spoke up.

"Gentlemen, I may not have a chance to see you again before debarkation. I want to wish you well, with all my heart. Also, please convey my fondest regards to the young lady."

"Thank you, sir," Victor said.

Barthou offered his hand to Nathan, who shook it solemnly. He then briefly wrapped Victor in a bear hug. "Take care of yourself, my boy. And your sister. And my good friend Mr. Nathan."

"I'll do my very best."

When Victor and David got back to their stateroom, they found Tina still in bed, still asleep, looking small and vulnerable in Nathan's pajamas.

"Think we should wake her?" Victor asked.

Nathan looked at the sleeping figure. "No need to. We can tell her all about it tomorrow."

Then he thought about tomorrow. Tomorrow, they'd dock in New York. Tomorrow, they'd say good-bye . . . and that, no doubt, would be the last time he saw the brave and pretty girl who was lying there on the bed, asleep in his pajamas. The thought was like a sudden, sharp pain.

Now that his job was done, how could he prevent the parting and keep the relationship going? He could take her out for a drink or dinner or to the theater or for a carriage ride. That's the sort of thing people did in New York.

His problem was asking her. He had absolutely no idea how to do that. He knew how she must see him — as a substitute parent, and a usually disapproving one at that. How could he make her see him differently?

He looked at her sleeping there, and he was suddenly overwhelmed with tenderness. He hadn't told her how proud of her he was, not really. He hadn't even given her a hint that he felt anything toward her other than the burden of guardianship.

But if he said something to her, she might smile at him the way she had smiled at Arthur Shepard, then find a way to politely let him down. And that he dreaded. Maybe the best thing he could do was just keep his mouth shut.

NIGHT

The *Normandie* had made great progress since jettisoning Jaekel's Mercedes-Benz, barreling along the coast of Nova Scotia, past Cape Sable, the Gulf of Maine, Cape Cod, Nantucket, Block Island, and down the South Shore of Long Island, where tens of thousands had spent that very day, the last Sunday of the summer, frolicking on the beaches of Westhampton, Fire Island, Jones Beach, and Rockaway.

It was well past midnight when the great liner steamed past the Ambrose Lightship, which was permanently stationed at the edge of New York's outer harbor.

This was the point from which transatlantic distances were calculated, and it was here, four years ago, that the *Normandie* had first captured the Blue Ribbon of the Atlantic, making the 2,907-mile journey from Bishop's Rock Lighthouse off the British coast in four days, three hours, and two minutes, averaging 29.98 knots over the entire voyage.

This trip in late August 1939 had been a fast one for the *Normandie,* but no record-breaker. Despite the zigzagging and the steam line problems, she'd made the voyage in four days, fifteen hours, averaging 29.71 knots. But that was none too fast for those who had been waiting for her and worrying about her ever since radio contact had been lost.

At Ambrose Lightship, Coast Guardsman Tony Curcillo, who had the watch, was the first to see her.

"I have a three-stacker in the glasses, sir," the curly-haired young man called to his commanding officer, who was sleeping on a cot nearby, ordered to do so by Coast Guard authorities in Washington.

"Freighter or liner?"

"Can't tell, sir. Can't tell if she has portholes. Maybe they're blacked out."

Now that's interesting, Captain Janowitz thought. He got out of bed and rubbed his face, not surprised to feel the heavy growth of beard. He'd been on duty for seventy-two hours. "Let me have the glasses," he said.

Janowitz focused the binoculars on the ship, glancing back and forth at the *Normandie* silhouette in the big ship identification book. There wasn't much moonlight, but the sky was clear and the visibility was good enough for him to see the pointed prow and the tiered decks near the stern.

"Damnit, that's her, that's the *Normandie!*" he said. "Look for yourself."

Curcillo looked through the binoculars again. "You know," he said, surprised, "I think you're right. I can see the whaleback, covering the forward part of the decks. And the superstructure is definitely curved."

"I think it's time we got on the radio," Janowitz said.

Ten minutes later, one of the President's assistants woke him and handed him a radiogram. Roosevelt read it, smiled, and asked the assistant to send a message to Claude Swanson, Secretary of the Navy: Call off the destroyers; she just steamed into New York Harbor, apparently safe and sound.

In lower Manhattan, the phone rang in the office of Maurice de Murville, head of the French Line in the United States.

"The Coast Guard just radioed," his secretary told him. "The *Normandie* has just passed Ambrose."

"Any damage, any signs of battle?"

"They said she was proceeding normally."

"Thank the good Lord," de Murville said, taking a very deep breath. "Audrey, would you get me the *Gouverneur-Generale* in Paris? At his home?"

"Yes, sir."

Fifteen minutes later the *Gouverneur-Generale* of the *Compagnie Generale Transatlantique* spoke, by phone, to French Premier Daladier. "The ship is safe, Edouard," he said.

There was a long pause. "Thank you, Marcel. And please convey the gratitude of the French people to your captain — what is his name?"

"Barthou."

"Yes. And my personal thanks as well."

The *Normandie* dropped anchor at quarantine — the mandatory inspection point at the edge of New York's outer harbor — at about two A.M. Three small cutters were on her almost immediately: a Coast Guard boat bearing officers of the U.S. Public Health Service, whose job it was to spot anyone aboard who might be carrying an infectious disease; the *President,* a mail boat, whose job it was to hurry the French liner's mail to shore as quickly as possible; and the *Alice M. Moran,* the tugboat that carried harbor pilot Anton Huseby, who'd been guiding liners into New York's inner harbor since the days when the *Mauretania* and the *Lusitania* dominated the Atlantic.

"We've been worried about you," Huseby told Captain Barthou, as he stepped aboard the French liner. "Is everything okay?"

"More or less," Barthou said with a weary grin.

Huseby took that as a yes. "Listen," he said, "the French government made me promise to deliver this radiogram as soon as I set foot on the ship. It's for someone named Segonzak . . . Jean-Louis Segonzak."

"I'll take it," Barthou said.

Huseby handed over an envelope and the captain opened it.

TOP SECRET TO SEGONZAK

Negative on your entire list, except for "Simon Rothmann." Sources say he is actually Kurt Jaekel, a Kriegsmarine commando. He is an explosives expert whose target may be the ship itself. Be warned: he is armed and dangerous. Known to have killed a man in a wrestling match. Good luck. Signed Foucault, SDECE.

To Huseby's considerable surprise, Barthou crumpled up the message and tossed it overboard. "No longer applies," the captain explained.

Day Eight

Monday, August 28, 1939

MORNING

At about eight A.M., when most New Yorkers were just finishing breakfast or hurrying to work, the *Normandie* weighed anchor, gave three belly-wrenching blasts on her great whistle, and began the slow and majestic journey from quarantine to her final destination, Pier 88, at the foot of Forty-eighth Street in Manhattan.

Glistening in the brilliant morning sun, she glided past Fort Hamilton, at the southern tip of Brooklyn, where just inside the ramparts thousands of new recruits were engaged in dismounted drill. She passed between Staten Island and Brooklyn, and was seen and noted by the occupants of thousands of motor cars on Shore Road, stuck in rush hour.

Across The Narrows, a handful of soldiers stationed in Fort Wadsworth momentarily suspended bayonet drill to watch the beautiful liner steam past. And a group of aged sea captains from the Sailors' Snug Harbor, resting on the benches of Grimes Hill, one of the highest points on the Atlantic seaboard, saw her and began talking—again—of their own bygone careers.

433

Two small vessels paused to let her pass: the Staten Island Ferry, Manhattan-bound with a load of secretaries, stock clerks, and garment center workers; and the Bedloe's Island Ferry, headed out to the Statue of Liberty with a boatload of midwestern tourists eager to get in a full day's sightseeing.

At Battery Park, the *Normandie* turned up the Hudson. Here, she was joined by six powerful Moran tugs, working boats whose job it was to assist her in the docking process.

The giant ship and her escorts now swept upriver, past the splendid Woolworth Tower, past the squalid tenements of the lower West Side, past the dilapidated Hoboken docks on the Jersey side of the river, past the crowded ethnic enclaves between Eighth and Twelfth Avenue in the Twenties and Thirties.

On board the *Normandie,* passengers spent half their time packing their steamer trunks, the other half eagerly looking through their portholes at New York City, watching it roll by as though they were seeing a movie.

Europe was four days behind them now, but it was much farther than that; it was a totally different world, an older world, a tired world, a suicidal world. This world was young, strong, and alive. Here, nothing was impossible. Here, there was hope.

In cabin 67, Tina, Victor, and David Nathan had gotten up early, aware that there'd be no little Maurice Cosset around to help them pack.

While they packed their clothing, Victor told his sister about his close call the night before, and in the space of about five minutes, she went from curious to shocked to relieved. Then, by mutual agreement, they dropped the subject. Enough of all these past troubles. It was a new day.

They'd almost finished packing when Tina came to the pajamas she'd worn the previous night . . . Nathan's pajamas. "What would you like me to do with these, David?"

Nathan took the pajamas from her. "Oh, I guess they go in here." He stuffed them into the laundry bag he kept in his suitcase.

It was a simple, polite exchange, but they both regretted it almost immediately.

It occurred to Tina, an instant too late, that she'd missed an opportunity for a little affectionate flirtation, a chance to give David an opening. She might have asked if she could keep the pajamas. In return, he might have told her to keep them warm or something. Then they'd be off and running. Instead, she'd just handed them over as though it didn't matter.

Nathan had a remarkably similar thought. Why didn't I tell her to keep the pajamas and wear them whenever she liked? he asked himself. Then she might have said something coy or cute and I could have responded in kind, instead of reacting gruffly, as usual. Now it was too late.

Nathan retreated from the scene, walking out onto the stateroom's small private balcony. There, while the *Normandie* slowly steamed upriver, he leaned against the rail and studied the Manhattan triptych, which was spread out before him.

Before long, Tina slipped through the balcony door and came out to stand beside him, her blond hair waving in the breeze. She was wearing the blue silk dress she'd had on when they boarded the ship. She looked fresh and lovely.

"It's a beautiful city," she said, sharing his view. She was determined to talk to him, to make contact somehow.

"It's good to be back home."

"Where do you live?"

He pointed into the heart of the city.

"Looks crowded," she said.

"It is. But that's one of the things I like about it."

Tina looked at the man standing beside her, at his slightly crooked nose, his shiny black hair, his rough good looks. It felt good to be standing next to him. "So you like crowds?"

"I like people," he said. He thought about smiling at her and telling her that of course he liked some people more than others, but the damn words just wouldn't come.

"Do you have many friends here?" Now, that was a silly question. Of course he had friends in New York. She knew that. She'd really wanted to ask him if he had a girlfriend here, but she couldn't bring herself to be that direct. Maybe that was the problem—a girlfriend. Or maybe it was that he thought she was just a kid—and a smart-ass kid at that.

"I have all kinds of friends here," he said. "Childhood friends, school friends, work friends. I've lived here all my life, you know." He wondered what his friends would make of Tina. Now, that would be something to see.

"It looks like a very exciting place." She almost added that she'd like to see it and would he mind showing her around. She could picture herself with him, walking through the city streets, her arm in his, or sitting across from him at dinner, or snuggled up beside him in a movie theater, grabbing his hand if something scary happened up on the screen.

"Most exciting city on earth," he told her. For a moment, he imagined Tina walking up Fifth Avenue, turning the head of practically every man she passed. Of course, that was the simplest and most natural approach. He'd just ask her if she'd like to see the sights.

"Listen, Tina, after we dock, would you like—"

There was a knock on the stateroom door. "Steward here to collect your luggage," a voice called. They came in from the balcony, and Nathan helped the steward load the trunks and the suitcases on a hand cart.

Just before ten A.M. the *Normandie* and her tugboat escorts drew even with Pier 88, slowed, and stopped. Three of the tugs lined up on the ship's port quarter, took the offered hawsers, and began their struggle to hold her stern in place against the downstream rush of the tide. The three other tugs pressed against her starboard bow and side.

Slowly, the bow came in and the stern swung out. Her propellers barely turning, the giant liner nosed into her slip and stopped dead. Around the ship, the water turned black. She was, as the old salts put it, "smelling bottom."

Now, a steel cable two inches thick was cast down from the ship and looped around a bollard on the pier. An electric winch began turning, drawing the *Normandie* closer and closer to the pier. Then more lines, dozens of them, were thrown down and made fast. The *Normandie*'s one hundred thirty-ninth crossing had come to an end.

At 10:45 A.M. the *Normandie* gave one long and two short blasts on her powerful whistle, signaling the tugs that their jobs were done and giving notice to all that she had, indeed, arrived.

Now began the rush toward shore, the disembarkation. Deckhands and stevedores ran out the gangways, one for each class—"the longest gangplanks in the world," the French Line called them—connecting the vessel with the upper story of pier. Just above the waterline, at ground level, the ship's cargo ports opened up and broad rubber conveyor belts were inserted into them.

At this point, passengers and baggage began to flow into the cavernous spaces of Pier 88, the *Normandie*'s American home. One category of cargo, however, remained in place: the gold bullion. As the French government had arranged earlier, a fleet of armored trucks would come to the ship tonight, while New York slept. The French troops would load the gold aboard the trucks, which would transport it to the United States government vaults under the Wall Street branch of the Federal Reserve Bank.

All in all, the arrival in New York of a major ocean liner rather resembles the final dismissal of the student body at a large high school at the beginning of summer vacation, or what happens after the final out of the World Series, when everyone struggles to get out of the stadium simultaneously.

It's the end of the adventure, it's good-bye coach, hello pumpkin; it's will he really call and what the hell will I say to him if he does; it's how much do we tip the steward and will they miss a couple of towels; it's I can't wait to tell them and God I hope he never finds out; it's the party's over now and it's time to start rewriting the memories.

It's thousands of people, not just passengers and crew members, but friends, relatives, sightseers, well-wishers, souvenir-hawkers, and pickpockets. It's fifteen thousand pieces of luggage trundled out of the hold by armies of longshoremen and sent off in search of a cab.

That's what disembarkation had been for nearly a century, on both sides of the Atlantic, not only in New York, but also at Boston, Southampton, Liverpool, Le Havre, Cherbourg, Bremerhaven, Hamburg, Genoa, and Palermo.

But on this twenty-eighth day of August, 1939, there was an additional harmonic — the profoundest sense of deliverance, the sort of feeling someone awaiting execution must have when the real murderer confesses . . . for this group of passengers, at least, had lifted its head just before the guillotine fell.

Because of the war scare and the rumors surrounding the ship, another group of people, a group unaccustomed to meeting arriving ocean liners, was also here in force — some of New York's most famous newsmen, the full gamut of reporters, broadcasters, photographers and columnists, including several famous names.

They had come to Pier 88 not only to witness the mooring of the *Normandie* and interview her illustrious passengers about conditions in Europe, but also to report on the arrival of the *Bremen*, the mighty German liner that was expected to dock right next to her French rival within the next few hours, probably before the last of the *Normandie*'s luggage was ashore.

As the passengers swarmed across the gangways, however, it was they who questioned the reporters, not the reverse — at least at first. "Has the war started?" "Has Hitler marched?" "Have London and Paris been bombed?" "What is Stalin doing?"

No, they were told, there's no war in Europe — not yet. But everyone is massing troops, practicing evacuations, cutting off phone service, closing borders. War could break out any minute.

The passengers couldn't absorb all of this. All they really heard were two key words: no war. The European passengers cried with joy, but the American reaction was mixed. Evidently, the radio blackout had led many of them to bet with each other about whether or not Hitler had marched. The winners were elated, the losers dismayed.

It was only after the war news had swept through the crowd of departing passengers that the reporters were able to regain the upper hand. One such fellow, trying to gauge Europe's mood, buttonholed Lilly Daché, the fashion designer.

"What are European women doing in light of the current situation?" he asked.

The glamorous lady flashed a casual smile in his direction. "The women of France," she said, "are using their most potent weapon to prevent war: clothing."

Another reporter managed to waylay Thomas J. Watson. "Will there be a war in Europe?"

"I couldn't say," the IBM president told him. "But if there is a war, it will destroy civilization as we know it."

A reporter and a photographer from the *New York Graphic* stopped Marlene Dietrich as she exited the gangway. "What do you think Hitler is going to do, Miss Dietrich?" the reporter asked.

"I don't know," she said with a saccharine smile. "And for all I care, he can go stick his head up his ass."

Count Andre Cherbatoff came off the ship with his young lady friend on his arm. He quickly found their baggage and engaged a porter to help them with it. Then he and his young lady went searching for the largest taxi they could find. A long line of boxy yellow cabs had queued up at the curb, their trunks open like the mouths of newly hatched birds.

"Excuse me, sir," a newspaper reporter said, intercepting the aging aristocrat before he could get to a taxi. "Could you tell me anything about the mood in Europe?"

Cherbatoff gazed at the man with undisguised contempt. "We do not choose to be interviewed by the common press," he said.

"We don't?"

Cherbatoff pushed past him and engaged a taxi.

Just inside the French Line terminal, an unfortunate press photographer from the *Daily Mirror* decided to turn his Speed Graphic on Salvatore Barzinni, who, as usual, was accompanied by his bodyguards.

Actually, Barzinni reacted hardly at all to the unexpected flashbulb in his face. He merely wiggled a finger in the photographer's direction. One of his men plucked the bulky camera out of the photographer's hands and tossed it to his colleague, who dropped it out the terminal window and into the Hudson River.

"We're not going to have any problem about this, are we?" the first bodyguard asked the photographer, grinning dangerously.

"Ah, no, no, sir, not at all."

Three of New York's most enterprising journalists avoided the *hoi polloi* and made directly for the bridge, to quiz the ruddyfaced, silver-haired captain himself. All three demanded a private interview, a problem Barthou neatly solved by agreeing to see them simultaneously, in his quarters. He brought Martel along.

The most senior of the reporters, a man from the Hearst newspapers, took the first shot. "The passengers are saying the *Normandie* zigzagged during her voyage," he said in his urbanely accented English, reading from a notepad. "Is that true?"

Barthou smiled gently, as if the very thought were ridiculous. "If there was any zigzagging," he said, "it was the passengers who did it — after spending a little too much time at one of the ship's bars."

The reporter frowned, and scratched out the note.

A reporter from the *Herald Tribune* was next at bat. "We've had reports that the *Normandie* traveled far to the north of its usual track, to avoid submarines. Is that true?"

"Well, there was a stray iceberg that drifted a little farther south than usual," Barthou said. "But it was on the wrong course, not the *Normandie*. Anyhow, it was a little one. Quite harmless."

"What about avoiding submarines?"

The captain shook his head. "We didn't avoid anyone. And I can assure you that if we had seen a submarine, we would have waved a polite hello."

Disappointed, the reporter noted the reply. The captain wasn't exactly a fountain of news.

A *New York Times* reporter stepped to the plate. "Captain, I don't exactly know how to put this . . . it's a question from my editors. It would never occur to me. But, ah . . . could you tell me whether or not the *Normandie* carries any hidden artillery?"

"Marius, would you like to answer that question?"

The young deputy captain stood up and pulled his trouser pockets inside out. "I don't know about the captain," he said, "but this is the only concealed weapon I carry." He held out a neatly folded white handkerchief.

Barthou actually laughed. "I couldn't have answered that question better myself," he said.

The three journalists looked at each other in dismay. No runs, no hits, no errors.

While the journalists were questioning Captain Barthou, a bearded man wearing a brown overcoat and clutching a pine box left the ship via the third-class gangway. He stood in the French Line's main waiting room, peering through the crush of people, looking for . . . for someone, he did not know whom.

Then, suddenly, he spotted a man across the room, a man who was waving at him, a man dressed in a long black overcoat, a man with a curly black beard and the payess, long curling hair at the sides of the temples required of those who closely obeyed the strictures of the *Torah*.

He waved back, tentatively, then pointed to himself. Do you mean me? he gestured. Are you waving at me? The man on the other side of the room nodded vigorously, yes, yes!

They pushed through the crowd toward each other and met somewhere in the middle.

"Reb Pinchas Nachman?" the man asked.

"I am he."

"Reb Nachman, I am Rabbi Herzberg."

Pinchas threw his arms around the man and began to cry.

David, Tina, and Victor were not among those who led the charge down the first-class gangway, but they were in the first group of stragglers.

A mild-mannered little man with wildly unkempt gray hair and sad, wise eyes was quietly waiting for them at the end of the gangway.

When he saw Victor and Tina, a grin lit his face and he

rushed forward, arms outstretched. David Nathan stood back, to give them what privacy he could.

"Victor!" said the little man. "How wonderful it is to see you. And Tina! Let me look at you! You're both so beautiful and so grown up."

"I'm very happy to see you, too, sir." Nathan was startled by the awe and respect in Victor's voice.

"You don't look a day older, Uncle Albert," Tina said, glowing. She kissed him warmly on the cheek.

"Well, you do, *liebchen.*" The man gave Tina a warm kiss in return. "I can see that you are not a little girl anymore."

To Nathan's absolute amazement, Tina blushed.

"And who's this?" Einstein asked Tina, noticing Nathan hovering close by. "Did you find a companion on the voyage, Tina? An admirer?"

"This is David Nathan, Dr. Einstein," Victor said. "He's the man President Roosevelt sent to rescue us from Germany."

Einstein and Nathan shook hands. "You seem to have done your job very well, young man," the scientist said warmly. "I can't tell you how grateful I am."

"It was my pleasure, sir."

Einstein turned toward Tina, grinning mischievously. "I knew the President would send a good man to bring you back, but I didn't realize he'd be such a handsome fellow."

Now Tina blushed again, astonishing Nathan a second time and giving him new hope.

At that moment, Wallace Westbrook stepped off the gangway, just a few feet away from them. Catching sight of Einstein and David Nathan together, he stopped in his tracks.

Westbrook pointed an accusing finger at Nathan. "I knew it! I knew you were lying!"

Nathan was astounded by the man's gall. "What in the hell are you talking about?"

"Well, you told me you owned a couple of Philadelphia

apartment houses."

"That's right, I do."

"But there's a lot more to you than that or this man wouldn't have come out to meet your ship."

"This man?"

Westbrook peered intently at Albert Einstein, trying to remember where he'd seen the face. "Harry Houdini," he said. "You're a friend of Harry Houdini. So you're a big promoter, right? And you're bringing this girl back from Europe to put her in some kind of production."

Nathan couldn't help laughing. "Right again, Westbrook. You know, you're a darned perceptive little fellow."

The diminutive reporter knew he was making a fool of himself, but he didn't know why and he didn't want to make things worse by continuing to speculate. So he instead tried to settle the score by fixing Nathan with a murderous glare. Then he stomped off, muttering to himself.

There was a twinkle in Einstein's sad eyes. "What in the world was that all about?"

Tina answered him. "It's a long story," she said. "We'll tell you all about it sometime soon. I promise."

"If you don't, I may have to tickle it out of you," the scientist threatened playfully.

Tina teased him. "I wouldn't try that, Uncle Albert. I'm bigger than I used to be."

"And stronger," Victor added ruefully.

"Oh ho," Einstein said, grinning. "We'll have to see about that."

"You're certainly looking well, sir," Victor told him. "America seems to agree with you."

"I am keeping busy, Victor. And I have a lot to tell you."

Victor caught his meaning. "Listen, Tina, maybe you could go on to the hotel and—"

Einstein interrupted. "Mr. Nathan, I wonder if we could impose on you for just a little while longer. This young

444

man and I have some technical matters to discuss. Perhaps you could look after Tina this afternoon."

"Look after her?"

"Yes, while Victor and I talk—seeing that she's a stranger in New York. Maybe you could show her a little bit of the city, then bring her back later to our rooms at the Waldorf—if it wouldn't be too much trouble, that is."

"Trouble? It wouldn't be any trouble at all."

Einstein nodded sagely. "Somehow, I thought you might say that."

Nathan took a very small risk. "How about if I bring her back after dinner?"

Einstein, smiling broadly, turned toward Tina to see her reaction, but she was looking at Nathan. "I'd like that," she said shyly.

"Good, said the scientist. "It's settled then."

Now they all began to walk toward the exit, Victor and his mentor slipping into animated conversation, the older man's arm around his protégé's shoulder.

Tina and David followed at a distance. After a few steps, he took her hand.

On Friday, September 1, 1939, four days after the *Normandie* arrived in New York, Hitler's armies invaded Poland from the west. Sixteen days later, Stalin's forces marched in from the east. World War II had begun.

As for the *Normandie,* there was no one hundred fortieth crossing. The French Line, worried about her safety, decided to leave her moored at Pier 88 for the duration. The crew returned to France via Canada.

A week after Pearl Harbor, Roosevelt decided that this valuable naval asset should be put to use on the Allies' behalf. The US government formally and legally seized the French liner, stored all of her furnishings and art treasures in Manhattan warehouses, and began converting her into a troop ship.

On February 9, 1942, a spark from a welder's torch ignited some kapok life jackets that had been temporarily stored in the Grand Lounge. The fire spread rapidly throughout the vessel's upper decks. Fire tugs inundated the ship with water, which promptly froze in the scuppers and was trapped on her upper decks.

The next day, in the early morning hours, the now top-heavy liner slowly rolled over on her side at Pier 88, in about forty feet of water. She lay there for a year and a half, her powerful engines rotting in the slime of the Hudson. By October 1943, she'd been pumped out and righted, but by then the Allies no longer needed her, and it would have cost too much to restore her to her former glory.

In 1946, the once-magnificent *Normandie* was sold to a scrap metal dealer for $161,000. He towed the fire-scarred hulk to Port Newark, cut her apart, and sold the scrap to the steel mills of Pennsylvania. Her famous furnishings and artworks survived her, however. Some were auctioned off during the war, and some were installed in the *Ile de France* during her post-war refit.

Those who would like a glimpse of the magnificence that was the *Normandie* can see half a wall of the glass paneling designed by Jean Dupas that once lined the ship's Grand Lounge. It's now mounted in the cafeteria of New York's Metropolitan Museum of Art. The handsome wood double doors that separated the Grand Lounge from the Smoking Room and the panels that surrounded them — jungle scenes carved, richly colored, and lacquered by Jean Dunand — are in the private dining room of Mr. Chow's Restaurant, on East Fifty-seventh Street in New York City.

ESPIONAGE FICTION BY WARREN MURPHY AND MOLLY COCHRAN

GRANDMASTER (17-101, $4.50)
There are only two true powers in the world. One is goodness. One is evil. And one man knows them both. He knows the uses of pleasure, the secrets of pain. He understands the deadly forces that grip the world in treachery. He moves like a shadow, a promise of danger, from Moscow to Washington — from Havana to Tibet. In a game that may never be over, he is the grandmaster.

THE HAND OF LAZARUS (17-100, $4.50)
A grim spectre of death looms over the tiny County Kerry village of Ardath. The savage plague of urban violence has begun to weave its insidious way into the peaceful fabric of Irish country life. The IRA's most mysterious, elusive, and bloodthirsty murderer has chosen Ardath as his hunting ground, the site that will rock the world and plunge the beleaguered island nation into irreversible chaos: the brutal assassination of the Pope.

Available wherever paperbacks are sold, or order direct from the Publisher. Send cover price plus 50¢ per copy for mailing and handling to Pinnacle Books, Dept. 17-362, 475 Park Avenue South, New York, N.Y. 10016. Residents of New York, New Jersey and Pennsylvania must include sales tax. DO NOT SEND CASH.